THE
TWIN
FURY

JEREMY THOMAS FULLER

THE TWIN FURY

THE METALWOOD SAGA
BOOK 9

JEREMY THOMAS FULLER

STARMIST★
ENTERTAINMENT

STARMIST ENTERTAINMENT

166 Geary Str STE 1500 #1259
San Francisco, CA 94108
United States

jeremythomasfuller.com
instagram.com/jeremythomasfuller
facebook.com/jeremythomasfuller
bsky.app/profile/jeremythomasfuller.com

CONTENT
WARNING

This book depicts the Great Awakening, when magic first arrives on Valaralda, setting the story in motion.

People are overcome with power, unable to understand what is happening to their very souls.

Magic is *extremely* powerful.

And it is not yet understood.

Content warning for domestic abuse, murder of family members, and violence directed at young children.

Power is in the hand of the destroyer.

—*A proverb of the People*

Paradoxically, farms were perhaps the worst hit by the changes the Awakening wrought. Sons became Talented overnight. Fathers went mad, either with rage or insanity. Mothers died to save their loved ones, and great Trees rose to take their place. Nobody understood what was happening.

By the time the ancient scientists of the day had realized what was occurring—or had fashioned some semblance of a theory, anyway—the damage was done. Aten's forward-thinking Department of Magical Research came too late for the poor pastoral towns that made up the majority of the agrarian society the elves once knew.

For magic—while powerful—does not come without its share of sorrow.

Excerpt from
   "Dawn of an Empire"
   by Iliaster Magnus,
   High Historian,
   Ilyrion Council of Mages
   18401 A.A.

PART
ONE

ONE

LUSVUNUB SPARKLED IN THE NIGHT, yellow floodlights and barbed wire and tar spreading out beneath a starless sky. Banzab paused, sniffing. There was too much smoke in the air—not when most of the People should be lining up, preparing to enter the gate. The trashburners shouldn't be operating at all right now—the smoke always disturbed the infants. She turned toward Second District, seeing the orange of flames in that direction. Cookfires, she thought, not trashburners, though they were larger than normal. Perhaps the People were frightened, nervous, anxious about what was to come.

She couldn't particularly blame them.

Banzab strode through Martial Square, reclaimed armor clinking musically as she walked, her proper jata hair falling beautifully against her back. It was lighter than the others—too blonde—but she'd made up the difference with extra dirt. She'd never been afraid of getting a little dirty.

Martial Square was full of preparations. Weaponmaster Galab was overseeing distribution, handing a weapon to each person who passed. Only some of them were guns, and those not very reliable. Lusvunub didn't have the same cache of military reclamation as some of the other Settlements—Falnarub in the east, in particular. Banzab had tried to reach out to the People there, to see if they would help, but it was no use. The People on that side of the continent preferred their isolation. They hadn't been visited by Magona, yet. They didn't know what was to come.

But Magona had said that it would be enough. So they were going with what they had: a few dozen rusted semi-automatic rifles, some pistols, fifteen compound bows. The rest were armed with knives and axes—fool's weapons, in Banzab's eyes. No machetes, like the People of the west coast. It was all they had, and Magona hadn't wanted to go find more.

Banzab approached Weaponmaster Galab, catching his eye as she neared. "Is it ready?" she asked, the guttural tongue of the People rolling from her lips.

Galab nodded. He slapped the man in front of him hard on the back, sending him forward into the line of troops that were forming around the gate. "Have it right here," he said, reaching under the table.

The blade he pulled out was thin and gleaming, impossibly straight, with a dark pommel and handle that glittered strangely in the yellow floodlights that surrounded them. Banzab took the weapon from the man, marveling at how light it was. Her fingers crept around the handle, and for a moment she was somewhere else. For a moment she was seeing dark shapes, cement, hearing the tearing of steel. Her hand clenched as she relived the memories, fragments of her past life crashing in around her.

Then she clipped the blade to her belt, and the vision disappeared. "You did well," she said to Galab. "I knew the power was within you."

He nodded, staring at her. Was that worry in his eyes? "The blade," he said, his voice rumbling. "It is not for you, is it?"

Banzab shook her head, jata dreadlocks waving from side to side. "It is for an old friend—one who is long dead. I cannot use the magic in this blade, but I can still *kill*." She bared her teeth.

Galab's mouth formed a straight line. "Kill you shall," he said, breaking into English for one brief sentence. He wasn't supposed to do that.

"Thank you, my friend," Banzab said. "It is almost time."

"Your place is at the head," Galab said in the People's language. "You should be up there." He nodded toward the gate, glimmering in the darkness at the far end of the square.

"My place is with the People," Banzab said. "Head or tail, it does not matter. Be well." She clutched a fist to her chest in the People's salute.

Galab returned the gesture. "Be well." Then he turned to see to the next soldier in line.

Banzab left the weaponmaster to his duties. He was one of her only friends in this place, this town of dirt and metal. At least he would not be joining them to die. She *was* needed at the gate—Galab was right. But something kept her from heading in that direction. She was not ready to go—not yet. Perhaps she was not yet ready to die. So instead she skirted the weapons station and headed north, out of Martial Square.

The air changed as she entered Second District—it became thicker, sweeter. She walked through a narrow, dirty street, pushing aside tattered clothing that hung drying from lines overhead. Her slim blade clanked quietly against her armor as she walked, adding another layer to the already noisy night.

For a moment, Banzab thought she felt a disturbance in

the air, as if a soul had wandered through her, unable to pass into the beyond. She shivered, imagining what it must be like to die—to die, but have nowhere to go once you were done.

It had been like this ever since the incident two years ago. A friend of hers—her lover, if she was being honest—had killed herself in this district, right near where Banzab was standing. She gritted her teeth, refusing to reflect on the memory. Tonight of all nights, she needed to do her best. She needed to banish thoughts of death.

Maybe she just needed a drink.

The edge of Second District was where the rickhouses started. She could smell them immediately, wood mixed with esters and alcohol. This was where they aged their bourbon, using a technique handed down from the original inhabitants of Lusvunub some three hundred years ago, before the Sundering.

Back when the town had been called Louisville.

Now it was Louisberg in the English tongue; Lusvunub in the language of the People. But they still made bourbon. They had almost never stopped. They used it now for trade, and quite a lucrative trade it was.

Particularly when they were selling it to Orym.

Banzab ran her hand along the outer wall of the rickhouse she was near, feeling the rough texture of the wood beneath her fingertips. This was their livelihood, their way of life. Without this to anchor them, the People here would likely turn to fighting. She'd seen it before, in other Settlements. It was never pretty, and it only served to further fracture the already tenuous society the People had tried to build.

There would have been no society at all if Magona hadn't arrived. She was an enigma—different than she had been before, when Banzab had first met her some years ago. She seemed more confident now, more mature, as if her impetuous nature had been stabilized by time.

Banzab had worried the woman might be dangerous, but thoughts of danger had quickly dissipated. A tinge of purple overtook her mind as she reflected, and for a moment she was no longer there.

The People had been wild without Magona. Chaotic. The woman had given them something they had sorely lacked, something they couldn't find for themselves.

She had given them a *plan*.

Banzab turned away from the rickhouse. She could go in, maybe take a barrel sample, maybe sit a while. But it was time to go. Time to lead her People. So she stifled her desire for liquor, turning instead and heading in the direction of the gate.

Banzab had heard the stories. When Magona had first left them—two hundred years ago or more—she had told them she would return. And when she did, she had said, she would have need of the People. It would be their time, she had said. They would be needed at long last. They would be needed to fight. And now, as the Sky Cities shadowed the Earth, as potent forces fought in the heavens, as the animals themselves responded to a great call, Magona had been true to her word.

The People's god had returned.

And she was magnificent.

Banzab approached the gate. It was a great circle of brilliant orange light, shimmering and flickering in white around the edges. She could see a desert through the gate, hot and wavering as if seen through imperfect glass. The People were lining up in pairs, filing slowly through the gate, heading to where they were needed. Heading into battle.

Magona herself was standing beside it, watching all, jet

black skin gleaming in the reflected sunlight from the magical beyond. She had a faint smile on her face as the People trudged through, stepping onto a new world. She seemed pleased. She turned as Banzab approached, lips curving into a smile that never touched her empty eyes. "It has already begun," she said, her voice low.

Banzab looked at her, at the tightly curled black hair, at the shirt that bared a portion of her stomach. The woman almost reminded her of someone else. Someone from long ago. She didn't seem to be a god—not here. A twinge of purple interrupted her thoughts.

"The People are obedient, if nothing else," Banzab said.

Magona quirked an eyebrow. "You speak as if you are not one of them."

Banzab surveyed the troops as they continued filing through the gate. "Some days I believe none of us are truly a part of anything."

"And now?"

Banzab turned back to her. "Now we do your bidding. We fight, but we know not for what."

"Power," Magona said, almost as a whisper.

"What?" Maybe Banzab hadn't heard her correctly.

"We fight to end oppression," Magona said. "We fight for a better future."

Banzab had heard those words before, and not from her. "We will not be so easily controlled."

Magona's eyes narrowed. Banzab could see the blindness in them, white where there should have been black. The woman could not see her, but she acted as if she did. "I do hope that was not a threat."

"Of course not," Banzab said, bowing slightly. The last thing she wanted was to anger Magona. "I simply mean that we wish to be full partners with you on this venture. Whatever it may be."

"Full partners…" Magona mused. "I assure you, all will be held equal. When I finally have Guruthos, all will be made well. The People will be held in high esteem. You will have all you ever wanted."

Banzab ground her teeth. All this talk of Guruthos, and she still didn't know what it *was*. She had been too rash in ordering the warriors of Lusvunub to fight. She should have waited it out, should have asked more questions, should have—

Magona's head swiveled suddenly, a look of alarm crossing her face. "What—"

"Is there a problem?" Banzab asked.

Magona didn't answer. She was looking through the gate, staring as if she could see someone else on the other side. She cocked her head as if listening to something.

"No," she uttered. "The boy. He can't *do* this!"

Banzab thought she heard screaming from somewhere far beyond the gate. The People continued stepping through into the desert sands, seemingly oblivious to their god's discomfort. Had Magona gone mad?

"The gates must…stay…open…" Magona said, but now her eyes were closed and she jerked as if she were being tortured. Banzab thought she heard another piercing scream from far away, then the woman's eyes suddenly snapped open, focusing on her.

Focusing on her.

Magona was no longer blind.

"Get everyone through the gate," she said, irises tight. "*Now.*"

"We can only move so fast," Banzab said, before yelling

commands at the People. They tried to pick up the pace, but it had already been at least an hour of marching. It took a *long* time to get so many thousands of People through a single gate.

"I will leave this splinter here as long as I can," Magona said. Banzab had no idea what that meant. "My powers may be needed elsewhere. You might see me flicker or disappear for a moment. Do not be concerned."

Banzab looked at her, trying to understand. What magic was this? It was nothing she had ever heard of. Perhaps Magona really *was* a god. "I will go through last," she said. Magona simply nodded.

They were silent for a long time. The People continued leaving, the line dwindling until there were only a few remaining. The others were arrayed out in the desert on the other side, weapons at the ready, as yet unsure what they were there to do. And if something happened to Magona, Banzab realized, perhaps they would never know.

They'd be stranded on an unknown planet.

Banzab felt a chill rush through her. Should they be doing this? Should they be following their mystical savior into the bright unknown? Why would the People fight someone else's war?

But the choice had been made. Everyone was already there. Everyone but Banzab, at least. She was last, and now it was her turn to go.

She took one final look at Magona. The woman was breathing erratically, newly-healed eyes locked on a distant target, muscles flinching periodically for reasons she could not discern. There was something happening, something Banzab could not know, something that was perhaps only in the purview of the gods.

Banzab did not want to be a god.

So she stepped through the gate.

Just as she did, Magona let out a scream. She fell to the ground, writhing in agony, the gate flickering in the air. Beam completed her step, feeling the horrid heat of the desert wash over her, feeling the chill of the gate itself pierce her flesh. There was a moment of confusion as her thoughts went blank, as the gate's magic did impossible things to her mind. Then she was back, already sweating in the sun, squinting and trying to see Magona's twisted shape as it lay on the ground in Lusvunub.

She wasn't moving. She wasn't breathing.

She was completely still.

Was she—? No. It couldn't be. Banzab watched her for what seemed like an eternity, but the woman did not move. She stared as the life seeped out of Magona's face, as her eyes returned to blindness, closing.

Magona—their god—was dead.

It had all happened in a moment.

Banzab put a hand to her mouth, feeling conflicting emotions warring in her mind. Confusion that a god could die. Relief that they would not be controlled by such a god. Fear that they would be stuck here on this unknown planet, trapped in a desert that they did not understand. Even now the gate was flickering and fading, threatening to strand them. Banzab could order the People to retreat back through it, but she knew that only a few of them would make it before the magic would be gone. She felt defeat as she realized her worst fears had already been realized. Sorrow as she beheld the body. And as she looked at the corpse of their savior, as she saw a spider crawling across the woman's prone form, she felt another emotion.

Revulsion.

She turned away as the gate snapped shut, as purple clouds finally lifted from her mind.

TWO

ELANIL WAS STILL STRUGGLING to get used to the fact that she could fly. The others had left them in the Thesserin Desert, in the strange complex someone had called the Palace of Memory. They had all left as if seeking something urgently, getting into flying cars with a bunch of strange-looking people dressed in robes. Apparently whatever they were looking for wasn't important enough to tell Elanil about.

Typical.

"Are you okay?" she asked Rylan. He was sitting in an office chair, sweat beading lightly on his brow. Cariel—the wolf in sheep's clothing, apparently Arra's long-lost mother— had just possessed him. They called it a "soulbind," but Elanil thought that was way too nice a word for what it was. It was mind control, plain and simple. It had been awful to watch.

But Trey had come in and saved the day, as usual.

Rylan took a ragged breath. "That was...*crazy*," he said. Then he actually smiled.

Of course he would take it like an adventure. A woman had just been inside his *mind*, inside his *soul*, but he had already rebounded from it like a rubber ball. Like an elastic band.

Like an underkid.

Elanil didn't think she could be that strong.

She pulled Rylan into an impulsive hug, almost picking him up out of the chair. He wasn't big—not like Trey or Orym or her poor, dead father. He was her size, kind of short, with hair all raggedy and dirt on his face. And there was a brightness in his eyes, something that spoke of intelligence, determination. Fun. That spark had been missing when Cariel had a hold of him. She shivered as she remembered it.

Then he was kissing her, kissing her like his life depended on it, and she was melting into his arms, and for a moment she forgot all about the metal and machines that surrounded them. She forgot about the madwoman who had tried to kill them all. She forgot about the fourteen Books of Amplification that even now were arrayed around the wall, lined up like perfect peas in a high-tech pod.

Rylan's lips felt so *good* against hers. His body felt so good. His hands. He wasn't quite like Martan, like the Remnant boy she'd thought she'd loved. Rylan was a bit stronger, yet at the same time gentler. But it wasn't really his looks or his manner that had drawn her to him, all that time ago when she had died. It wasn't his messy hair or the dirt, though that did help. It wasn't his innocence, feigned or otherwise.

It was his eyes.

She melted into his embrace, grateful that she had this time. Grateful that she wasn't dead anymore. That she wasn't trapped in Ambarhal, doomed to an oblivion of wavy purple and evil gold. But there was something wrong with her nose. She wanted to itch it, to take a breath, to sneeze, but Rylan was still kissing her and she didn't want to interrupt the moment, and...wait.

Was something *burning*?

She pulled out of the kiss, keeping one hand on Rylan's waist as she looked around the room.

The Books of Amplification were all on fire.

"Is that supposed to happen?" she asked, and Rylan turned to see what she was looking at.

"Uh," he said. "We used them to heal Cariel's eyes. Why would they be—"

He lunged forward toward the nearest Book, pulling it out of its placement on the shelf. He threw it to Elanil and she caught it awkwardly, watching as he grabbed a second one for himself. These two weren't badly singed, since the fire had just started. Elanil beat the flames out with her hand.

But the twelve other books were really on fire now, the pleasantly sweet stench of burning parchment filling the room.

"What happened?" Elanil asked. "Why are they doing that?"

The fire wasn't in any danger of spreading, since the Books were entirely surrounded by metal. Still, it meant that twelve irreplaceable magical Artifacts were being lost right before their eyes.

But at least they still had two.

"I don't know," Rylan said. "Maybe they were rigged to do that. Or maybe it was something about the magic we used—I don't think soulsoothing is meant to replace broken body parts. *Especially* eyes."

Eyes were the window to the soul. Elanil had heard that expression somewhere before. And it was true, she realized. It was why she loved Rylan.

Loved...

She hadn't meant to use so strong a word. But it was true, she realized. She was only fifteen, and so was he, yet the emotion felt as pure as anything else she'd known in her short life. She loved this boy, and it wasn't just because of his eyes.

"We should get out of here," she said, willing her mind to change the subject. She might kiss him again if she let herself continue. Although—would that be so bad?

Rylan was nodding. "Something's going on out there—I can feel it. Something important."

The entire structure rocked just then, vibrating as if in a minor earthquake. "What the—" Elanil said, but then the vibration intensified. It intensified a *lot*.

"Do you still have primewood?" she asked, struggling to keep her balance. Rylan nodded. "Then let's fly."

They set out into the air, leafrunning and fallfoiling magic blending seamlessly together, moving them effortlessly through space. Being a Prime Mage sure did have its benefits. It was really fun.

They flitted a few feet out of the Palace, hovering in the air like two bees. But then they heard someone yelling, and Elanil turned.

It was Imra. The woman was gesticulating wildly, trying to get them to stop. "Wait!" she shouted, and Elanil moved closer to her. She was standing on the same shelf they had been, yet somehow Elanil had completely ignored her. She chastised herself for being a fool. Too many people ignored Imra, to their peril. Elanil had fallen into the same trap.

"Sorry!" she said, flying down to the shelf again and alighting next to Imra. "We want to go check out what's going on."

"They were heading to Ilyrion," Imra said. "The Department of Magical Research took them."

"Oh," Elanil said. So Imra had been more aware than she had been. It figured. Imra always had been bright, like Arra was, even if Arra always got all the attention. "I think I can take you with us, if you want to come."

"In the air?" Imra asked, lips twisting into an almost frown. Elanil nodded. "Okay," Imra said. "Try. But I don't guarantee that I won't throw up."

Elanil smiled at her. "I'll be as gentle as I can."

THREE

"THAT'S DONE IT," Donar Cresius XV said, motioning to someone behind him. "Ilyrion is now under executive order from the Department of Magical Research. Note it down."

A mage in a purple robe typed it in the air, dutifully copying down what Cresius had said. Arra hadn't noticed him before.

She had been too focused on the Twins.

The world *shook* as Arra stood there, watching as the two Anubis Twins smiled at each other, raising their maces and destroying everything around them. Trees shook. Trees *fell*. Brush and leaves and metal and dirt flew everywhere as Velion and Nelenor took great, striding steps away through the Ecological District, swiping at everything they passed.

They were killing the forest.

How much else would they destroy?

"Tarathiel," Cresius said, "you really shouldn't have done that."

But Trey was just standing there slack-jawed, watching the Twins rip through everything around them. Arra saw another tree fall, and another. Then the Twins hit a building, sheets of glass shattering, metal skin buckling as Arra watched. She felt horror rising up in her stomach. Fear worse than when her mother had appeared. Terror greater than when Cariel had drawn her Palace of Memory out of the sand. This was worse. This was *far* worse. The Twins were making their way east, toward the Airon Sea, and they were destroying *everything* in their path.

The city would not survive.

People were screaming in the distance, pouring out of buildings and into the streets outside the forest. She heard cries of agony, shouts of alarm, everyone clamoring to get out of the way of the rampaging Twins. And still more buildings erupted into shards, abruptly silencing each and every soul within them.

Ilyrion, and everyone within it, was dying.

"Where is he?" she heard a voice say. A loud voice, echoing off the remaining buildings.

It was Velion.

"Show your face, Imprisoner!" the other Twin said. Nelenor turned, face dark, eyes alighting on everything as if he were searching for something. "Come into the light! We know you're here. We can *feel* you."

Arra had no idea what they were talking about.

She looked at Trey. Saw his stark white face as he realized what he'd done. Saw him standing there helpless, clueless, as stupid as the day she'd first met him—both times. He was always doing this: rushing headlong into things, seeking after fantasies, obsessing over his latest discovery.

This time he'd gone too far.

"You did this," Arra said, her voice shaking quietly.

Trey heard her. He turned, lips parted, eyes frantic. "I didn't know."

"You didn't...know." Her words were almost drowned out

by more crashes and explosions. Metal and glass and branches and leaves rained down on the world, falling further east in the Ecological District. Soon the Twins would be out of the District and into the city proper. Soon they'd be killing people by the tens of thousands.

And there was no one who could stop them.

"They're gods," Arra breathed. "*Evil* gods, and you unleashed them."

Trey took a step toward her. "It was supposed to turn on the Defense Mechanism," he said. "Edrafen...the Key. It was supposed to kill Guruthos."

Guruthos. The Weapon. The bane of all living things.

The Fall.

Guruthos was a big hunk of gray metal, dozens of feet long at least now held by the impossibly tall Anubis figures of the Twins themselves. The elven gods come to life. Elven gods who looked startlingly like Egyptian mythical creatures.

It was all a bit too strange.

"It corrupted you," Arra said. "Didn't it."

Trey hung his head. "It happened again."

He was speaking of Quynn—his "father"—who was actually a Cothellon boss and the person who'd mindmastered him almost into killing Arra. Trey had been easily corrupted then, and he was easily corrupted now.

Trey was weak. Arra knew that now.

Perhaps she'd always known.

"Imprisoner!" one of the Twins shouted from up ahead. They were almost out of sight now, their heads barely visible above the tops of trees. Which meant they were at least two hundred feet tall, which was somehow the *least* strange thing in this situation. "We will kill you when we find you! Your soul is here!"

"Who are they *looking* for?" Arra asked.

"No idea," Trey said, "but it's obviously not you or me."

"I have a feeling we don't want to find out who it is."

"Guys," Cresius said, "we need to leave. The Twins look to be destroying the whole city indiscriminately. We aren't safe here."

"Where can we go?" Arra asked.

Cresius' lips formed a thin line. "The Department has a place prepared for this kind of eventuality," he said. "Come."

So they ran, heading for the spaceport. It was Arra and Trey, and Lashel, and Cresius and his cohorts with the Department of Magical Research. They ran, feeling the world shake beneath the wrath of their resurrected gods.

Arra hoped the Department had some kind of solution for what was about to happen.

QUYNN STAGGERED and almost fell as the forest lurched around him. He cast about, confused. One minute he'd been on Eryn, the sweltering jungle planet, staring up at a huge Prime Tree. Then he'd done something to *unlock* the Tree, it seemed, and a portal had opened up and now he was here.

He had no idea where *here* was.

Saul was gone, having already run off somewhere. Magona, that great black witch of a woman, had disappeared before the portal even arrived. She had clearly been using magic more powerful than Quynn was familiar with. Now it was just Quynn, alone in a strange forest that was surrounded by skyscrapers, reeling as the ground thumped and jumbled underneath him.

Well, he wasn't *quite* alone. There were two big Anubis things off in the distance, so tall their heads cleared the trees, yelling something about wanting to find someone so they could kill him. And there were others in the forest, others of a more normal elven size. He couldn't quite make them out, though. Was that Orym, crouching over a corpse? Had he seen Trey in the other direction? Everything was moving too quickly, leaves and branches and tree trunks and shards of plate glass windows flying every which way, whirling through the air like the dust of a particularly deadly storm.

Those Anubis things. The giant yelling freaks. They were destroying *everything* around them. It was as if they'd just been woken up early from a nap and were *incredibly* cranky about it. Or as if they had a personal vendetta to settle against each and every one of the elves on this world.

It was probably the latter.

Quynn could understand, to a point. He'd been mad before. He was often mad these days, it seemed. And he'd killed, if not quite so effectively. He'd even destroyed buildings, if not exactly with his own hands. He knew what it was like to be so violent, how it felt to hold someone's life in your hands and twist.

So he knew that he needed to get the hell away from here.

He recognized this place now, barely. He was in Ilyrion, on Valaralda, in the big forest that took up the center of the city. He turned southwest, saw the high spires of the spaceport in the distance. He'd stood there, mere days ago, surveying the alien city with a strange man by his side.

Another crash rocked the forest, the Anubis people shouting once again for someone to show themselves. The Imprisoner, they called him. Quynn wasn't sure if they were looking for the one who'd put them to sleep or the one who'd woken them up. Either way, he hoped they weren't somehow after him.

He was, after all, still missing most of his memories.

There was no telling what he may have done.

He looked again at the spaceport. It was his only way off this planet. And from the looks of it, this planet was likely doomed. Earth would be safer by far, so long as he didn't show his face in the United Sky Cities. If he could get to Earth, he could find somewhere to live out some semblance of a life.

Yes. Good. That is what he'd do. He'd go to the spaceport. Once there, he'd find a pilot and convince him—or force him—to take him home. Or, failing that, he'd find a way to sneak on board. But first he needed some way to get there.

A car. Surely they had cars here? Something he could drive.

More leaves and branches fell around him as he sprinted out of the forest, heading toward the nearest street he could see.

ORYM CROUCHED with Lorelei on the forest floor as the last life left Cariel's body. She had used her dying breath to perform great magic, sending a cascade of gates over and around their brains.

Now all their memories were coming back.

Orym felt them wash over him, a great torrent of a hundred thousand years coming back to him as if poured from a great waterfall on high. His mind was brimming with them, filled with the past, full to overflowing with a life long lived.

Orym wasn't his name.

It was Aten.

The world of the now began to fade away, replaced with memories of a past long forgotten. And as the forest blurred and his old life rose to take its place, he caught a glimpse of Lorelei's face.

The same thing was happening to her.

KYTHAELA SURVEYED the group surrounding the mentorfire. The trees were mostly gone from Pano Sylrantheas—having been burnt down in the battle Quynn had brought—leaving the square empty, barren. But it wasn't trees that made a village.

It was the people.

She stood beside the mentorfire, knowing that this could be her final firestory. The moments were drawing to a close. After all this time, the Twins had finally returned.

She could feel them.

"History," she said, her storyteller's voice rolling richly across the circle. "What can be said of it? So often the distant past is just that—distant. So often it matters not to us what happened in that time. For people grow and change, doing great and terrible things. But with the passage of time also comes something else: death.

"All people die, do they not? And when they do, the only thing that remains is what they did, what they achieved, who they affected. What they built. Their spirit lives on in us, but it is just a memory.

"And with time, memories fade.

"But there are some for whom death does not come. For when they die, their spirit lives on in *more* than just a memory. There are some whose memories do not fade with time—or for whom those memories can be recalled.

"There are some among us who have walked with us as gods."

She turned, looking at each person in turn. There were Remnant humans mixed with elves, each sitting at rapt attention as she began to spin her tale. It was overly dramatic, of course, as her tales so often were. It *seemed* that way, at least.

Sometimes truth was far more dramatic than fiction could ever be.

"The story I am about to tell you takes place one hundred thousand years ago, on the planet Valaralda. It is a tale of our ancestors—or of our gods. It is a tale of death and vengeance and life and horrible injustice. It is a tale of love.

"Everything I am about to say is true."

FOUR

WAVES of golden grain bent and flexed, shimmering as the sun caught them, brushing against Lara's face. She giggled as they tickled her nose, holding out one hand to feel them waving in the wind. The sky above was brilliant blue, clouds flecking at the edges like the remnants of a dream.

Lara—Lorelei? No—her name was Lara then. She knew it as she descended back into the dream, into the memory, into a time so very long ago.

Into the golden abyss of her past.

Lara sang a little song as she took off running through the grain, red gingham dress swishing delightfully around her legs.

She was twelve years old.

Today was her birthday. Today Ma would bake her a special treat—cake, if she was lucky, but it would probably be honeybread. Pa always said real cake was too expensive, on account of the sugar. They had to ship it in all the way from Tanomar, that newly-discovered island in the far south of the Airon Sea. Pa always spoke of it in wondrous tones, of the elves there who harvested something called Sugar Cane, shipping it all over the world in great vessels they called Boats. Pa said it was an incredible discovery. He said it would change the world.

But sugar was still *dreadfully* expensive.

"Lara!" someone called in the distance. A girl's voice. Her sister.

Cara.

Lara felt the vision of her world twist as she remembered her sister's name. For a moment she was back there with her, watching her die on the forest floor, seeing the blood seep out of her neck. Cariel was such a vicious creature.

But she had not always been so.

"Lara!"

"Right here," Lara shouted back, annoyance flashing through her. She wanted to be out here with the grain. She wanted to run next door. Jon would be there again, the strapping young neighbor with the bulging biceps. He'd have his shirt off as he mucked the horse stalls, as he fed and watered them and brushed them and gave them a run. He might even let her ride with him, if she was lucky.

Cara finally arrived, blonde hair a stark contrast to Lara's raven brown, her dress a pretty white, eyes green. Cara had gotten the looks in the family. Pa said Lara would grow into it, that she had the makings of a temptress, but she had no idea what that meant and besides—she knew that he was lying, anyway.

"Jon's feeding the horses again," Cara said, flashing a smile at her. Her sister was making fun.

"So?" Lara feigned innocence.

"He's too old for you," Cara said, picking at her white skirt. "Pa says if he sees you with him again, he'll—"

Lara stepped forward suddenly, grabbing Cara by the scruff of her dainty white collar. "You didn't tell him," she breathed.

Cara got a frightened look in her eyes, but it passed as quickly as it came. "He saw you riding," she said. "I didn't say *nothing*."

"Anything," Lara corrected, releasing the girl. Cara was just a year younger than her, yet somehow she was always getting in the way. "I'll be home in an hour."

"Ma says to come home now." Cara's voice took on something of a whine.

Lara stomped her foot. A piece of errant grain waved against her cheek and she flicked it away, annoyed. "It's my birthday," she said. "I want to see Jon." She slapped a hand across her mouth as soon as the words came out. She hadn't meant to admit it.

Cara got a sly look on her face. "I wonder what Pa will say when I tell him?"

Lara felt storm clouds cover her face. "If you say anything, I'll kill you," she said, her voice low.

Cara didn't look frightened this time. She curtsied slyly, white dress swishing against the grain. "If you want to stop me," she said, "you'll have to beat me home!"

She turned and took off running, heading back toward the farmhouse.

Lara paused for only a moment before chasing after her.

IT WASN'T hard to beat Cara in a footrace, even when the girl had a head start. Lara was taller, after all, and a better runner.

Cara had never been very athletic, but she made up for it in smarts. Lara had always felt as if her sister harbored an evil spirit inside her. It was probably just jealousy on Lara's part, though—she *hated* it when someone was smarter than she was.

Pa hoisted her in his arms when she arrived home. "Oof," he said, setting her carefully back to the ground. "You're getting too big for that. Happy birthday, Lara-bear." He wrapped her in a big hug.

Lara felt her anger dissipating. This was home. This was her family. This was love—why was she seeking it elsewhere?

Then her sister clattered into the house, and she remembered why.

"Cara," Pa said, frowning at the girl, "what have I told you about being quiet in the house?"

Cara stepped into the room, head hung. "Sorry, Pa."

"Now go help your mother get dinner on the table."

"Yes, Pa." Cara flashed a glare at Lara before spinning and leaving.

"Lara-bear," Pa said, sitting on his big wicker chair and patting his leg, "do you know what day it is?"

Lara jumped into his lap, snuggling her head against his big chest. His beard tickled the top of her head, reminding her of grain. "It's my birthday, silly," she said.

"Not that," he said, and she pulled away, frowning up at him. "Today is not just your birthday, little one. It is also the Eternal Equinox."

Oh. That again. Why did Pa always bring up God at a time like this?

"You are lucky to have been born on such a day," Pa continued. "After dinner we will go to church, as we do every year. But unlike every year, you are finally old enough to attend the firestory."

The firestory. The older kids always gloated about it, said it was the most amazing thing to happen all year. They would gather around a big bonfire and eat pig cracklings and listen to the most wondrous story. You had to be twelve years old to attend. The older kids gloated about it, but Lara figured they were full of it. There was no way a stupid *story* could be worth all the fuss.

They were probably just trying to make her jealous.

"But Pa," Lara said, "I don't *want* to go to the firestory. I want to stay here with you and eat cake." Or go riding with Jon.

"There is no cake," Pa said. "Only dinner and the story. Now come along."

This was quickly shaping up to be the worst birthday Lara had ever had.

FIVE

"DID you get all your chores done today, *Lara-bear*?"

It was Belar, and he was making fun of her. Though everyone in Errenmel had chores, for some reason it sounded worse when Belar talked about them. He always had to find some reason to make her feel bad, if he could.

"Of course I did," Lara said, walking briskly past him. "Not that you'd know anything about *work*."

She made her way to the far side of the bonfire, sitting on a log with the other new twelve-year-olds. She hadn't *wanted* to sit with them—not and call attention to her age—but Belar had provoked her. She couldn't sit with him or his friends now.

So she sat with Talila, also twelve, who she hadn't talked to very much in the past. Talila was shy and kind of ugly— daughter of Deryth, the village pastor. She wasn't exactly looked down on as a result...she was just pretty well avoided.

No one wanted to anger God.

"Uh...hi," Talila said. It was very unlike her to be the first to speak.

Lara sighed, turning to her. "Is this going to be as stupid as I think?"

A look of confusion flashed on Talila's face, then she righted herself and smiled sweetly. "I—I don't think so. This is my first time, too. I hear the stories are great."

Lara turned back to face the fire. "I wanted cake."

"You have *cake*?"

Lara sighed loudly. "No. No, we do not. But I thought *surely* Pa would get some sugar this time. For me. I asked him so many times."

She saw Talila's mouth working silently out of the corner of her eye. "Father would *never* get me sugar," the girl said eventually. "It's a sin!"

Lara looked at her sharply. "Sugar is *not* a sin."

"It's the devil's work," Talila said, face white in the orange firelight. "Everyone knows that."

"Not everyone," Lara said, but she let the matter drop. This was why no one wanted to associate with the pastor's daughter.

But could Talila be right? No one really knew what God wanted, did they? No one really *knew* what things were sins.

Right?

A hush came over the crowd as Kila entered the square. She was tall and stately, long brownish-blonde hair swept back in a tight ponytail, revealing finely-pointed ears. She was wearing a flowing white dress with a high-necked collar and long sleeves complete with lace around the edges. High cheekbones and upturned nose gave her an elegant look, sharp eyes looking out at the crowd with distinct intelligence. She was the very picture of innocence and beauty. Lara at once loved her and hated her.

Kila was relatively new to Errenmel, having arrived just one year ago. She was enigmatic, unwilling to speak much of her past. Yet she had quickly risen in the ranks of the Church, gaining Deryth's favor in a way that even his wife didn't seem to have. Lara thought something fishy must be going on.

Still, it was hard to dislike Kila. She was poised, smart, and gorgeous, and there was not a hint of evil in her. Lara watched her as she stepped around the fire, and she found herself wishing that Kila was *her* mother.

She banished the thought as quickly as it had come.

"Greetings," Kila said, her voice round. She swept her piercing gaze around the bonfire, and Lara swore she met each and every person's eyes. There were at least a hundred people there—all age twelve and up, of course, and all waiting anxiously for Kila's story. Lara had never heard one of her stories before, but she knew there was no way it would live up to its reputation.

"Thank you for being here," Kila said. "Tonight we celebrate the Eternal Equinox, the moment when God first came to man ten thousand years ago." She paused again, continuing her pace around the fire. "It is said that God came as a man himself, ears pointed and hair long. It is said that when he came, the deserts erupted with sandstorms, the oceans divulged great salty tears. Those things are true, but they will happen with or without a god to make them so.

"No—when God truly came, he came in quietness. In peace. His footsteps were gentle. His manner compassionate. For God is not a god of war, but a god of love. Here now, I shall tell you the *true* story of the Eternal Equinox. The true story of how elvenkind first encountered the One.

"Everything I am about to say is—"

Kila stopped suddenly, looking up at the sky. "No," she whispered. Then: "Yes." Then she just stared upward at the stars, beautiful face poised as if she were seeing God Himself.

Lara didn't know what was going on. Talila took a sharp

breath inward next to her and Lara glanced her way, saw the starkness of her expression. She, too, was looking at the sky. Lara followed their gaze. Was there something up there? Were they actually looking at God? Had he come again, as He had promised ten thousand years ago?

She craned her neck, squinting and trying to see. She heard gasps all around the fire, people shifting position on their logs. But there was nothing up there. Just stars, just the two moons. Just an ordinary night sky. Was everyone going mad, or was Lara the one who was insane?

Then she saw it.

It looked like an orange ball of light, glimmering far away in the darkness. It was small, but bigger than the stars. Just a little bit bigger—not nearly as large as the moons. But it was *wrong*, out of place, somehow an alien in the familiar Valaraldan sky. Lara felt her heartbeat speed as she wondered what this omen must portend.

But then she noticed Talila's face. The girl was staring at Kila for some reason, with a look of murderous intent. "She brought this on us," Talila said quietly. Then she continued, louder. "Kila has brought the end of the world upon us!"

SIX

THE SQUARE ERUPTED INTO CHAOS, people scrambling up and yelling at each other, kicking dirt into the fire, screaming at Kila to stop her magic. Two men grabbed her, restraining her, but Kila wasn't resisting. She was just staring up at the sky with an open-mouthed expression.

Lara had thought they were looking at God in the heavens.

Apparently Talila thought they were looking at Satan.

Pastor Deryth finally arrived, having been absent until now. He was an older man, a bit pudgy and stooped, with a fringe of white hair around his balding pate. He shuffled into the square, looking with consternation at the crowd milling about. Talila found him, speaking urgently into his ear, and his eyes finally found the heavens. Lara saw his expression change to one of fear.

"A great evil is upon us," he stated, though Lara was sure nobody was listening.

The men had wrestled Kila closer to the fire. "Burn the witch!" they shouted. "Kill the defiler!"

Deryth looked at them, lips pursed, and for a moment

Lara thought he might agree. She felt her heart leap in her chest—Kila didn't deserve to die! She wasn't doing any magic. She was just telling a stupid story! An orange light in the sky wasn't cause for alarm, was it?

Why was everyone suddenly so afraid?

"No," Deryth finally said, speaking to the men holding Kila. "Take her to the jailhouse. We will keep her there for questioning. We will not burn anyone tonight."

Lara leapt off the log she was sitting on, coming over to stand next to the pastor. The square was clearing out now, everyone running back to their homes. Something about this light had driven fear into everyone's hearts, and Lara still didn't understand why.

"Kila didn't do this," she said to Deryth. Kila was standing calmly, not resisting. "She was just telling a story."

"Where is your father, young lady?" Deryth asked. "Go home. Darkness has visited us tonight, and we will not be the same."

"But it's not darkness," Lara said. "Can't you see?" She pointed at the sky, at the orange ball that was still small, no bigger than a speck of dust. "It's light."

PA CAME to get her in the buggy and took her home. The mood in the farmhouse was tense, quiet. Ma had lit candles, an unusual luxury at this time of night. Cara was in her nightgown, huddled on a wooden chair with her knees up to her chest, shivering. It was cold in the house.

Pa had let the fire die. He sat in his chair, picking up a knife that had been lying on the table next to him. It wasn't a carving knife, either—it was a butcher's knife. Lara felt a chill roll through her as she saw it.

Not this again.

"What is it, Pa?" Lara asked, hearing the trepidation in her voice. She had seated herself at the table, hoping there might still be time for her birthday treat. Everyone seemed to have forgotten about her.

But now Pa had taken up a knife.

He looked at her as if startled from a daze. "I don't know," he said. "Pastor thinks it's some kind of evil, come to punish us for our sins."

"Is that what you think?"

"I don't know," he said again, shaking his head, the knife held rigidly in his hand. "Olithir thinks it's something else. He had that looker of his out, pointed at the sky."

Olithir was something called a "scientist." He was from Ilyrion, the big city south of Errenmel. He was visiting the farming village, doing some kind of research for the University. No one knew what exactly he was doing, and no one trusted him. Anyone who could see great distances simply by holding a cylinder to his eye could not be trusted.

"What did Olithir say?" Lara asked.

"It's a celestial object."

"A what?"

"Like a star, only this one's moving."

"But what *is* it?" She had to be careful. She didn't want to push Pa too far.

But he just shook his head. "Olithir doesn't know. He thinks it could be some kind of craft, way out there in space."

"But is there...could there be...a *person* in it?"

"That's heresy," Pa said, his voice sharpening. "Valaralda is the One True World. There is no other."

Cara let out a little whimper from her place in the chair.

"So someone could be visiting us," Lara said. Why did she

insist on pushing the subject? The last thing she wanted was for Pa to get angry.

His eyes got very cold. "This is Kila's doing. She brought this on us."

"How can you say that? How can a person do anything like that?"

Pa stood suddenly, the knife brandished wickedly in his hand. Lara cringed, her body shrinking into itself, her face turned reflexively away. There was no reasoning with Pa when he got like this.

Not even on her birthday.

She was just glad Ma wasn't in the room.

"Is Kila really a witch?" Cara asked suddenly. "Can she really do magic?"

"I'm afraid she can," Pa said. He appeared to think better of things, sinking back into his chair and putting the butcher knife down. Lara let out a sigh of relief, hoping it wasn't too loud.

"But Olithir said—" she started.

"Olithir is a crazy old man," Pa interrupted. "Maybe he's a witch, too. We'll soon get to the bottom of this."

"What are you going to do?"

"There are tests. We will find out if Kila is a witch. And if she is, we'll test Olithir as well. This town cannot harbor evil. We will not allow it."

"Are we all going to die?"

"Shush," Ma said, stepping in from the kitchen, long dress sweeping the floor. She had a big covered plate in her hands. "No more talk of witches and death." She set the plate on the table. Lara eyed it curiously.

"This is serious," Pa said. "We could all be in a lot of trouble."

Ma turned to him. "It's Lara's birthday, dear, unless you

forgot. If this is the end of the world—which I very much doubt—it can wait until tomorrow. Now wish your daughter a happy birthday."

She pulled the cover off the plate.

Lara squealed with delight. It was *cake*! An actual cake was there on the plate in front of her! It was small, of course, but it glistened there in the candlelight, gooey frosting practically dripping off the edges before her eyes. She could feel herself salivating.

"It's not fair!" Cara cried, getting off her chair and padding over to the table. "Why does *she* get a cake?"

Ma's smile dimmed as she looked at her younger daughter. "Be nice to your sister," she said.

Cara just glared at Lara. "She's never nice to *me*."

"Your sister is an angel," Ma said. "Now apologize to her, and wish her happy birthday."

"I will *not*," Cara said, stamping her bare feet on the wooden floor.

Pa stood, towering over all of them. "You will respect your mother's wishes," he said, voice rumbling. "Apologize."

"Make Lara apologize first."

"For *what*?" Lara squeaked. She had done nothing wrong.

"For always being so rotten!"

"Silence, Cara," Pa said. "Go to your room."

"But I—"

"*Go.*" He raised a threatening hand, and Cara's face paled. She turned and left the room.

Lara wasn't sure what had gotten Cara so riled up. It was her birthday—of *course* everyone was being nice to her. They would have been just as nice to Cara on *her* birthday, right?

Right?

LATER THAT NIGHT, Lara found herself shivering on the street just outside the jailhouse in Errenmel. She should have brought her winter coat, but it would have made too much noise to get it out of the closet. She had broken so many rules getting here: out of the house after bedtime, taken a horse without permission, stolen some of the cake Ma had made— which wasn't *precisely* against the rules, but with sugar being so expensive, it would definitely get her a lashing. But the worst sin was what she was about to do.

She was about to deliver cake to a *witch*.

She stood on tiptoes, careful not to drop the small paper-wrapped package in her hand. She was just barely tall enough to see into the window that looked out onto the street. It was barred with iron, of course, glass being far too expensive for something like a jail. So Lara thought maybe she could pass a bit of cake through the bars.

She liked Kila, though she didn't know why. She hadn't heard the woman's story, which was doubtlessly boring and stupid. But she'd seen the woman around. She'd been living in Errenmel for a *year*, after all. Kila had always been nice, courteous, even magnanimous. Even to her, a kid. Kila seemed to have a special place in her heart for kids, actually. Maybe that was why she liked her so much.

And now she was some kind of witch? It made no sense. Witches were supposed to be mean, sneaky, evil things with bad teeth. But Kila's teeth were *perfect*.

There had been cake left over. Lara's cake, to do with as she pleased. At least that's what she had told herself when she cut a piece off and wrapped it in paper. It was her birthday. She could do what she wanted.

She thought she'd seen Cara peeping out at her just as she left, but she couldn't be certain. If her sister *had* seen her, Lara would be in immense trouble. Maybe Pa would even go looking for her. She'd be lashed for sure, maybe stuck in the house with naught to do but chores for a month. So she hoped she'd been imagining things. She hoped Cara hadn't really been there. She had probably been asleep.

She stood on tiptoes, trying to see into the cell. It was dark in there, and nothing moved. She couldn't see anybody inside —nobody sitting on the floor, nobody leaning against a wall. She cast her eyes everywhere, trying to see into the dark corners of the room, but everywhere she looked was empty.

"Kila?" she whispered into the night.

There was no answer.

Had they moved her? They were taking her to the jail-house, they had said. Had they already taken her out, done something horrible to her? Lara felt icy fear shoot through her as she envisioned them torturing her, beating her, burning her at the stake. She didn't want that for Kila, even though she couldn't exactly say why.

She called the woman's name again, but there was still no response. Nothing moved. Nothing shifted. Nothing disturbed the straight lines of the stone cell.

Kila was gone.

SEVEN

ATEN SHOVED the notebook in his bag, jamming it in between the three other books and the quill pen and loose papers and things. He let out a curse as the pen stabbed him, piercing the skin and drawing blood. He pulled his hand out and sucked on the finger. Stupid, moons-forsaken bag. It was nowhere near big enough for what he needed to take with him, but he couldn't afford a new one. He would have to make do.

He shouldered the bag, keeping his finger in his mouth as he left the teachers' lounge and burst out into bright sunlight. He had to cross the vast central lawn and pass three more big brick structures before he would reach Suldusk Building, where his students would already be waiting.

Aten had a class to teach, and he was already late.

He hurried through the quad, brushing past students as quickly as he could, only tripping two of them in his haste. He caught their glares out of the corner of his eye, feeling a little spike of pleasure when he saw their stupid, hurt faces. So they'd tripped. They hadn't even fallen. They hadn't been paying attention well enough. It served them right. Maybe they'd try harder next time.

He swept into the classroom just six minutes and thirty six seconds after it was supposed to start, not bothering to look at the seven students that had decided to attend. It was a class on astronomy, which, if Aten was being honest, was not the sexiest of classes. Even if it *was* one of the most difficult. It dealt with science that was unproven, theoretical. And there was still a very large religious stigma against it, to Aten's great displeasure.

The church never did him any favors.

"Books open to page two hundred twenty three," he said, dusting chalk off the chalkboard. The previous professor in here had been messy, as usual. Nobody knew how to keep a clean workspace. "Today we will be learning about the moons."

"Uh, Junior Professor?" one of the students said from the front of the room.

Aten turned, grinding his teeth. He *hated* it when they called him that. "What?"

"Um. Did you hear about last night? Sir?"

The boy added that last part almost as an afterthought. Aten felt his face heating. "No," he snapped, "I have no idea what you're talking about."

The boy had the decency to cower, at least. "There was a, uh..."

The girl next to him took over, placing a hand on his arm. "Unexplained phenomenon in the sky, sir," she said. Her voice was clipped, precise. It helped that she was also cute. "An orange ball of light was first reported by residents of Errenmel. The resident astronomer said the object appeared to be moving. It's not a star."

"Of course it's not a star, if it's moving," Aten snapped, but thought better of it instantly. The girl didn't react, anyway. Cute *and* strong. Why was Aten in such a bad mood today, anyway?

"People are saying it's Satan," the first boy said.

Aten frowned at him. "That's stupid."

"Well, that's what I thought too, Professor, but—"

"There's no such thing as Satan."

"People need an explanation."

"That's why science exists, dammit," Aten said. "To provide explanations. But science takes *time*." He turned to the board, having forgotten what his lecture was going to be about. "I need to view this phenomenon for myself."

WHEN ATEN RETURNED TO THE TEACHERS' lounge, a crowd was there waiting—and not for him.

"Do you know what it is?" Cilivren asked, brushing past Aten and attaching herself to Thallan's arm. Those two were a couple, and full professors besides.

"They're saying it's the devil," Thallan said. He looked scared, hands wringing, face falling.

"Did you bring your looker?" another woman asked. Aten didn't even know what her name was.

Everyone was milling about, speaking excitedly to each other about the celestial object in the sky, wondering with amazement what it could possibly mean. But none of them had thought to ask the only professor at the entire place who taught astronomy.

They weren't there for him at all.

Aten cleared his throat, looking around the room. Nobody noticed him. So he tried again, louder. Still nothing. He did it a third time, not even needing to fake the phlegm rising in his throat. This time one of the older men glanced at him, covering his own mouth with a look of disgust.

Nobody else noticed. Nobody else cared. Nobody even knew who he was, much less what he taught. So Aten turned in disgust and slammed through the doors, almost dropping his bulging bag in the process. If he wanted more data on this strange orange thing in the sky, he would have to gather it himself. He would have to use his own telescope—not a *looker*, damn those imbeciles. He would formulate his own opinion, and then he'd deliver it to a rapt audience, hanging on his every word.

Nobody noticed him leave.

ATEN COULDN'T HIRE a buggy to get to the promontory, because of course he couldn't afford one. Because the University didn't pay him peanuts to teach the hardest class they had. Okay, maybe not the *hardest*. That honor probably went to Advanced Math IV, which he could also have taught. But the honor of teaching it went to full professors, not junior adjuncts like himself. And if astronomy wasn't hard, it was certainly the most *advanced*.

Most people didn't even *believe* in the subject.

He caught himself sighing as he climbed up the rocky hill —Piedmont Point, or some stupid name like that. It was a mile outside the University, easily within walking distance if you didn't have better things to do with your time. And it was the highest point in the vicinity. Also, it was nighttime.

He cursed as he tripped on a rock, struggling not to drop his bag and the telescope and the notebook he'd already taken out. He had no room for a lantern or a candle or anything—

he had to navigate by moonslight. Which *should* have been easy, but he hadn't been paying attention.

He managed it eventually, staggering to a stop atop the rocky ridge that overlooked Ilyrion. The city glimmered in the night, lanterns and candles and a handful of remaining bonfires flickering in the chill, dark air. The night smelled faintly of woodsmoke and cooked meat. Aten felt his stomach rumbling. When had he eaten last?

No matter. He had a job to do up here. A discovery to make. He needed to see what the devil had made everyone so upset all day. Some fire in the heavens? It had to be a load of cow shit. It had to be nothing. But he had to be sure—because if it wasn't, if people were actually *right* about all this, it could be the most important discovery he would ever make.

EIGHT

WHEN LARA GOT HOME, things weren't quite the same.

For one, everyone was awake. Two, all the lanterns were lit, and the fire, and even two candles. But the worst part of it all was Pa.

Pa was standing at the door with an axe in his hand.

"I—" Lara said. This was worse than the butcher knife.

"Get inside, young lady," Pa said.

She obeyed, shrinking as she stepped underneath his axe. Pa scared her sometimes, when he was mad.

Tonight was one of those times.

She caught Cara smirking at her as she entered the main room, but her sister ducked her face as soon as she saw Lara looking. That bitch. So she *had* seen Lara leave the house. And she'd wasted no time telling on her.

It figured.

"You have some explaining to do, young lady," Pa said, motioning for her to sit at the table. There was no "Lara-bear," no kindness of tone. Pa meant business, birthday or no. The axe was still in his hand.

Stories flashed through Lara's head, possible lies she could tell. But there was Cara over in her chair, legs drawn up into her chest, face pressed into what was not supposed to be a smile—but Lara could read her sister better than that. Cara was proud. Proud that she'd finally caught her sister out on something. Proud that she could finally be the one with the advantage. So Lara decided to do the one thing her sister wouldn't expect.

She decided to be honest.

"I went to the jailhouse to take a bit of cake to Kila," she said. But she couldn't resist adding *one* little embellishment. "I figured if Kila was going to be burned, she might as well have a taste of real sugar before she died."

Pa looked at her with clouds covering his face. "You are not to leave the house without permission," he said. "You know this. You are not to give away our food without our knowledge. You are not permitted to take a horse without supervision—you could have been killed! And you are *especially* not allowed to consort with known witches! What might have happened to you? What did she say?"

Lara felt herself bridling. "Kila is *not* a witch," she said. "And anyway, she wasn't there."

"She wasn't—but where did she go?" Pa started lowering the axe.

Lara shrugged. "No idea. She wasn't there when I arrived. The cell was empty. And the horse is tame, Pa. He knows me. I ride him all the time! How would I get *killed*?"

"You are too young to—"

"And this is *my* birthday cake, Pa. I know it's expensive. I know it was hard to make. But you gave it to *me*, and if I want to give it to someone else, that is my decision to make. I'm not a child anymore, Pa."

He stared at her for a long moment after that, jaw muscles twitching. The room was silent. Ma had her hands clasped in front of her, head bowed, not daring to look her in the face.

"You are my daughter," Pa finally said, anger barely simmering beneath the surface, "and you are strong. In the future I want you to ask me before you take such a trip on your own. You *are* a girl, Lara-bear." His voice had softened. "You'll always be my girl, and I worry about you." He stepped forward and picked Lara off the bench, gathering her into his arms. "I was scared," he whispered to her.

"That's *all*?" Cara screeched. "She broke *four* rules at once! You aren't going to even whip her? What is *wrong* with you?"

Pa whirled on her, Lara still in his arms. "Silence," he said. Lara could feel his voice rumbling in his chest. "This is my house to do with as I will. Now go to your room."

Lara could see tears gathering in Cara's eyes. She almost stuck out her tongue at her sister, but she didn't want to push her luck. Cara was already upset enough. Lara had been lucky.

"It's not *fair*," Cara said, her voice a whine.

"Now," Pa said.

Cara got up, padding silently to her room, sending one final glare to Lara before she did. If looks could kill, Cara had just killed Lara *twice*. Maybe Lara hadn't been so lucky, after all.

Maybe, for once, she'd been *smarter* than her sister.

NINE

CARA WOKE THE NEXT DAY, bleary-eyed. She slid out of bed, bare feet cold on the wooden floor, thoughts taking moments to resume.

There it was. The anger.

Her sister had broken the rules, and for that she hadn't gotten so much as a slap on the rear. Her sister was *always* doing that, always doing what was wrong, and she almost never got in trouble.

Because Pa liked Lara more than her.

The worst part was the helplessness. There was nothing she could do. She couldn't break the rules herself, because Pa would always punish her. She'd tried tattling on her sister, but Lara still managed to sweet-talk her way out of it. So there was no winning. Unless...

She padded into the kitchen, long night dress skirting the floor. Ma was out there, stirring something fragrant in a big metal pot. She turned as Cara arrived, a loving smile on her face.

That was when Cara knew her plan would work.

Something caught her eye on the street outside. The

kitchen window faced the dirt road, one of the side roads that led out to four different farmsteads. Their house was rare in that it was relatively close to town—and close to the road. Cara sometimes liked to just stand at this window, watching horse-drawn carts roll by.

But this time there was something else going on. There were people outside, and not in carts. She saw four people, two men and two women. The women were just walking through the long grass, dazed expressions on their faces, hands held outstretched in front of them as if they were waiting for it to rain.

The two men, meanwhile, were chasing each other. One was chasing the other, actually, hair waving as he ran, shouting something and gesticulating wildly.

"What's going on?" Cara asked.

Ma shook her head. "It's this new moon," she said. "Driving people crazy."

Cara looked up at her. "More than this?"

"Your father was at the market early this morning. He said there were no stalls set up, and all the farmers were either missing or wandering about aimlessly."

"But today's Market Day!"

"Exactly. They should have been ready to go—it was only a few minutes before the market was supposed to open. But nobody was doing anything. Pa took one look at everyone and left."

"But that means he won't sell anything today."

Ma pointed out the window. "Do you think he would have gotten any customers?"

Cara shook her head. Something strange was definitely going on. She'd heard about the new moon, the little orange thing that had appeared in the night sky. Lara had been raving about it, about how it had disrupted the firestory and everything. She'd been too proud, so Cara hadn't listened. Now she wished she had.

Shouts erupted suddenly from outside. One of the men had caught the other, wrestling with him next to a big poplar tree. It didn't look like it was going well for the man on the ground.

"We should help them," Cara said.

Ma nodded firmly. "Stay here," she said, brushing her hands off on her apron and leaving through the kitchen door.

Cara waited about thirty seconds before following her.

ATEN WOKE SUDDENLY, coughing and shivering as the coldness hit him. He sat up, brushing dew off his jacket. He had fallen asleep on the damn hill. He'd been watching the orange light in the sky, trying to figure out what it could mean and how he could see it better. His telescope hadn't given him nearly enough magnification to make the object out.

Now it was morning, and he was freezing, and he was no closer to figuring out what in the two moons the stupid thing was.

He packed up his telescope and notebook, growing further annoyed as he saw how soaked the bag was. How had he managed to sleep in such cold? Why hadn't he just gone home?

He knew the answer to that one. Because home was just a tiny, piddling room in the Adjunct Suite, a fancy name for what amounted to a boarding house for poor, young Junior Professors. He hated it. It was almost worth spending the night on Piedmont Point if it meant he could escape the judging eyes of the full Professors, of the students, even of the janitor who cleaned the front room of the Suite. He didn't clean *Aten's* room, oh no. That honor was reserved for Aten himself.

He was worth so much more than that.

Movement caught his eye as he shouldered the bag. Something was happening out in the distance, way out in the middle of Ilyrion.

It looked like a tree was *growing*.

WHEN CARA STEPPED OUTSIDE, she could hear the two men screaming. One was on top of the other, grappling with him underneath the poplar tree. They rolled around as she watched, screaming something at each other. Something about...weeds? She couldn't make out the words. She thought they were arguing about weeds.

What in God's name was going on?

Ma hadn't seen her yet. She had rushed over to the men, shouting at them to stop. But they didn't listen, of course. Why would they listen to a woman? Some kind of madness had taken hold of them. Cara could almost see their thoughts, tinged with red. A little shudder rippled through her as she envisioned it. What was happening to the world?

The men managed to stand, and Cara realized she knew them. They lived on their street, actually—they had the next two farms. The aggressor, the angry one, was Ruven. He had a big cornfield, and pigs. The other man was Jonas, from the farm further down. His farm was mostly beans this year, with a smattering of squash. Normally the two of them got along famously.

But now they were facing each other, faces twisted into expressions of hatred or fear. Jonas almost tripped on a tree root but he recovered quickly, fists raised, eyes wary. Ma was still watching them, standing about twenty feet away, her hands balled into helpless fists. Cara took a few steps forward so she could hear what they were saying.

"My corn was doing just fine," Ruven said. He was the angry one, his feet in an aggressive stance.

Jonas cowered a little behind his defiant glare. "I didn't do anything to the weeds," he said.

"Yes you *did*. I *saw* it, dammit!" Cara cringed at the curse. "You touched them."

"You're crazy," Jonas said.

"I am *not crazy*!" Ruven said. But he was clutching his head as he said it, his body rocking as if in pain. "They're trying to kill me." His hands formed into fists.

"What? Who's trying to kill you? Put your fists down, man. I didn't do anything to your crops."

Ruven lowered his fists. "I can feel them," he said. "They're coming."

"Who's coming?"

"The stars."

"Man, you have got to quit the liquor. What in the two moons has gotten into you today?"

The men stared at each other for a pregnant moment. Ma and Cara just stood there, watching the scenario play out. There was something very much not right about all this.

"I can feel them," Jonas said.

Then, suddenly, Cara could feel them too.

ATEN RUBBED HIS EYES, wondering if he was seeing things. Maybe it was the lack of food—when had he last eaten, anyway? He could have sworn he'd seen a tree *grow*, getting larger and larger by the second before his eyes. There it was now, waving slightly in the wind, towering hundreds of feet above Ilyrion. It was an ash tree, round crown prominent and green. It was almost as if the hand of God had reached down to pluck this one tree out of oblivion, raising it to new stature.

Or it would have been, if he had believed in God.

Rubbing his eyes didn't help. The tree was still there. It was brighter than trees normally were, somehow. It was more vibrant, as if the colors were reaching into his eyes and pulling forth newer, better passions. He could almost feel it calling out to his soul.

He put a hand to his head, awareness whirling for a moment. Had he ingested something? A mushroom of some kind, an herb? Was he still dreaming? Was he even still alive? Trees weren't that big. They weren't that green. And they *certainly* couldn't speak into his soul.

Aten turned abruptly and began picking his way down the hilltop. First the orange light now this. *Something* was going on, and he intended to get to the bottom of it.

CARA FELT as if her soul were trying to expand.

She felt sparks of it shooting outward, heading for the sky, the trees, the fields. She felt her mind enlarging, her feelings bursting, awareness sharpening. There was a *calling* out there, a life, a time. Two lives—no, three. They shone out like pinpricks, like mirrored lanterns, like stars. She felt the heart of them, felt their feelings decay. She felt the sanity of their minds.

Then the feelings were gone.

But everything in her awareness had shifted impercepti-bly, as if she were seeing the world through slightly colored lenses. A portion of her mind had turned on, just then, blinking into existence where there had been none before.

She felt refreshed now. She felt whole, clear-minded, purposeful. She didn't understand the purpose—not yet. But she would. She knew she would. It would happen when it was time.

She felt as if she had just awakened.

WHEN ATEN GOT BACK to the University, things had changed. People were bustling about, which they always were —but this time they were talking to themselves, clutching foreheads, crying. More than a few of them were kissing madly underneath the trees—but that in and of itself was not so unusual. What *was* unusual was their faces.

Their eyes were all wide open.

Aten felt dread crawling through his stomach. He pushed it aside, ascribing it to hunger. And he *was* hungry, after all, so he headed for the professor's lounge to try to get some food.

When he got there, Professor Antioch was staring at him.

"What?" Aten demanded.

"Your face," Antioch said.

"What about it?" Aten could hear the surly tone in his voice. Did he always sound like that?

"You look like you've been sleeping in the dirt."

"Oh," Aten said, brushing self-consciously at his cheek. "Well, I, uh—"

"You don't have to explain anything to me," Antioch said. "Have a seat. They're still serving breakfast."

"Thanks."

Aten sat across from Antioch at the long cafeteria-style

table, conscious of his proximity to the other professor. Antioch was a full professor, not a junior like Aten was. They didn't talk much, but they knew who each other were. They didn't talk much because Aten didn't usually associate with other professors. Come to think of it, he didn't really associate with *anyone*. He reflected on that for a moment, lost to the world around him. Why was he so antisocial? What did he think he could possibly gain by that approach?

"Lost you again," Antioch said. "You know what they say about big minds."

Aten came back to himself, eyes sharpening on Antioch's face. He was an older man, cheeks craggy with age, eyes a gray that had seen a cold lifetime. He had been through troubles, Aten realized. Intuition leaped before him, revealing the lines and shadows of a life gone by. Thoughts and feelings flitted across the page of Antioch's eyes: a flick and a finger, a glint, a pause. The man was interested in Aten; he was lonely; he was very intelligent; and he was a little bit afraid.

Aten pushed back suddenly. Where was all this new awareness coming from? It was like a whole new world had opened up before him, as if he were suddenly prophetic, a visionary, an oracle. As if he could read people's minds.

Aten felt as if he'd just awakened.

TEN

CARA BLINKED. Her eyes cleared. The world was the same as it was.

Almost.

Jonas and Ruven were still standing beneath the poplar tree, Ruven clutching Jonas' neck with one hand. They weren't speaking anymore. They were just staring at each other, breathing dark thoughts.

Ma was standing there, too.

Cara fidgeted with her dress. Should she do something? Should she step forward, maybe shout, maybe scream at them to stop what they were doing?

Would anything she did have any effect?

No. She was just a kid. She was just a girl.

There was nothing she could do.

"I can see you," Ruven said. "I can *feel* you. Get out of my mind. I don't like you this close."

"I'm not...doing...anything," Jonas said. His voice sounded pained, shortened, as if the life were being drawn out of him. He flicked his eyes upward to the sky as if seeking some kind of resolution there.

There was nothing to be found.

"I need you," Ruven said, "to die."

And he pulled a knife out from somewhere.

Cara let out a little shriek. She couldn't help it. She wanted to be strong, but she didn't like knives. She'd seen Pa with knives far too many times. He always got that certain glint in his eyes, that quirk of the mouth that said don't come any closer, Cara. Don't say the wrong thing, or this knife might miss. It might accidentally slay you where you stand.

Metal. Knives. Fear.

These were things that Cara knew.

"You wouldn't," Jonas said. He was up against the tree, breathing heavily, not even struggling to get away. He wanted to—Cara could see that—but he didn't know how. He wasn't strong enough.

"Ma," Cara whispered.

"Shh," she said. Evidently she had decided not to intervene. Not that Cara wanted her to now. Her mother might die if she intervened now. The situation was too far gone.

"Look," Jonas said, "I don't want to fight you. I didn't touch your crops. I didn't destroy the weeds like you thought I did. I *might* have...I don't know. Something is happening, here. Something beyond you or me. I could almost feel the soul of the plants...but that's crazy."

"Shut up," Ruven said. "Plants don't have souls. *You* don't have a soul. You've always been jealous of me. Jealous of my land, my farm, my money. You've always wanted me out, but it's not going to happen. I'm not going anywhere!"

He pushed the knife up against Jonas' throat.

"Listen," Jonas said, his throat struggling against the knife, "we can work this out. I don't want to fight. Kill me if you must, but think what that will do. How will you live with yourself?"

"You're giving me *permission* to kill you?"

The air was silent for a moment. Cara was conscious of her own breathing.

"Yes," Jonas said. "If it will right whatever is wrong with your soul, kill me. Do it. Just know that when it is done, I will haunt you. My soul will find you in the afterlife. And God will punish you for your sins."

Then he lifted his face up to the sky and closed his eyes. He was a willing sacrifice before the devil with the knife, chest heaving as he held himself against the poplar tree. Cara watched the scene pause as she stood there, as the two men held themselves poised in a frieze for all eternity.

Then the knife slashed across the throat.

A line of red. A gasp.

A sheen of blood, welling, falling.

Streaming.

Crying.

Somebody was crying. Somebody was falling. Jonas. Blood was flooding down his neck. He was falling, slumping to the earth, thick red liquid mingling with the poplar roots and the dirt and the grass. Ruven just stood there, knife in gleaming hand, eyes set, brow unwavering. He was breathing, thinking about what he'd done. Regretting? No. Cara saw a smile spread across his face. Ma was the one crying. Cara found herself smiling along with that horrid man.

She stopped herself as soon as she realized what she'd done. She stilled her mouth, closed her eyes, wondering how in the two moons her mind had gone in that direction. It had been a mirroring, as if she had *felt* what the killing man had felt, as if she herself had held the knife, as if she had pulled that murdering blow.

She wondered how that darkness could lie inside her.

Then she opened her eyes.

Something was happening. Something in the ground, underneath her feet. Something was—

The entire earth began shaking.

ELEVEN

"SOMETHING JUST HAPPENED," Antioch said. "Didn't it."

Aten shook his head, trying to clear it. It worked, for the most part. "Something strange is happening on campus."

"You mean the eyes."

That was an odd response. Aten thought about it, thinking back to his walk through campus. The students had been making out, kissing rampantly underneath the trees. And their eyes had been open.

"It's strange," Aten said. "Why are their eyes open?"

Antioch squinted at him. "What? Oh, you mean the kissing fools. Yes, I thought that was odd, myself. But that's not what I meant."

Someone delivered a tray of food to Aten just then: scrambled eggs—probably cold—a hard roll, a smattering of greasy potatoes. Orange juice. He picked up his fork and started poking at the food.

"It's the eyes," Antioch continued. "Not just the students —*everyone*. Didn't you notice it? It's as if you can see into their souls. As if suddenly their thoughts—no, that's the wrong word for it. It's as if their *intentions*, their proclivities

—no. Their...desires? Needs. Yes—needs. That's it. It's as if their *needs* were suddenly apparent to me. To everyone I've talked to, at least on campus. It's as if I can peer into their very soul."

"You're not making any sense," Aten said around a bite of mealy potatoes.

Antioch frowned. "Tell me you haven't seen it too."

"I—" Had he? Aten paused mid-bite, thinking. He *had* noticed something different, something unusual as he had passed through campus. And there had been something new just now, just a moment ago, when he'd watched Antioch speak. Like a new awareness burgeoning in his mind.

"It's that celestial object," he said. "It has to be."

"What?"

"The bright light in the sky, the one that appeared last night. It's a perfect correlation."

"Correlation does not equal—"

"Yes, yes, I know. Of course I know. But you can't deny the circumstances. This thing—this strange thing—it appears, and suddenly everyone goes berserk."

"Maybe there's something in the water."

"Maybe there's—you know what, Antioch?" Aten put down his fork. "That's your problem. You lack *vision*."

ATEN PICKED his way through the undergrowth of Ilyrion Park. Whatever had happened, the eyes were only a part of it. Only the smallest part. The bigger change—quite literally—was the maple tree in the middle of the park. It was mostly forest, the park was, land that hadn't been converted into houses from its natural state. At the rate things were progressing in the city, Aten figured that it was only a matter of time before the forest disappeared entirely. He wasn't sure how he felt about that. Progress was progress, which was almost invariably good—and often far too slow—but there was something terrible about killing trees.

When he arrived at the maple, he realized there would be no killing this particular tree.

It was *huge*. Huge in every dimension: the trunk was hundreds of feet wide, and it had to be at least a thousand feet tall. It was impossible to estimate from where he was on the ground, but Aten remembered what it had looked like from his vantage on Piedmont Point. It was many times taller than any other tree in the vicinity, towering over everything by an order of magnitude.

He'd never seen anything like it before.

What could cause a tree to grow this large? It looked like an ordinary tree, other than its extraordinary size. Although there *was* something different about it now that he was paying closer attention. It wasn't just the size; the *color* of it was different, too. As if a painter had driven deeply into his paint supply, pulling out stronger colors, brighter hues, more vibrant shades. He blinked, wondering if it was just his eyes. But no—his eyes were fine. Something about this tree was very, very strange.

It was almost as if it held a great power of some kind. But it was just a big, dumb tree. Big, yes, but still dumb. It was just a plant. It couldn't be anything special.

Still, he had to admit it was very strange. And Aten did not like unexplained phenomena. Especially ones that just appeared out of thin air.

He bent to pick up a piece of bark that had fallen off the tree. It felt warm to his hand, probably because it wasn't a particularly cold day. He had a sudden flashback to his father, dead these past five years. His father had built homes for a living, houses and barns and things. He was always using his hands to put things together, feeling more at home with a hammer and a saw than with a book. He had always whittled at tree bark just like this in the evenings, carving faces in the flickering light of an oil lantern. He had said the faces were the spirits hidden in the wood, that he was just bringing them to life with a knife and hand. He had even taught Aten how to do it, though Aten never believed in the spirits himself. He was far too pragmatic for that.

Aten had been the one who had enjoyed books. But he had helped his father, dutifully putting up wooden frames and roofs and walls and floors. It had been backbreaking work, but it had made Aten strong, at least in his youth. Now his nose was in books all day when he wasn't teaching, and he had lost what muscle he once had had. Perhaps it was time to pick up a hammer again, a knife.

Perhaps it was time to find the spirits in the wood.

He felt around in his cheap bag, brushing past the books and papers and quill pen. There was a knife in there, a little carving knife that flipped open with an ingenious mechanism that Aten himself had created, long ago. It kept the knife from cutting you when it was in a bag like this, its blade sheathed into its handle when it wasn't in use. His father had said he was a fool for wasting his time on such an invention, but there had been a smile on his face as he had said it. Sometimes his father was pragmatic, too.

Aten pulled the carving knife out and flicked it open. The mechanism still worked, all these years later, opening as smoothly as it had the day he had built it. He didn't know why he'd kept it in his bag for so long—maybe because it was his first real invention. Or maybe because it reminded him of his father.

His father had always told him that he would go far in life, that he had a good head on his shoulders, that his intellect and curiosity would leap him far above the rest of the world.

Unfortunately, his father had been wrong.

He brought the knife up to the piece of bark, not really knowing what he intended to do. His father had always carved faces into the wood—it wasn't thick enough to do much else. Maybe, if he used the knife just right, there would be a face waiting in the wood for him to find.

Suddenly he felt as if he could see it.

A face peeked out at him from the bark. A soul, an elf, maybe an elven spirit of some kind. He could almost feel it reaching out to him, through the wood into his hand. He almost dropped the bark in his surprise.

But there was nothing there. It was just his imagination. He took a deep breath, wondering if something was the matter with him. First the eyes now this. Maybe the stress of working at the University was finally getting to him.

Or maybe his father hadn't been crazy after all.

He made a cautious flick of the knife, feeling it bite into the wood. The shape of the face was still there, burned into his mind. He felt his knife could almost do the carving on its own, a pure extension of his will. His hand and the knife were one. The face of the spirit in the wood would come to life.

He felt something spark into the wood as he carved. Some kind of energy, a new kind of warmth. It felt distinctly like *power*, almost as if the wood were somehow on fire. He almost dropped it again, but there were no flames. Everything was fine. Yet the wood still felt pregnant with energy, as if Aten could wish it to do his bidding and it would. Or as if the soul inside it would. The face.

He looked around him at the forest, at the massive tree that should not exist. Had his father been right all along?

Were there hidden spirits living in the trees, waiting for the right mortal to happen along and unlock their power? Aten had always thought of himself as the smarter one, the one who had studied, who had always been driven to learn about the world and how it worked. His father had been the builder; Aten had been the discoverer. But maybe his father had had the right of it all along.

Aten felt a tear come to his eye as he envisioned the man, sitting in his chair in front of the fire, a glinting golden lantern on the wooden table next to him, a piece of old tree bark in his hands. He had been a good man, his father had. He hadn't deserved to die so young. Aten wished desperately that he could see him again, just one more time.

He felt a spark ignite in the wood in his hands, energy channeling through the fibers, through his hands, into the air.

And suddenly his father was standing there before him.

TWELVE

"MAGIC," Kythaela said, the firestory fresh on her lips. "Or technology beyond his understanding—but Aten felt it was probably magic. That was what Aten had discovered in the forest that day. He brought as much wood as he could back with him to the University, stuffing it in his bag and carrying armloads of it besides. A branch had fallen from the tree, so he brought a saw back into the forest to cut it up and bring it back with him in pieces.

"Then he tried again, skillfully carving shapes into the wood with his carving knife. And once again the wood flared up, as we all know it does, Investing with power ready to be used. Aten had truly Awakened.

"He was the first mistweaver. But it would only be a matter of days before the second mistweaver arose."

MORE PEOPLE DIED over the next few days. Cara tried not to think about it, tried to just go about her day. But she could smell it when they burned Ruven for being a witch. They did it over by the church, but the smoke and smell carried far. Everyone was there—everyone except for her. Even Lara was allowed to watch the burning of their murderous neighbor.

And more trees grew.

Ivran was next. He was the town baker, the one who had made Lara's cake. He had picked a piece of bark off the poplar tree outside their farm, walking with it and humming to himself. The next day they had found his wife dead, impaled by a fork through the heart. A *fork*. And Ivran wasn't a fighter. He wasn't angry. He *loved* his wife.

And he had killed her.

Something strange was going on.

Cara had picked up a piece of poplar wood, wondering if it would cause someone else to die. The wood had felt warm, almost as if there were some kind of life inside. But nothing else had happened. Nothing as crazy as killing, anyway. Lara had glared at her, but Lara was always doing that. So Cara had put the wood in her pocket and forgotten about it.

SHE WAS BRINGING Pa's hammer to the barn one day when it happened.

She heard shouting at first. It sounded as if Pa were in some kind of trouble. He was always quiet when he was out in the barn, tinkering around with things or maybe milking the cows when it was raining. He never shouted. He never exclaimed. So Cara almost burst through the barn door to see if she could help.

But something stopped her. There was a peculiarity in Pa's voice, something in his tone that seemed *off*. So instead of going in the barn, she chose to take a peek through a gap in the wall.

Pa was standing there with a piece of wood in his hand. A small branch, probably taken from the tree just outside the barn. It had grown there overnight a few days ago—a massive maple tree now far larger than any tree had a right to be. Cara had looked at it curiously when she'd first seen it. She hadn't been the only one to notice the blood along the roots.

And now Pa had a piece of it in his hands, looking at it as if entranced. Something was rumbling in his throat. He was singing to it, crooning at it, almost worshipping it. Why would he do that? What was so special about the wood?

He obviously wanted to be alone. She saw him glance around, checking if anyone was watching. He couldn't see her through the crack in the boards.

He turned back to the wood, holding it up to the sunlight streaming in from the window in the second story of the barn. The wood looked normal to Cara's eye, although maybe it *was* a little bit browner than it should have been. What with gigantic trees growing up all over the village, a bit of color wasn't enough to surprise her. The wood seemed normal enough to her.

Pa was a builder. He always had been. He was a farmer too, of course, but his first love had always been for building things. He had built this barn, and he had built their house. He was always out here tinkering, putting pieces of things together and nailing them or tightening. That was why Cara was bringing him his hammer, so he could have something to nail with. He'd accidentally left it in the house.

So it wasn't a great surprise when Pa put the piece of maple on his work table, one end sticking several inches off the edge. Then he picked up a saw and commenced cutting.

A minute later, he had two pieces of wood. Then he cut again and again, expertly creating squared-off edges and symmetrical shapes. He did it all freehand, with his saw and his eyes. He was good at it, and he seemed to enjoy it. And as he worked, Cara thought she could almost feel a palpable sense of power in the room.

Then something...happened. It was hard to describe. Cara thought it started as a mist, an almost effervescence in the room, hovering around Pa's head. The mist coalesced as he worked, merging and forming into the shape of something she recognized. No, not something—someone.

It was Ma.

She was standing there next to him, wavering slightly in the air, an expression of love on her face. Pa hadn't noticed her yet.

He continued working, fashioning the wood into some kind of object on the table. He had glue, and metal fasteners, and he didn't even seem to need the hammer Cara was carrying. She didn't know what it was that he was building, just that he seemed to know exactly what he was doing. He was in his element, in his moment, creating things in the privacy of his barn.

More shapes whirled in the air around him as he did.

There was a bird—a raven, perhaps, reminding her of Lara's hair. Then it disappeared and two moons took its place, hovering in the air behind Pa, shimmering in what was not a night sky. Ma was standing there the whole time—the image of Ma, at least—watching him work. Her clothes had changed, though. Now she wore something tighter, skimpier. Now her body had thinned, curving around the bust and waist. Her hair was longer, her skin firmer. She was an idealized version of Ma. A younger version.

It wasn't until then that Cara realized that Ma was an illusion.

What was Pa doing? *How* was he doing it? Was it something in the wood, something that made these magic shapes appear? How was any of this possible? And should Cara go in there and give him his hammer?

No. She couldn't do it. Not with Ma standing there, illusion or no. She would just watch—just watch, and see what else Pa had inside his mind. She shifted her feet, trying to get in a better position to see what was happening, and accidentally dropped the hammer.

It clattered loudly on the ground, narrowly missing Cara's foot. She almost squealed, but managed to keep herself quiet. The hammer, though, made quite a sound. As she bent to pick it up, she caught Pa looking in her direction.

He looked *scared*.

The illusion of Ma had disappeared. She watched as Pa cast about the room, a strange new awareness in his eyes. He was actually shaking with fear. What had gotten into him?

She went to pick up the hammer again, but this time she accidentally bumped her head on the wall itself. "Ow," she let slip, then put her eye back to the gap in the boards.

There were two Pas standing there.

One of them was holding a piece of wood. A piece of too-brown, probably magical wood, wood that Pa had cut with his own two hands. One of him was standing there holding it, and the copy of him was just standing there staring.

Both of them looked scared.

But neither of them were looking at Cara.

She put a hand to her mouth, trying to stifle the exclamation of shock that almost came out. What was going on?

Then she heard something like a screaming sound. It was Pa. Pa with the wood. Pa who she thought of as the first, the one who was creating this strange magic. Pa1 was screaming.

Pa2, the image of her father, looked real enough. He was not misty or wavering, and he was not a younger version of Pa. He was the real deal, an exact replica of her father. Except

Pa2 didn't have any wood. He just stood there staring, doing nothing as Pa1 screamed himself out.

When he finally finished screaming, Pa1 looked *extremely* angry. "Where the fuck did you come from?" he demanded.

Pa2 looked at him in fear. "Who—what—"

Pa1 took a step forward. "You're me. How is this possible?" He looked at the wood in his hand.

"I don't know," Pa2 said, lifting a finger and pointing at the wood. "I think there may be power in the—"

The piece of wood turned to dust.

Cara watched it sprinkle to the ground, pieces of it flying in the air and catching the sun rays through the window. It looked so innocent, that dust. It looked so harmless. But somehow there were *two* fathers in the barn. Cara thought about backing away, of leaving, but part of her wanted to stay. She *needed* to stay—to stay and see what happened here.

THIRTEEN

"IT'S MAGIC," Aten said, rubbing a piece of maple wood between his fingers. It felt warm, as this particular wood always did. Only wood from that massive maple tree felt like this to him—other, normal maple, did not. There was some kind of power in the wood, some kind of latent energy. Energy that he could tap into, use.

The magic created illusions, but only when it was activated by carving it. Aten wasn't sure *why* it worked like that, but it did. He'd done the experiments. He was sure. And it wasn't just blind carving that did the trick, either—it had to be skilled carving. He had to picture his intent, see the face in the wood before he started any motion. Only then would the power react. Only then could he create images out of nothing.

"This is heresy," Antioch said. The older professor was sitting across from him—not at the university cafeteria, this time. Tonight they were at the tavern just outside the campus. Tonight they needed something stronger than orange juice.

"It's not heresy," Aten said, lowering his voice. Even the people in Ilyrion could be a superstitious bunch. "It's *science*. Whatever is going on here, it needs to be studied."

"You think it's related to the orange light in the sky."

"It has to be. The Trees didn't start growing until it arrived." Aten had started thinking of them as Trees, with a capital letter in front. They certainly were big enough for it. "Listen," he continued. "This is my chance. My opportunity to prove myself. If you will sponsor me to the Dean, maybe I can get some funding."

"You've written a proposal?"

Aten nodded. "I want to start a new branch of research. A new department, if you will. I intend to study this power, to conduct controlled experiments, to figure out what's going on with all this...wood."

Antioch pursed his lips. "What do you hope to find?"

"I don't know," Aten said.

"But without a hypothesis," Antioch said, "it isn't really science."

Aten frowned. The man was right. "We need to start with experimentation. We need to find out what this magic can do, who can use it, how it works, what its limitations are. We need to test the other Trees—the others that have been sprouting up all over the place—and figure out what that wood can do. And we need to figure out why some people can use the magic, and others cannot."

"You already know that much?"

"That part was easy. I can use maple, for example. I can make illusions, if I carve. But I've tried some of the others: poplar, oak, yew. They don't do anything for me. They don't feel warm like maple does."

"That's progress already."

"See? You don't need a hypothesis to do good work. But I'll give you one anyway: my hypothesis is that the orange light in the sky is some kind of advanced technology—far beyond anything we elves understand—and it is the source of this power. It operates at great distance, enabling some kind of link we didn't know about. Something to do with trees, and…and…"

"And what?"

"And me. Us. Elves. It must be something to do with our… souls."

Antioch sat back in his seat, frowning. "That's a hell of a hypothesis."

"You asked."

"I did. But why are you involving me? Surely there are other, more qualified professors you can go to."

"None of them will listen to me. Hell—none of them even *talk* to me. You're the only one."

"I'm the only—moons, Aten, are you *that* disliked on campus?"

Aten took a sip of beer. It was good—it tasted good—but he found himself wishing there was some other kind of liquor. Something stronger. Maybe it was something else he should research.

"General dislike for me seems to be part of the package," he said. "It's what I do."

"Well, you are prickly, but surely—"

"I push people away, Antioch. Moons, I *hate* most people. I'm too stubborn, I'm too smart, and I'm too *limited* by this moons-forsaken campus and its draconian rules. That's why nobody likes me. Because I don't like *them*."

"Well at least you're self-aware about it."

Aten raised his glass. "The world hates me, and I know why, but there's not a damn thing I can do about it."

They drank.

"What will you do?" Antioch asked. "If you finally achieve your wildest dreams, what will you do?"

"What are you on about, Antioch?"

"You have them. Dreams. Don't bother trying to deny it. *Something* is driving you—I almost shudder to know the extent of it."

"My dreams are none of your concern."

"They are if you want my support."

Aten paused, sighing. "I want," he said, "to matter. It's as simple as that. I want to make a difference. To have someone write about me. To have cities built in my name."

"Cities? Good God, man. Don't you just want to *live* somewhere? To have a home? A wife?"

Aten frowned, but then his expression softened. "Perhaps. I've always wanted to try living in the desert. If life can flourish there, life can do anything."

Antioch took a drink. "You're a very strange man." They were silent for a moment. "What will you call it? This new department of yours—what will it be?"

Aten caught Antioch's eye. "Does that mean you're agreeing? You'll support me to the Dean?"

"Perhaps."

Aten looked down at the piece of maple on the table in front of him. Powerful maple. Strong maple. It was the first among Trees, the best of its kind. A Tree that was somehow connected to the primal forces arraying out from the orange light in the sky. Yes—that was a good name for the power.

Prime.

"It will be a new department," Aten said, picking up the wood and rubbing it between his fingers. "I'll call it the Department of Magical Research."

Antioch rubbed the edge of his glass. "It's as good a name as any," he said. "It sounds downright civilized." He mused for a moment, deep in thought. "I wonder how the farming villages are handling all of this."

PA2 WAS STARING AT PA1.

It was really starting to give Cara the creeps.

"Who are you?" Pa2 asked.

"I'm you."

"I can see that, but—"

"Have you always been this stupid?" It was Pa1 talking. He seemed angrier than Pa normally was. Sure, Pa had his anger spells—more often than not, it seemed—but there was something different about this version of Pa.

Something darker.

"I'm not stupid," Pa2 said, taking a step back. "I'm just trying to figure out what's going on. One moment I was standing where you are now, and the next I'm—"

"You're asking stupid questions. While you're here, can you at least help me with this?" Pa1 turned back to the wood he was working with.

Pa2 cocked his head at him as if wondering if he were about to step into a trap. Then he walked up to the workbench, looking at the wood with a frown on his face. "What are you doing?"

"I'm trying to make a bird house," Pa1 said. "These new trees, the wood is firmer and more pliable at the same time. It's hard to explain. It's like the tree is just easier to work with, somehow. And I've worked with maple before, many times. It doesn't work like this."

"A bird house?" Pa2 repeated.

"Don't be stupid," Pa1 said, picking up his saw. "You're repeating me."

"You like...bird houses?"

Pa1 looked at him. "You're me, remember? You know as well as I do that we *hate* bird houses."

"Then why are you making one?"

"It's for my daughter, idiot. Are you sure you came from me? Lara loves birds. So I thought I'd—"

"Okay," Pa2 said. "I'll try to help."

"Thanks."

The two men stood next to each other at the table, the moment growing long between them. Pa1 was the first to speak.

"Well, pick up the glue, idiot."

Pa2 sighed and picked up the can of glue that was sitting on the table. "Why aren't you nailing it together?"

"Oh now he knows how to build things," Pa1 said. "Because my hammer is still in the house, idiot."

"Oh."

"Put the glue here." Pa1 held up a piece of wood. "On the end."

Pa2 did so. His hand shook as he applied the glue, using a small brush to spread the sticky stuff across the rough edge of the wood.

"Now hold these pieces together." Pa1 showed him how.

Pa2 did as he was bid, putting two pieces of the perfectly cut wood together, joining them where he'd laid the glue. But when Pa1 stepped away, Pa2's hands started shaking.

"What's the matter with you?" Pa1 demanded.

"I don't—"

"Moons, you're stupid."

"I—"

"Hold it steady, damn you!"

"I'm trying!"

Cara couldn't figure out why Pa was acting this way. Sure, he did get mad sometimes—scary, even, especially when he had his knife. But he was never needlessly hurtful—not unless he'd been drinking first. Had he been? She hadn't seen him drink anything, not today. No, Pa1 was just being angry for anger's sake, it seemed. It was very unlike him.

Pa2's hands were really shaking now. He put one hand to his head, touching his brow. The other hand barely held the two pieces of glued wood together.

"Now what's wrong?" Pa1 demanded.

"My head," Pa2 said. "It hurts so *bad*."

"Shut up," Pa1 said. "I thought you said you wanted to help."

"I do," Pa2 said. "I—" Then he screamed and dropped the wood, both hands clutching his head in apparent agony. The pieces of wood split apart when they hit the floor.

"You motherfucking idiot," Pa1 said. Cara blanched at the unfamiliar curse. Why was Pa talking like this? "You *meant* to do that, didn't you? You're just trying to screw me up."

That's when Pa1 finally drew his knife.

It wasn't the butcher knife—not this time. That knife was safely inside, ensconced in its wooden block in the kitchen. The knife he had now was a hunting knife, a skinning knife, short and fairly stubby, with a drop point at the end. Pa had told her about knives. She could recognize them. This one wasn't nearly as massive as the butcher knife, but she knew he could still do a lot of damage with it if he wanted to.

Especially since Pa2 wasn't carrying a knife of his own.

"What?" Pa2 managed, hands still clutching his head. "What are you doing?"

"I'm going to kill you, idiot," Pa1 said. "You can't even hold together simple wood."

"But I didn't mean to—I wasn't—why do you want to kill me?" It sounded like Pa2 was really in a lot of pain. Cara felt her heart speeding in her chest.

"Because there can only be one of me," Pa1 said, "and you're not it."

He plunged the knife into Pa2's chest.

FOURTEEN

THE HOUSE WAS STRANGELY EMPTY. Lara wandered about, trying to figure out where everyone had gone. Ma was in town getting something from the General Store. Pa was out in his shop doing whatever it was he did out there in the afternoons. Cara had been outside doing her chores, but Lara was pretty sure she should have been done by now. Was everyone outside playing except for her?

She was about to head outside when Pa suddenly stormed in.

He looked to be in a bad mood. A *very* bad mood. His face was blotchy, his hair awry. He was carrying his hunting knife.

And there was blood dripping from the blade.

Lara screamed, and Pa looked at her, and Lara thought that surely this was Satan himself, come to Valaralda.

She ran.

CARA SNUCK into Lara's room sometime later. Lara could

hear somebody banging around downstairs—heavy footsteps punctuated by crashes, things breaking. It could only be Pa.

Cara had a frightened look on her face. She closed the door quietly behind her and came to sit on Lara's bed. She didn't even ask permission—she just did it. Something unspoken passed between them. Right now there was a larger problem, something that superseded their sibling rivalry.

"What happened to Pa?" Lara asked, her voice a whisper.

Cara was visibly shaken. "He did something in the barn," she said. "I saw him. Something with the wood from that big maple tree. He was cutting it, building something. I don't know."

"What got him so angry?"

"I don't know," Cara said. "One moment he was putting pieces of wood together—gluing them, I guess. Then there were suddenly *two* of him. They fought."

"Wait—*what*? Did you say there were *two* of Pa?"

Cara nodded her head soberly. "He did other things first. I saw Ma in there, only she was younger. Much younger. And there was a mist, and—"

"Cara, you're not making any sense."

"I think it was..." She leaned forward, dropping her voice even further. "*Magic.*"

Another crash sounded from downstairs. It sounded like a plate breaking. Why would Pa break their good ceramic? They couldn't make more themselves—they'd have to go into town and buy replacements. Pa was normally very, very careful with the dishes.

None of this was making any sense.

"I...I think Pa *split*, somehow," Cara said. "It was the wood. The magic. Somehow he split in two, and then there were two of him. Only—" She paused as if in thought.

"Only what?"

"Only, I think one of Pa was good, and the other one was *evil*."

Lara shrank back, suddenly growing very afraid. "What happened?"

"They fought," Cara said. "They shouted at each other. Then—" She started crying. Lara reached out to comfort her and Cara allowed it, scooting forward and nestling herself in Lara's arms. Lara hadn't done anything like this since before Cara could talk. It felt...strange.

"It's okay," Lara said, smoothing Cara's blonde hair. "You can tell me."

Cara looked up at Lara, tears dripping from her bright blue eyes. "Pa1—the evil one—he killed Pa2. Stabbed him. I saw it happen. I didn't scream."

Lara felt something cold rush through her veins. First Pa was using some kind of *magic*—which was preposterous on its own—and now he had somehow killed half of himself? It was impossible. Had Cara eaten something that disagreed with her? Had she gone insane?

Or could there really be witches walking amongst them?

THERE WAS no dinner that night. Ma took one look at Pa and told him to sleep it off, thinking that he must be drunk. Maybe he had been, actually—it would explain a lot. But it wouldn't explain what Cara had seen.

Ma and Pa had had a staring match right there in the kitchen, and for a moment Lara had been sure that Pa was going to kill her mother. But in the end he had done as he was bid.

He went to bed.

Late that night, Cara found Lara in her room.

"Are you asleep?" Cara whispered. Lara didn't answer—she just turned over and stared at her sister. Cara's eyes were glowing faintly in the moonlight coming in through the window. She looked like a little blonde demon, if such a thing were real. "I want to find the body," Cara said, tiptoeing over to the bed.

"What?" Lara asked. "Why?"

"Because I want to be sure he's dead."

"Pa?"

"Pa2. His good side. If he survived, maybe he can help us. I want to go look for him."

"Where?"

"Outside. In the barn. Or near it."

"And you want me to help?"

Cara nodded, and for a moment she was once again a scared little girl. Not the manipulative bitch that Lara had grown to hate. Cara actually did want to do some good. She actually wanted Lara's help. She *needed* her.

It was the first time Lara had felt like a big sister.

"Okay," Lara said, swinging her legs off the bed and standing on the cold floor. "Let's go."

They put on shawls and shoes and snuck downstairs and out the kitchen door. The house was silent, luckily. Pa was not awake. Getting out was easy.

They searched the barn, but it was empty other than a dark patch of blood, black in the moonlight. Lara snuck a look up at the sky, at the little orange dot that was still visible up there. Was this the source of all their newfound pain? All the deaths, all the trees?

Was it the source of this strange new *magic*?

"There's nothing here," she said, and Cara shook her head.

"There must be," her sister said. "Maybe he hid the body somewhere."

"Or maybe the good side got away."

"Let's hope so," Cara said.

"What now?" Lara asked. She was deferring to Cara on this, she realized. It almost rankled her, but Cara had been the only one to see everything happen. Had she made it all up? Had Pa just been in one of his moods? Had he been drunk? Was Cara trying to trick her, to lure her out into the barn and kill her? Was this one of her plans?

She turned to look at her sister.

Cara was holding a knife.

FIFTEEN

"HE PUT IT BACK," Cara said, and she lowered the knife. "He cleaned it and put it back in here." She set the knife down on the table.

Lara let out the breath she'd been holding. Her sister was not trying to kill her.

Not today, at least.

"So he was at least somewhat aware of his actions," Lara said.

"There was a lot of blood," Cara said. "The other half of him couldn't have survived."

"Do you think he hid the body?"

"Maybe. Let's go look."

They left the barn, glancing anxiously at the house to make sure nobody had discovered their absence. There were no lights lit. They were safe.

So they headed around to the back of the barn, taking care to step quietly. The ground was all just dirt out here, dirt that led eventually into brome grass before turning into crop fields. The forest stretched out in the distance, bordering their farmland. If Pa's other half had gotten away, he could be hiding there.

"What's this?" Cara asked, poking at the dirt with a stick she'd found against the barn. It looked like plain dirt to Lara —dark dirt, of course, with it being night and all. Only...there was something darker on it, a discoloration. Cara was poking at it more.

"Don't do that!" Lara said, suddenly fearful. What if part of Pa *was* buried there? What would they do? This whole experience was so surreal. None of this should be happening. None of this was even possible.

Not until the orange light had appeared in the sky.

Lara wondered again where Kila had gone, that night when she'd disappeared from her cell. Had someone helped her escape? Had she been let out? Or had she, like Pa, been using magic?

She shivered.

Cara was digging in the dirt.

"Stop!" Lara almost shouted, managing to keep her voice quiet at the last second.

Cara looked at her sharply. "What?"

"We can't do this," Lara said. "What if Pa is down there? What will we do then?"

"We have to know," Cara said. Her eyes were glowing again. "We have to know if the magic is real."

Lara sighed, knowing her sister was right. She went back to the barn and found a shovel. If they were really going to do this, they might as well do it the right way.

IT ONLY TOOK them twenty minutes to find the body.

"It's him," Lara breathed. "It's really him."

It really was.

They pulled the body out of the hole in the ground, struggling to lift it between them. Pa wasn't fat by any means, but he was an adult man. He was heavy. They got him onto the ground next to the hole and laid him on his back. His body was cold and already starting to smell. There was a great gaping wound in his chest.

"He looks just like Pa," Lara said. They were both breathing heavily.

"They're identical," Cara said. "At least they looked that way to me."

"So if that's really Pa up there asleep in the house, and this is really Pa down here, dead…"

"You heard him breaking things. That's the *evil* version of Pa." Cara looked down at the body. "This was the good."

"If this is all true," Lara said, "then all of us are in a lot of trouble."

Cara nodded at her, glowing eyes glistening with tears.

THE NEXT MORNING, Lara and Cara sat at the kitchen table for breakfast, exchanging looks. They had reburied the body, shedding tears as they said goodbye to the part of Pa they'd loved. Neither of them had gotten any sleep.

"What's gotten into you two?" Ma asked. She was standing in front of the wood stove, cooking eggs in a cast iron pan. She was wearing her nightshift, a loose gray dress made of spun wool that waved about in the air as she moved. Her hair was down, cascading along her back in thick brown rivulets. Lara had gotten her mother's looks. Cara had gotten Pa's.

"Nothing," Lara said, stifling a yawn. Inside, her mind was going a mile a minute. If Pa really had been reduced to his evil nature, could they stay? He had already had violent tendencies, even before this strange split. She wasn't sure they could stay with him now. It wouldn't be safe. But she was just a little girl, beholden to her parents for everything. How could she possibly survive on her own?

Pa entered the room suddenly, heavy steps announcing his presence. He was shirtless, which was strange, revealing his hairy chest and thick arm muscles. Lara watched him as he walked into the room. Was there anything different about him? He looked the same, although he was walking with a certain unusual swagger.

"That smells good," he said, walking up behind Ma and wrapping his arms around her. "You smell good." He ground his crotch against her rear end.

"Stop that!" Ma protested, though Lara could hear the smile in her voice. "Not in front of the girls!"

Pa reached up and began massaging Ma's breasts through her loose nightshirt. "I'm hungry."

Ma turned, anger written on her face. Pa still held her tightly, their faces inches away from each other.

"This is inappropriate," Ma said. "Let me finish breakfast. We can talk about this later." Pa didn't move. He just leered at her, hands creeping lower on her body. Lara wanted to look away. "I said *stop*," Ma said, her voice firm.

Pa slapped her across the face.

Ma reeled, slamming into the pan and sending it crashing to the floor. Lara could hear the sizzling of flesh as Ma touched the hot metal. Her mother screamed, flailing and falling to the floor in a jumble of limbs and hair and shift. Then she lay there, holding her badly burned arm, hair in her eyes and fear on her face.

Pa loomed over her.

Eggs littered the floor.

Ma was only eyes and breath and fear.

Lara saw it all as if in slow motion.

"You'll give me what I want, bitch," Pa said. Pa1. It was Pa1, the evil one. Lara was sure of that now.

"Stop this," Ma said, tears and pain in her eyes. "This isn't you."

He bent over her, mouth curving in a leer. "I've never felt better. Now take off your clothes, or I'll do it for you."

"Go upstairs," Ma said, burnt arm clutched limply in her hand. "I will clean this up and then we can talk. I can..." She let out a sob. "I can take my clothes off for you then."

"No," Pa1 said. "I'm the man, and I want you now. Here. The girls can watch."

"What has gotten into you?" Ma asked.

"Strength," Pa1 said, straightening. "Power." He began unbuttoning his pants.

"You're insane."

Lara saw Pa1's face darken into red. She saw his muscles clench before he did it, before he kicked her mother savagely, kicked her hard enough to send her slamming into the kitchen wall. Lara heard ribs crack. Ma's mouth opened in a wordless expression of horror and fear and pain. Her eyes began to glaze.

And Pa1 reared back to kick her again.

"Stop!" Cara screamed, running over to Pa1 and grabbing his arm. "Don't hurt her!" The girl was crying, blonde hair flying out behind her as she pulled again and again on Pa1's massive arm.

He looked down at her, big hand reaching downward, fingers finding Cara's neck. She yelped soundlessly as he lifted her off the floor with just one hand, her feet kicking, her hands beating uselessly against him. He was choking her. He was *killing* her.

"Nobody tells me what to do," Pa1 said, and in his voice Lara heard the words of death.

Lara had a choice to make. This was her one moment of opportunity. She could escape—she could dart to the front door and get away. She was sure she could make it before Pa1 could drop Cara and get to her. She could escape and leave this carnage behind.

It might be her only chance.

But he would kill them both, she knew. Ma and Cara would be dead, and Lara would have done nothing but run. Nothing but be a coward.

But if she stayed, she would probably die too.

It was the hardest choice she would ever make.

SIXTEEN

CARA COULDN'T BREATHE.

She was dangling in mid-air, the kitchen tilting around her as darkness crept around her vision. Pa was holding her. Pa1 was choking her.

Her father was going to kill her.

The evil inside him could not be stopped. First Ma now her. What would be next? When would it end? Would he ever be sated, or would he continue to rampage unchecked, killing everyone that didn't give him what he wanted?

And there was Lara, standing over there beside the kitchen table, just watching as Cara had the life choked out of her. Would Pa1 kill Lara next? Maybe not. She was his favorite, after all.

She ceased struggling, waiting for her time to die. There was nothing else she could do.

"Pa," Lara said. Her voice held a quiet intensity, as if the word itself were imbued with irresistible command.

That was all she said. Just one word.

Pa looked at Lara, and Cara saw all the color drain from his face.

He set her down. He even did it gently. Cara tried to breathe and started coughing instead, bright stars bursting around her as air returned to her lungs in fits and starts. She clutched her own neck, feeling the burning pain where Pa1 had held her. She envisioned the death that had almost come, saw it pass by her in a rush of wings and teeth.

That had very nearly been the end.

"I—" Pa1 said. He was still looking at Lara. "I'm sorry."

His face fell, and Cara realized that Pa1 *did* love Lara more than her. But it was more than love. It was something else, something deeper.

It was respect.

Pa1 stared at Lara for a long moment, then seemed to gather his wits about him. The cloud of evilness that had pervaded him was gone now, and Cara didn't understand why.

"Oh, God," Pa1 said, looking around the room. "What have I done?"

But Cara was still looking at Lara. The girl had a look of smug satisfaction on her face. There was fear there too, behind her eyes, but Cara could see her holding it back. She'd stood up to Pa1. She'd done it, and he'd backed down. She'd succeeded where Cara had failed. And Lara was proud of that fact. Her chest had swelled, her eyes firm.

Cara realized then that Lara would grow up to be a force to be reckoned with.

She wasn't sure she wanted to be around to see that happen.

PA LEFT to get a doctor for Ma. She refused to speak to him or anyone else, huddled on the floor and shivering. This man, this unexpected violence, had been more than the poor woman could take. Cara felt terrible for her, but there was nothing she could do. Ma was on her own.

Later that night, after Ma had been seen to as best the doctor could, Pa was sitting in his chair with Lara on his lap. Cara watched them there, fuming and not a little bit nervous. By all accounts they seemed happy, normal. Or as normal as they ever were.

But Cara knew that this was anything but normal.

What had happened? Was that still Pa1, or had he somehow reclaimed part of his former self? She didn't understand it. Ever since Lara had reprimanded him with a single word, Pa had seemed changed. She watched Lara sit and giggle as she played with a wooden bird Pa had made for her. Lara seemed oblivious to the danger—or maybe there wasn't any. Pa always did treat Lara better than the others, after all. Maybe Lara was somehow immune to his darker side.

Cara watched him. She watched his eyes. They didn't crinkle like they used to. The merriment was there on the surface, but it was only on the surface. She still saw evil lurking at the edges as he talked and laughed and entertained his older daughter. He was a bit too quick—a bit too sharp. His movements were too forceful, too abrupt. His eyes were a bit too calculating.

He stole a glance at Ma as Cara watched. Ma was slumped on the couch, numb from the willow leaves she'd been chewing. There was a huge willow in town now, one of the many trees that had been transformed. Pa had gathered the leaves on the doctor's orders. They were more potent than they should have been, and now Ma was nearly comatose.

Perhaps that was for the better.

When Pa looked at her, Cara saw something flicker in his eyes. The darkness stirred, uncoiled one wing, flexing a talon when it gazed on Ma. And in that moment Cara knew that Pa1 was still there. The man she'd known as her father was truly gone, and in his place was nothing but hate and hurt and pain.

She wondered how long it would take for Lara to notice.

"You always treat her so well," Cara whispered. Too late, she realized she had said it out loud. Pa1's eyes flicked over to her, the evil unfurling its other wing.

"What did you say?" he asked. Lara stopped playing, turning to look at her.

"Nothing," Cara said. "Sorry. I'm going to bed."

Pa1 gently lifted Lara off his lap, setting her down to stand on the floor. Then he stood, darkness settling into his eyes. "You said I treat Lara so well. What do you mean by that?" His voice was cold.

"Nothing," Cara said. "I'm glad you do. You're nice to her. You two are good together."

"*Liar*," Pa1 said, taking a step forward. Now he was standing right in front of her, his head towering too close to the ceiling. His eyes were dark. "You hate your sister, don't you? You always have."

"I—" He wasn't wrong. But what good would it do to admit that in front of Pa1? All it would do is get her a beating, if she was lucky. "I love my sister."

"You used to be a better liar," Pa1 said, and he slapped her *hard* across the face.

Cara scrabbled, seeing stars, trying to get away from the man somehow. But he hit her again and she lost her balance, crashing through an oil lamp and sending a small table hurtling toward the floor. She felt hot oil burst against her skin; felt the stinging pain of Pa1's hand; felt the table where it had hit her in the arm. She heard the screams that were her own, her lungs frantically shrieking as the floor rose up to meet her, as Pal's fist rained down, as his boot met her stomach.

"No!" she heard Ma shout. Cara was dimly aware of her mother getting up from the couch, her face a blur. Pal delivered one last kick at Cara's midsection before turning to Ma.

A knife was in his hand.

SEVENTEEN

WHEN CARA OPENED HER EYES, it was pitch black everywhere. For a moment, she almost screamed. Where was she? She felt panic rising. Everything was dark, formless. Every part of her was on fire with pain.

Then she remembered.

She had hidden in the barn, in her special place in the hay loft. It was just a wooden box—nothing special. Normally it held seed, kept off the ground so as not to get damp. But it was empty now, the seed having been used for planting. And nobody bothered to look in the box when it was empty.

She had crawled out of the house while Pa1 beat up Ma. She had struggled, bleeding from her impact with the table, reeling from Pa1's slap, her chest and stomach in horrible pain from the kicks he had inflicted. But for all the damage he had done to her, he was surely doing far worse things to Ma.

She probably hadn't survived the hour.

Now Cara was alone in the barn with no one to look after her. She had no idea where Lara was, but the girl seemed inexplicably safe from Pa1 and his terrible wrath.

Cara was alone.

She managed to get out of the seed box without hurting too horribly. Her wounds were superficial. They would heal. She couldn't say the same for Ma.

On her way out of the barn, she picked up Pa's hunting knife. It was the same knife he'd used to kill his good twin, the magical illusion that had somehow become real.

Cara thought it fitting that she would use the same knife to kill the evil half.

WHEN SHE GOT INSIDE, she saw that Ma was dead.

There was a great gash of a wound on her stomach. Blood had splashed all over the couch and pooled on the wooden floor. Her hair was torn, her face a mangled mess of bruises and blood, her nose bent at an impossible angle. Her arm was broken. Her dress was torn to shreds. And one of her hands was lying on the floor five feet away from her, cut cleanly at the wrist.

Ma wasn't just dead. She was *destroyed*.

Cara threw up all over the floor.

The room spun wildly for a moment, pain in her heart colliding with the pain in her body. Blood. There was so much blood.

She would never see Ma again.

She staggered, almost falling, but managed to right herself just in time. Vomit mixed with Ma's blood, pools of acid and grief on the rough wood floor.

Pa was a murderer.

She had already known that, though. She'd seen him kill *himself*—he was definitely capable of it. But he was more than just a killer. He was wild, strange, given to impulses that no ordinary elf should have. He was lustful and angry and quick-tempered and even happy for a few minutes when he'd held Lara. Then he was violent, destructive, and horribly, horribly murderous. He had no care for family. He had no care for anything but what he wanted in the moment, what his hands and weapons could do.

Pa was *insane*.

She stood, swaying, and wiped her mouth. She tasted bile. She smelled blood. Her eyes took one last look at the scene before her, at Ma's broken, mangled corpse. At her eyes. At least he'd left her eyes.

Eyes that would never look at Cara again.

She fingered the knife in her hand, resolve growing within her.

CARA HAD LONG AGO LEARNED how to sneak up the stairs without making a sound. There were exactly seven major creaks and two minor ones on the way up, and she had memorized them all. And so it was that when she entered her parent's room at the top of the stairs, no one had heard her coming.

Pa was asleep on his back, one bloody hand outstretched on the white sheets. He was naked and uncovered, body carelessly displayed for anyone to see. His chest rose and fell as she watched. His breathing seemed easy.

He clearly had no remorse for what he had done.

Pa—no, Pal; she had to remember to think of him that way—was a killer. A stone cold, horrific killer. If he hadn't already killed Lara, he would do so soon. If Cara didn't get away, she would probably be next. And with Ma gone, there was no one to stand in his way.

But Cara held the solution to all of that in her hand.

She took a step forward, feeling a kind of coldness taking over. Her muscles were sure. Her hands were steady. Her heart was ice.

Her mind was clear.

He didn't hear her as she stepped silently to the bed. He didn't stir as she reached forward, as she brought the knife out, sharp edge up, as she ran it smoothly across the skin of his throat. Only then did his eyes flick open, pain and confusion and surprise flickering across them like broken leaves. Then he clutched his neck, and blood was flowing, and the sheets were red.

It didn't take long for Pal to die.

He stared at Cara the entire time.

Then there was a little scream, and she turned and saw Lara standing there, shock evident on her face.

"You...*killed* him?" she asked. She looked stupid in her wool nightgown.

"He killed Ma," Cara said, her voice cold. The knife was dripping on the floor, on her feet. "He would have killed us next."

"He was nice to me," Lara whispered. "He would never have hurt me."

"He always loved you best," Cara said. "Perhaps I should kill you, too."

"No!" Lara shrieked, and she began to turn.

Cara felt something warm in her pocket just then. She reached down instinctively, pulling the thing out to see what it was. It was a little piece of wood. Poplar. A shard of it from the big tree in their yard. The tree that had formed that day their neighbor had murdered someone right in front of them. The wood had always felt warm to her, but now it felt even warmer. It was almost as if there were a kind of *life* inside it, an essence, a being.

As she held the wood, she could almost feel the soul that was inside.

Lara hadn't left. She was peering at Cara curiously, clearly wondering what her sister was about to do. She must look rather funny, Cara realized, standing there with a knife in her right hand and a piece of wood in her left.

"I'm going to turn you in," Lara said. "You won't get away with what you did."

"You wouldn't," Cara said, raising the knife. Lara was too far away for her to reach with it, not unless she threw it at her. But she was terrible at throwing things, least of all knives. She'd never thrown a knife before.

And besides, she didn't actually *want* to kill her sister.

"You're as evil as he was," Lara said. "You've always had it out for me. Now I will get away, and you'll never get what you wanted. You'll never see me dead. You'll *pay* for killing Pa."

She ran out of the room.

And Cara felt a surge of emotion tunnel through her all at once. Fear. Rage. Sadness. But mostly fear. If Lara really turned her in, Cara could get in a lot of trouble. They might jail her like they had with Kila. They might kill her outright, even though she was a child. How could she prove what had happened? She was standing in her house with two dead parents and a murder weapon in her hand.

There could be no coming back from this, not if Lara got her way.

All this happened in an instant, before Lara was even out the bedroom door. And suddenly, instinctively, Cara knew what to do.

She threw the knife.

She felt magic coursing outward from the poplar in her hand. Magic from the soul inside, connecting to the universe and the orange light in the sky. Magic that slipped effortlessly into her hand, into her body, into her mind. Magic that formed a web in the sky, cradling the knife as it flew through the air.

As she had feared, her aim was terrible. The knife headed right for the wall, two feet away from where Lara was still running. She was out into the hall now. She would be heading down the stairs. Soon she would get help, and Cara would be done for if she couldn't hide somewhere.

But the web of magic was still holding the knife.

And she really didn't want Lara to win.

So she pushed it, urged it, Willed the magic in the air to move the knife, to turn it, to propel it neatly *not* at the wall, but through the door, and around the corner, and into Lara's waiting shin.

The knife stabbed deeply into Lara's leg, and she went down in a tumble of wool and screams.

Cara wasted no time. She had to get away. She had killed her father and stabbed her sister. There was nothing left for her here. Maybe she could hide in the forest, find somewhere else to live. She had to do something to survive. She had to leave this horrible, disastrous place that had once been her home.

Lara was screaming and crying, huddled on the floor at the top of the stairs, holding onto her leg. The knife stuck out of it like a stick in thick mud. It was a clean cut. It wasn't even bleeding yet. Lara would be fine.

Cara hadn't actually wanted to kill her.

She brushed past her sister and clattered down the stairs, heading for the back door where she could escape unseen. She didn't have time to get food or supplies or anything— Lara would be recovering soon. She would shout for help, and there were still neighbors near enough that someone might come.

Cara had to get away.

She clattered down the stairs and collided *hard* with something. She shrieked, pushing wildly with her empty hands—where had the wood gone?—but it was no good.

She had run into a man.

Hands grabbed her roughly, pulling her off the stairs, pulling her toward the door. She got a look at him as he wrestled her easily out of the house. It was Athtar, the doctor. He must have come back to check on Ma.

"I saw what you did," Athtar said as he held her tightly. "You're coming with me, *witch*."

Cara felt new fear flooding through her as she realized how much trouble she was in.

EIGHTEEN

THE NEXT DAY, Pastor Deryth organized a group of people to clean up the house. Lara watched as they carted out Ma and Pa's bodies, wrapping Ma's hand separately. Then they scrubbed the wood, burned the sheets, and sent Lara away.

She felt numb inside.

Doctor Athtar fixed up her leg, wrapping it in a cloth bandage and applying some herbs to ward off infection. It was a clean wound and well-struck, he said. Cara's knife work was excellent.

But Lara had seen it. She had seen the knife curving through the air, sailing through the door and around the corner, then angling down and striking her in the leg. Nobody could throw a blade like that.

Cara had used magic.

And that made her a witch.

Now she was off in jail, waiting a few days until she would be burned. The village had taken to doing the burning in batches, grouping the witches together once a week so they could do them all at once. It was easier, that way.

There weren't many villagers left.

Lara wondered why Cara was a witch and Lara wasn't. Was there something innate about it? Some kind of hidden talent? Or had Cara secretly been practicing, maybe practicing with Kila, learning the dark arts of magical knife throwing? What else could she do?

And did that make Cara truly evil?

She'd killed Pa. She'd stabbed Lara. Cara had shown more strength and grit than Lara had, but she had gone too far. She'd had no right to take someone else's life into her hands. Even if that person *had* killed Ma.

She brushed a tear from her face, willing the numbness to return.

They'd given Lara a spare bed at Pastor Deryth's house, sharing Talila's room. Talila, the girl who had first decided that Kila had been a witch.

Perhaps she had been right.

But Lara didn't like Talila. She didn't want to talk to her. So she kept her back to the girl, crying herself to sleep every night, staying as silent as she could.

She knew her life would never be the same.

The night before Cara was to be burned, Lara decided that she wanted to see her one last time. To talk to her. To ask her why she'd killed their father. To ask her why she was so cold. To ask her how this pain in her heart could be taken away.

She brought a small loaf of bread with her, having stolen it from Deryth's kitchen. His wife would never miss it—she baked dozens of them every day, handing most of them out to the needy. Well, Cara was needy enough. Even though she was a murderer and a witch, she still deserved a loaf of bread.

Lara arrived at the jailhouse, sticking to the shadows as well as she could as she approached. There didn't seem to be anybody guarding the jail. She didn't know if that was normal or not—perhaps they trusted the cells to hold their prisoners without a guard. The jail hadn't been used much, Lara knew. There hadn't been much crime. Not until the orange light in the sky.

She drew up to what she knew was Cara's cell—the one facing the outer wall. There was a barred window there, open to the street. Talila had shown it to her earlier that day as they were walking by. Lara had stood on tiptoes and seen her sister there, huddled in a corner with her hair around her face. She hadn't said anything to her then, but later she had changed her mind. She wanted some last words with her sister before the burning started.

She stepped up to the window, loaf of bread in hand. She had prepared the words to say in advance. She summoned them now, hoping her sister wouldn't try to fight or argue. She just wanted to say her peace and be done with it. Then her sister could burn.

She stood on tiptoes, neck craned and nose stuck between the bars. She looked around the cell, searching for her sister. Her blonde hair should be standing out in the moonslight shining in. She had been in the far right corner earlier that day, but she was not there now. Perhaps she was in another corner? No. They were all empty. Lara couldn't find her anywhere. She cast about the cell one last time, wishing that just this once, things had gone the way she'd planned.

But it was not to be.

Cara was gone.

She would never see her sister again.

PART TWO

For it was not into my ear you whispered, but into my heart.
It was not my lips you kissed, but my soul.

— *Judy Garland*

Of all the Fourteen Gifts that magic has given us, perhaps the most dangerous—and misunderstood—is mistweaving. For even more than mindmaster magic, mistweaving is a power that can warp the very soul. Be on guard. Your life may depend on it.

Excerpt from an internal department memo
by Antioch Silverstream,
Interim Chief Researcher,
Department of Magical
Research,
Ilyrion University
10 A.A.

NINETEEN

KYTHAELA LOOKED around the fire at the faces there. Some were sleepy, some were bored, but most of them were staring with rapt attention, listening as the story unfolded around them. Kythaela smiled.

"Although the tale is not yet over," she said, "there is already a moral to be told. Every magic has a weakness. Every Aspect has a darkness. There are things you have been taught —things to avoid, things that are dangerous to do. Mist-weavers are taught to never project an illusion of themselves. Leafrunners are told to never hover, to always be moving. Soulsoothers are cautioned not to heal themselves too many times.

"Now you can see the reason behind these prohibitions. What Pa did is called a soulsplinter, and it is very, *very* dangerous."

She paused, checking to see if the crowd had understood her words. They had.

"Let us speed up the story now," she said. "For although much happened while our heroes grew older, not all of it must be told in so much detail. So let us continue, flitting through the next ten years of our heroes' lives.

"Everything I am about to say is true."

AND SO IT was that Cara escaped into the forest that bordered Errenmel. She never saw the person who freed her—they were cloaked in shadows, somehow impervious to light. The person spoke no words, they just opened the cell and motioned for Cara to leave.

She was happy to do so.

She lived for a time in the forest, finding nuts and berries and mushrooms to eat. She stole a bow and a hunting knife from a nearby farm. She found another poplar tree that had transformed and she took as much wood from it as she could, noting that the wood grew back almost instantly whenever she cut some off. It was warm in her hand, as she knew it would be. It was magic.

Her diet improved vastly after that. She was able to hunt, even with no prior experience with a bow. She fashioned arrows and shot them, using her magic to make them go where she needed them to go.

And so it was that for some time, Cara was almost happy.

But she was still alone. And after months of solitude, she couldn't stand it anymore.

But she couldn't go back to Errenmel. She didn't want to go to Ilyrion, not without a place to stay, or money. And any other settlements were miles and miles away. So she had no choice but to stay in the forest. She had no choice but to remain alone.

Perhaps forever.

ONE DAY CARA met someone in the woods.

It was a hermit, a man who had a shack in the far reaches of the Errenmel Forest. He offered Cara a place to stay, should she so desire it. And though he was old, and smelled bad, and though he had a funny manner about him, Cara needed elven interaction. So she agreed to come with him.

As it turned out, this was a very poor decision.

For the hermit made her touch him, and he touched her, and he made her do things that are inappropriate to repeat. He fed her and clothed her in rags, but his true intentions were of a more carnal nature. And Cara, in her innocence, in her want for attention and for love, did not know that what she was doing was wrong.

And so the years passed. And while Cara grew larger and stronger, the edges of her soul began to fray.

LARA, meanwhile, stayed at Pastor Deryth's house. She decided to do something different, something that would enable her to get ahead in life, despite losing her parents and her sister in one fateful day. Something that would help her finally win.

She decided to lie.

And so it was that Lara became the assistant to the pastor, beating out even his own daughter for the position. Lara was not a witch, and so the people of Errenmel respected her, loved her. Deryth groomed her to replace him one day, for he thought he saw great faith in her heart.

But Lara had other plans. She wanted to go to the University in Ilyrion. There, she reasoned, she could finally get the thing she'd always wanted: respect.

Deryth protested, at first. But Lara had done so well in his eyes, working with him at the church, that in the end he took a special offering from the villagers. The money would go to a good cause, he said—perhaps the greatest cause of all. It would go to fund Lara's education in the big city.

And so it was that Lara left Errenmel to seek her fortune in the University and beyond. She took one last look at the forest before she left, wondering if her sister had survived.

ATEN GATHERED ALL the astronomers he could find, as well as all of the Awakened. With them he founded two groups: the Department of Magical Research, of which he was the head, and the Doctorate of Magic program. The Dean, as it turned out, had been quite amenable to Aten's requests. Antioch had been very persuasive.

Aten had everything he'd ever wanted.

But it wasn't enough. He had respect, he had a full professorship—he even had a few friends. But his magic was so limiting, so weak. As part of his research, he'd given each power a name. His was called mistweaving: the power of illusion. But it could do nothing. It was useless. And as his knowledge of the other powers grew, he found himself frustrated that he could not perform any of them.

He resolved to change that, if he could.

ONE DAY CARA finally realized how terrible her life was. It came to her all in a flash—the abuse, the uselessness, the powerlessness. The loneliness, even with the hermit around. She was just a toy to him. Just a plaything. She could feel the darkness of it gnawing at her soul. And so it was that Cara did the one thing she always did in situations like this.

She killed the hermit.

He died easily, bleeding all over a yew tree that was right outside. She cut his throat, like she did her father's, and for a moment she saw Pa's face as the old hermit died. She saw Pa's face, white and bleeding in the cold forest air, and she felt nothing.

She felt nothing at all.

But then the tree *changed*. It grew, but only a little. The wood darkened, becoming somehow shiny, as if metal had been fused into the fabric of the wood. As if the moonlight— or the orange light looming in the sky—had somehow driven its way into the very core of this tree. As if the hermit's soul had become trapped inside of it.

The tree was gnarled now, twisted and misshapen. It was ugly, dark, nightmarish, strange. Yet somehow to Cara it seemed the prettiest thing she had ever seen.

She took some of its wood, noting that it did not regenerate like the larger trees did. And she experimented, trying to do things with the wood. Trying magic. It took her only a week to figure out what this new wood was for.

Mind control.

LARA WAS HAPPY AT SCHOOL. Happier than she'd ever been at any period of her life. Here were people she could actually converse with, people who were smart and driven and successful.

People she could control.

She gathered them around her like flowers, like falling leaves, like trees. She cultivated them like a garden, doing what she'd done at the church in Errenmel. Garnering their love. It didn't matter to her that most of it required lying.

And so it was that Lara was finally happy.

Until the day her sister reappeared.

IT DIDN'T TAKE LONG for Cara to figure out how to use this new mindmaster magic. She wasted no time—she went to Ilyrion, using her power to convince several people to give her all their money. Then she got a room at a boarding house, convincing the landlady that it was normal for a teenage girl to appear out of nowhere, thin and dirty, hair and clothes unkempt and woefully out of date. She got a room, she got cleaned up, and she bought new clothes. And as she stood in front of the mirror, wondering where her life was going, she decided it was time to change her hair.

She fashioned it into a braid.

If she wanted to succeed—if she wanted power of any kind in this world—she knew she needed knowledge. Knowledge and connections. And there was no better place to get those things than at the University here in Ilyrion. That was why she'd come here to begin with.

The next day, it took no more than a few moments of magic to gain entrance to the school. And so it was that the sisters finally met again after ten long years.

The events that followed would resound throughout history.

TWENTY

10 A.A. (AFTER AWAKENING)
ILYRION UNIVERSITY
VALARALDA

THE ORANGE LIGHT in the sky was getting larger, faster. Aten had given up watching it himself—he left that job to the Corps of Astronomers. They had separated themselves from the Department of Magical Research two years ago, claiming that they didn't study magic. And they were right, Aten knew. They didn't study magic. They should be separate. And yet as he looked into the night sky like the astronomers did, he felt sure that magic was staring him directly in the face.

It had been ten years since the day the light had appeared. Ten long years since the Trees had begun transforming, since the time when mages first began Awakening. And in all that time the orange light had held steady, moving only ever so slightly, growing larger ever so slowly. And though there were still many mysteries yet to ascertain, one thing had become clear quite quickly.

The orange light was heading for them.

Aten's position had certainly improved. In one fell swoop he'd gone from Junior Professor to the head of a new Department. The year after that he'd started his own degree program. Now he was looked up to, respected, even admired. Now students bowed to him when they passed him in the halls. Now people wanted to eat with him in the dining room. Now nobody was ever late to his lectures.

But it was not enough.

He turned from the chalkboard, surveying the class. It was full, as usual. This was Magical Theory 101, and any student could take it—even if they hadn't Awakened. Some students might Awaken later—Aten had found that many people were delayed, for reasons he had yet to discover. Some would never Awaken, but the knowledge of magic was still useful to them. So anyone who wanted to could take this introductory course, and as a result the class always had a wait list.

Except—that was odd. There was a new girl up front— pretty, with a blonde braid running down her back. She was a spindly little thing, looking like she hadn't had enough to eat for the last decade or so. She was seated next to Lara, the raven-haired young beauty. Yes, Lara had certainly caught his eye more than once. But who was this new blonde?

This was the third week of class, and it had had a wait list of at least thirty people the last time he had checked. New students couldn't be admitted to the class unless someone else had dropped out. He did a quick headcount—there was indeed one extra student today. The blonde. Somehow she'd weaseled her way into a full class, bypassing the entire wait list. How?

Something fishy was going on.

He turned back to the chalkboard, preparing to begin the lecture. He'd ask the Program Administrator later how the blonde had gotten in. It was a mystery, but an unimportant one.

He opened his mouth to speak, but whispering interrupted him.

"How are you here?"

"How else? I walked."

"But...you're still alive!"

"In the flesh, sister."

Aten turned to see who it was that dared disrupt his class. As he had suspected, it was the two girls in front: the raven-haired beauty and the new blonde. Apparently they were sisters.

Things were getting more unusual by the minute.

He cleared his throat suggestively, but the girls just kept whispering, oblivious to the fact that everyone was staring at them.

"Where have you been? I haven't seen you in *ten years*!"

"Oh, here and there. I learned a few things while I was gone."

"You were in the forest, weren't you."

"Yes."

"I looked for you, you know. I even visited your cell the night you were to be burned. But you weren't there."

The brunette's name suddenly entered Aten's head. Lara. Her name was Lara. He cleared his throat again, tapping his hands together, but the girls still didn't listen.

"How did you *get* here, Cara?" Lara asked. "And why?"

The blonde—Cara—smirked. "I came for the same reason I imagine you did—to learn."

Lara looked at her sister for a long moment. "No," she whispered. "You came here for power, didn't you."

"Didn't you?"

"I don't have to answer that."

"No," Cara said, "I suppose you don't. I just thought religious people were always supposed to be honest."

"What do you know of religion?"

"I know that you pretended to be an assistant to Pastor Deryth. I know that when he wasn't looking, you pilfered money from the weekly offerings. I know you slept with the doctor's boy—what was his name—Corym? And I know that if Deryth had found out, he would have excommunicated you from the church. God frowns on sinners, Lara."

Lara looked taken aback. "How could you *possibly* know all that? Nobody has seen or heard from you in ten years."

Cara leaned forward, her face taking on a menacing tone. "You know how," she said. "I'm a *witch*."

That was enough. As interesting and strange as these two girls were, Aten had a class to teach. "Ladies," he said, making his voice as firm as he could, "that is quite enough out of you. Both of you report to the Dean."

"Now?" Lara asked, her face dismayed. She looked around, finally aware that their entire conversation had been heard by the class.

"Now," Aten said. "Speaking out in class is forbidden. I will inquire with the Dean immediately after this lecture to find out if you obeyed. Now go."

"I don't want to go with *her*," Cara said.

Aten surveyed her. There was an intelligence behind those eyes, and there was also something else. A hunger. A drive. And something even deeper: darkness. Aten suppressed a shiver. How could one so young already look at him with eyes so old?

"You should have thought of that before you disrupted my class," Aten said. "I will hear no more from you about this. Go now, or I will devise a worse punishment for you."

"Fine," Cara said. She and Lara got up from their desks,

picking up their books and leaving the room. Aten watched them go.

Cara had called herself a witch. She had gotten into his class when the rules were strictly against her. She possessed information that her sister said she should not have. How could this be? What power did Cara hold?

Perhaps there was more to magic than Aten had yet uncovered.

TWENTY-ONE

THE DEAN MADE them wait for an hour before he would see them. Cara was forced to sit next to her sister, fuming, trying not to look at her or speak. Maybe it had been a mistake to reenter the world after all this time. Maybe it had been a bad idea to attend the University—she'd known Lara would be here, after all. But there was something in her, some driving force that insisted she needed more. More knowledge, more power. More control of her life. And she was convinced that the only way to obtain any of that was by going to school. She just hoped they didn't burn her at the stake.

Lara was refusing to speak to her—not that she minded much. But she felt it was only a matter of time before her sister's anger erupted into actual violence. The girl was still clearly mad about Pa's death.

When the Dean finally let them in, they sat in his office and blinked at him across his rather large oak desk. The Dean was a larger man, bald, his wrinkled face littered with age spots. But his eyes were sharp and blue, and his look carried an intensity that made Cara suddenly nervous. Perhaps she shouldn't have angered a professor on her very first day of class.

She fingered the dark poplar in her pocket.

"Your names?" the Dean asked.

"Cara," Cara said.

"Lara."

"I'm Dean Aubric," the Dean said. "This is the first time I've seen either of you in here. Why were you sent?"

"They were sent for disrupting class," Aten said, suddenly bursting through the doors. He frowned down at them. "I'm glad to see you two can sometimes follow instructions."

Cara looked at Aten, really paying attention to him for the first time. He was tall, with blonde, slicked-back hair that gave him a severe look. His cheek bones were high and prominent, his eyes blue. He was rather cute, for an older man. Rather cute indeed.

But his expression held no love for her. "These two girls—sisters, yes?—held an entire conversation in front of the class." He had turned back to the Dean. "While I'm sure what they had to say was very interesting, I had a class to run."

"A rather minor offense, wouldn't you say?" Dean Aubric said.

Aten's brow furrowed. "Only if you consider the effective teaching of students to be *minor*."

Aubric sat back in his seat. "Very well," he said. "Detention for both. Really, Professor Aten, you could have given them that yourself. Students, report to the professor's office directly after last period."

Aten was fuming—clearly he had expected some harsher form of punishment. Cara was looking forward to it, though. It would give her a chance to speak with this cute man. But Lara—Lara was downright angry, her mouth open in shock.

"But I—I can't serve detention tonight!" she said.

"And why not?" Aubric asked. "What could a freshman have to do that is so important?"

"What, indeed?" Aten asked.

Lara hung her head, her face reddening. "I, uh. Well. I was supposed to meet this—"

"It's a boy," Cara said, giggling. "Isn't it?"

Lara didn't answer.

"It's always a boy," Aubric said. "See that you attend detention, or there will be consequences."

"Yes, Dean," Lara said.

Cara beamed. Finally her sister was being put in her place.

LARA STORMED out of the Dean's office, angry beyond words.

"This is your fault," she said to Cara. "If you hadn't shown up here, none of this would have happened."

"What, detention?" Cara asked. "You're afraid of a little detention?"

"How do you even know what detention *is*, you little backwoods bitch? You're an orphan! You've never lived anywhere that wasn't a farm or a forest."

"You're an orphan too," Cara said. "Lest you've already forgotten. And I've always been a quick learner."

Aten had left, Lara noted. Clearly he had no further desire to get involved with their argument. Lara wished *she* could leave—leave and be done with her sister forever. Cara had been dead, hadn't she? Dead or gone.

She should have stayed that way.

"Who's the boy?" Cara asked, winking at her.

"What boy?" Students were giving them a wide berth, stepping around them on the grass. Lara noticed a massive oak tree next to them—one of the magical ones. Strange that it should be right here on campus like this. She didn't know what oak was supposed to do.

"The boy you had a date with," Cara said. "Were you going to fuck him, too?"

"Probably." No reason to lie about it. "Which is more than *you* can say."

Cara had a hand in her pocket. "I can get any boy any time I like."

Lara doubted that claim. "You've always had it out for me," she said. "And it seems that even after all this time, nothing has changed." She took a step toward her sister, fists balled. "Well, I'm not going to stand for it. This ends *now*."

She punched her sister in the face.

But Cara dodged the blow, returning it with one of her own: a swift slap to Lara's right cheek. It hit her *hard*, sending her reeling. Her cheek stung. How was Cara so *strong*?

Then Cara was on her, hitting her again and again, tripping her and throwing her to the ground. She tried to hit Lara's face, but Lara kept her hands up, guarding against the blows. They grappled together, rolling around on the University grass. Students formed a ring around them, watching.

Cara got another hit in, this time on Lara's stomach. "You were always Pa's favorite," she shouted, aiming a punch at Lara's nose.

Lara dodged weakly, turning the punch into a glancing blow along her cheek. She felt the pain resounding in her head, mingling with her anger. "That's why I didn't kill him," she returned, trying to kick at Cara but failing to hit her with any strength. Cara tackled her, twisting until she was behind her, putting Lara into an efficient head lock. Now she was stuck, winded and afraid. There was no more fight left in her —not against this demon girl.

"How did you get so strong?" Lara asked, breathing heavily. Her cheek hurt terribly. "How did you learn to fight?"

She could hear Cara's teeth grinding in her ear. "The man I lived with liked to hit me, too."

Lara didn't know who she meant. And she didn't know where this was leading. Cara had her trapped now, held tightly in her arms. The girl was just too strong. Evidently a decade spent living and hunting in a forest was enough to make you into quite a fighter. Lara should have known it was a mistake to get involved with her sister. It never turned out well.

"Let me go," she said.

And, for a wonder, Cara did.

Lara lurched away, suddenly free from Cara's arms.

"Now I see why the boys like you," Cara said from behind her. "They must like an easy lay."

Lara felt the blood boiling between her ears.

She lunged forward, grabbing an oak branch that had fallen from the massive tree. Then she turned, acting on pure instinct, not quite sure what she intended.

Cara had that look in her eyes.

It was the same way she'd looked that night, that fateful night when everything had gone wrong. It was the expression she had had just before she'd killed Pa.

Which meant Cara was planning on killing *her*.

It might not happen now. It might not even happen soon. But it would happen, eventually. It was only a matter of time. It was as clear to her as the roughness of the oak wood in her hand.

Lara felt fear racing through her, but she decided that now was not the time to surrender to it. No—now was the time to take matters into her own hands. If Cara was planning on killing her, Lara needed to prevent it while she still could.

She needed to kill Cara first.

"You will *not* be the death of me," she said, hearing the authority in her voice.

And she swung the stick. She swung it with all her might. She intended to hit her sister with it, to bash her across the head as hard as she could. Cara might be strong, but she could not resist the hardness of oak. She was but skin and bone before the might of Lara's fury.

She swung the stick, but then something *else* happened.

She felt something flashing through it. Energy, maybe. Power of some kind. A force, an element, maybe a soul. She felt it all in an instant, the energy pouring out of the branch and into her body. She swung the stick, feeling her strength grow and grow, feeling her instincts improve, her eyesight sharpen. Her hearing got better—the jeering of the students around them got clearer, louder. Her muscles seemed to expand, her heart beating firmly in her chest. She swung the stick, and she knew that this power in her had made her *strong*.

This blow would kill her sister.

But the wood suddenly disintegrated into dust.

Lara was fast now, though. She didn't even pause—she converted the swing into a punch, aiming it directly at her stupid sister's face. Lara didn't even feel it when it hit—her bones and skin and muscles were too strong.

Cara's face crumpled, and she sailed a dozen feet across the lawn. The light flashed out of her eyes.

Lara froze.

No.

She hadn't actually meant to kill her sister. There was some kind of power roiling through her. Some kind of... magic. The oak had done this to her. It was the wood's fault.

It had made her into some kind of monster.

She took a step forward, hand outstretched, intending to go to Cara. Maybe she wasn't dead. Maybe there was still time.

"What is this?" a woman asked, stepping in suddenly from somewhere out of sight. She had long, blonde hair and a rather pronounced chin. Lara was sure she'd never seen her before. The woman bent down over Cara, inspecting her destroyed face. "Oh, my," she said. "This poor girl has been done in."

Then she waved her hand over Cara's face, and the girl's skin blurred. When her hand passed, Cara's features shifted, falling back into place. Lara took two steps forward to make sure what she was seeing was correct.

Cara's face was back to normal.

Her sister took a gasping breath, her back arching as life returned to her body. Then she coughed, and the strange blonde woman knelt to see to her.

"There, there," the strange woman said. "You'll be fine. I hope I never meet the fist that did this to you."

"What—" Lara said. "How did you—"

The woman looked up at her, a serene expression on her face. "Did you know this girl? The poor thing. She'll be alright." The woman stood, helping Cara up. Cara looked around as if confused. Maybe she was still gathering her thoughts.

"Who are you?" Lara asked.

"Nelenor," the woman said, bowing to Lara. Then she looked at the huge oak tree behind Lara, cocking her head at a curious angle.

A man swept in from somewhere. He had blonde hair as well, and the same chin as Nelenor. He was rather dashing, actually. But Lara had never seen him before.

"Oh," Nelenor said, turning to the man, "let me introduce you to my twin brother. This is Velion."

Velion gave a bow of his own. "Quite the beautiful planet you have here," he said, his gaze finding the oak tree as well. "I am curious, though. Do all your trees grow this large?"

Suddenly the sky became intensely orange. Lara had to squint to see anything.

Nelenor looked up, long blonde hair backlit by the strange orange glow coming from above. "Brother," she said, a wide smile on her face, "it is here. We arrived just in time."

TWENTY-TWO

LARA HAD to shut her eyes for a moment. The sky was just too bright. She could see orange through her closed eyelids, as if Persephone had suddenly grown, inundating the sky. The glow was searing, intense. Then it was suddenly gone.

She opened her eyes.

A big boxy thing was lying on the ground a mere fifty feet away from them, nestled in the grass. It was long and silvery, with sharp, squared-off edges. It looked to be made of some kind of metal, but the light struck it strangely. The whole thing was maybe twenty feet long and a foot square, and the edges were set at angles to each other, forming a sort of trapezoid. Two handles were set into it, one on either end.

It was the strangest thing Lara had ever seen.

She turned her eyes from the metal device, looking at the two strangers who had identified themselves as twins. They certainly looked alike, albeit of differing genders. Nelenor, the woman, was still bent over Cara in the grass.

"Are you her?" she asked. "You have the hair, though your face is not what I recall. Things are so muddy to me."

Velion knelt next to her, picking up a piece of Cara's hair. "Golden," he said. "Is it her?"

"Am I who?" Cara asked, sitting up. Her face seemed fine from where Lara was standing. Somehow it had been completely healed.

The blond twins stood. "We are looking for our sister," Nelenor said. "She is here somewhere. We can feel her. Are you her?"

"I'm Cara," Cara said. "My sister is over there." She pointed at Lara, and the strangers' heads swiveled to look at her.

"She is not her," Velion said, beckoning toward Lara. "She does not have the look."

"You don't know who your sister is?" Lara asked. This was all very strange.

Nelenor shook her head sadly. "In our haste to escape, some pieces of our reality got mixed up. We know we have a sister that we dearly love. She is likely blonde, like me. But her face—we lost her face in the escape."

"How can you lose a face?"

"It is...difficult to explain. Much happened when Starmist Prime was destroyed."

"I have no idea what you're talking about," Lara said. Cara was standing, looking shaken. Curious students were gathering all around them.

"We know she is here," Velion said. Although he was clearly a man, he was almost woman-like in his appearance, with long, flowing hair and fine features. He was very pretty, Lara realized. His blue eyes were open and full of light, without a hint of malice in them. Lara felt as if she could look into those eyes forever. "We felt her presence," Velion continued. "Guruthos followed her here, though it is not as fast as the vessel she used. Nor, for that matter, are we."

Lara approached them, trepidation falling away. The strangers seemed kind. Gentle. Concerned. She didn't have anything to fear from them, despite the strange things they were saying. "Are you from up there?" she asked, pointing at the sky.

Velion nodded. "We traveled a long way to reach you, much of it while asleep. This place—she must have been drawn to it."

"She?"

"Our sister. The one we are looking for."

"Why would she be drawn here?"

"The souls," Nelenor said, waving a sweeping hand around at the crowd that was growing by the minute. "The souls are strong, here."

"You know something about our...souls?" Lara pressed a hand to her heart unconsciously. Was this some kind of religion?

"There is much we know," Velion said, "and much we do not. Your souls are indeed strong—and not just yours. Even the plants in this place have stronger souls than we expected. Even the trees."

"Especially the trees," Nelenor said.

That was interesting.

"And this sister you're looking for," Lara said. "Are you triplets?"

"She is older," Velion said. "She is—was—our guardian." Tears crept into his eyes. "We miss her greatly. We have been searching for so long."

It was only then that Lara realized what was so strange about these two.

They looked like elves. *Exactly* like elves. Yet by their own admission they were from the sky, from outer space, from the place astronomers only theorized about. If that were true—

and surely it could not be true—but if it *were* true, how could these beings look exactly like them?

Unless there was some kind of magic going on.

"This is not her," Nelenor said. "We must continue looking. We will search this whole world if we must. I can feel her, brother. She is here. She is close."

"I hope you find what you are looking for," Lara said, and Velion smiled at her.

It was a smile that could warm the coldest heart.

ATEN WAS DUSTING off his diploma when Antioch bustled into his office. "Something strange just happened," the man said, making himself comfortable in Aten's leather chair. He had the grace not to put his feet up on the desk, at least. The older man had gotten far too chummy with Aten over the years. Perhaps he felt it was deserved.

Perhaps it was.

Aten turned, feather duster in hand. The frames on his wall held many precious things, not least of which was the diploma that officially made him the world's first Doctor of Magic. The "MrD" designation was a bit odd—it stood for Doctor of Magistry, which wasn't *quite* the right term for "mage"—but it made the point all the same. Aten had created the program, and he was its first graduate. It was his life's greatest accomplishment to date. And though he kept the frame clean, and though he looked at it many times a day, feeling that familiar warmth of accomplishment blossom inside him every time he did, it was not enough.

He knew there *must* be more.

"What do you want?" he asked.

Antioch shot him a glare. "I wanted to tell you about the

strange things happening on campus." He shifted in the seat, leather creaking. "But if you have no interest, I'll take my gossip somewhere else."

"Fine, fine," Aten said, waving a hand in the air. "Tell me. What is so interesting that you thought to come all the way to my office?"

"I work across the hall from you," Antioch said.

Aten just quirked an eyebrow at him.

Antioch sighed. "You're quite prickly today. Wake up on the wrong side of the bed?"

"You know, I never could make sense of that saying," Aten said. "What difference does the side of the bed make? And besides—my bed is against a wall, and it's only big enough for me. There is only one side, Antioch."

"Maybe that's your problem."

"What is?"

Antioch giggled, an unbecoming trait for an older man. "You need a bigger bed."

Aten crossed his arms and cleared his throat, feather duster dangling from one hand. "Whatever you have to say, spit it out. Was there magic involved? There must have been, if you're coming to me."

Antioch smiled. "Oh, yes," he said. "There was definitely magic involved. Two strangers appeared on campus today. They've just been arrested."

"Why do I care about two strangers?"

"I've heard accounts that they healed a girl—Cara, I believe it was—from a mortal wound."

"Soulsoothing. It's one of the Aspects. So?"

"Nobody knows who they are. They appeared next to some *machine*. They say they're looking for their long-lost sister."

"None of this matters to me. I see hundreds of strangers every day."

"And they claim to be from outer space."

That stopped Aten cold. He looked around the dimly-lit office, jaw muscles clenching unconsciously. When his gaze returned to Antioch, he felt excitement coursing through his system. This. This could be what he'd been waiting for. This could be the thing he'd been missing. "You say they were arrested?" he asked. "On what charges?"

"They were finding all the blonde girls in the school," Antioch said. "They were...questioning them."

"Is that all?"

"Well...that's why they were arrested. You'd have to ask them if that was *all*."

Aten glanced at his diploma, eyes narrowing. He didn't know why, but he had a feeling about this. This was big. This was somehow important. Although he couldn't yet answer why he felt this way, he'd learned over the years to trust his instincts. And his instincts were telling him that this mysterious pair might be the most important thing to ever enter his life.

"They're at the police station?" he asked.

Antioch nodded. "The police are asking for you. Since the pair has already been seen using magic, they think you'll be the best person to interrogate them."

"Good," Aten said, jaw muscles relaxing. A smile creased his face. "Give them a call for me, Antioch, if you don't mind. Tell them I'll be right there."

TWENTY-THREE

AN HOUR LATER, Aten was sitting across from two of the blondest people he had ever met. They were both thin and wiry, impossibly pretty, with long hair and crystalline blue eyes. They had an air of great intelligence about them, as if they'd seen things no one else had ever seen. Wonders. Technology beyond his wildest dreams. Aten longed to ask them about it, to learn all he could from these mysterious beings, but first he had to ascertain just who, exactly, they were.

"Who are you?" he asked.

It seemed the simplest approach.

The police chief was standing in the corner, watching the proceedings. It was unusual for a civilian to be interrogating suspected criminals, but in this case the police had felt the exception warranted.

"I am Nelenor," the woman said. "And this is my twin brother, Velion."

"Twins," Aten said. Nelenor nodded. "And where are you from?"

"The planet Starmist Prime, in the Starmist solar system,

Sector 421. The planet was destroyed, and a few things...
escaped. We mean no harm to this world."

"I'll be the judge of that," Aten said. "Why are you here?"
He should probably have asked them *how* they were here, but
he could get to that later.

"We are looking for our older sister. Her name is Kaela.
She left the Starmist system before we did, in a much faster
spacecraft. It took us time to catch up to her."

"How do you know she is here?"

"We can feel her," Velion said. "We share a connection, as
siblings. It is...difficult to explain."

"Try."

Velion cast about the room as if searching for answers.
"There is a part of every living thing," he said, putting a finger
to his chest. "The spark. You might call it a...soul. The souls
can touch, you see, reaching out in a vast web of interconnec-
tions. Some are stronger. Some are intentional. Our connection to Kaela is not intentional—it is a part of nature. It is the
family bond, the bond that cannot be broken."

"You speak as if you really are from another planet, yet
you look like us."

"We—" Velion seemed taken aback for a minute, as if not
sure what to say. He looked at his sister for support.

"You are right," Nelenor said. "We had not thought on it
until now. We should have expected an alien race, people we
could not even converse with." Her eyes were downcast,
looking at the wooden table. "How could we be so stupid?"

Velion put a hand on her arm. Their love for each other
was evident even to Aten, who did not put a great deal of
stock in such things. "This must be one of them," he said.

"A Seed Planet," Nelenor said. "But the records didn't—"

"The records were destroyed. We don't *remember* the
Seeds anymore."

"You are right, brother. Still, I wonder: how did Kaela find her way here?"

Velion stroked his smooth chin. "That is a very good question, sister. She must have been drawn to the souls here, like we told that raven-haired girl in the park."

"The trees."

"Yes."

"You haven't answered my question," Aten said.

Velion turned to him. "Long ago, Starmist was attacked by a great threat: marauders. Aliens, warlike beings bent on destruction. They were called the Xelle by us, though they had other names. The people on Starmist Prime were able to fend off this threat, but only at great cost. And we knew that it was only a matter of time before the Xelle returned, this time bringing larger forces, greater weapons.

"And so, knowing that they could not face this threat in war, the leaders of Starmist Prime devised a plan to carry on our race. It was a multifaceted plan: first, they sent members of our species to several Seed Planets—planets far away from Starmist. Each generation ship was filled with people who were ready to start a new life on the planets they found, knowing that they would never see Starmist again. In this way, even if Starmist Prime itself were destroyed, our race would still survive.

"The second portion of the plan involved our technology. Starmist Prime had developed many great feats of engineering, devices which would look like magic to you. Many of them operate with advanced quantum tunneling, allowing power and information to transfer across vast distances in the blink of an eye. We couldn't let these devices fall into the enemy's hands—they were too powerful. So we made plans to send them away—as far away as possible—when the Xelle reappeared."

"You brought one of those devices here," Aten said. He'd seen the long metal thing in the school quad, looking for all the world like alien technology. They'd tried picking it up, moving it, but it was too heavy to lift.

Velion nodded. "Guruthos. It is one of several Starmist technologies—one of the more powerful. This particular device responds to sparkthreads, allowing certain users to control the output."

"Sparkthreads?"

"Pieces of the soul. Tendrils, if you will. Strands. You might think of them as soulstrands, if you prefer that term."

"I see." Aten didn't see at all, but he wanted to let these twins talk more. They seemed eager to share, after all. Were they lying to him? It seemed far-fetched. If it was a lie, it was the strangest lie he'd ever heard.

"We were surprised to find the people here already communicating with Guruthos," Nelenor said. "Ordinarily it requires great training over hundreds of years, and an immense amount of soul energy. Not just anyone can activate the device. This is probably what drove Kaela here: curiosity."

"It wasn't until we arrived that we realized how you were doing it," Velion said.

"And how *are* we doing it?" Aten asked. There was much he could learn about magic from them, he realized. He had landed on a treasure trove. He felt anticipation building.

"It's the trees," Nelenor said. "Souls of great strength, if muted and slow. The trees of your world latch onto souls as they pass, opening a conduit to Guruthos. It is through this conduit that your people are able to attune themselves to the device, to utilize its energy."

"Through the wood," Aten said. Everything was starting to make a strange kind of sense.

"Yes," Nelenor said. "Yet still, not all can do this. Each

person has an affinity, a certain portion of their soul that is stronger than the rest. For those that are strong enough, it is this part that expands outward, communicating with Guruthos."

"We call them Aspects," Aten said.

Nelenor smiled at him, making her even more beautiful than she already was. "You have learned much in a short time. You are a strong people."

"If what you say is true," Aten said, "we're *you*."

Nelenor nodded. "Indeed. Yet even on Starmist Prime itself, the home of countless wonders beyond your wildest dreams, there exists no one who can harness the power as quickly and effortlessly as you have done."

"Perhaps we diverged over time," Aten said.

"Or perhaps there is something else at work. But no matter—we must find our sister now."

The twins made as if to get up, but Aten stopped them with a gesture. "We're not done here."

"But we must—"

"Velion. Nelenor. We would like to learn from you, if we can. Perhaps we can even teach each other. Maybe you would like to learn more about this tree magic."

"We are scholars, like you," Velion said. "Yet our errand is an urgent one. We *must* find Kaela. We must reunite our family. We will speak more once that mission is complete."

"No."

"No?" Velion's eyes narrowed.

"I need more from you," Aten said. "You're not free to leave."

Velion sighed, quirking his fingers in the air briefly. Then he reached down and pulled something from his pocket, laying it on the table.

It was Guruthos.

Except it was *tiny*, maybe two inches long.

"Is this what you wanted to discuss?" Velion asked.

TWENTY-FOUR

"HOW THE HELL did you do that?" Aten asked.

Velion shrugged. "Guruthos can fold itself through its private dimension. This allows it to appear smaller, if necessary. We can also make it disappear."

He quirked his finger and the metal object blinked out of sight.

"Bring it back," Aten said.

Velion obliged, the device popping back into existence on the table.

"A separate dimension?" Aten asked. "I don't know what that word means."

"Ah," Velion said, spreading his hands on the table. "That would take a long time to explain. Let us say that it is like an alternate reality—a pocket in space, in time, that matter and energy can be transferred to. Guruthos generates its own small dimension, just enough to allow for tricks like this."

"Can...*people* visit this dimension?" Aten asked.

Velion frowned. "I suppose, if it were enlarged. But why would you want to?"

Some kind of loud sound erupted outside, shaking the

police station briefly. Aten started, looking in the direction of the sound, trying to discern what it might have been. Was it an explosion? It had come from the university.

"I'll check it out," the police chief said. Aten had already forgotten his name.

Aten nodded, returning his gaze to the twins.

"The power is very strong now," Nelenor said. "Though you were quick to learn how to access it, I think perhaps you are not so quick to learn how to *control* it. With Guruthos so near, I fear you will destroy yourselves."

"We must find our sister and be off," Velion said. "This power is too much for you."

Another explosion rocked the building as if to punctuate his point.

"I can't allow you to leave," Aten said.

"You can't force us to do anything," Velion said. "But we are a peaceful people. We will not resist you, so long as you do not endanger our sister. We will try to help where we may."

"Perhaps we should turn the device off," Nelenor said.

"You can *do* that?" Aten asked.

"Of course," Nelenor said. "It is a simple matter, though it requires both of us."

"Why both of you?"

"Guruthos requires two souls bound to it in order to operate. This was done as a failsafe, you see—the device is too powerful to be in the hands of one person alone."

"I see."

"But no matter. We are both here. We will turn it off now." The twins reached for the device on the table.

"No," Aten said, his voice loud in the silent room.

Nelenor looked at him, alarm in her eyes. "No?"

"Don't turn it off," Aten said. "Give us a chance to learn.

We'll find who is causing the disturbance and make them stop."

"We don't wish to *make* you do anything," Nelenor said. "The power is too strong for you. You must take the time to learn."

"Please," Aten said, realizing that all he had were words. If these strange twins wanted to turn Guruthos off—if they wanted to kill him or escape—there was nothing he could do. They were far too powerful to resist. And yet there was one thing they did not seem to have, something that could give Aten an advantage.

They weren't willing to lie.

"It's my mother," Aten said. "She is sick. There is a soul-soother by her side day and night, taking away her pain. Trying to heal her. But we are new to this, you see. We do not yet know how to correct the sickness that is in her. Without this...magic...she will die."

"Let us see her," Velion said. "We will heal her straightaway."

"No," Aten said. "Seeing you would give her great fright. She is unused to strangers, you see. I fear that if you arrive suddenly, it could be the end of her."

The twins looked at each other, as if sharing an unspoken thought. Then they nodded, turning back to Aten. "We will leave Guruthos active," Velion said. "For the time being. But know that any destruction wrought by its power is not our responsibility."

Aten dipped his head in acknowledgement. "I under-stand. Thank you for this." He suppressed a sob. "My mother thanks you."

"We wish her well," Nelenor said.

Aten smiled inwardly. Powerful though they may be, this pair of blondes were the most gullible people he'd ever seen.

LATER THAT NIGHT, Aten crept into the room the twins were sleeping in. The police chief hadn't wanted to hold them in jail—they hadn't harmed anyone, after all, despite how creepy it had been that they'd been going after young girls. They seemed wholly innocent to Aten—too innocent, almost. Nobody was that forthcoming, that honest. He was sure they were hiding something.

But he was even *more* sure that they had power. Lots of power. Power that Aten wanted. Power that would make him into the person he had always wanted to be.

And so it was that he found himself creeping into their room at the University, the room that the Dean had graciously offered them after hearing the police report. He snuck across the room, wincing as the floorboards creaked, watching their faces as they slept. They were peaceful. They didn't move.

Which made sense, since Aten had drugged them earlier.

Guruthos was sitting on a bedside table, still a mere two inches long. He picked it up, struggling with it briefly as he did—it was shockingly heavy for such a small device. But he managed to get it into his pocket and get back out of the room.

The twins never awoke.

ATEN TOOK Guruthos to his office. The twins didn't know where the office was, but he was sure they could find it once they awoke. They were bound to the device, they had said. He could see the two little handles worked into either end of the metal. They were probably symbolic, but they got the point across. Two wielders. Two souls. And if the twins could feel their sister's soul across millions of miles of space, he was sure they could feel the presence of Guruthos itself.

Luckily, the sedative he'd given them should last a few days.

He wanted time to research Guruthos, to see if there was anything he could learn from it or do with it. Perhaps he would need to kill the twins to accomplish his goal. Or maybe they would help him with it—they had been very accommodating, after all. Perhaps he should have just left them awake, asking their permission to play with the device. But a part of him knew that they wouldn't approve of what he was about to try. And a larger part of him just wanted to be alone.

"This dimension they spoke of," he said. "How can I gain access to it?" He had a habit of speaking to himself, especially when he was trying to solve a tough problem. "I know you're in there somewhere."

He probed the device, touching it with his fingers. It felt oddly warm, as if heat were radiating out from the metal itself. And the machine was quite heavy, despite being only two inches long. It was because it was folded into its other dimension, he reasoned. Although it reduced the apparent size, it hadn't entirely reduced the mass of the object. This other dimension—that was where he wanted to explore. It sounded like a potential source of additional power.

Touching the device did nothing. He needed to do something else. Something involving this "spark" the twins had spoken of? The soul. Everything was connected to the soul. So it was there that he must start.

He picked up a piece of primewood—maple, of course. The only kind of wood he could use. He took his carving knife and flicked a flake off of the prime maple, envisioning the shape of a leaf. Familiar power flooded into the wood as he did, power he had felt hundreds of times before. Except this time he focused on it differently. Instead of concentrating on what he could *do* with the magic, he tried to focus on how the magic *felt*.

And there it was. He could see it, almost. It was a line, a bright line, bursting outward from himself and shooting into the wood. Then it went out from the wood, across a few inches of air, connecting directly with the metal device on his desk.

It was simple. Easy. And it was exactly as the twins had described.

Well, then. He could work with this. But how? He kept the magic flowing, not doing anything with it yet, trying to figure out what to do. Illusion magic—mistweaving, he'd named it—was pretty useless. Causing people to see things that weren't there—it was a good party trick, but it didn't really *do* anything. For the millionth time, he wished he could access the other Aspects. The more useful ones. But first, he needed to get into this other dimension the device held.

"Hmm," he said to himself, stretching his mind along the length of the soulstrand that was linking him to Guruthos. There was almost a connection point there—not at the handles, but right in the center. Instead of using his mistweaving magic, what if he used the power to bind his soulstrand to the device? He could attach it right *there*, and then—

The link slammed into place, and suddenly Aten found himself in another world.

TWENTY-FIVE

THE SKY WAS PURPLE. The ground was green. Everything waved around him in hazy shapes, as if the world couldn't quite decide what it wanted to be. The land seemed to undulate in curves, rising and falling in rolling hills. But that was it: purple and green as far as the eye could see.

Aten looked down, but his feet weren't there. His body wasn't there. *He* wasn't there—he was seeing all of this from a vision. But he could feel something, as if his soul were somehow expanding in this place. As if it wanted to be free, to soar, to strike like lightning, to blow like wind.

Then everything collapsed into a pinprick of purple light, and the strange dimension was gone.

He was back in his office, staring at his desk. Guruthos was still there, shiny and silver and small. And the wood in his hand had disintegrated into dust. The soulstrand was gone.

But he'd *seen* the other world. The little dimension that Guruthos held around itself. And he somehow knew that this dimension held the secret he was looking for.

He needed to experiment. He needed more data.

Suddenly he had an idea.

"WHAT'S THIS ALL ABOUT?" Antioch asked. It was the middle of the night, and he and Aten were walking through the university campus. Guruthos was in Aten's pocket, the weight of it heavy as he took each step. In his left hand he held an activated piece of prime maple—a large piece, which would last longer.

His right hand concealed a knife.

"An experiment," Aten said. "I've been learning about magic from these twins that appeared. They have a machine that generates the power."

"A...*machine*? But that's impossible. No machine can do these wonders."

"Think, Antioch. What would our machines look like to someone from ten thousand years ago? We take steam and turn it into motion. Our lanterns burn oil to make light. Hell, even *fire* would look strange to one who had never seen it before."

"These are not magic."

"Of course not. But what is magic, if not technology that we cannot yet understand? This device did not come from Valaralda."

"So it *is* true."

They were nearing the edge of campus, where a grove of trees had been planted to act as a screen bordering the city. Aten stopped, looking up at the branches overhead. "It's true," he said. "They claim to be from a planet called Starmist Prime."

"Starmist? What a strange name for a planet. Perhaps it's a mistranslation."

"You know the strangest thing, Antioch?" Aten said. "I don't think they're translating at all."

"You think they speak our language on their planet? But that's impossible."

"They said Valaralda was a Seed Planet. That their people settled here, thousands of years ago."

"Thousands of years? But we would have records of that."

"They didn't specify the time frame. Who knows when it was? They obviously managed to keep it a secret from us—which would have been very simple. All they had to do was *not* write anything down."

"There might be remains," Antioch said.

"There may be. I suspect Thylmanas will be where we will find anything, if it exists."

"We should mount an expedition."

"Feel free to do so, my friend. I will stay here and continue researching this device."

"My 'friend?'" Antioch asked. "Why the sudden conciliatory tone?"

"I'm in a good mood," Aten said, taking a step toward the other man. He had to take care not to trip over the roots of the elm tree he was under—they were everywhere, stretching almost out of the ground in their haste to find water. "These...twins. They say they fought a great threat in the past, a threat that would return. They couldn't let their greatest technology fall into the wrong hands, so they sent it out from their world. They sent it here."

"Making us the lucky beneficiaries."

"Just so," Aten said, taking another step. Antioch's eyes were glittering in the moonlight, branches shading his forehead. His neck was bare. "I think they're withholding information from us," Aten said. "I think they're withholding *power*."

"Of course they are," Antioch said. "Wouldn't you?"

"I certainly would. That's why I've taken matters into my own hands."

"Always the experimenter. That's good."

"Yes," Aten said. "Experimentation is the only way we can learn. See, I have a theory."

"You always have a theory."

"You know me so well. See, I think there's a way to unlock the soul. To gain access to every Aspect."

"You think...*what*?"

"I want more power, Antioch. I *need* it. Mistweaving isn't enough. I want the others. I want it *all*."

"You're a madman. You know that isn't possible!"

"Magic is new. We don't know anything about it."

"We've been studying it for *ten years*!"

"And now we have the source—the *true* source of the power. Now the real study can begin."

"I don't understand," Antioch said. "What did you have in mind?"

"This," Aten said, and he slashed the man wickedly across the neck.

It didn't take Antioch very long to die.

Blood streamed from his neck, dripping from his slumped body and mingling with the roots of the elm tree. Aten concentrated on his bond with Guruthos, on the soulstrand that connected him to it. He needed to observe everything that happened in the next few minutes.

That's when the tree *changed*.

It didn't grow. Actually, it shrank. And it grew darker, twisted, more angular. Moonslight shone from it, rippling off the surface of the wood as if it were made of a strange kind of metal. As if the power contained within it were dark and twisted like the tree itself. But that wasn't the part that Aten was focusing on.

He was focusing on Guruthos itself.

He could feel it open, as if the dimension it held was enlarging, somehow. He closed his eyes, feeling through the wood in his hand and the device in his pocket. He could actually see what was happening; he could visualize it as it happened. Lines of energy were pouring out of Antioch as he died. They were captured by the tree, which had a soul of its own. That soul was reaching out to Antioch, pulling his soul into its embrace. And as Aten watched in his mind's eye, he saw the two souls merge, saw a spark of energy shoot out from that merging, saw it slice into Guruthos, into the dimension it had made. He felt the doorway to that dimension opening, widening, accepting this new pairing of souls, this energy.

Then the door contracted, and it was done.

Aten opened his eyes. A darkprime tree stood in front of him, ready for anyone with the requisite Aspect to utilize its magic. Aten almost reached for it, but he knew it would be useless. He couldn't use dark elm magic. He knew it would be impossible.

He needed to unlock his other Aspects.

And he was beginning to develop a theory as to how.

AND SO IT was that Aten experimented. He managed to hide his kills, at least for the first few days. He managed to keep the twins sedated for twelve hours before he had to return Guruthos. If they suspected anything, they didn't let on. He had gotten away with everything—so far.

But he was having no luck. He was making no progress.

He needed to figure out this strange dimension—what it could do, how it worked. It enlarged every time a soul died. He could feel them making their way into that dimension, as if they were being absorbed by the device. But he could make no sense of it beyond that.

He needed to get inside.

And the only way to do that was to die.

He needed another way.

"Tell me," he said, facing the twins across a desk, "how can I visit this immortal plane?" They were maddeningly calm, not even suspecting Aten's intent.

"Ambarhal," Velion said. "That's what it's called. You can't visit it."

"What if I want to?"

"What do you hope to accomplish?"

There was no particular reason to hide his intentions from them, Aten reasoned. Might as well tell them what he wanted —perhaps they could help. "I want to unlock the other Aspects of my soul."

"Oh," Nelenor said. "I think that's quite impossible, at least for you."

Aten gritted his teeth. He was tired of being told what was possible and what was not. "So one cannot visit this... Ambarhal?"

"No," Velion said. "I do not believe it is possible. Certainly no one has tried before. On Starmist Prime, users train for *decades* to unlock further Aspects. It is quite doable—you just need to put in the work."

Aten slammed his hand down on the desk, hard. "I don't have *time* for decades!" he shouted.

Nelenor sat back in her chair, obviously surprised. "Why?" she asked, beautiful eyebrows quirked in a question. "Why are you in such a hurry? We can teach you the spark-ways. You can unlock your soul through discipline and dedication."

Aten took a deep breath. There had been no reason for that outburst, truth be told. He'd just been on edge lately, for reasons he could not define. He felt the weight of time pressing on him, and he had no idea exactly why.

"I don't know," he said, trying for once to be honest with them. They were good people. They deserved it when he could. "I just feel like there's a discovery here, waiting to be found. I want to be the one to unlock it."

"You're hungry," Velion said. "I recognize that trait in you. I saw it from the start." He leaned forward, eyes intent on Aten's. "Beware this path, Aten. It is a dangerous one. Too much hunger...too much yearning for that which is beyond you...it can only lead to folly."

Aten took a deep breath, steeling himself against the retort that had sprung into his mind. "You are right," he said, careful to keep a measured tone. "That is my great folly: I always leap ahead. There is time—I just need to allow for it. Still, I am curious. Has no one from Starmist ever delved into Ambarhal?"

"There is no need," Nelenor said. "The device is operating within its intended parameters."

"I see," Aten said. "What would happen if you were killed?"

Both twins sat upright in their chairs, faces rigid, eyes still.

"Why do you ask this?" Velion said.

Aten spread his hands on the desk in a gesture of what he hoped was obeisance. "I am just trying to understand how all of this works. You two are bound to the device, are you not?"

"We are."

"And you have said that you are the only ones that can control it."

"Yes."

"You can turn it off."

"Yes."

"And then you could turn it on again?"

"We could."

"So I'm just trying to understand the last option—what if you were dead?"

"It's okay," Nelenor said, placing a hand on Velion's arm. "He's just trying to learn more about Guruthos."

"I'm not so sure," Velion said.

"If we were killed," Nelenor said, squeezing her brother's arm, "the binding would be incomplete. We would be gone, but the binding points on Guruthos would still be filled. And with us dead, the device would cease to operate. In other words, killing us would render the device permanently inoperative."

Velion leaned forward. "I hope that's not what you were planning."

Aten gave what he hoped was a friendly smile. "Of course not," he said.

Inwardly, he seethed.

TWENTY-SIX

"UNBEKNOWNST TO ATEN," Kythaela said, "the Department of Magical Research—the very department that he had founded—was already working against him. They had formed a plan to eliminate Guruthos by flinging it away from Valaralda. It wouldn't end magic—that much they knew, for Guruthos had an *extremely* large range. But it would prevent the device from landing in the wrong hands.

"Hands like Aten's."

She looked around the fire, which was still burning strongly after all this time. Everyone was paying attention now—none had heard about the origins of magic before. This was new.

Perhaps she should not have waited this long to tell it.

"Let us continue the story."

ATEN'S PLAN WAS SIMPLE.

Since the twins couldn't be killed without permanently deactivating Guruthos, and since he didn't know how to forcefully sever their connection to the device, his plan was to imprison them.

He was growing increasingly sure that Ambarhal was the key. The souls that visited there grew, somehow, unlocking their latent potential. He'd felt it time and time again, observing as a person died. He felt their soul encounter the tree, felt their souls merge and blend, felt them enter the dimension created by the great machine. Beyond that, he wasn't sure. He couldn't visit Ambarhal without dying himself, and he wasn't quite ready for that.

But he needed to keep the magic alive, and he needed the twins out of his way.

It didn't take much effort to concoct a believable story. A story in which the twins were enemies, beings sent to Valaralda to sow doubt and discord amongst the citizens. People whose goal was to dismantle religion, society, faith and fitness and good intention. Of course, anyone that actually *met* the twins would know that his story couldn't possibly be true—they were just too nice, too forthcoming. That was why he did his best to limit their exposure to the outside world.

And their sister, this elusive girl they'd come here searching for? Well, he supposed she was nowhere to be found.

Aten needed help with his operation. He needed mages of all types, mages who could keep a secret. And, perhaps most importantly, he needed mages who could do the rarest of magics: the primal powers.

The Department of Magical Research had discovered them. Each side of magic had a primal power, one that transcended the others. One that was rarest. One that was probably the most dangerous. On the light side, from the trees that formed when a willing sacrifice was made, they had discovered soulsundering. It was the ability to tear a soul away from its body, trapping it forever in Ambarhal.

This was the bulk of Aten's plan.

And on the dark side, for the trees that formed when a soul was killed by murder: gatesending. This powerful magic allowed someone to transfer to somewhere else with both body and soul. It was a powerful magic, but very, very few could do it.

As it turned out, both Lara and Cara had that power.

So that was his plan: first to transport the twins far away —to other planets, if he could work out how—then to soul-sunder them, but only part way. With this technique, he reasoned, he could trap them forever in the trees they seemed to love so much.

Then he could be free to research Guruthos as long as he desired.

"ARE you sure this is a good idea?" Cara asked. She and Lara were sitting on Lara's bed in her dormitory, legs swinging off the side. They had a pitcher of beer on the bedside table, stolen from the nearby pub. Cara was good at stealing things —Lara had learned to respect her for that.

"Aten is powerful," Lara said, "Or he will be, at least. If we help him, he will help us."

"I think he's lying to us," Cara said.

"You do know how to spot a lie."

"What's that supposed to mean?"

"Nothing," Lara said. "I probably do, too. I think it's in our blood."

"That's not the only thing," Cara said. "Did you know about the gatesending?"

Lara shook her head. "I didn't know a lot of things. I wonder if Pa could do it."

The room was silent for a moment.

"I'm sorry," Cara said after a while. Lara looked at her. "He deserved to die, but you deserved to have a say in it. He was good to you, after all. I could have left."

Lara shook her head, feeling her eyes begin to burn. "No," she said, "you were right. Pa would have eventually turned on me. He'd already hit me once."

"I didn't know that," Cara said.

"You had the right of it. You had the sense of him. Something changed, that day when he split his soul."

"You think that's what it was? His soul split in half?"

"That's what you told me," Lara said. "It was something with the magic."

"That's why we need more knowledge. We need to research it more."

Lara nodded. "Aten's plan needs to move forward."

"He needs us."

Lara reached out and took Cara's hand. It had been a decade since she'd touched her sister without fighting, without trying to hurt or kill. Cara's fingers were cold and hard, the hand of a girl who'd had to live on the edge of things for far too long. "Aten will help us find what we're looking for," Lara said. "We should help him."

"Yes," Cara said. "Yes."

They stayed like that for quite a while.

TWENTY-SEVEN

AND SO THE Imprisonment continued as planned. The Corps of Astronomers found Aten two likely planets, far away from Valaralda but within range of their new telescopes. Aten sent students through as a test at first, making sure they could actually arrive on those planets through the gates. It worked. It was startlingly easy. The students complained of headaches when they came back through, said that maybe they felt a little dizzy, but that was to be expected when such magic was involved.

Everything was proceeding according to Aten's plan.

He used his students. They were his core of trusted magicians. They respected him like few others did. They didn't think to question him. And with their talent so new and raw, he could form them into anything he wanted. But the stars of his regime were the gatesenders: the sisters Cara and Lara. He was lucky he had found them, and so easily.

He sent Cara to a planet called Eryn. Although she was new to the University, he needed her gatesending magic. She seemed trustworthy enough.

He sent Lara to a planet called Mar. Aten accompanied

this group, but he did not participate in the magic himself. He wanted to make sure he found the perfect place to imprison Velion. He carried with him a cypress sapling to use as the prison itself.

And so it was that the expeditions succeeded in reaching their destinations. Velion was sent to Mar, and Nelenor was sent to Eryn. They were powerless to resist, for Aten had drugged them yet again. The poor twins were too guileless to anticipate one such as he.

They had never found their sister.

THE WORLD they sent Cara to was an endless, sweltering jungle. She stayed behind the expedition leader, a Junior Professor by the name of Elbereth. He and one other were carrying Nelenor between them, the woman's long blonde hair blowing out behind her as she trudged forward. She, like her twin, had been drugged into a stupor. But she could still walk.

Cara still wasn't quite sure why all this was happening. The good-looking professor had somehow gotten it into his head that these alien elves were not to be trusted, that they needed to be locked away for the safety of all. But not just locked away—he wanted their souls sundered from their bodies. He wanted them imprisoned forever in trees. He wanted to send them to the place that not many people knew about.

But Cara was good at listening, especially when no one was expecting it. She knew about Ambarhal, the magical world that was attached to Guruthos. She knew that Aten wanted to open it up, widening it and feeding on its power.

And the way he intended to do that was simple: by giving it more souls.

Cara was willing to go along with his plan, so long as she saw a benefit to herself. And there *was* a benefit, assuming everything went the way Aten thought it would. First, Cara would make herself useful to him. Then she would use her close proximity to gain knowledge. She would know the moment Aten discovered something new, and she would be at his right hand to help him. With that knowledge would come great power, as they unlocked the mysteries of Guruthos and the magic it contained. And Cara knew that both she and Aten agreed on one thing.

Power was all.

"There's a good spot up ahead," Elbereth said. He was struggling with Nelenor, trying to keep her upright as she tottered through the jungle. They had found a path of sorts—probably a hunting trail, one used by the animals of this planet. They hadn't seen any wildlife yet, but she knew it was out there. She could hear it. She wondered if the animals here were dangerous.

"Here," Elbereth said, stopping the group.

They were in a clearing, the thick jungle parting ways for a brief moment. The animal trails all ended here, as if this were a special place for the denizens of the jungle. Perhaps they met here, or killed each other, or mated, or whatever it was that unthinking creatures did. Either way, it would serve their purpose.

"You have the sapling?" Elbereth asked her.

She'd almost forgotten about that.

She swung her backpack off, seeing the tiny willow tree's foliage wave as it stuck out through the top of the bag. "Why'd we bring our own tree?" she asked. "There are plenty of them here."

"Ask Aten," Elbereth said. "It probably has to do with the magic. Willow and cypress are the seventh trees, you know."

She did know—and she knew the reason Aten wanted these specific trees—but she pretended to be dumb. She found she could learn a lot more that way. "What now?" she asked.

"Now," Elbereth said, "we begin the ritual."

Nelenor stepped forward suddenly, wrenching free from Elbereth's grasp. Her eyes were wild, darting. She seemed to be coming out of her daze. "You can't do this to us," she said. "What have we done to deserve this? We are only looking for our sister. We have caused no harm."

Elbereth backhanded her hard, and she went reeling. Cara could see a red welt appearing on her cheek. "Stay silent," he said. "You twins know too much. Aten wants to study the machine you made."

"We are happy to tell him all we know," Nelenor said. "Why treat us this way? We have been nothing but peaceful."

"You interrogated girls."

"We *asked* them if they were Kaela. And all of them said no. We did not lay a hand on any of them."

"That's not what I heard."

Nelenor sighed. She was free of her captors now, and it would seem that she was free of the stupefying drug. Yet even now, even when she could lay waste to them all with her unimaginable power, even now she just stood there meekly, peacefully, trying to talk her way out of the situation.

Cara almost felt sorry for her.

"Please," Nelenor said, her voice full of sorrow. "We only wanted to find our sister. We will leave this place. We will leave you alone. We are not here to interfere with a Seed Planet. We just want to find our sister and go."

Elbereth grabbed her suddenly, fingers digging into her

arm. Cara could see pain rippling across her beautiful face. "You Awakened us," he said, his face close to hers. "You gave us magic. So many of us have died because we did not understand what was happening. So many have been lost. And now when we are so close to true understanding, when we can finally turn this power into something *good* now you want to *leave*?"

"We will help you, as I said."

"No. You will not help us with your words. With your veiled words, words which do nothing to explain. We need Ambarhal, *girl*—we need to get inside. And Aten believes that imprisoning you will grant us access. It is how we will Awaken the other parts of our soul."

"He does not understand the—"

"*He understands it all!*" Elbereth shouted, slapping Nelenor again across the face. Cara shrank back, suddenly afraid of this man. Where had Aten found him?

Nelenor held a hand to her face, tears leaking from her eyes. She was so elven, so like them. She was not an alien. Yet somehow she was from an alien planet. A planet that had created technology so far advanced from anything they knew. A planet that, according to Nelenor, had been destroyed. She did not deserve the treatment she was getting here.

"Who *are* you?" Nelenor asked, rubbing her face.

Elbereth smiled. "I am Aten's Executor," he said.

Executor. Cara didn't know what that meant, but it didn't sound good. Aten was known for creating orders, for founding groups of like-minded individuals. He had created the Department of Magical Research, the Corps of Astronomers, *and* the Doctor of Magistry program at the school. Perhaps this was yet another one of his ideas.

"Go on with it then," Nelenor said. Her eyes had dried. Her back was straight. "If you insist on treating my people in this way, we will not resist. We are not like you. We are not opportunistic. We are not cruel. We *listen*. We discuss. We are rational beings."

"You mean you're better than us."

Nelenor crossed her arms. "That may be so," she said. "You may proceed—I will not resist. But know this: we *will* escape our prison. It may take years. It may take centuries. It may take *eons*, but we *will* be free. And when we do, you can be sure your kind will pay for what you've done here."

"Threats? From you? I thought you were more *rational* than us."

"While you may learn much with us imprisoned," Nelenor said, "have you considered what might happen for us in Ambarhal?" She leaned forward, face perilously close to his. "We might learn *more*. And I promise you this: we will find our sister. And if you continue with this misguided action, everything and everyone your kind holds dear will *pay*."

"Drug her," Elbereth said, stepping back. He looked visibly shaken. Had Nelenor's words actually gotten to him? Cara knew them for what they were: pure bluster.

But then she looked in Nelenor's eyes, and she saw that perhaps she was wrong. There was something feral in those eyes, something that bespoke great mystery and power. There was *cruelty* there, but it took great measures to draw it out.

"Let us begin," Elbereth said.

And Cara realized that this—this Imprisonment—might be the very thing that would turn poor Nelenor into elvenkind's worst enemy.

TWENTY-EIGHT

"YOU WON'T GET AWAY with this," Velion said.

Aten laughed at him. "It doesn't look like you're doing much to stop me."

Lara stood to the side, not wanting to get involved. It was clear these blond creatures from another planet had power, but they didn't seem willing to use it. They were just too nice, too patient. Too weak. Aten had jumped on the opportunity.

They were standing in a cave. A cave that was deep underwater—some place Aten had found. The group had used forcefinding magic—one of the dark magics—to get them down this far. Lara hadn't understood exactly what was going on, or why they were going here of all places. The planet seemed uninhabited. Couldn't they just deposit Velion anywhere? But Aten had insisted that they needed to hide him, to put him in a place where no one else would ever see.

And so they were here, deep underground in an underwater cave, about to imprison someone who could very easily be a god.

Lara wondered how it had come to this.

"Drug him again," Aten said, and his assistant obliged,

shooting Velion in the arm with some kind of chemical. Lara watched as his eyes rolled up into his head.

"Always wanting to talk, these ones," Aten said, turning around and brushing his hands off. "Now—where's the sapling?"

Lara had it. She swung it around, handing the pack to Aten. He looked at her for a moment as if studying her resolve.

"Thanks." He set it down, unpacking the tree and placing it on the ground. "Now," he said, standing, "it's time to begin."

"We would have cooperated," Velion said. "There is much we can teach you." Evidently the drugs weren't preventing him from speaking.

"You're like a dog," Aten said, "always ready to please. Perhaps if you were stronger, this would not be happening to you now."

"Are you really this cruel? Why can you not see reason?"

"Reason is exactly what I'm after," Aten said. "The reason this power works. The reason you are here. The reason Ambarhal only admits the souls of the dead."

"You think by imprisoning us, you will find your answers?"

"Given time, I will. I always find my answers."

"You are young," Velion said. "You do not even know the right questions to ask."

"Don't patronize me," Aten spit. "You're better than that."

"Have it your way," Velion said, sighing. "Know that we will fight this, though. We will find a way free. You should have learned more before leaving us to this fate. You have no idea what this even means."

"Silence," Aten said. Lara could see Velion's eyes beginning to glaze over. "Still you talk, like a little dog. Perhaps it would be better if the world saw you as such."

He waved his hand, and Lara saw a wood carving in it. As she watched, Velion began to transform before her very eyes.

He grew taller. Thicker. *Much* taller, actually—soon he was easily thirty feet tall, towering over everybody, his head nearly brushing the top of the cave. And his face—his face had changed. He no longer looked elven. Instead he had a dog's face, with a long, canine snout and pointed ears that stuck out from his head. He looked like some kind of monster.

Like some kind of god.

"What are you doing?" Lara asked, watching Velion's arms thicken with muscles. It was all an illusion—right?

"I'm making them into what they ought to be," Aten said. "Their true form."

"You're using mistweaving."

"I am doing what is necessary. Now let us begin the ritual."

The ritual. Soulsundering. They were about to sever this poor man's soul from his body, dooming him to live an eternity in the terrible dimension called Ambarhal. And all so Aten could study Guruthos.

"Wait," Lara said. Aten looked at her. "Should we be doing this? They've said they'll help."

"It's the only way to widen Ambarhal," Aten said. "Each time a soul enters it, the dimension grows larger. I believe with these two in it, it will become *truly* useful."

"Why not just wrest Guruthos from their grip?"

"Can't be done," Aten said. "Even if I kill them, Guruthos will remain bound to them. There might be a way to sever their connection…but I need more time to figure out how."

Lara fell silent. His arguments made sense. He wanted power; he wanted magic. And if trapping these two innocent aliens was the key, then Lara would do her best to assist.

She wanted power, too.

AND SO THE expeditions proceeded apace. The students exercised their new soulsunder magic, severing the soul from each twin's body and imprisoning it in a tree.

Velion was imprisoned in a cypress tree, a tree they had planted in a cave deep within the oceans of Mar.

Nelenor was imprisoned in a willow tree, high on a hillside in the jungles of Eryn.

Their souls were caught, transferred forever to Ambarhal. And though Aten had not brought Guruthos with him—he could not risk it falling back into the twins' hands—he could still feel Ambarhal enlarging. His plan had been a success—now the source of all their magic was imprisoned, stuck forever in a place where time and magic could not touch.

But back on Valaralda, something else was happening.

The Department of Magical Research found Guruthos, the object of Aten's research and affection. And they executed their plan, casting it far away from Valaralda using great leafrunning magic. Their intent was to shoot it away in a straight line, but their knowledge of space and physics was woefully limited in this ancient age.

The gravity of the nearby planets caught Guruthos, transforming its straight line into a near-parabolic orbit. An orbit which was close to escaping the solar system, as the Department had intended—but it was not quite enough.

And so it was that Guruthos was destined to return.

But that was not the only unexpected thing that happened.

For soulsundering magic was—and always has been—poorly understood. And so it was that, through no particular error of their own, every single student who imprisoned the poor, blond twins was killed.

Aten watched them die.

He saw their souls ascend, saw them transfer into Ambarhal. He saw the great Trees form from their corpses, from their blood. From their willing sacrifice. He watched it as his students died, and for the moment he was satisfied.

For in their passing, the gates to Ambarhal yawned wide.

TWENTY-NINE

ATEN STUMBLED through the gate just as it closed. Lara—who had made the gate—was gone. Luckily it seemed the magic stuck around for a minute after the mage had died. Now he was back on Valaralda. Now he was free to study Guruthos without interference.

He fingered the glass ball in his hand. It was smooth and warm, glimmering with a strange, unearthly light. This was something he had kept to himself throughout the imprisonment proceedings—it was the *real* trick he'd figured out. He'd taken to calling the glass Edrafen.

The Key.

It held a piece of two souls: a piece of Velion and a piece of Nelenor. He'd nabbed them while they were asleep. The technique was difficult to describe; he'd been acting mostly on instinct. You had to visualize the souls, to really see their circular shapes with the pie-like slices that represented the Aspects. And if you were sensitive enough—and careful—you could carve a tiny piece of the soul off, trapping it in the glass. Aten wasn't entirely sure how it worked, just that it did.

The twins hadn't even noticed.

Except something had gone wrong. Aten wasn't sure what it was, exactly, but he had a suspicion.

A tiny part of *his* soul might be trapped in Edrafen, too.

But there was nothing for it now. It was either there or it wasn't—he couldn't do anything about it. He needed to keep Edrafen as it was, even if his soul was somehow part of it. For if the twins somehow ever regained access to their whole souls, he was sure they would escape their imprisonment and inflict themselves upon the world.

And this time, they'd be *mad*.

So Aten buried the Key, hiding it from every prying eye. Hiding it from himself. Yet it called to him, even over great distances. He could hear it in his mind, in his sleep, in his dreams. It wanted him. It needed him. And as the years passed, his thoughts grew darker and darker.

He continued his research, using his knowledge to build and do great things. His power grew immense, though he was still maddeningly restricted to just one type of magic. And so time passed, and Aten's influence grew.

And the Twins were never seen or heard from again.

THIRTY

ATEN LOUNGED on his favorite cushions: the tan ones on the balcony, hundreds of feet up at the top of his palace. From here he could gaze out on all of Nekhrumet, the great jewel of the desert. The metropolis in the sands.

The city he had built.

Prime Trees ringed the city, leafy crowns sending waving shadows across the sweltering desert landscape. They seemed to survive well out here even with very little water; the magic kept them strong. Buildings of sandstone, brick and adobe stretched out beneath the leaves, dotting both sides of the Iteranu River. Bright cloths and tapestries dotted the city, waving in the air. People milled about everywhere, dressed in robes and headscarves, carrying food and spices or haggling in the streets. Members of the Eglaria—the religious group that doubled as the local militia—made their way from street to street, keeping the peace.

Everything was running according to Aten's plan.

"Soon," he said to himself, stroking the cheetah that he kept as a pet. "Soon my next experiment will be ready."

Even now he could see the pyramids being built in the distance, great triangles of sandstone. The people of the desert loved him. They worshipped him. They obeyed him as they would obey a god. It had taken just a few short centuries to make it all happen.

And a lot of magic.

Selenia stepped into the room, wearing the flimsy, see-through gown he loved so much. Her long, blonde hair was braided down her back, her nails painted a lovely cerulean. She wore the small, dark glasses she had popularized in the city. For most people, the lenses kept the glare of the sun out of their eyes. But for Selenia, it did something different.

It hid her blindness.

Nothing hid the rest of her. Selenia's breasts bounced pleasingly as she swished into the room, left hand out to touch various pieces of furniture as she made her way to the balcony. The brilliant sun shone on her tanned skin, and Aten reached out to cup her ass as she stood next to him. Her skin was smooth, her butt cheeks firm. He felt himself stirring as he gazed out on the city he had made.

Come to us.

"What?" Aten asked.

Selenia turned to him, blind eyes hidden. "I didn't say anything. Not yet." She bent and licked his cheek. The cheetah purred loudly to his left.

"I thought I heard something. Never mind."

"You seem tense, my love." Selenia stroked his bare shoulder. He wrapped his arm around her waist, bending his neck back to kiss her on the lips as she bent down. She'd lost her eyes in a childhood accident, she'd said. He hadn't bothered to pry further. Her blindness almost made her more attractive. One less person to interfere with his plans.

You are so close.

"They are falling behind again," Aten said. "The pyramids won't be ready on schedule."

"What's the hurry, my love?" Selenia wrapped her sinuous arms around him, settling down with him in the cushions, her breast pressed tantalizingly into his arm. "They are merely monuments, are they not?"

"You know they are not just decorations, my love," Aten said. "I have seen you listening at the doors."

Selenia had the decency to blush, at least. "I beg your pardon, my lord. It is simply that I desire to know your plans for us all."

"Yes." He doubted that was all. "Well, you already know that the pyramids are more than just buildings. More than just statues. They are, in fact, part of a grand device of my own imagining. The Pyramid Offensive System."

"Will it bring us closer to the gods?"

Yes.

"Yes," Aten echoed. The voices in his head were growing worse. "It will grant us power unimaginable. It will grant us our freedom."

"Are we not already free?"

He looked at her, at the smile on her face. At her chin where it curved into her throat. At her lips, open now in a partial smile. He had found her begging on the streets a year ago. She'd been lost, out of her mind. But she'd been smart, well-spoken, a fantastic lover despite her blindness. He felt safe around her, safe in a way he couldn't be with anyone else. It might have been her eyes—he didn't want to ascribe too much to it. But it might have been.

Yes.

"Come, my dear," he said. "Let us retreat inside. The pyramids will be done when they are done. It is not for the gods to decide."

They went inside, Aten's hand in its customary position on her ass. She fed him grapes when they had settled into bed, white bedsheets billowing around them like rare clouds in a desert sky.

"What does your great device purport to do?" Selenia asked. Her fingers were tracing a line down his bare chest.

Aten wanted to purr like his cheetah. "There is a great evil," he said, "imprisoned many centuries ago. Elvenkind thought this evil defeated, but they yet still cling to life. They are attached, attuned, connected to a magical weapon—the source of our power. And while their connection remains, we elves remain their subjects."

"You speak of the Twins," Selenia said.

Aten nodded. "Their evilness knows no bounds. And so it is that I have devised a great machine which will sever them from their weapon, returning control to us. And then we will see what *true* power means. Nekhrumet will grow beyond all possible imagination."

"And where is this weapon of which you speak?" Her lips were close, her breath fragrant in the afternoon air.

Aten gave a little growl. "Lost to us," he said, "for now. Those idiots who purport to *research* the magic instead threw it away. But it will return—mark my words. It will return. And when it does, we will be ready for it."

"Power becomes you," Selenia said, her hand reaching

lower. "You grow with it day by day." She swung on top of him, dark glasses reflecting the sun.

Yes, the voice said, and Aten couldn't help but utter the word himself.

"Yes."

THIRTY-ONE

SELENIA WATCHED Aten sleeping from her viewpoint at the corner of the room. The bird there was inconspicuous, discreet. Aten never suspected she could see through her soulbinds. His chest was rising and falling in a regular rhythm, fast asleep despite the early hour. Her exertions had exhausted him, as she had intended. Now she could be free to roam his chambers uninterrupted.

She still didn't understand his plan. It involved Guruthos —that much she knew—and it somehow included all those pyramids he was building. She also knew his darkest secret, the one he thought he had kept from everyone.

He was gathering souls.

Before the pyramids were even built, he'd been gathering them. Killing people—often in the guise of religious persecution, usually by the very Eglaria he employed. He had them killed, and he siphoned their souls into the repositories at the center of the pyramids. She didn't know how it worked. She didn't need to. She just needed to understand the plan.

She grimaced, feeling phantom pain behind her eyes. It came and went at unpredictable times, a constant reminder of the horrors she had faced on Eryn. Of her enslavement by the rylak. Of her almost-rape and blinding, of her survival in the jungle when all hope had been lost. Of her death by the hands of Svalya, pack leader. Of her subsequent trip through Ambarhal, speaking with the Twins themselves.

The Twins that even now were calling to Aten.

Oh yes, she knew of that as well. She knew they were speaking to him. She recognized the signs.

They spoke to her too, from time to time.

You will do our bidding, Velion said. She recognized his voice now, coming to her as it was from so very far away.

"Patience," Selenia said into the sultry afternoon air. "You will have your reward. As will I."

Yes.

Edrafen. It had to be here. Or if it wasn't here, it had to be somewhere within Aten's reach. He couldn't have destroyed it —she knew that much. It contained a portion of the Twins' souls, making it impossible to destroy. He had probably hidden it, but she didn't know where. There were so many mysteries, so many things yet to discover. But she had time. She had so much time. She had been through Ambarhal. She had paid its price, and she had reaped its benefit. She had time to search for what she needed.

Because unlike Aten, Selenia would live forever.

"HOW DO THE PYRAMIDS WORK?" Selenia asked. They were eating breakfast on the balcony overlooking the city, reclining together on his ample cushions. Aten barely left his chambers lately, choosing instead to make his servants and deputies come to him. Selenia worried that he would grow fat from all his time up here. She intended to make sure that didn't happen.

Aten sat up on one elbow, looking at her as if trying to delve into her soul. Her angle was bad—the cheetah was off to his left, as usual, trying to appear asleep while keeping its slitted eyes open—but it seemed like Aten might be angry. Then his expression softened, and he reached out for her.

"I have told you," he said, "the pyramids are a great machine. A machine which will strip the gods from their magic."

"The Twins."

"Just so. I have experimented and thought and tried so much, Selenia. And what I have discovered is that the Twins may have been many things, but they were first and foremost *liars*."

"What?"

"Their connection to Guruthos, my dear," Aten said. "The Twins told me that it could not be severed—not even in death. But I have learned that this is not true."

Selenia felt her heart begin to speed. She sat up, not wanting Aten to feel it, disguising her sudden interest by reaching for his crotch. He always like it when she did that. Typical man.

"I have a theory," Aten continued. "With enough souls, I can strip the Twins of their magic. I can break them from Guruthos, and when it returns, I alone can take control of the great weapon."

"Souls are power," Selenia said, continuing her ministrations.

Aten gave a little gasp. "Yes," he said. "But it is not the power that is needed, here. It is the *quantity*. My research has led me to believe that with sufficient numbers of souls—hundreds, maybe thousands—the connection can be broken.

Even the smallest souls could do it, if there were enough of them."

The smallest souls.

Selenia traded glances with herself, the cheetah gazing briefly at the cactus wren on the balcony.

The smallest souls.

She yielded the conversation to him then, letting him continue to illuminate his plan while her mouth went to work on his organ down below.

It was by far the best way to get the man to talk.

THIRTY-TWO

THE VOICES in Aten's head were growing worse. He tried to silence them. He tried to ignore them. But every day they gnawed at him, insinuating their raw desires into his mind.

Free us.

Unlock the Key.

Come to us.

Your soul is ours.

He tried moving Edrafen further from him, burying it hundreds of miles away, far out in the desert sands. Still it called to him—distance made no difference. He could pinpoint its exact location. He could find it amidst trillions of tiny grains of sand. He could locate it *anywhere*. It was tied to him, and he to it, and he wanted nothing more than to be rid of it for good.

It was intruding too deeply in his thoughts.

He left Valaralda, using an Eglaria gatesender to send him back to Mar. He lived there for a time, hoping that such great distance might finally quiet the voices in his head.

It did not.

So he returned.

He was bound to Edrafen too strongly, and he did not know how to sever the connection. His plan was nearly ready now—the pyramids were complete, gathering the souls the Eglaria fed to them. They pulled people off the streets at night, taking them to the pyramids for a ritual sacrifice. And the device Aten had created soaked up the souls, binding them and holding them for later use.

He had learned much from his study of magic. Even with Guruthos gone, Aten was still able to make great advances. All it took was perseverance and experimentation, and he had that in spades.

But still the Twins would not leave him alone.

SELENIA TWIRLED her fingers lazily in a bowl of lavender water. She / the cheetah was stretched out next to the open door, keeping watch down the hallway. She / the cactus wren looked inward from the balcony, cocking her head slightly. These were her quarters. They were positioned somewhat lower than Aten's were, but they still offered incredible views of the city below.

She popped a grape into her mouth, pondering her next move. She'd figured out Aten's plan—or most of it, anyway—but he knew next to nothing about her. He didn't know she was a Prime Mage, for one. He didn't know that she'd visited Ambarhal and had spoken with the Twins. He didn't know she'd learned the miracle of soulbinding. And he *especially* didn't know her biggest secret: the incredible power she'd discovered while she was in that mysterious purple realm.

Selenia had the power to hop between worlds.

It was very simple, actually. Surprisingly so, once you figured out the basic mechanics of soulbinding. Instead of binding an animal or a person, all you had to do was bind a tree.

There were many things you could do with a tree, once you had bound its soul. You could turn it into a Prime Tree, for example, with no blood spilled. You could even choose its allegiance: light or dark. But that wasn't the *true* power the trees held.

For once you'd created a Prime Tree, its soul straddled the line between worlds. Every Tree existed in two places at once: in the mortal plane, and in Ambarhal with the gods. And if you spoke to the soul in the tree *just right*, you could transfer yourself across the veil.

You didn't even need to die.

This was how she'd escaped Ambarhal in the end. This was how she was here, on Valaralda, and not back on Eryn where she'd been killed. This was how she'd followed Aten, using Ambarhal to transfer to Mar and Eryn and the other Seed Planets. She could do all of this and more, and Aten had no idea.

But the one thing she couldn't do seemed to be the thing he wanted most: to defeat the Twins once and for all, to wrest their power from them. Aten's plan seemed as good as any—the device he had made was immensely complicated, incredibly cruel. He had been responsible for so much death. Compared to Selenia, Aten was a bloodthirsty warlord. Yes, Selenia had killed hundreds of rylak during her time as Cariel —but Aten had killed *thousands*.

So she had a choice: devise her own plan, continue to learn more about magic, and hope she figured out some way to defeat the Twins herself. Or she could let Aten's plan succeed, but with one small twist. She would take control of the Pyramid Offensive System at the last possible moment, turning his victory into hers.

And to do *that*, she needed to keep him close. He was a good looking man, at least, and he had a wonderfully cruel streak to match his razor sharp wit. She enjoyed her time with him. And so it would not be too large of a stretch for them to marry.

A smile crept across her face as she imagined the scene. She would go to him tonight, in his bedchambers, dressed in the flimsy gown he loved so much. She would get on her knees, hands outstretched, mouth wide. And she would profess her undying love for him. She would propose. And Aten, in all his lustful glory, would accept.

Then they would be together forever, and nothing would come between her and her ultimate reward.

THE VOICES WERE WORSE NOW, interrupting Aten's thoughts in an almost constant stream. Edrafen was pulling at him endlessly, and he had no way to break its tether to him.

Not without taking extreme measures.

He had buried it in a secret place, far from anyone's prying eyes, underneath one of his pyramids. He had built traps around it, ensuring that only he would be able to gain access to it again. He knew that others sought it—even pretty Selenia, who he had found as a blind beggar woman—even she was after Edrafen and its magic. He had seen her prowling about when she thought he wasn't looking. He knew she wasn't who she claimed.

But Edrafen was safe now, or as safe as he could make it. Now there was just one thing left to do. One thing that would finally make the voices in his head go away.

Yes.

TARATHIEL
20,000 YEARS AGO

SELENIA SMOOTHED OUT HER DRESS, the transparent fabric leaving nothing to the imagination. Her cheetah padded around her, watching her from all angles and purring with approval. She looked good. It was time.

She stepped into Aten's room, freshly lacquered finger-nails holding the object she had brought to commemorate the occasion: a golden ring. She opened her mouth, ready to utter the words she had prepared. Her cactus wren flew in from a side window, adding its eyes. All was ready. All was about to fall into place.

Selenia let out a horrible scream.

Aten. He was in his room, where she had expected him to be. But he was not in his bed.

He was hanging from the ceiling.

His eyes were bulging, his face white, distended. A thick rope was wrapped about his neck, choking the life out of him. His legs were kicking as she watched, his mouth wide and struggling to breathe. His wrists were slit, too, as if being hung were not enough. Blood dripped from his arms, collecting on the floor underneath him. He was dying. He was almost dead.

It was a horribly gruesome sight.

The ring slipped from Selenia's fingers, clattering on the stone floor as she rushed forward, reaching up to him. She could save him. He didn't need to die. She didn't *want* him to die, and not just because if he did, she might never find a way to defeat the Twins. No—it was more than that.

It was in that moment that Selenia realized she actually had *feelings* for Aten.

"No!" she screamed, wishing tears could fall from her destroyed eyes. She reached for him, trying to lift him up, to hold his weight. Blood covered her, slippery and sweet. She needed a chair, a ladder, a knife. She needed to get him down. She needed wood so she could heal him. She sent her bird in, pecking uselessly at the rope. She used the cheetah to lift her up on its back, granting her enough height to lift him.

But it was too late. It was not enough.

Aten gave one last, final kick before he died.

Then something strange happened.

A tree appeared on the floor underneath Aten's body. It was small, glowing a brilliant, shimmering white, the outlines of it brighter than anything she had ever seen. She / the cheetah shrank from it instinctively, afraid of this new source of light. She / the bird shrieked, flying out of the room, disobeying the bond.

And she / Cariel shielded her eyes, as if the glow of this tree could pierce into her very soul.

Then it grew. The brilliant glowing outline of it became larger, more mature, filling all available space, cutting through the room. Its scintillating image flew right through her body, filling the air, growing and growing. Soon it was so large that she imagined it towering over the palace, over Nekhrumet, over everything. Her cactus wren was still outside—it confirmed what she suspected.

This was the largest tree she had ever seen. It was as big as the entire city, and still growing.

But it wasn't real. It was a ghost. The image faded into nothingness as she watched through the wren's eyes, leaving her alone with the corpse of the man she'd loved.

WHEN ATEN ARRIVED IN AMBARHAL, he quickly realized three things.

First, his Aspects were now unlocked. He could feel them, every portion of his soul, reaching out to the Trees that dotted the strange green and purple landscape. He knew that he had achieved his goal: all of magic was now his to control.

Second, Edrafen was gone. Its voice was silenced. His bond with it had been severed. It had only taken death—a small sacrifice in the scheme of things. The Twins were no longer in his head.

The third thing was even more interesting.

The moment his soul crossed the veil to Ambarhal, connecting through the sapling beneath his feet, he had felt a new kind of binding take place. It was as if his soul had reached out, traveling millions of miles through space, seeking the source of the new dimension it was in. Guruthos. And it found it, and bound itself to it, and Aten felt a new pathway open in his soul.

Aten had access to every magic. He was no longer tormented by the Twins.

And he was also now immortal.

WELCOME, Nelenor said from up ahead. **WE'VE BEEN WAITING FOR YOU.**

THIRTY-THREE

"IT IS HERE that we must proceed more quickly," Kythaela said. "For I have already kept you here for longer than I had any right to do."

Most of the children had already fallen asleep around the fire, nestled into their parents' arms. Many of the adults had drooping eyes, too. Perhaps Kythaela should not have gone into quite so much detail. But this was perhaps the longest—and most important—story she had ever told. She had to do it what justice she could.

"There is yet one more part of the tale that I must tell you," she said, "to catch us up to today."

IT TOOK Aten two days of subjective time to figure out how to escape Ambarhal.

When he emerged, two hundred years had passed.

Nekhrumet had grown. Its citizens had heard of Aten's death and had taken it to be a great sacrifice. They had elevated his name, changing it to Akhenaten. Now they worshiped him as a god.

Imagine how they reacted when their god returned to life.

Akhenaten was quick to use this to his advantage. He expanded the Pyramid Offensive System, feeding it countless more souls. With enough power, he was sure he could sever the Twins' connection to Guruthos. It took him the space of just one year to fill the pyramids, and then he was finally ready.

He stepped through the gate he had made. There were three of them, placed in different parts of Valaralda. Each gate rotated its destination according to a pattern only he knew—yet another trick he had learned in his time studying magic. If you went through the wrong gate at the wrong time, you'd be sent into oblivion. You'd die.

It was just one more layer of traps he'd placed into the system.

For he knew that Selenia was still out there, still trying to obtain Edrafen and unleash the Twins. If she ever succeeded at releasing them, he knew the Twins would be angry. They would be *incredibly* angry, and there would be no matching their power. For whoever held Guruthos also held the strings.

They could even turn all magic *off*.

So he stepped through the correct gate at the correct time, the one that he knew would lead to the Control Center—the place where he could turn the Pyramid Offensive System on. There he hesitated for just a moment. This was it—this was the culmination of all his work. With one flick of a switch, the System would activate and the Twins' connection would be forever severed. Then Akhenaten could take the power for himself, and he would be lord and master over all.

The time had finally come.

He flipped the switch.

And nothing at all happened.

AKHENATEN DID NOT KNOW what had gone wrong. The machine simply didn't work. Was something blocking it? Had he made a mistake? He didn't know. Perhaps, he reasoned, he simply did not have enough power.

And so he expanded the system, building pyramids on Mar—Earth—and Eryn. He fed souls to each of these pyramids, too, their great insides filling to the brim with death. And when he was again ready, when his empire stretched into Egypt and Nekhrumet and Falganr on Eryn, when he had countless tens of thousands of souls ready to power his arcane machine, he once again entered the Control Center and flipped the switch.

And nothing happened.

Akhenaten cursed and rampaged, but there was nothing he could do. His vast, incredible machine didn't work at all.

And he had no idea why.

SELENIA EVENTUALLY SHOWED her face again in Nekhrumet. She tried to disguise herself, but a blind woman was a rarity in the desert. And so it was that Akhenaten knew who she was.

Selenia demanded Edrafen. Akhenaten refused. The two of them fought for centuries, back and forth across the desert sands. Akhenaten strengthened the defenses surrounding Edrafen, for now he knew who Selenia really was.

She was an immortal, like him.

And so it was that Akhenaten constructed seven traps,

seven tests that he knew Selenia could not withstand. He built them specifically for her, because he knew her true nature. He knew her tricks, too—often she would send others to him, other men and women, people she had soulbound. They were puppets, hollow men, beings bound by string to Selenia herself. Her methods became increasingly tricky as time went on, but Akhenaten had foreseen them. His tests prevented all.

Eventually he tired of their endless conflicts. It distracted him from his true purpose, which was to get the Pyramid Offensive System working. He needed to focus on that, not on their petty squabbling.

And so he arranged his death. Again. Only this time he didn't really die.

It was really rather simple. His original magic—mist-weaving—came in handy for this. And so it was that Akhenaten died before Selenia's blind eyes, and she was not smart enough to see through his deception.

Now he was finally free of her.

MILLENNIA PASSED. Tens of thousands of years. Akhenaten took up many names across that time, retreating into shadows. The denizens of Nekhrumet continued worshiping Akhenaten, but even that religious fervor eventually faded, for all things must come into an end.

Selenia did not give up. She, too, took many names and forms. One day she was Mirra, a brown-skinned woman living in the desert. The next she was Magona, the jet-black warlord who enjoyed killing people to pass the time. Still later she was Selenia again, feigning sight, infiltrating Ilyrion politics with deft precision. But in all that time, she never knew that Akhenaten was really still alive.

And so it was that in the eightieth millennium after the Awakening, a boy named Tarathiel was born. And when the Sending came, Akhenaten decided to accompany them through the gates. He wanted to check on his pyramids, to see if there was anything else he could do to get the System to work.

Always before, Akhenaten had used treebinding—world-hopping—to travel to Mar. He had gone through Ambarhal, using the same technique Selenia used to traverse vast distances across the universe. But in that day the dangers of gatesending were still poorly understood. And so it was that Akhenaten decided not to use a treebind to accomplish his task. He stepped through the gate.

And instantly lost all his memories.

This, he had not been expecting.

And so the years passed. He became a Prime Tree for a time, living a bewildered life in Ambarhal. When his Tree was finally destroyed in a raging forest fire, his soul arrived back on Mar again, naked and alone and confused.

The year on Earth was 1715, and he needed a name.

Orym sounded good.

PRESENT DAY

ORYM TOOK IN A SHARP BREATH, meeting Lorelei's eyes as she looked up at him from the Ilyrion forest floor. Wait—this wasn't Lorelei. This wasn't Lorelei at all. This was *Lara*, that girl he'd met so long ago at the University. He finally recognized her. And her sister had been...no. It couldn't be. How could he have been so blind?

Cara was Selenia.

How had he not put it together in all this time? Cara was the one who'd been trying to steal Edrafen from him. Cara was the little girl who had so brazenly interrupted his class all those eons ago. Cara had been a cute, pigtailed girl. Cara had been his sultry, blind mistress in the palace of Nekhrumet.

Cara was dead beneath his hands.

The ground shook suddenly, nearly throwing him down. Cariel's skin was cooling now, the last breath gone from her body. And all around them, destruction reigned. The Twins had been released.

And they were *mad*.

"Imprisoner!" Velion shouted. They were still in their Anubis forms, the illusion Orym had made for them just before he imprisoned them. "Show yourself!"

"They're after you," Lorelei said. "They want you dead. I remember now. I remember *you*." She was shrinking back from him as she spoke, horror dawning in her eyes.

"I meant no harm," Orym said, but he could hear it for the lie it was.

"You," Lorelei said. "You're just like *her*." She gestured at her sister, dead on the forest floor. "All you want is power, power at any cost." She scuttled backwards, fright on her face.

"Don't," Orym said. He reached down to Cara's lifeless hand, finding a piece of dark willow there. "Do not breathe a word of this to anyone. To them, I am still just a scientist."

"They must know," Lorelei said. "I must tell them." She got to her feet, balance shaky. In the distance, more rubble rained down. The Twins had no idea where Orym was.

He stood, a smile blooming on his face. "Go ahead," he said, shrugging. "Tell them all you know. Who do you think they'll believe: the woman who almost destroyed an entire planet? The woman who tried to steal Trey's heart? The woman who killed Arra's sister?" He took a step forward, smile turning into a sneer. "Or will they believe *me*—the man they know. The man they trust. The man who helped them save the world,"

He clutched the willow in his hand, staring at Lorelei for one final, fateful second.

Then in one small flash of light, he disappeared.

PART
THREE

THIRTY-FOUR

TREY STEPPED LIGHTLY out of the spaceship, half expecting gravity to be different. But they hadn't actually left Valaralda —they had simply used the spacecraft's immense speed to vault themselves quickly out of Ilyrion.

This, Cresius had explained, was the headquarters of the Department of Magical Research.

It was a series of low buildings, unassuming in their austerity. Flat cement structures no more than three stories tall filled an area several city blocks wide. The whole area was fenced in and paved, with a large, sliding gate on one end. The gate was guarded by two pairs of what appeared to be soldiers, standing stock still with huge machine guns held upward at an angle.

For a department purported to be all about magic, Trey had not expected guns.

"Will the Twins be after us?" he asked as they disembarked, strolling off the landing pad and heading toward the heavily guarded gate.

Cresius shook his head. "Not unless you're this Imprisoner they're asking about."

"Do we know who that is?"

"No. It's the first time I've even heard the reference."

They continued walking, bright sunlight burning into Trey's forehead as they approached the complex.

"You'd think something like this would be prettier," Arra said. "This has to be the ugliest set of buildings I've ever seen."

Trey saw a faint smile on Cresius' face. "Beauty is in the eye of the beholder," he said. "And besides—this is a magical research facility. Don't believe everything you see."

"What I wouldn't give for a pair of sunglasses," Lashel said.

The guards let them in without exchanging any words or identification. The gate slid aside and a shuttle appeared from somewhere to the left, the driver dipping his head in a nod to Cresius. They boarded the small car, and soon everyone was heading through the campus.

"How far from Ilyrion are we?" Trey asked.

"Fifty miles as the crow flies," Cresius said. "This facility is located in the northeastern stretch of the Faedori Forest, north of Ilyrion."

"The Twins could be here in minutes."

"Based on our knowledge of the Twins," Cresius said, "the Twins could be on another *planet* in minutes. At least this place is somewhat under our control."

"Somewhat?"

Cresius shrugged. "We're up against great power. There are no guarantees. But if the Twins do come here, at least we'll stand a fighting chance."

He led them into a building marked with a big number 6, and from there to a conference room. The room held a long table and expensive-looking chairs, and there were video screens placed around the perimeter.

"As it happens," Cresius said, "many of our researchers are on holiday this week. The vanguard of our fighting squadron is likely still in the Thesserin Desert—we deployed what we could on short notice, in order to meet the threat imposed by Cariel. So you'll find this building, at least, to be relatively empty. Make yourselves comfortable."

He stepped over to the wall, flicking switches and hitting buttons. Trey heard a beep and a light came on. "There," Cresius said. "We'll have some coffee in a minute."

Trey and Arra sat at the long table, Trey feeling a bit awkward in his big, black chair. The end of the world had arrived, and they were going to have a *meeting* about it?

"This will give us a safe place to regroup," Cresius said, joining them at the table. "Others will be arriving soon, I expect. Others from the Department."

"How old is this place?" Trey asked.

"This particular facility is about ten thousand years old," Cresius said, "though we have others that date much further back. Our order as a whole was founded one hundred thousand years ago, shortly after the Awakening."

Trey gave a low whistle. "Whose idea was it?"

"The DMR was founded by a man named Aten," Cresius said.

Trey and Arra exchanged a look.

"Isn't that the guy who left the note and the soulmirror?" Arra asked.

Trey nodded. "And the person who setup all those traps or tests or whatever they were. The guy who rigged that pyramid to sink."

"That does sound like something he would have done," Cresius said. "He was nothing if not enigmatic. And immensely creative."

"I wonder what happened to him?" Trey asked.

"He died," Cresius said. "Well, that's not entirely correct. He committed suicide, then came back from the dead, then died again."

"I...see," Trey said. He didn't.

"Right now we need to figure out how to combat this new threat," Cresius said. "The Twins have power like we've never seen. They control Guruthos itself—the source of all magic. It's only a matter of time before they find out about us and chase us here."

Trey opened his mouth to ask another question, but there was a sudden clanging in the hall outside. "One of the researchers?" he asked.

Cresius furrowed his brow. "It could be, but they'd all know the code to get in. I don't know what would make a noise like that."

"Maybe they ran into something."

Cresius didn't look convinced. He crept over to the door, one hand fishing in his robe's deep pocket. When he pulled it out, he was holding a mergegun. Trey recognized it immediately. Cresius was a mergemelder.

He keyed open the door.

"Show yourself," Cresius said as it slid aside. "You can't hide. We have cameras on everything, so come out now and save yourself later embarrassment."

Nothing happened for a long minute. Trey could only hear the quiet whirring of air conditioning vents in the ceiling. Then there was a footstep, then another.

Quynn stepped out of the shadows.

Trey and Arra both stood quickly, chairs bouncing backward and almost toppling to the floor. Trey reached for his Tree Ring Staff, but it wasn't there. He saw Arra clenching her hands, probably wishing she'd brought a bow with her. Cresius, meanwhile, had his mergegun up to Quynn's head.

At least one of them had thought to bring a weapon.

"How did you get in here?" Cresius asked.

Quynn gave him a level stare, no fear evident on his face. "I was hidden in that vessel of yours." His lips curled in a sneer. "It wasn't hard."

"It should have been," Cresius said. "Who were you with? Who let you in?"

"Nobody. The hatch was open, so I went in. Maybe your captain was too distracted by the Twins destroying your famous city."

Cresius clutched the gun tighter in his grip. "What do you know of the Twins?"

Quynn gave a short, clipped laugh. "Nothing. And neither do you, it would seem. We're all in a shit lot of trouble. And your gate guards really need to learn how to turn their heads."

Cresius frowned, dropping his gun. "I want to hear how you circumvented our defenses," he said. "Come in and sit. Now."

Quynn took a step into the room, though he didn't look happy about it.

Cresius glanced at Trey. "Do you know this man? You and Arra look like you've just seen a ghost."

"That's Quynn," Trey said, eyeing him as he stepped into the room. How long had it been since Trey had seen the man? It must have been just after the Cothellon were defeated, back on Earth. Trey hadn't thought of his former "father" in all that time. "How'd you even get to Valaralda? Weren't you in a prison in New San Francisco?"

"It's a long story," Quynn said, coming up to stand beside them at the table. "I took a trip to the wild side for a bit. Met an interesting woman by the name of Magona. Then I—"

He stopped, as if suddenly afraid.

"You what?" Arra asked.

"I...think I helped release the Twins."

"You found a Prison Tree," Cresius said. "Didn't you."

"What do you know of it?" Quynn asked.

"Not enough," Cresius said. "Just that the Twins were said to be imprisoned in Trees, on faraway planets. We hadn't pieced together enough information to know more. This Imprisoner the Twins want...whoever it is, they have a good reason to be angry."

"Cariel must have planned all this from the beginning," Trey said. "She knew where the Trees were, and she knew she needed mages there to unlock them. It was Quynn and Orym. She got you there."

"Could Cariel be the Imprisoner?" Arra asked.

"Possible," Cresius said. "But if that were true, we have a problem."

"This...Cariel," Quynn said. "Who is she?"

"A very powerful mage," Trey said. "Dead now. She was Magona, too. You met one of her splinters."

"If she truly is who the Twins are after," Cresius said, "all they'll find is a corpse."

"Magona used me for her own ends," Quynn said, "and I allowed her. But that doesn't matter now. Now I'm afraid I must be going."

He bolted out of the room.

But Arra was there to stop him. She dove at him faster than Trey could blink, trying to tackle him to the floor.

Except Quynn was far faster than anyone had expected.

He dodged her initial attack, defending himself with a great deal of skill. No wonder he had been so difficult to defeat back at the Prime Forest—the man was *good*. For one brief moment, Trey wished Quynn had actually been his father. Maybe that way Trey would have been a better fighter.

Quynn and Arra grappled for a minute, but Quynn

quickly got the upper hand. He pulled Arra into a rough chokehold, his arm around her neck and his body positioned behind her. Her arms were pinned and his teeth were bared.

It had taken only a few seconds.

Trey had thought Arra was the best fighter he had ever met. Apparently Quynn was even better.

Cresius lowered his gun, unwilling to risk hitting Arra. "Let her go," he said. "We aren't going to hurt you."

"Like hell you aren't," Quynn said, pulling his hold on Arra tighter. She whimpered, her face going white. It was obvious she was in a great deal of pain.

"Let her go," Trey said, his voice quiet.

Quynn looked at him, surprise registering briefly before it was replaced with a smile. "You," he said. "You were always too weak to resist me. Even now, you can't speak."

"Let. Her. Go," Trey said, taking a step forward, willing his voice to have more strength. He was only partly successful. For some reason he always had trouble facing Quynn. Quynn, the man who'd pretended to be his father.

Maybe that was why.

"Or what?" Quynn sneered, his voice adopting a whiny tone. "Will the great *Prime Mage* kill me? You couldn't do it before. Oh, wait now I remember. It's because you're only *half* a mage."

"Shut up," Trey said, taking another step forward, a headache blossoming in his mind. "Don't hurt her."

"You might want to step back," Quynn said. "You could hurt yourself."

"I'll kill you," Trey said.

"How's your head?"

Pain shot through Trey's head as if on command, searing pain that made it difficult to think or move. But he pushed through it, willing himself to continue on. Quynn was holding Arra. Arra, the woman he loved. Arra, the woman who could never be taken advantage of. She was strong. She was fearless. But *Quynn* had somehow managed to do it anyway. Quynn, the bastard who had been so cruel to Trey. Quynn, the man who had made him kill a cat.

Headaches didn't matter.

Killing Quynn did.

He launched forward, anger blazing in his eyes, muscles contracting, fist reared back. He intended to hit Quynn, to pummel him, to destroy him if he could. He saw surprise in Quynn's eyes as he flew through the air, unexpected strength propelling him. Quynn shifted his grip and Arra twisted away, and Quynn's eyes opened wide as Trey leveled the hardest punch he could at the horrible man's face.

But when they touched, it was like a spark connected them. Trey had a vision of two circles, wavering in the air, each with slices cut out of them like a pie. One circle had three slices on the left, the other had three slices on the right. They floated in his vision, moving together until they were superimposed, outlines burning in the air.

That was when the memories began returning.

THIRTY-FIVE

KYTHAELA WATCHED the remaining group around the mentorfire, the loyal few who had stayed to listen to her entire story. They were looking at her now with mixed expressions on their faces: confusion, worry, fear. Maybe they thought she was going insane.

Maybe they were right.

"The night air grows chill," she said. "But if I may keep you for a moment longer, there is one thing yet which we must discuss." She bent to pick up a willow branch that was laying at her feet. It somehow seemed appropriate. "Consider the splinter," she said, firelight flickering as she peeled a portion of the wood away from the branch. "It worms its way into our skin, piercing our body, causing pain. But what is a splinter, if not a part of something larger?"

TARATHIEL—20,000 YEARS AGO

"WHATEVER HAPPENS," Tarathiel said, "know this: we will always be together." It wasn't a lie—not precisely. He *hoped* they'd find each other after the Sending, after the Prime Trees were made. He knew their souls were destined to be together across the eons of time, no matter what planet they were on. But he didn't know how the magic worked. He didn't know if it was possible.

He felt tears coming to his eyes.

All around them, he could hear the other elves saying their last goodbyes. Their words were quiet, but he could feel the emotion behind them. The fear. The grief. The mystery of it all. Some of them were even excited to make this journey into the great unknown.

Tarathiel was one of them.

But he didn't know if their mission would succeed. To find the Defense Mechanism, to stop the Fall in its tracks. To save the galaxy from great destruction. This was what he had set out to do, but he didn't know if he could. It was too much for any man.

Alleria squeezed his arm. "This will be an awfully big adventure," she whispered.

She was right. She was perfect.

"I love you," he replied.

QUYNN—PRESENT DAY

QUYNN LOOKED at Trey looking at him. His eyes...they looked so familiar. It must have been the decades he'd spent with the man, pretending he was Quynn's son. The fool had never quite lived up to expectations. Hell, Phoenix had done a better job at age five than Trey had ever done. She'd had more power. And what of the others? Quynn had had so many "children." None of them were real, of course. None that he knew of, anyway. He wasn't exactly shy about spreading his seed.

But why was he thinking of Phoenix now? He hadn't thought of her in fifteen years.

That was when the memories came crashing down.

It felt like Quynn was swimming through the years, moving forever backwards through the nightmares of his past.

TREY

TREY STARED into Quynn's eyes, conscious of the coldness of the floor. Arra had recovered quickly, scrambling up, her hands touching her throat. She hadn't been hurt.

But something had passed between Quynn and Trey. It had happened when he'd punched the man—some kind of blazing light had flashed through his brain. Now they were on the floor, and his fist hurt, and his head hurt, and all he could think about were the strange memories that had begun slipping through his brain.

Time.

Time was such a fleeting thing.

It felt like Trey was flying through his life, running through experiences in reverse.

TARATHIEL—20,000 YEARS AGO

TARATHIEL STOOD on the mountain in mainland China with the others. He did not know the mountain's name. He did not even speak the language of the natives they had found there. He had not had time to marvel at this new planet's beauty, to make drawings of the strange animals he had already seen.

The elves needed magic. And he had volunteered, as he knew he would.

As Alleria had.

That, he had *not* expected.

He squeezed her, feeling the warmth of her body next to his. He looked out at the rest of the Fourteen, gathered there to commit their ultimate sacrifice. He bowed his head as the ritual words were uttered.

He barely felt it when the knife slashed his throat, spraying hot blood onto the tree. And as he died, he uttered one final prayer to the Twins.

He held Alleria's hand until the end.

His soul was dimly aware of the great Tree rising in his place.

QUYNN—6 HOURS AGO

QUYNN LURCHED, almost losing his balance in the jungle. There was a breath, as if all the air on the planet had been instantly replaced. As if reality had for a moment been disrupted. And when it reasserted itself, when the world was back to being a world, Quynn noticed that the night sky had *changed*.

"Did we just—"

"We did," Saul said, giving him a grim smile. "Eryn is now in the Persephone system."

"But a gate of that magnitude...shouldn't we have lost our memories?"

Saul shrugged. "Gatesending is a fickle magic. Who can tell what will happen? But did you not feel yourself disrupted for a moment?"

"I did." Maybe he *had* lost some memories. How would he even know? "What now?" he asked, looking up at the massive nightmare Tree they were standing in front of. Magona had already left. Whatever the plan was for Quynn, he figured it must be time.

"Almost," Saul said. "Just a few minutes more, I believe."

Quynn gritted his teeth, his gaze never leaving the strange Tree. It was black, but the black was somehow *glowing*. That shouldn't be possible. "What—" he started, but then something else happened.

He felt a connection. A merging of souls as if from very far away. An intrusion in his mind, as if someone wanted in. And for a brief minute he felt power seeping out of him.

It was mindmaster magic.

TREY

A LINE of thick red hung between Cariel and Arra, pulsing with viscous blobs that looked like blood. Cariel had her arms outstretched in front of her, palms out, face turned up to the sky, fierce wind blowing through her hair.

Cariel was hurting Arra.

Cariel was killing her.

But Trey was only half a Prime Mage. He didn't have the necessary power to stop her.

His headache was splitting now, stronger than it had ever

been before, and he was tired of headaches. So he gritted his teeth, questing outward with his mind, *wanting*, *willing*, *forcing* the magic to come. It would come!

It. Would. Come.

And for a fleeting second, from a million miles away, he felt an unfamiliar surge of power.

He struck with it, struck as hard as he could, activating poplar and oak. Purple shot out from his hands, spreading rapidly in the air, undeterred by the sandstorm whirling around them. Purple clouds shot toward Cariel, going right through her forcefield, suffusing her body, merging and mastering everything within her.

This, Trey realized, was *true* power. This was where *true* control lay.

This was mindmaster magic.

But where had it come from?

And how?

THIRTY-SIX

TARATHIEL—11,312 YEARS AGO

TARATHIEL STEPPED out into the world, blinking in the sudden sunlight. The sky wasn't purple. The black and gold Trees were gone. He was in a mountainous region of some kind, covered with grass and different types of trees. The air was cold.

Where was he? What had happened? He struggled with the memory.

This was China. He recognized it now. But when? What year?

He had been killed. He had been a Prime Tree—one of the first. Alleria had been killed, too, but where was she? He didn't see her anywhere. He didn't see *anyone*.

His Tree. Where was it? It should be right here, but all he saw was grass. Then he turned, and there it was—but it was no longer a whole Tree. It was split in half and smoking, its wood charred and its leaves burned off. It looked like it had been hit by lightning.

Could Prime Trees be killed? He had never thought of

that before. What happened when they died? Wait—he knew the answer to that one. He knew it because it had just happened to him.

He was the soul that had fashioned the Tree. Now here he was, alive again, standing in front of the remains of his former home.

But he could still feel something. Some kind of connection, like a thread reaching out from his soul. He was tied to Ambarhal now, he realized. Tied forever. It was holding his life, keeping him in balance. Keeping his cells from aging. He could somehow feel it through the bond.

It felt like he would live forever.

But it was more than that. His soul had fully Awakened. His trip through Ambarhal had unlocked it all. Every Aspect. He knew that if he had the right kinds of primewood, he could do *anything*.

He felt incredibly powerful.

But now what? What should he do? He couldn't stay up on this mountain. He needed food. He needed to find Alleria. He needed to find out what other kinds of magic he could do.

He checked the angle of the sun, orienting himself to the west. Toward where he knew life had first formed on this planet. A place they had called Mesopotamia.

Maybe he could find his answers there.

QUYNN—3 YEARS AGO

THEY'D INSISTED on having the wedding at Grace Cathedral, probably because Lorelei had been the one to insist that Grace Cathedral should exist to begin with. They hadn't *needed* to rebuild San Francisco from the ground, keeping everything the same, but for some reason Lorelei had wanted it to be that way. Quynn never had figured out why.

Maybe she was just nostalgic. Quynn didn't know how old Lorelei was, exactly. She seemed to have a lot of knowledge— knowledge that she couldn't have gotten in the past five hundred years, or maybe even at all—but he couldn't question her. She was in charge. And she made sure he remembered it every time he saw her.

He smiled to himself, thinking to the last time they'd been in bed. She was ravishing, as she usually was, red lipstick and black hair and those tight dresses that made him squirm. And her breasts—Twins, the tits on her were to die for. He found himself salivating and stirring all at the same time, but now was not the time for that.

He was here to watch a wedding.

He was Trey's "father," after all. And Lorelei was not Lorelei at all, not the Cundu, leader of the Cothellon. Lorelei was Lora, Trey's fiancé. Which meant Quynn would have to share her in the future.

His mouth twisted in disgust.

Still, it was better than not having her at all. And though Trey himself was far too meek and mild for Quynn's taste, he had to admit that the man *was* handsome. It was even somewhat believable that they were father and son, though Quynn knew that it wasn't the case. They shared certain similar physical traits, though their temperaments couldn't be more different.

Quynn's lip curled again. Trey was a total and complete pussy.

Still, this was the next phase of his plan. Trey and "Lora" would get married. While this in and of itself would not result in a Prime Mage, Quynn was hopeful that the next part would.

They needed to have a child.

TREY

TREY STEPPED through the doors of the church, trepidation overtaking him. Everyone was already there: the pastor, the wedding party, even Lora was already in a side room getting ready. And Simon. Simon was at the door, watching him as he entered. Simon, his father. Simon, the man he hated.

Trey studiously avoided looking at him as he passed, instead looking around the cathedral. It was beautiful, white archways atop wooden pews—real wood!—leading up to the vaulted ceiling high above. The sanctuary ended with a huge pipe organ, reproduced in every exacting detail from the original organ in the ruins below.

The ruins that the virus had made.

Trey turned, surrounded by finery he felt no part of. There was so much wood, so much tradition in this place. Yet he felt apart from it, adrift in a floating world that did not know his name. He belonged in his bookshop, not in a graceful church like this. He belonged alone.

"You're supposed to be happy on your wedding day," a woman said.

He felt a hand on his shoulder, and he turned. It was Lora, his beautiful bride-to-be, not yet changed into the brilliant white wedding dress she'd picked out months ago. She smiled up at him, red lips beckoning. He obliged her, kissing those lips as deeply as he could. Somehow it was not enough.

"It's the church, isn't it?" Lora asked. "I told him it was too much."

"My *father* was the one who insisted on Grace Cathedral?"

Lora nodded. "Simon's an odd one, sometimes."

"That's putting it mildly."

She poked him in the stomach. "You need to get dressed, young man."

"So do you, little lady." He reached out and touched her hair. She really was beautiful. He felt sometimes as if he didn't quite deserve her—or maybe he didn't quite belong.

She reached her arms around him, pulling him in close. "We have a few minutes before everyone gets here," she said. "I want one last snuggle with you before I have to call you 'husband.'"

He squeezed her, feeling her soft body pressed up against him. "Maybe we can do more than cuddle."

Lora looked up at him, a smile on that perfect face of hers. "Now you're talking, mister."

TARATHIEL—6000 YEARS AGO

NOISES IN THE FOREST. Footsteps. Tarathiel turned, trying to see what was behind him, but there were only Queñua trees as far as the eye could see. Whoever was in the forest with him had been tracking him for hours. They were closer now, and growing more careless. Or perhaps they were just more bold.

He turned back the way he was heading, trudging uphill through the forest. He shouldn't be out here at all. He should be safe at home, warm in front of a fire. Cook dinner. Maybe even have some of that new popping corn that trader from the north had brought.

But he couldn't do that now. He'd come out here for a reason. He thought he'd seen someone at the village edge, a face he hadn't seen in thousands of years. A face he remembered loving.

Alleria.

But she had run, and now he was out here in the forest trying to find her. And she was nowhere to be found.

Alleria. He remembered her name and her face, her hair. He remembered knowing her, loving her. He remembered the feeling of her arms, but he couldn't seem to remember anything else. Who was she? Why had she been gone for so long? Why was she here after all this time?

A twig cracked sharply behind him, and Tarathiel turned.

Only to find a knife's edge placed against his throat.

The assailant gave a wicked slice, and Tarathiel felt a searing pain. He tripped on a tree root, crashing to the ground in a cascade of blood and bones. The world dimmed, and then he was back. Back in a world of purple skies and green, of malevolent Trees and wavy lines. He was dead again. He was a Tree.

Which meant he had failed.

He might never see Alleria again.

TREY—16 YEARS AGO

TREY WALKED DOWN NEW EMBARCADERO, holding his latest hardbound book closely to his chest. It was growing cold as evening settled over the city, and Trey's light jacket wasn't quite sufficient to keep it out. He kept on walking, lost in thought.

His life seemed so numb right now. His father was gone more often these days, leaving Trey to run the bookstore. And his mother was usually holed up in the kitchen, doing whatever it was she did with the strange pieces of metalwood Simon brought home. So Trey just worked at the store, ate dinner at the Pig and Whistle, then trudged home. Every day. For years.

Something about his life didn't seem right.

So on this rare day, he had decided to make a change. He'd taken the 5 into New Union Square, then the cable car up to Old Fisherman's Wharf. Now he was walking east around New Embarcadero, passing shantytowns and Planner buildings and the very few restaurants that dared build out on the Edge. They were expensive establishments, both because of their proximity to the Shield—and the nanovirus it kept out —and for their view of a world three thousand feet below.

Trey had never been inside a restaurant like that. He was too afraid of heights to try.

He should have brought Callan with him. At least then he'd have had someone to talk to. This morose hike so near the Edge wasn't helping matters much, though it was nice to see a different part of the city for a change. Trey really should get out more.

Maybe he needed a girlfriend.

Something was happening up ahead. As he continued around the bend toward New Market Street, it seemed like there more people in this area than he'd expected. Was that normal? There were hundreds of them, milling about. Did some of them have signs? As he got closer, he heard that they were chanting something. He crossed the street so he could hear what they were saying.

"Phoenix! Phoenix! Phoenix!"

Phoenix. It was a mythological beast, a bird that was purported to burn to death, then rise back to life from its ashes. What would cause a crowd like this to be chanting after a bird? What would get a crowd here in the first place?

Some of them had torches, he saw. Further in the distance, a few fires were going. The crowd grew larger as he reached New Market, people crammed together so tightly that they could barely move. Most of them were looking up into the sky. His mouth fell open as he followed their gaze.

There was some kind of glowing red sphere flying over-head, like a bubble made out of fire. He saw *people* inside it: three women. Two of them had swords out, blades clashing as the bubble soared overhead, grim expressions on their faces. It looked like they were engaged in some kind of battle, encased as they were in a magical floating fire thing.

What in the hell *was* all this? Was Trey dreaming? Was this whole *crowd* dreaming? Or could magic somehow actu-ally be real?

He clutched the book to his chest, a smile forming on his face.

QUYNN

QUYNN TOOK IN A DEEP, shuddering breath, wincing as he felt searing pain slice through him. He saw the gate flash out of existence in the corner of his eye, and two soulsoothers were on him in an instant. He shuddered as rivers of ice poured over him, closing the two pinblade wounds and fixing his other cuts and scrapes. Then he was whole and the soothers stepped away, flinging shit off their fingers, grimaces on their faces.

The sound of clicking heels announced Lorelei's approach. "You weren't in the Under for more than ten minutes," she said, "and already you're covered in shit?" Her bright red lips curved in a distasteful frown. "Get cleaned up, then meet me in my quarters."

"Of course, my lady." Quynn gave a little bow, shit dripping off his nose. "Your wish is my command."

"My lady?" Lorelei barked a laugh. "You've been spending too much time in the Under." She took a step closer to him, pretty nose wrinkling as she smelled him. "Do be sure to get *very* clean." She licked her lips and turned away.

Quynn smiled as he thought about what was to come.

THIRTY-SEVEN

KYTHAELA

"THE WORLD IS a strange place for a magician," Kythaela said. She was still holding the branch in one hand, a splinter in the other. The faces around the fire were interested, but confused. Perhaps this story was too much for them. "So much is unknown," she said. "So much is forbidden. Eons of time are lost to us, Sent as we were to this new planet. The old rules, the old laws, are naught but shadows. The mechanisms of magic, vanished to the ravages of time, are nothing more than a glimmer in our mind's eye.

"Who is to say what is right and wrong? Should power be sought for power's sake, or should we operate under some moral imperative? Do those who do evil in magic's name really sin, or are their actions simply those of a people who do not belong in this place?

"We elves, we forsaken few: what do we know of magic? What do we truly know of gods? Who are we to describe the contours of a soul?"

TARATHIEL—5011 YEARS AGO

TARATHIEL AWOKE, gasping, hand reaching automatically for his throat. But it was whole. He was whole. He was alive.

He was in a forest, a gorgeous forest of lush trees. The air was thin and rather hard to breathe. There was a huge tree stump behind him, cut or chopped by someone's hand. It must have taken days to destroy that Tree.

Where was he? He remembered nothing. Nothing at all. He looked at his hands and saw foreign hands. He didn't know those hands. He looked at his feet and saw a stranger's feet. They weren't his own. Then he looked to his left and saw the most beautiful girl he'd ever seen.

But he had no idea who she was.

"What is this?" a voice said, and he saw a man trudging toward them through the woods. "Who are you?"

But Tarathiel did not understand the words, for they were in a language he did not know. So he shrugged, and mimed his ignorance as best he could. Next to him, the girl did the same. She obviously had no memories, either.

"Come," the man said in his foreign tongue. "You are my kind—I can see it by the tips of your ears. You can stay with me until we find out where you belong. I am feeling generous, for today is an auspicious day. Today my son was born. Talanaar."

Tarathiel and the girl went with him, though they did not know his words. He seemed like a kind man.

And so the days passed, and the months, and gradually Tarathiel began to learn the strange man's language. He was given a new name: Usunaar. And the girl he'd been found with was called Koranaar. They were treated as family, growing up with their new baby brother. But something strange occurred as the years passed: Usunaar and Koranaar did not age.

And so it was that Talanaar and Usunaar and Koranaar soon looked to be the same age.

That was when the Kotosh attacked.

They were a band of warriors, sweeping in from the coast south of the Supe Valley, intent on death and destruction. They killed indiscriminately, burning and raping and pillaging as they went. There appeared to be no purpose to their fight; there was land enough for everyone. And yet they came onward.

The elves found them first, before the humans in the nearby village of Caral were alerted to their presence. And the elves, ever a peace-loving race, almost left the intruders to their own devices.

But the Kotosh went too far. They captured a band of elven Hunters, among them Koranaar.

So the elves enacted war upon them.

It was during this war that Usunaar Awakened, becoming a Prime Mage. He battled and fought, his new power amongst the greatest in known history.

In the end, they succeeded at driving the Kotosh away. But the victory came at great cost: Koranaar's death. And so it was that Usunaar left the village, speaking to no one, setting out on his own into the forest to look for his sister. Talanaar searched long for him, but Usunaar could not be found.

And Usunaar, the last living Prime Mage, was never seen or heard from again.

Years later, when Usunaar had faded from all thought and memory, a pair of new Prime Trees was discovered, in the forest where Talanaar's tears had fallen. They grew together in that forest, intertwined like two long-lost lovers. They were the greatest Prime Trees ever to grow, towering far above the Queñua forest. The elves marveled and worshipped at their roots, giving thanks to the Twins.

For Usunaar had finally found what he'd been searching for and had forgotten. He found her underneath the purple skies, beneath the branches of black and gold.

Koranaar was there.

Alleria.

QUYNN—50 YEARS AGO

QUYNN HAD HIS "SON" tethered to a chair.

Trey was squirming, fear in his eyes, face pallid and covered in sweat. The boy opened his mouth as if to shout or scream, but no sound came. He was a coward. He was a fool.

It was always like this when it came time for a memory wipe. Quynn would put his hands on Trey's forehead—like *this*—and he would utter some meaningless words that had no effect other than to soothe Quynn's own conscience.

There was less and less of that left, these days.

"This will be over soon," he said. "This is all for your benefit. I'm just trying to unlock your potential."

Just trying to make a Prime Mage.

Trey's eyes were darting back and forth, his lower lip trembling. He was so weak, so different from Quynn himself. It was a wonder anyone believed the boy was his son.

Not a boy. Not a boy. Trey was probably several hundred years old at least—there was no real way to know. Elves stopped visibly aging at around one hundred, and it wasn't until they reached five or six hundred that they started showing signs again. Trey could be anywhere in that middle ground.

Quynn stroked the rounded tip of Trey's left ear. The ear that he'd had cut off, moulded to look like a human's ear.

Trey had no idea who he really was.

And now this round of the experiment had failed. Quynn had tried being nice to the guy, pampering him and giving him every luxury. That strategy hadn't worked—all it had landed him was a spoiled brat who was still a coward. A brat who was not a Prime Mage at all.

He brought up a piece of prime poplar, purple clouds surrounding Trey's head as the mindmaster magic went to work. He couldn't directly wipe out memories, but he could make them much harder to access. And he could make *other* memories—fictional memories—more prominent. All it took were a few minutes of focused magic.

So. This round of Trey's apprenticeship had failed. What options did that leave him? Quynn could try torture, brutality. He could try giving Trey a job, maybe a relationship. Or perhaps if Trey had offspring, maybe *that* kid would be a Prime Mage. He'd tried it with others in the program, but so far none of his breeding had been a success. Probably it was just a matter of finding the right pair—but who?

He would try everything—there would certainly be time. The Cothellon were taking forever rebuilding New Tokyo—at this rate it would be another fifty years before Lorelei's plan was ready to come to fruition.

Quynn *would* learn how to make a Prime Mage. It was only a matter of time.

TREY

TREY SAT THERE in the chair, leather straps pinning him down. Simon—his father—was looming over him, a calculated smile on his face, and there was a piece of that strange metalwood in his hand. Trey wasn't supposed to know the stuff existed, but his mom was always using it. It was like a drug to her, somehow. He didn't understand it.

How had he gotten here? What did his father want with him? He'd treated him kindly up until now, pampering him, giving him everything he'd ever wanted. Now he was acting differently—meanly—leering at Trey like some kind of storybook villain.

None of it made any sense.

Had he been in this room before? Something about it seemed so familiar to Trey.

A purple cloud rose up around him, and all his thoughts went blank.

TARATHIEL—4995 YEARS AGO

USUNAAR—NO, Tarathiel, his name was Tarathiel—stepped out into the forest, once again free from the purple skies of Ambarhal. He turned, expecting to see the smoking ruin of his Prime Tree behind him, but everything was normal. The Tree towered over him, its immense trunk filling his entire vision. It wasn't destroyed or even damaged. It looked perfect. Beautiful.

So how was he here?

He remembered something, vaguely. He'd been touching a Tree in Ambarhal, feeling the soul inside it. The Tree's soul. It had one, too. That was how Tarathiel could access magic. He could see it, ropes of colorful power ranging across space. The Tree's soul made it all possible.

Tarathiel had reached out through the soul, out into the world beyond. To Earth. To the mountains of Peru where this Tree stood. He had visualized it, he had seen it clearly, and he had asked the Tree to let him through.

And it had.

Now he was free, and his Tree was still alive. But wasn't there someone else? Someone he'd been trying to find?

He couldn't remember.

He couldn't remember anything.

And so he trudged into the forest, hoping he would see a friendly face somewhere in the world.

TREY—293 YEARS AGO

HOW HAD HE GOTTEN HERE? He couldn't remember. What was this place? What was his name? Something with a T? No. Maybe it was a U. Usunaar? No—that was a stupid name.

What had happened to lead him here? He remembered being trapped in some kind of purple world with wavy lines and trees all around. Then there had been a massive golden light, and he'd seen thousands and thousands—millions, billions—of souls streaming into the world. He'd felt overwhelmed by them, about to panic, but then his Tree had called out to him. It was in pain. Its soul was dying. No—its soul was *retaliating* for all the pain it had just caused. It was pouring forth its power back into the world from whence it came, and he was being called along with it.

Then he'd been shot back into the real world, his Prime Tree collapsing into gray nothingness all around him. Now it was dead, and he was alive. One soul traded for another. So he had wandered, remembering nothing but miasma skies of purple, wondering where he was.

And where all the people were.

Finally he'd found some of them, further south on the coast. They were building a city there, a strange city that was all staged up on stilts, with an immense framework of upside-down buildings underneath it. It almost looked like a city built with a mirror of itself. It almost looked as if the city were intended to fly.

But none of that made any sense.

So he'd wandered inside, and now he was exhausted. He was sitting with his back pressed to a small building, looking at the whirlwind of construction around him. He didn't know why he was here. He didn't know what to do.

"Son," a man said, stepping up to him as if out of the blue, "what's your business here?"

QUYNN

NEW TOKYO II was coming along well—if slowly—but Quynn wasn't in the city for pleasure. He had a job to do. The droplift came to a halt and the passengers streamed out, Quynn taking up the rear. He branched off, heading toward the construction foreman's office nearby.

As he neared the office, he noticed there was a very dirty man sitting out front, leaning against the wall, looking out of place. He was an elf, somewhere in his early twenties or maybe fifties. Age was hard to pinpoint with elves.

Quynn walked up to him, feet kicking up dust on the pavement.

"Son," Quynn said, "what's your business here?"

"I don't know," the disheveled elf said. His accent was strange.

"How did you get in here?" Quynn asked. "This area is off-limits for civilians."

"I just...wandered in one day," the man said. Quynn frowned, looking him over. There was something strange about him. Something almost...ancient. But how could a twenty-year-old elf be ancient? It made no sense.

"What's your name, son?" he asked.

"I don't think I have a name."

"What's the first thing you remember?"

"I remember...bright lights. Golden lights. Sounds. Explosions. Screaming. I remember the screaming." He put his hand to his head as if in pain. "The Trees. They were dying."

Quynn made up his mind in that moment. The foreman could wait. This was far more important. This was his chance, his opportunity to start that big project he knew he needed.

Quynn held out his hand to the man sitting on the ground. The man looked up at him, a confused expression on his face.

"Let me help you," Quynn said.

THIRTY-EIGHT

TARATHIEL—4912 YEARS AGO

SOME TIME after his latest release from Ambarhal, Tarathiel found himself in the Sahara Desert, in Egypt. The pharaoh at the time was a man by the name of Sneferu. He was presently engaged in some campaigns of ill repute, capturing foreigners, mostly from Libya and Nubia, and putting them to work. He was starved for labor, needing thousands of people to build his pyramids and ships and other improvement projects. Tarathiel thought it was an awful shame that so many people from neighboring countries were being subjugated, but he wasn't exactly in a place to do anything about it.

At one point he was almost captured himself. He didn't look anything like the Egyptians—his skin was far too white and his eyes were wrong. And so it was that Tarathiel was almost made to be a slave like the others.

But luckily, Tarathiel was a Prime Mage.

He wielded the Fourteen Powers—as long as he could find primewood to supply him, at least. Magic yielded to his beck and call, and he rejoiced in it. And one power in particular was useful in this situation.

Mistweaving.

Tarathiel made himself look like a local. And so it was that he was able to infiltrate Ineb-Hed without being noticed. The city was beautiful, though very strange to Tarathiel's eyes. Everything was still so backwards, so primitive. The humans on Earth had not yet risen to the technological heights that Tarathiel sometimes dimly remembered from a past life he'd had. His memories were a blur now, confusing and strange. He knew he was different from these people, but he didn't know why. Or how.

Or when.

Why was he here, again? There were other, more hospitable places on Earth to be. What was it about this place that had drawn him? Oh, yes. Now he remembered.

It was the sand.

There was some kind of magic here, something the locals had uncovered. The local *humans*, which made it doubly strange. Tarathiel hadn't known any humans who could perform magic before. He'd heard it was something with forcefinding magic—something that was *very* advanced.

There was some kind of secret society out here. Someone was supplying them with darkprime wood—an elf, most likely, as elves were the only ones who could create the stuff. He had followed them here, to Ineb-Hed, but now the trail had run cold. He wasn't sure where to go next. And if he ran out of prime maple, his illusion would drop. Then he'd be in a lot of trouble.

He stood at the edge of the city, looking out into the desert. If he were a secret society, would he be in the great capital of Egypt? No—he'd find somewhere else to hide. Somewhere that was much more difficult to find.

He shaded his eyes, scanning the horizon. A whirl of sand caught his attention, spinning up like a bright tornado in the sun. He watched it move, growing larger, blowing faster. Soon it would turn into a sandstorm, rampaging across the desert. But then the sand did something unexpected: it changed into a shape.

The shape of a *person*.

It only happened for a second. If Tarathiel hadn't been looking straight at it, he wouldn't have even noticed it. Now it was back to being a cyclone, just blowing around in circles in the sand. But Tarathiel had seen. He knew that this was what he'd been looking for.

He'd found the practicers of this strange force magic.

Now he had just had to infiltrate them.

QUYNN—500 YEARS AGO

QUYNN LACKED PURPOSE. He lacked motivation. He lacked...*style*. While the war was raging up in the American-Canadian frontier, Quynn was down in Boston, trying to figure out what he wanted to finally *do* with his life.

It wasn't that his life hadn't had meaning before. Maybe it had. It was just that Quynn couldn't *remember* his damn life. How old was he? He had no idea. He didn't know where he was born, or even what his original name was. He didn't know a damn thing except that he was an elf, a very talented mindmaster, and that nothing in this world seemed right at all.

He'd heard about a new faction—well, not *new* exactly, but it was the first time he'd heard about them. Apparently they'd been around for at least two hundred years already and it was just now getting to him. They were a progressive group, a group that was interested in science and exploration, in exploitation and magic and research and in pushing the envelope. He'd heard they were a group that didn't care one whit about humans, which made them unique amongst the elves. The only tricky part was that they were so difficult to find.

"Mr. Smith," a man said, appearing suddenly out of the shadows. It wasn't raining, but he was carrying a large umbrella. He wore a black suit with a long, black overcoat and an empire hat that was far too tall for his skull. Quynn had always had trouble following human fashions.

"Yes," Quynn said. "I am Mr. Smith."

"Your application was very...unexpected, Mr. Smith," the man said. "Right this way." He turned and started walking down the street.

Quynn suppressed the smile that came unbidden to his face. Now was the time—if he could just get into the man's good graces, Quynn might finally be allowed to join the Cothellon.

TREY

TREY CHECKED HIS RIFLE. It was clean, as it always was, and loaded, as he'd done about half an hour ago. He wasn't with the troops—they were a mile further north, billeted under the open sky. General Hull only had two thousand men, but he was sure the march to Fort Malden would be a total and complete success. He hadn't even deigned to take on any volunteers during the stopover in Detroit.

But Trey was after something else. He'd seen someone—

someone he thought he'd been looking for, but he couldn't remember why. A girl. He didn't know her name.

But he knew she was out here, somewhere in the wilderness in the southern reaches of Canada. And the war didn't matter—the United States would win, of course, at least if you listened to President Madison and General Hull. They were confident, assured of their victory over the paltry British troops. The British were too busy with Napoleon, the reasoning went. And it made sense—Napoleon was quite a force to be reckoned with. Trey had met him. He knew what the man was capable of.

Distant memories whirled for a minute—desert sands, chariots, spears. The fall of a city named Babylon. Had Trey been there? It had been so long ago. Maybe a fragment of his soul *had* been, was now calling to him from that distant past. Stranger things had happened, and they always seemed to happen to him.

He had sudden thoughts of home, of the home he'd long since forgotten. Of sunlit hills, of moonlight processions, of that girl and her hair and her eyes as she looked at him. Of Ilyrion, glittering in the dark.

Then he was back, flooding through that whirlwind of memory, seeing trees and purple skies and fire and death and pyramids and women and sands in the shape of men.

For a moment, it was too much for him.

Then he felt a cold muzzle pressed against his neck.

Trey stood and looked behind him, seeing a man standing there with a rifle pointed at him. It was Ben Jefferson, one of Hull's soldiers. He should have been with the others.

"You owe me fifty cents," Ben said, spitting chewed tobacco in the grass. They were standing underneath a large maple tree, Trey noticed idly. It seemed important.

"An amount I intend to pay back," he said, turning to the man. Now the rifle was pointed at his face.

"You'll pay me back *now*," Ben said. "No more excuses."

"I don't have the money now," Trey said. Why was this man so intent on fifty cents? Why now, when they were so close to war?

"You're a cheat," Ben said. "You always were a liar. You swindled me. Admit it."

"I'll pay you back," Trey said. "Let's just get through this fight with the British, take some new territory, then when we get back home I promise you I'll have the money."

Ben pressed Trey back against the tree with his gun, a sneer written on his face. "I'm going to kill you."

"Why?" None of this was making any sense. They were supposed to be fighting soon, at least once their march was concluded. They were supposed to be taking this region for the United States. Then the British would finally treat them with respect. Then they would give America its due.

"I'm going to kill you," Ben said, his finger tight on the trigger, "because I *want* to."

He pulled the trigger, and Trey knew no more.

TARATHIEL—3811 YEARS AGO

IT WAS NIGHT, and the scent of smoke was in the air. Tarathiel looked through the small archer's slot, trying to get a gauge of the enemy's distance without exposing himself. The Hittite army was coming fast, and he could see King Mursili in the lead. His chariot was the largest, the most ornamented, his battle leather the most pronounced. Two men rode with him, large spears outthrust and ready to strike.

"The King is at the vanguard," Abarat said from Tarathiel's left. Abarat was an elf—a mistweaver, like Tarathiel was, though not a Prime Mage. He and Tarathiel had become friends many years ago. Abarat was looking for something, but he had never told Tarathiel what it was. He had a strange fascination with pyramids.

"Is that unusual?" Tarathiel asked. He didn't know much about the Hittites, though he knew he should. They had long been a thorn in the side of Egyptians and Babylonians alike.

"Not particularly," Abarat said. "But it does make him easier to kill."

Tarathiel watched Mursili approach, his chariot speeding forward, long hair streaming behind him. "Why are they attacking the city directly? Don't the Hittites normally prefer open ground?"

Abarat nodded. "Easier to use those chariots of theirs. They have grown bolder of late, and our army is in shambles. Perhaps they sense weakness."

"Not much of a trick, that," Tarathiel said. "Hammurabi was the only reason this pile of shit was sticking together in the first place."

"Just so," Abarat said. "It's always the same—empires come and go."

Tarathiel looked at him. "You speak as if you've lived a very long time."

Abarat smiled. "Perhaps. You are not the only enigmatic elf to have visited these parts over the years."

Tarathiel frowned. Abarat was clearly hiding something, but what? Tarathiel had known him for years, and he had never spoken like this before. Perhaps this night really was the dawning of something new.

The Hittites were drawing closer.

"What should we do?" Tarathiel asked.

Abarat was staring through the archer's slot. "Unless you want to fight," he said, "it's probably best to hide."

"But we have magic," Tarathiel said.

"Magic that we cannot reveal."

Tarathiel sighed. "You're right."

And so the Hittites came.

Tarathiel did his best to fight with a bow, defending the city against all comers. Abarat used a spear, matching the Hittites in skill with the awkward weapon. Tarathiel wondered where Abarat had learned to fight—it wasn't here, not in the years Tarathiel had known him. Perhaps Abarat really had been alive an extraordinarily long time.

Could he be a Prime Mage after all?

Crashes and screams sounded at the front gates of the city. Tarathiel surveyed the field from his position atop the wall: the Hittite forces had easily overwhelmed the city's external defenses, laying waste to the infantry and the few chariot forces that the Babylonians had mustered. Now the Hittites were gathering at the gates with torches and bows and a battering ram.

The city was about to fall.

"This battle is lost," Abarat said, climbing up to where Tarathiel stood. The man wasn't even winded. He'd been outside the city just a moment ago, fighting on foot.

"How did you—" Tarathiel started to ask, but Abarat interrupted him.

"We need to get down from here," he said. "Come. It will be close combat in the streets next." Abarat scanned the city. "It won't go well. The Hittites are too good."

"And we've been too lax."

"Just so," Abarat said. "Come."

They jumped down from the wall, scurrying through the streets toward the gates.

"Why are we doing this?" Tarathiel asked as they ran. "Why are we fighting? This isn't our home."

Abarat flashed a smile back at him. "Don't you ever do things just for fun?"

Then he was off, Tarathiel struggling to keep up. "My definition of fun is much different from yours, it would seem," he said as he ran. Abarat didn't give any indication that he had heard him.

Then the gates were breached, and the Hittites flowed into the city.

It was hand-to-hand combat, as Abarat had foreseen. Tarathiel was decent with a sword, but these Hittites insisted on using their damn spears—even at close quarters. They looked stupid, but Tarathiel had to admit they were very good at using them. He didn't stand a chance.

And so it was that he found himself trapped in a dark alleyway, surrounded by enemy forces with only a sword in his hand.

There was no way he would survive this.

He was still holding his illusion; he'd gotten used to doing it after all this time. It made him look like a local, changing his features and skin and hair. The magic itself came not from primewood in his hand, but from a nearby Prime Tree. Tarathiel had discovered that the Trees could provide passive illusion magic, as long as you were near enough to them. It only worked to change your own appearance, though—and even then, only slightly. It was just enough to pretend to be a human, and a local. It was not enough to transform into anything else.

Luckily, Tarathiel had some prime maple in his pocket.

He reached for it, watching the soldiers approach. They were coming in from both ends of the alley, cornering him. There were five of them against one of him.

But what if there wasn't just *one* of him?

The maple blossomed in his hand.

He made illusions of himself, scattered down the alley. Five of them plus him made six, and for some reason the magic didn't want to make any more. They looked like him, but they were dim, transparent, obviously just images. That wouldn't do. He needed these illusions to be realistic, to present the appearance of an even fight.

So he made the magic stronger.

He felt himself start to split, as if the pieces of his soul were tearing apart at the seams. His illusions needed essence to become real, needed souls, needed form. And Tarathiel could give that to them if he tried. If he pushed. If he Willed the magic to do its deed. He felt them coalesce, saw them taking form in front of him. The Hittites had paused now, confused at this army suddenly materializing before them. And Tarathiel kept pushing, kept channeling the magic into his other beings.

His soul was crying all the way.

Then there was a hand on his shoulder, and the maple was knocked out of his grasp. The five forms shuddered for a moment, wavering, then collapsed back into him with a sucking sound and a sigh. Then he was back. Whole. One person and not six.

Abarat was standing next to him.

"How did you—"

"I'm very sneaky," Abarat said. "Now get that sword ready, my friend. For tonight, we fight!"

The Hittites were advancing now, confusion on their faces replaced with anger.

"This is a fool's fight," Tarathiel said.

"Only a coward would say that," Abarat said. "Are you a

coward? We will make it through this fight alive. And Tarathiel, you must make me a promise."

The soldiers were close now, torchlight gleaming on their spears.

"What?"

Abarat clapped him on the shoulder. "You must promise to never use that magic again. Casting illusions of yourself...it is very dangerous, my friend. You must promise."

"I—"

The Hittites attacked, and Tarathiel was never able to complete his promise. Yet the experience of that night stuck with him, even as he survived the sacking of Babylon and the subsequent upheaval. As he traveled north, north into Europe, he remembered the words Abarat had told him. Never use that magic again, he had said, and Tarathiel remembered why. No one should have their soul ripped apart. No one should be six at once. It wasn't natural. It wasn't right.

And so he kept the promise he had not uttered. He did not use mistweaving magic to make a copy of himself. And while he never saw Abarat again, Tarathiel stayed true to his word.

He managed to keep that promise for 1542 years.

THIRTY-NINE

KYTHAELA

"WHAT IF WE could choose which parts of our personality we keep?" Kythaela asked, carrying the tree branch in one hand. "If you could excise a part of yourself, would you do it? Your hate, your despair. Your tendency toward anger. What if you could split them off, like this branch, and watch it burn?"

She cast the branch into the fire.

"What if you could change who you truly were?"

TARATHIEL—2269 YEARS AGO

TARATHIEL HAD FOUND ALLERIA. He had finally found her, after millennia of searching. He'd lost count of his deaths over all that time, of the Trees he'd been. The violet sky of Ambarhal wavered in his mind's eye, an ever-present reminder of his immortality.

He wanted it all to end.

But he could be happy now. Now they could make a new life together, finally free to just be themselves. Yet something gnawed at him, keeping him up at night. Something filtered through his dreams, a dim past he wasn't sure was his.

There was something important he was forgetting.

They were sitting at their dinner table, surveying the remains of their recently finished meal. Tarathiel was still struggling with things as simple as cooking food—he felt out of phase, as if the technology around him didn't match up to his expectations. The ovens, the open flame, the lack of simple utensils or even napkins—it didn't make sense. How did he know about these things if they didn't exist?

He was floundering. He had to get a grip.

"I want to join the Romans," Tarathiel said, sitting back in his wooden chair.

"You've said that before," Alleria said.

"This time I mean it."

"You know how I feel about the Romans. Why the sudden insistence? Why now?"

Tarathiel flexed his fingers, feeling as if something should be between them. "Something's wrong," he said. "Everything feels out of place. I keep getting these…urges."

Alleria narrowed her eyes. "Explain."

"There's something I'm meant to be doing, but I can't figure out what it is."

"And you think fighting with the Romans is it?"

Tarathiel felt anger closing in. She was always like this, always second-guessing him. "I don't *know*, dammit," he said. "I just need to get out of here. I need to *act*."

"Then get outside," Alleria said. "Get some exercise. Help with the farming. Butcher a sheep. You've been cooped up inside with your books for far too long."

"I've tried those things, Alleria," he said. "Nothing works.

I feel as if my life were meant for some great purpose, but I can't figure out what it could possibly be."

Alleria stood, gathering the dishes. "It's magic, isn't it," she said. "You've always been obsessed with it."

Tarathiel absently reached into his pocket, pulling out a piece of prime maple—sycamore, in this part of the world, but it amounted to the same thing. The wood felt warm in his hand as it always did, exuding possibility. He rubbed it between his fingers and thumb, lost for a moment to imagination.

"Tarathiel," Alleria said, her hand suddenly on his shoulder. He jumped back, startled, almost knocking over his chair in his haste to get away. The dishes she was holding clattered to the floor, shards of broken pottery scattering everywhere. "Twins dammit, Tarathiel," Alleria said, "those dishes were *expensive*! What in the world is wrong with you?"

"Sorry," Tarathiel said. She had startled him, was all. He enjoyed her touch—just not when it took him by surprise. "I'll help you clean it up."

"I'll take care of it," she said, her tone cold. "Just get outside. Find something useful to do."

"I want to help," Tarathiel said.

Alleria looked at him for a long moment. "I don't think you do," she said. "You've always been self-centered, but lately you've taken it to the extreme. Half the time I don't even know who you are—one minute you're in my arms, nuzzling my hair, and the next you're rampaging around the house, railing against society. I don't *get* you, Tarathiel. You say we've been together for thousands of years, but *how*? Why?" Her voice dropped to a whisper. "Why would I have been with such a terrible person?"

Tarathiel felt his face heat, his heart drop. He felt hurt, deep hurt suffusing him, but he pushed it aside.

He let anger take its place.

"We loved each other," he hissed, towering over her in the small room.

Alleria looked up at him with something like sadness in her eyes. "You can't tell someone they love you."

He hit her, then.

He hit her in the face. Not hard, or at least he didn't mean it to be. But she reeled from the blow, hair flying as she fell to the floor, shards of sharp pottery digging into her skin. He saw tears flash into her eyes as she went down.

And he felt pain overwhelming him. Not pain in his head —his head felt clear. It wasn't a bodily pain at all, not the kind you can feel.

It was almost like a pain inside his very soul.

"I'm sorry," he tried, but the words echoed off the walls in pieces, broken. Alleria was sprawled on the floor, head down and back facing him, shoulders shaking as she cried.

"What have you become?" she managed.

"I don't know," Tarathiel whispered. "I'm not this person. I just...I just. Don't. Know."

He felt tears coming to him, then. Seeing his wife like that, broken on the floor, seeing the pain he had caused her, knowing that *he* was the reason she was hurting, knowing that *he* was the monster—it was too much.

He imagined the lines of his life, like a building taking shape. Some pieces were murky, distant. But others were near, painted in sharp relief, a blueprint of his soul. The reading, the studying, the kindness he *knew* was still inside. Those things clashed with his anger, his pride, his desire to be in control. Part of him wanted to dance, while another part wanted to kill. Half of him wanted to love Alleria, while the other half wanted to destroy her.

He couldn't handle it anymore.

He needed it to end.

And as the spires of his horrible personality rose in his mind's eye, he felt the maple in his hand flare into life.

Suddenly there were two of him.

FORTY

TARATHIEL2

TARATHIEL2 STARED at the copy of himself. How had this happened? Was this some infernal property of mistweaving magic? Tarathiel hadn't meant to use it—he was just so *emotional*, so fed up with his very existence. He had sought a means to shed himself of every bad trait, everything that had made him such a poor partner to Alleria.

It had worked.

Tarathiel2 could feel his new soul, his half-soul, welling up within him. The desire to build, to design. The desire to slice and pierce and rip. The need to be in control. These were the parts of him that remained, and he instinctively knew that Tarathiel1 had everything else.

Tarathiel2 was the outpouring of everything Tarathiel had hated about himself.

Who was now the better man? A smile spread across his face as he realized the truth. For while Tarathiel1 might now be happy, might even be able to love Alleria again, Tarathiel2 was the strong one.

Now he could finally do great things.

"You," Tarathiel1 said, staring at him with shock from across the room. "You're me."

"Yes," Tarathiel2 said, and he launched himself at his twin.

TARATHIEL1

TARATHIEL1 LIFTED his hands to block the fists of his strange clone, but his movement was uncoordinated, off. Pain burst through his head, shooting into his skull before the other man had even made contact.

Then he felt a fist impact his jaw.

He reeled, seeing sparks, feeling nothing but pain. The room tilted up to meet him as Tarathiel2 continued hitting him, beating him horribly.

"Stop!" Tarathiel1 tried, but his voice came out too weak. "You're hurting me!"

Blows rained down on him, driving him to the floor. As his consciousness began to fade, Tarathiel1 wondered what he had done to deserve this. All he'd wanted, in that one desperate moment, had been to rid himself of his negative aspects. He'd wanted to become a better person.

He'd wanted Alleria to love him again.

But what Tarathiel hadn't counted on was just how dangerous concentrated evil could be.

TARATHIEL2

TARATHIEL2 STOPPED JUST short of killing his twin. He could have done it, but the woman was looking at him with a kind of shock in her eyes. Something about her made him pause, as if rethinking his life's decisions. She was beautiful, he realized as he leered at her. He could bed her right now, take her body as easily as he had taken his twin's.

But there had been something else there when Tarathiel2 had formed. As his body had been created out of magic and illusion, an imperative had been sent. There was a command embedded in the magic, a command that Tarathiel2 could not disobey.

Tarathiel1's final wish was for Tarathiel2 to leave.

So he stood, surveying the scene. Alleria was on the floor, long auburn hair messy around her tear-stricken face. Tarathiel1 was unconscious, bleeding over the crushed pottery and partly-eaten food. And Tarathiel2 was standing above it all, a smile on his face.

He was the strong one now.

He turned and left the house, whistling a little tune. He was finally free. Now he could do anything, *be* anything. Now he would no longer be held back by structure or good behavior.

Now he could be the person he had always wanted to be.

He struck out north, wandering aimlessly, the pathways of his life opening out ahead of him. He needed a name, he realized as he walked, as he breathed the fresh night air. He wasn't Tarathiel, that sad sack of pathetic shit. That name no longer belonged to him. He needed something new, something he could call his own.

He'd always liked the name Quynn.

TREY—PRESENT DAY

TREY STARED AT QUYNN, seeing his blue eyes, his brown hair, the way his nose curved just *so*. The blemish on his cheek that Trey didn't have. The chin that was a different shape. The hard set of the jaw. The determined, villainous streak. The sneer.

Hadn't Allain's twin looked different in just a few short weeks? Hadn't one of them been surly, difficult to talk to, even mean? Hadn't one of them been unable to perform even the simplest mistweaving magic?

Trey's breath came faster as he realized the implications. All of this had been in front of him the entire time.

He was half a Prime Mage.

And so was Quynn. The man had never used forcefinding or transmuting or shockstriking. In their battle in the Prime Forest, Quynn had been able to mergemeld, to shoot through other objects. He was a mindmaster, a power Trey did not have. And he must also be a mistweaver, the final thing Trey could not do.

It made so much sense.

The answer had been staring him in the face.

"You," he breathed as the memories resolved into focus. "You're *me*."

PART
FOUR

A soul, once shattered, finds the shadows creeping in.

— *Fragment of a Remnant ritual story*

FORTY-ONE

ARRA STARED at the two men staring at each other.

Everything had just changed.

"Impossible," she breathed. But fragments of a memory were coming to her now. She remembered bits of pottery, food on the floor. She put a hand to her face as she remembered the sting of being hit.

"I never saw you again," Trey said.

Quynn was backed up against a wall, eyes flashing, chest heaving. "I never *wanted* to see you," he said. "Twins. What happened to us? Why don't we remember?"

"We died," Arra said. "We all did. We became Trees, maybe several times. Ambarhal can really screw with your memories."

"Maybe we used gates, too," Trey said. "Shit, there is so much I can't remember."

"I *thought* you looked familiar," Quynn said. "That day when I found you, looking so pathetic in New Tokyo II. You seemed important, so I took you in."

"You became my father." Trey stepped away.

Quynn's expression was wary. "I needed to find a Prime

Mage. It was some instinctive part of me, some innate desire. And I thought you were the best chance I had."

"You tried it with Phoenix, too," Arra said. "You thought *she* could be a Prime Mage."

Quynn nodded. "I experimented on dozens of people, Phoenix included. I didn't always sleep with them when I did."

"You're a monster," Trey said.

"No," Quynn said, "I'm *you*. I'm the part of you you wanted to hide. And I think, Trey, that by making me come into existence—that makes *you* the monster."

Cresius cleared his throat. "Is there going to be a fight? Do I need to worry about you two?"

Arra watched Trey. He was breathing deeply, staring into his twin's eyes. *This* was why things had felt off between them, she realized. This was why Trey hadn't even remembered the parts she'd remembered: the leering at Lorelei, the anger issues, his tendency to ignore her. He'd been living with *Quynn* inside of him.

But now Quynn was gone.

"We won't fight," Trey said. "Not unless he starts it."

"No guarantees," Quynn said. "I always knew you were a sack of shit, but Twins. I'd never even *imagined* you were me."

"We should probably stop taking the Twins' name in vain," Lashel said.

"Trey," Arra said, "I just realized something: Lorelei."

Trey and Quynn stared at each other for a pregnant second.

Then Quynn burst out laughing. Trey's face was red.

"What?" Lashel asked. "What am I missing?"

"They both slept with Lorelei," Arra said. "It all makes *sense* now. Hell, that woman has been after my husband for *eons*. Of *course* she would find his splinter, too! She's like a spider."

"I fail to see the analogy," Lashel said.

"She's a good lay," Quynn said. "That's about all I care about."

"I thought she was my wife," Trey said, still blushing.

"I'm over it," Arra said. "I think I understand now. So many pieces of the puzzle are finally clicking into place. If you—wait a minute." Her face grew cold.

"What?" Trey asked, responding to her look. He was worried, suddenly, and well he should be.

"You—Quynn—slept with Phoenix. I met her son, Trey. So have you. His name is Rylan."

"Oh, shit," Quynn whispered.

"Trey," Arra said, "*Rylan is your son.*"

RYLAN alighted on a pier at the eastern edge of Ilyrion, Elanil and Imra setting down easily beside him. The Twins were somewhere to the west, destroying building after building in their haste to find this "Imprisoner" they were so interested in. A thick line of refugees was making their way north out of Ilyrion, heading into the Faedori Forest. At least some people had survived—so far.

Rylan was sure the worst was yet to come.

"Now what?" he asked.

The Airon Sea spread out ahead of them as far as the eye could see, glittering in the morning light. Waves lapped gently beneath the pier, and he could see boats bobbing in the water.

The boats themselves were strange: he'd never *seen* a boat before, but he hadn't expected them to look like this. They were wrought in a silvery material, three masts thrusting upward from the hull. But instead of sails, the masts bore massive, glittering leaves, dozens of feet wide. They were made out of the strange metallic substance, too.

"Those aren't sailboats," Elanil said.

"How do you know?" Rylan asked.

"No sails."

That made sense, at least.

"They're leafboats," Imra said. "I've heard of them. They do races with them a few times a year—apparently it's a very popular sport on Valaralda."

"Why are they called leafboats?" Rylan asked.

"Oh!" Elanil said. "I guess you don't need wind when you have *magic*."

Leafrunning magic. Of course. That was how the boats moved. It was an extravagant waste of magic, but what was magic if not extravagant? It must be nice to just have a little fun with it, instead of constantly trying to save the world.

Explosions sounded in the distance, as if responding to his thought.

"They're getting closer," Imra said. "We should leave."

"And go where?" Elanil asked.

More explosions sounded, and they turned just in time to see the buildings bordering the pier collapse, one by one falling to the ground in a cascade of thundering wood and metal. One of the Twins poked his head up, glaring at them. He was easily as tall as the buildings had been.

"You," the Twin said—it was Nelenor, Rylan thought. "Do you know where the Imprisoner is?"

Rylan shared a look with Elanil. The Twins really creeped him out. "No," he called back to Nelenor. "We have no idea what you're talking about!"

"You lie, children," Nelenor said. "You have met the Imprisoner. I can feel his imprint on you."

"What in the Twin's name is he talking about?" Elanil said.

"Shh," Imra said. "Maybe we should stop using their name as a curse."

"Good point. What should we do?"

"Tell me what I want to know," Nelenor said, his voice rolling loudly across the pier.

"Let's take a leafboat," Elanil whispered.

Rylan glanced back at the boat, at its glittering, leafy shape rising above the waves. He was a leafrunner now, after all. He could help propel it.

"We can't outrun them," Imra said.

"Well," Rylan said, "we can at least try."

FORTY-TWO

LARA—NO, Lorelei—was having trouble reconciling memories of her past life. She'd been so many people, but then again so had her sister. It seemed false identities ran in the family. But even Arra and Trey had been other people—many others, by the sound of things. All of them had descended into myth, and all because of a strange technological device from another planet.

Lorelei wished it had never existed to begin with.

She got up from the forest floor, brushing leaves and twigs from her knees. Cara—Cariel—was dead on the ground, her skin cooling. She had had a long and terrible life, but in the end Lorelei had been the stronger one.

No. That wasn't fair. She needed to stop thinking about things that way, always trying to win. She didn't need to *win* anything. She just needed to survive.

She turned, surveying the destroyed Ecological District around her. The Twins were still rampaging over by the Airon Sea—she could hear them yelling for the Imprisoner. It sounded like they were having a conversation with someone.

She ran a hand through her hair, picking more twigs from

it. She felt aimless, alone. She had no friends, and probably never had. Her great castle in the sky—the floating cities on Earth—were gone, taken from her. Her entire *purpose* was gone.

What was she supposed to do?

Had she loved Tarathiel? She'd pushed back when Arra had brought it up, but it was only because the thought rankled. And like all thoughts that worm their way into your brain, that one had an element of truth to it.

She just didn't know.

She was about to pick a direction and just start walking when she heard the unmistakeable sound of a footstep in the forest. She froze, looking in its direction, wishing she had a weapon on her. Arra had taken the knife she'd used to kill Cariel.

Oh. Lorelei almost laughed. She was a Prime Mage now. She had *endless* weapons at her command.

She pulled a piece of light ash from the pouch strapped to her waist, readying a storm.

"I can hear you," she said.

A woman stepped out from behind a tree. She was cute and rather tall, with curly, dark hair and eyes that seemed to hold great mysteries. There was a kind of darkness to her, a darkness that matched her hair.

Lorelei found herself instantly liking her.

"Who are you?" she asked.

"Elasha," the woman said. "I am...was...the head diver on Orym's expedition to Atlantis."

Expedition to *Atlantis*? That was interesting. "You must tell me that story sometime," Lorelei said. "I'm Lorelei."

Elasha stepped closer. "What's happening?" she asked.

Lorelei winced as more explosions rocked the city. "The

Twins are back," she said, "and apparently they really want to destroy Ilyrion."

"They kept calling for someone," Elasha said. "Some kind of...Imprisoner?"

"Yes," Lorelei said. "You mentioned you were on Orym's team?"

Elasha nodded.

"We need to get out of here," Lorelei said. "Come with me. There's something I need to tell you about Orym: he's not who you think he is."

ALLAIN AND ERODAR were wandering in the Thesserin Desert. Allain was still unnaturally tired, owing to his exertions the evening before. Splinterleaping definitely took it out of you, and he'd done a *lot* of that. They'd gotten a few hours of sleep, at least, hidden in the bowels of Memory. The rylak and cavek and Remnant and every other thing that Cariel had brought into the desert seemed harmless now, milling about aimlessly as if lacking direction. Which they were, he knew.

Because Cariel was dead.

So they were safe. And now he was slightly more refreshed. But the desert was hot, and he thought he could hear some kind of muted *booming* sounds coming from the direction of Ilyrion.

"We should splinterleap to the city," Erodar said. "See what's going on."

"It doesn't sound good, whatever it is," Allain said. "Maybe we should go the other way."

Erodar gave him a flat look. "We need to at least see. I *live* there, dammit!"

"Fine!" Allain said. "You win. I'm not sure how far I can splinterleap, though. I'm still pretty tired."

"I'll help," Erodar said. "Let's go."

THEY LIMPED INTO ILYRION, flitting forwards in the air, splinters flying. Allain was carving a little dragon now, its wings taking shape as he flew. He wondered if he'd be any good at architecture, like Erodar was. It would certainly make mistweaving a hell of a lot easier if he could do it in his head.

"Twins," Erodar cursed as they approached the city. "It's gone."

Twins was right. Allain's mouth fell open as they neared Ilyrion and the sheer scope of the destruction became clear.

The city had been torn to shreds.

Most of the buildings had been reduced to rubble. All five Prime Trees that had graced the city skyline were dead, split in half or broken into massive wooden shards. Only one building remained standing in the Ecological District: *Turu-voite*, the combination restaurant and residential building Orym liked to frequent. It towered over the decimated forest, a reminder of the hubris of elves.

They should not have awakened the gods.

"It was Trey," Allain said. "It had to be. That Key he had—Edrafen—it released the Twins."

And there they were, standing near the coast, Anubis heads giving the constant illusion of merriment, of glee. Allain found himself wanting to give them a new expression.

But they were powerful. Far too powerful to fight—that much was readily clear. Even Cariel, in all her might, would have been no match for these two evil beings. Their hatred, their malevolence—it was obvious in their fox-like eyes, in the rampant destruction they had caused.

Allain had no idea why they were so mad.

"Who's that?" Erodar asked, pointing at the ground.

They flitted lower.

"Allain!" someone shouted up at him. Allain blinked, wondering if he was seeing things.

It was Small.

"Ho!" Allain called, settling down to the ground with a flick-flick of his carving knife.

Dill was there, too. "Ho, Allain," he said. "Me and Small were just watching the end of the world."

"Looks like it was quite the show," Allain said. But then he stumbled, weariness crashing into him once more.

"We all need rest," Dill said, stepping forward to catch him before he fell. "Come on, we'll find somewhere to sleep. We're underkids—well, some of us are, anyway. This is what we're good at."

Allain hobbled off on Dill's arm, grateful for the help. Hopefully the world wouldn't end while he was asleep.

FORTY-THREE

ELANIL HAD ALWAYS LIKED SAILING. Her father had taken her out a few times when she was younger, saying he liked the smell of sea salt in his hair. Silanar had been a very good sailor.

She missed him.

Elanil had picked up what she could, but since then she'd forgotten much of what he'd taught her. Luckily, this leafboat required none of those skills.

This boat required *magic*.

Leafrunning was her strength. It was her specialty. It was the thing Arra had always been jealous of, but now it was the thing that was possibly saving her life. She'd always known that leafrunning was the greatest thing in the world.

Now she had proof.

She was just so happy to be here, so happy to be free from those infernal purple skies. Happy to be back amongst the living, back using magic. Even if the world was coming to an end around them, even if they were fleeing from a dark and terrible foe, at least she had her life. At least she was free. At least she had *him*.

She grinned at Rylan, caught up in the moment, loving how the wind whipped his hair around as they flew across the waves. He had a look of concentration on his face, lips slightly parted as he burned elm chip after elm chip, lending his strength to their motion. She fought off a sudden urge to kiss him. He was cute, standing there. It almost seemed as if he'd finally found his purpose.

"Wind!" she shouted at him, and he turned.

"What?"

"We should call you Wind!"

"That's no undername I've ever heard of," he said, the boat slowing a bit as his concentration lessened.

Elanil Willed more magic into it, making up the slack. "It's not an undername, silly," she said. "It's a primename!"

He looked confused for a moment. "That's not a thing."

"Neither were Prime Mages, until recently. If we're the super heroes of this world, shouldn't we all have names?"

A small smile crept over his lips. "You could be Dance," he said. "It's what you're good at."

"Wind and Dance," Elanil said. "I like it!"

"Guys?" Imra called from her position on the bow. "Do we have any idea where we're going?"

TREY HAD A SON.

Well, *he* didn't have a son—his strange, evil twin did. Quynn, the violent, stern, lustful version of himself, the man who'd claimed to be Trey's father—he had slept around.

And now he had a son.

"Has this ever happened before?" Trey asked. "I—I don't know what to say or think."

Everyone looked at Cresius.

The Director of the Department of Magical Research gave a deep sigh, picking his purple robes up as he settled into his chair. "We tried to keep the knowledge of soulsplinters away from the general public," he said.

"Wait—you *knew* about this?" Arra asked.

Cresius nodded. "Truth be told, we use it in our drills. All our troops are trained to splinter into six and then reintegrate at a moment's notice."

"But that's a myth!" Lashel said. "Formations like that are literally in the ancient story books we're taught as children."

"Not a myth," Cresius said. "We just wanted to make it seem that way. In truth, it's a very useful tool—when the mages are properly trained. Accidental splintering is too common."

"Apparently," Trey muttered.

"As to whether a child has ever resulted from just one splinter before—I'm sure it's happened, though we have no record of such a thing. Frankly, I'm not sure what it means, exactly. You *are* the same person, and yet you are not. Should you choose to reintegrate, you would in fact become one. You would be Rylan's father. Is it not safe to say that you are both the father, even before a reintegration?"

Quynn was glowering at the desk, feet dragging on the floor as he sat. "I will *never* be him," he said. "Never."

Trey looked at him askance. "I don't want his personality in my head. Even if I'm a bit boring as a result. Even if there are things I can't do."

"Even though you are only half a Prime Mage?" Arra asked.

"Even with that," Trey said. "There was a *reason* I split myself in the first place. My two sides were never very well integrated, even when I was just one person." He stared at Quynn from across the table. "*He* was always stronger."

Quynn met his eyes at that, and some kind of unspoken communication passed between them. Hatred, Trey thought. Mutual hatred.

Or was it fear?

"Very well," Cresius said. "If you two will not reintegrate, I propose we take Quynn as a prisoner."

"Agreed," Trey said.

"No!" Quynn said.

"We have to," Arra said. "You're untrustworthy. Violent. You're a proven menace. We can't just let you go, *especially* now that we know who you really are." She leaned toward him, peering into his eyes. Quynn met her gaze awkwardly, muscles clenching in his jaw. "I know my Tarathiel," she said. "This side of him is truly dangerous."

"I'm so sorry," Trey whispered.

"Then it's settled," Cresius said.

Quynn bolted for the door.

But Arra was there to stop him yet again. She was so strong. Trey wondered if her strength had grown without his darker side holding her back.

She grappled with him for a moment, but this time she quickly got the upper hand. Quynn seemed disillusioned, stunned, moving as if everything in his life had just changed.

Which, Trey knew, it had.

Arra got him back to the table, slamming him into his chair with a glare on her face. Then she kept her hand on his shoulder, a warning should he try to escape again.

"Very nice," Cresius said. "You elves from Mar are harder than we are here. You will be invaluable in the coming war."

"I can't kill the Twins," Arra said.

"Nobody is asking you to. But we all will need to do our part."

"Listen," Quynn said suddenly, "I'm not going to hurt anyone."

"I don't believe that for a *second*," Trey said. "You've done nothing but harm people for your entire existence."

Quynn almost looked hurt at that. He opened his mouth as if trying to think of something to say. It took him a moment before he did. "You never met Phoenix, did you, Trey."

Trey shook his head. "I've heard a lot about her, but I never had the pleasure of knowing her. If she was Rylan's mother, she must have really been something."

Quynn looked down at the table, his voice growing quiet. "She was."

Arra must have sensed the change in mood. She took the seat next to Quynn, staying near enough to catch him if he tried to run again.

Quynn looked up at her. "You knew Phoenix." Arra nodded. "She was fierce. Not unlike you. She was fierce in every way: fierce in battle, fierce in love, fierce in loyalty. She was loyal to that girl of hers—Beam—in a way I'd never seen before. Still haven't. When Beam betrayed her with Queen—something I'm not proud to have had a minor role in, since I taught Queen everything she knew—it *destroyed* her. It unmade her. And only one person was there to help her pick up the pieces. To hold her. To tell her what she needed to hear. To just be there for her in her darkest moment."

Arra was studying him critically, eyes flicking back and forth as she watched his face.

"I pretended to be a man named Eric," Quynn said. "I did it because I wanted to feel what it was like to be someone—something—else. What it might be like to love. What it would be like to think of someone besides myself. I think Phoenix might have felt something for me, in that moment. We had a connection." He was still looking at Arra. "I'm not sure I've ever had anything like it before."

Arra's eyes were soft. "You did with me."

"I don't hate life," Quynn said. "And I don't hate you or Trey. I don't even hate the elves."

"You killed *so many* of us," Arra said.

Quynn hung his head again. "It's like a war going on inside me every single day. Can you imagine what it must be like? To have every ounce of goodness, of creativity, of happiness stripped away from you in one fatal moment—to feel nothing but anger and hatred and the desire to destroy? I sowed chaos. I committed horrible acts. I lied. A lot. And out of all of that, in all that time I spent as half of me, I only ever had that one moment of love. For one brief interlude, Phoenix showed me that life could be something more than ambition and pain.

"And then the moment was over."

Trey cleared his throat. "I can't believe you got through that speech without a headache."

Quynn turned to him, his face stolid. "I've never been in so much pain before in all my life."

The room was silent for a long moment.

"Quynn can stay," Trey said, "and not as a prisoner. He will be a full member of this...team, or whatever we're doing here. If he wishes, he can help us fight the Twins."

Quynn dipped his head in acknowledgement. "I will do my part. We each have our strengths—let me use mine."

Arra put a hand on his arm. "Never bring us harm," she said. "I'll be watching you."

"And I you," Quynn said, and for one brief moment Trey could swear that she was turned on.

Cresius clapped his hands together, breaking the tension. "Well done, all of you," he said. "Now that we're best friends, we have a fight to plan. Out of curiosity, where are all your other friends? There were a lot of you at Memory."

"That's a good question," Trey said. "I wonder where my son is, right now." He glanced guiltily at Arra. "*That* was the strangest thing I've said all day."

"I DON'T *KNOW* where we're going," Rylan said. They were skimming quickly across the waves—he had added a bit of fallfoiling, lifting them slightly out of the water to increase their speed. It took less energy than outright flight, at least. Now they were going *fast*.

"We should turn around," Imra said. "Go back to Ilyrion."

"The Twins are back there," Rylan said. "And besides, do you see this overcast sky? I don't even know where the sun is right now. How can we turn around?"

"Does anyone have a compass?" Imra asked.

"A what?"

"Never mind." She stared out at the ocean ahead, obviously frustrated. "We might be stuck out here. And we didn't even think to bring any food."

"We can transmute water," Elanil said.

"Oh." Imra stared at her for a second. "I'd completely forgotten about that."

"I vote we keep going," Rylan said. "Elanil, can you act as lookout? Maybe fly above us and scan in every direction? There must be *something* out there, maybe an island."

"Sure," Elanil said, and she shot skyward with a smile on her face.

"Damn Prime Mages," Imra muttered, going back to her position at the bow.

It only took a few minutes for Elanil to return.

"There's an island up ahead," she said, setting down lightly on the deck, her legs dipping in a little plié. Rylan couldn't help but smile at her.

"Well, that's convenient," Imra said.

"How far?" Rylan asked.

"Should be visible in a few minutes," Elanil said. She pulled out more wood, and the boat moved faster across the waves.

Ten minutes later, there it was. Just a dot, at first, but the dot grew and grew until it was large enough to make out a few details.

"That's...interesting," Imra said. "Are you guys seeing what I'm seeing?"

"I think so," Rylan said, feeling lightprime power flowing through his fingers as the boat continued to sail on winds of magic. "But I'm not sure if I believe it."

"Are those palm trees?" Elanil asked.

They looked like palm trees. He'd seen ones like them before—New San Francisco actually had two of them on New Embarcadero, looking cold and out of place. He'd never understood why they were there.

"How far did we travel, anyway?" Imra asked. "That looks like a tropical island."

"It's hard to tell," Rylan said. "I've never sailed one of these things before."

"Well, those are definitely palm trees," Imra said. "But either that island is really, really tiny, or the trees are really, really big."

"They're Prime Trees," Elanil said.

"But that's—"

"Impossible?" Elanil asked.

Imra nodded. "Palm is not a type of Prime Tree."

"Maybe it's just that no one has ever seen one before. Shouldn't *all* types of trees be eligible for Prime Trees?"

"I don't know," Imra said. "I don't really know how it works."

"Guys," Rylan said, "why are the Trees on fire?"

FORTY-FOUR

"FRIENDS," Cresius said, "we need a plan."

Arra sipped the coffee she had been given, wincing at the bitter taste. She hadn't drank coffee very often in Sylrantheas. Right now, she would have preferred beer. "You're the Department of Magical Research," she said. "You're telling us you don't have a plan?"

"We didn't *entirely* expect the Twins themselves to be unleashed on us. Like most people, we thought them to be religious myth."

"Entirely?" Trey asked.

"In truth, some of us did predict this."

"Let me guess," Trey said, "those people were ostracized, their programs defunded."

Cresius spread his hands out on the table in front of him. "Some of them were, yes. However: in recent years the Believers have been gaining ground. As Research Director, I thought it prudent to at least understand why. Could there be some element of truth to their belief?"

The Believers—or the Devout, depending on who you

asked—had attacked them in the desert. Arra wasn't sure anything about them should be believed.

"As it turns out," Cresius said, "the Believers were right."

"Weren't they originally pacifists?" Trey asked.

Cresius nodded. "Not so much of late, but yes. In fact the Believers taught that the Twins' righteous wrath would encompass all violence in the world—and that by performing violence themselves, the Believers would be diminishing their great return."

"That's fucked up," Quynn said.

"And almost certainly untrue. But you have to admit that even there, we see an element of truth. The Twins do seem to be here to enact revenge. On something."

"The Imprisoner," Trey said.

"We know exactly *what* they're referring to," Cresius said, "just not *who*. Which makes me wonder: if we could find out who this individual is—and if he or she is still alive—would turning them in stop this violence?"

"The Imprisoner must be alive," Arra said. "Didn't the Twins say they could *feel* them?"

"It's the soul connections," Cresius said. "We've been studying them for millennia, but we never seem to crack it. Somehow the true nature of it all eludes us. All we know is that there are strands connecting many, many souls—not just people, but plants, insects, animals. We *suspect* the soul-strands are somehow what enable magic to exist. But we can't prove it. Some are more attuned than others."

Arra took another sip of coffee. "How does this attune-ment help?"

"We believe mages of sufficiently high attunement—soul sensitivity, in other words—would be capable of greater feats of magic. Witness Cariel: most mages cannot do the things she did."

"Soulbinding," Trey said.

"That and other things. Shaped forcefields. Rapid Aspect switching. Simultaneous gates from multiple Aspects. These things are far out of reach for most mages. I should know—I train mages for a living."

"Aspect switching?" Arra asked.

Cresius nodded. "We covered soulsplintering already." He glanced at Quynn. "Now, when you splinter, your Aspects split. That's why Trey and Quynn here can't do each other's magic."

"Makes sense," Arra said.

"Now pretend you splinter yourself six ways—which is the maximum, because the soul only has six Aspects."

"But the seventh—"

"The seventh is a part of all of them," Cresius said. "It becomes diluted as you splinter further, but it is still present."

"Explaining why both Trey and Quynn can make gates."

"Correct. So pretend you've splintered yourself six ways. Now you've moved your various Aspects to several physical locations, maybe far removed from each other."

"Like Cariel did with herself and her Magona counterparts."

"Yes. Each splinter would only have one power available to them, right?"

Realization was beginning to dawn. "Cariel used multiple powers against us," Arra said. "Even Magona did, back on Earth when that volcano was exploding. Oh. I just realized what we saw, back then: one of Magona's splinters was coming to report."

"Not unusual," Cresius said, "assuming you want to remain splintered. The act of splintering requires enormous energy, and while you are splintered, your memories remain distinct, separate from each other. If Magona had reintegrated her splinter, she would have instantly obtained those memories."

"But she didn't want to do that."

"I would assume that's true. But back to the subject at hand: what if you were to change which splinter was using which Aspect?"

"Interesting," Quynn said.

"Can you do that?" Arra asked.

"Only highly attuned mages can, and then only after a *great* deal of practice, but yes. You can dynamically trade Aspects across splinters without reintegrating them."

Trey was staring at Quynn. "That's what happened to us," he said. "For a brief moment, when I was facing Cariel, I had mindmaster and mergemelding powers. It felt as if the Talent had come from a million miles away. Which…it had."

"I was on Eryn at the time," Quynn said. "I remember feeling something strange, as if part of my essence had left. This is crazy."

"You must have performed a partial Aspect switch," Cresius said. "I only have a handful of mages who can do that —our most elite. If you can practice that, hone it to perfection, you could be nearly unstoppable."

"Cariel nearly was," Arra said.

"So where does that leave us?" Trey asked. "We know the Twins are real, that they are vengeful gods. We know this weapon—Guruthos—is in fact the source of their power. Right?"

"That seems to be the case," Cresius said.

"So what do we do? How do we defeat them?" He clutched his head, suddenly.

"What's wrong?" Arra asked.

"I always get these headaches when I try to do something Quynn would normally have done," Trey said. "Building.

Destroying. Leading. Those are his Aspects, not mine. But this headache—this headache feels *different*."

"You were in contact with Edrafen," Cresius observed.

"Yes."

"They spoke to you during that time, did they not?"

"They did. I didn't know it was the Twins at the time, but yes. It was like something was gnawing at my soul, corrupting me. Shit. That's what this is."

"What?" Arra asked.

"I'm still connected to them. I can feel it now. Hell—I can *see* it. There's a little soulstrand still connecting me to them."

"That confirms it," Cresius said. "You are highly attuned. Only those individuals can actually *visualize* soulstrands. Let's just hope this one doesn't draw their interest."

"We can't defeat them," Lashel said. "They control *magic*, and what do we have?"

"Actually," Cresius said, "we have quite a lot. It's time I showed you."

FORTY-FIVE

THE WORLD WAS BURNING. Why was the world burning? The woman looked up at the hazy sky, at the violet light that even now shone down upon her. Life for her had been a blur. She was disconnected, forever roaming this strange place without a Tree, without a strand, without anything tying her down.

YOU HAVE TAKEN THE PATH OF SELF, the dark Tree on the hill had said. **YOUR ALLEGIANCE IS ONLY TO ONE**.

Herself.

Even now she remembered it, how it had felt. The shock of breaking through, her soul instantly connecting to the great machine. No Tree. No wood. Her own soul had done it, had somehow torn its way through the cosmos, linking up with the sky.

She was magic now.

The spear of light had left her, then, transporting her here to the land of violet skies. And she'd left something in her place, she remembered. A ghostly Tree, towering over everything, a reminder of what she'd done. Who she'd lost. Who she'd saved.

And so she had wandered this strange world, sometimes communing with the Trees on the hill, sometimes content to sit and think. Her thoughts flowed lazily in this place, her aims unclear. She had had a life, once, but she could no longer remember what it was.

She had learned things, though. Other souls passed through this place, and sometimes they would speak.

Once, she was sure she'd spotted Magona.

But then the Twins had disappeared. Their Trees had flashed away, leaving nothing but a barren hillside amidst the purple sky. At first she'd thought to panic, but nothing else untoward happened. So she'd settled down, sitting on the strange, flat grass and waiting to see if they would return.

She had waited for what seemed like an eternity, lost to the here and now. But eventually, as all things do, her time had come to an end.

That was when the Trees had started burning.

The Twins were gone, but the other Trees were there. Thousands of them, stretching to the horizon, each one linking a soul with the mortal plane. Each Tree in this place had its counterpart somewhere else, somewhere living beings could see. And with the Twins gone, it seemed that there was nothing left to hold them there.

The Trees were dying.

And so she stepped, staring into the flames, watching embers surge and wood crack, seeing in the fire remembrances of her past. Of her brother. Of her son. Of the life she had—until this moment—forgotten all about.

The flames roared higher, and she stepped through them.

The purple sky parted, and the sun shone through, and

ash and flames surrounded her as her feet stepped onto *real* grass, real dirt, as she felt a sultry breeze caress her face.

She entered the world once more, like a Phoenix from the ashes of a life now saved.

FORTY-SIX

THE PALM TREES really were on fire. Flames shot up toward the heavens as Rylan and the others approached, the leafboat sliding effortlessly through the water.

And were there *people* emerging from the Trees?

"This might be dangerous," Imra said.

"There must be magic at work, here," Elanil said. "Those are Prime Trees, and that fire doesn't look natural."

She was right. The Trees weren't burning like real wood should—they had the appearance of being in flames, but they seemed normal, healthy, not blackened or falling apart.

"Definitely magic," Rylan said. "Let's land this thing. We need to see what's going on. Maybe whatever this is can help us, somehow."

"I don't like it," Imra said, "but I agree—we should at least investigate. But guys, if anything goes wrong, you *will* get me out of there, right?" She was staring at Elanil.

"Of course!" Elanil said. "You're my sister's best friend, and my friend, too! I would never let anything happen to you."

"Thanks," Imra said. "Now, how do we land this—"

The leafboat hit the shore hard, knocking all of them off their feet.

"Well," Imra said, standing painfully, "I guess that's one way to do it."

ELANIL HOPPED out of the leafboat, using a little bit of fallfoiling to drop the long distance to the ground. The ship had landed at an angle, driving up into the sand with great force. It didn't look damaged, though. Whatever metallic material it was made out of seemed strong. Good—they would need this ship if they ever wanted to make it off this strange island.

Actually, wait. Why had they taken the ship at all? They were Prime Mages now. They could have simply flown. She shook her head, trying to clear it.

This Prime Mage stuff was confusing.

Rylan hopped down beside her, lifting his hand to beckon Imra out. She jumped, and Rylan caught her with a bit of magic. Then they were all standing on the beach, staring out at the burning Palm Trees.

It was not the strangest thing Elanil had ever seen.

Not by a long shot. Not after traversing Ambarhal, after flying around Cariel's great Palace of Memory. Not after her experiences at Fennas Elenathon. No, a cluster of burning Trees didn't rank very highly on the list of strange and unusual things in Elanil's life.

But Rylan was standing stock still, face white with shock. He was staring at something, and Elanil followed his gaze.

People were indeed appearing ahead of them.

They were emerging out of nowhere, out of mist, out of the flames surrounding the Trees. It was almost as if their souls were gathering, unlocked from a place far beyond. And with a sinking feeling in her stomach, Elanil realized exactly what was going on.

The Twins had been released.

Which meant Ambarhal could no longer hold its souls.

One of them was nearing, a woman striding toward them in the sand. She had flowing, brown hair and flashing dark eyes, and she carried herself with a certain air of danger. She was slim, and looked to be about Arra's age.

She was beautiful.

This was who Rylan was staring at, his mouth held open, eyes wide with shock. Elanil had no idea what would cause him to react that way.

"*Mom*?" Rylan said, and everything started clicking into place.

FORTY-SEVEN

CRESIUS TOOK them out of the conference room, down a hall, through a door, and into an elevator.

The elevator went down a long way.

"Where are we going?" Arra asked. She was leery of being trapped underground with a man she barely knew. And Quynn. And Trey. She was surrounded by men, and she was not convinced that they all had her best interests at heart.

"It will all become clear in a moment," Cresius said, and the elevator dinged.

The doors opened on the most incredible scene.

It was a forest underground. Huge trees—a few of them Prime—filled most of the space before them, hundreds and hundreds of feet high and at least a mile deep. The forest was densely filled with vegetation, bushes and flowers and ferns filling up the gaps between the trees. She saw birds flitting around in the air, chipmunks and other animals she didn't recognize climbing along the branches.

Three Prime Trees towered over everything, their crowns touching the ceiling of the vast chamber. Oak, maple, and ash were there, looking for all the world like the gods of the place.

But Arra knew that they were not gods—the real gods were outside, wreaking havoc.

Out around the forest, buildings grew. She saw skyscrapers—underground!—lining the edges of the forest. Some were straight, like those on Earth, while others were sinuous and curved, flowing in and around the vegetation like the buildings did in Ilyrion. *Had* done, Arra realized—now most of them were likely destroyed.

Electronics lined the outer walls of the chamber, glowing lights and viewscreens and wires and racks of equipment filling up every available space. The whole thing was an interesting amalgamation of nature, city, and technology. She wasn't sure what it was all for.

She wasn't sure, that is, until the mages came into view.

"Welcome," Cresius said, "to the Army of Mages."

Elves were suddenly everywhere. They descended from the ceiling, they crept out of hiding places in the forest, they strode in from doorways in the walls. Many emerged from underground, pulling aside carefully-hidden passageways that left no trace once they were closed. Soon there were hundreds of them climbing and flying and practicing with weapons of all kinds. And the mages just kept coming, flowing into the chamber from all sides.

"Three thousand of the best mages Valaralda has to offer," Cresius said. "They apply here by the tens of thousands, hoping to gain entrance to this, the best magical training facilities on the planet."

"That Senate bill," Trey said. "The one we gave away in order to pass the Sending. It defunded the Anthropological Society. It gave *you* those funds."

"I meant to thank you for that," Cresius said.

Trey just glared.

"Are any of them Prime Mages?" Arra asked.

"No. We thought Prime Mages to be a myth—until you showed up, at least. Now we know they've been hiding among us."

"Cariel's group."

"Indeed. And who knows—there may yet be more. I fear this game has been played across timescales no one ever anticipated, and no one knows how it will end. Now, come with me—there's something else I want to show you."

"This wasn't it?" Arra asked. The scale of this facility—it boggled explanation. The sheer amount of *money* it must have cost…

"Not all," Cresius said. "Come."

He shepherded them out of the room and back into the elevator, where he pressed another button.

The elevator started moving sideways.

"What—" Arra started.

"You don't have elevators like this where you come from?"

Arra frowned. "We don't have elevators at all."

Cresius laughed.

"They do where *I'm* from," Quynn said. "And none of them move sideways."

"It's nothing to be afraid of, I assure you," Cresius said.

The elevator dinged, and they got out.

The room they found themselves in was smaller than the first, but it was still large by any other standard. And it was *very* strange.

No forests or buildings filled this room. The chamber was black and dimly lit, with sharp, flat edges that went back further than she could see. She couldn't see the floor, either—they were standing on a ledge overlooking the room, and the room itself was much deeper than she'd expected.

In the center of the room was a series of floating cubes.

They were black as well, lit softly by lights she couldn't

see. Dozens of them were arrayed throughout the three dimensional space ahead of her, each cube positioned at a slightly different height and distance away from each other. Some of them moved slightly, bobbing in the air or sliding back and forth from place to place.

"What the fuck?" Quynn said.

"My thoughts exactly," Trey said.

"Glad to know you two can agree on something," Arra said. "What *is* this place?"

"Advanced training," Lashel said. "Or something like that. Am I right?"

"Right on the money," Cresius said. "This is where the Elite Corps of Magicians train. They don't have sessions today, but you can imagine what it must be like."

"I'm not sure I can imagine it at all," Arra said.

"The Elite train on advanced techniques: soulsplintering, Aspect switching—for those that can—pair magic, soulcircles, Aspect circles—you get the idea."

"Aspect circles?"

"Take fourteen mages and have them all splinter six ways. Then take those splinters and circle them by Aspect. Now you have six full soulcircles, one for each power."

"I thought none of them were Prime Mages?" Arra asked.

"Good catch," Cresius said. "In fact, much of what we do here is theoretical. If the Elite were somehow to *become* Prime Mages...they'd be a force to be reckoned with. As it stands now, none of those six soulcircles would actually work."

"Because only one of the six splinters would have any Talent."

"Correct. We modeled our training off the ancient books written just after the Awakening. Prime Mages did exist back then, and many of them invented techniques similar to these —and wrote them down."

"Everyone thinks they're just stories," Lashel said.

"They are just stories now. But once you get some Prime Mages into the mix…"

"We're not killing anyone," Trey said.

"Of course not," Cresius said. "But I happen to have a little bit of a theory about something."

"Don't keep it to yourself," Lashel said.

"If the Twins really have been released, what's keeping all the mages locked away in Ambarhal?"

IT *WAS* HIS MOM. Phoenix was striding forward, a bewildered look on her face, smoke trailing from her shoes. But it was her. She was really there.

She was *alive*.

Rylan couldn't help himself. He ran forward, arms outstretched, and grabbed her around the waist. "Mom," he said into her shirt, "I missed you so much."

She put her hands on his back as if trying to remember who he was. He pulled away, looking at her. Hadn't she been taller, before? Oh—no. It was he who had grown. Was still growing, in fact. Soon he'd tower over her, but now they were of equal height, face to face on this strange burning island with Palm Trees a thousand feet high.

Her look softened as she gazed at him, and he saw recognition finally dawn.

"Rylan!" she said, putting her hands on his face. "Oh, my son, my boy. You're here! You're really here! You're so much *older*!"

Tears were coming to Rylan's eyes. And even though underkids never cried, he let them come. He needed this.

He needed his mother back.

"How are you here?" he asked after a moment.

"I—I'm not sure," Phoenix said, still holding him. "I remember dying, but it was like my soul shot out from me, instantly connecting with…something."

"The Twins," Imra said. She was standing beside them, staring at Phoenix with an awed look on her face. "The source of magic."

"I don't think it was the Twins," Phoenix said. "I spoke with them many times while I was in their world. They aren't the *source* of magic—they merely control it. And by doing what I had done—by killing myself using magic—I had somehow bypassed them, connecting myself directly to whatever it was that they are using to do all of this."

"To *do* all of this?" Rylan asked. "I don't understand. It's magic!"

"No," Phoenix said. "I don't think it's magic at all. Who's this?"

Elanil had finally approached.

Rylan extracted himself, feeling suddenly protective of the girl. "This is Elanil," he said, putting a hand on the small of her back. "My…friend."

Elanil gave him a look that was halfway between love and embarrassment. He felt his face reddening.

"I see," Phoenix said, a smile growing on her face. "How long has it been? How long was I dead?"

"Five years," Rylan said.

"So you're…"

"Fifteen."

Phoenix's smile got wider. "Only fifteen, and already with

a girlfriend. It's nice to meet you, Elanil. I'm Phoenix." She gave a little bow.

Elanil blushed. "Nice to meet you, Phoenix."

"Hey, Mom?" Rylan said. "Who are all those people behind you?"

Forms were emerging from the burning palm Trees, people who were barefoot and seemingly confused. Dozens of them—no, *hundreds*—were heading to the beach even as Rylan stood there watching.

Phoenix turned to look, watching for a long moment. "Wait," she said, "I *know* these people. I was with them in Ambarhal. These are all the mages who had died. All of them are Prime Mages. Like I am now."

"You don't seem confused about all this," Rylan said. "You already know you're a Prime Mage. You know what Ambarhal is, how it works. How?"

Phoenix pursed her lips. "Guruthos," she said. "The device behind all this. I was *connected* to it, remember? It taught me, in its way."

"What way was that?"

She made a motion as if brushing him aside, turning away to watch the mages stepping out onto the beach. "What matters now is them. These mages. These fierce fighters. Here they are, ready to rain down justice on an unjust world."

"You don't sound like my mom," Rylan said, and she turned to look at him.

When Phoenix met his eyes, he saw worlds whirling inside them. Darkness and light, purple and gold, an amalgamation of destruction and creation, blizzards of brightness and eons of night. The sheer power contained within her...it almost took his breath away. She could level kingdoms. She could raze souls.

And she wasn't even the most powerful being on this planet.

"I am who I am," she said, her voice low, and Rylan felt a shiver travel through him.

Ambarhal had changed her.

It had changed them all.

He wasn't sure he liked who any of them had become.

"But who *are* they?" Imra asked.

Phoenix turned to her. "Every Talented person who was killed to make a Prime Tree—light and dark. Everyone who died in service to this horrible *magic*. Across all of time. Across one hundred thousand years. They're *all* here. They've all been released.

"The Prime Mages have finally returned."

FORTY-EIGHT

ELANIL WATCHED the Prime Mages come, stepping silently along the beach, somber expressions on their faces. Their initial confusion seemed to be fading as they beheld the light of Valaralda, as they breathed the salt-fresh scent of the Airon Sea.

Her mother was not among them.

Melenora had died—*truly* died—in Ambarhal. Elanil had been there. She had witnessed it. Even now she felt a tear trickle down her cheek as she remembered it. The Tree had consumed her. Forever.

She would never see her mother again.

But she was so happy for Rylan. Elanil had never met Phoenix, but Rylan had always spoken of her with love, with sadness, with great longing and respect. Dill had spoken of her, too. She was almost a mythical figure, one of the most powerful mages ever to exist.

Now here she was.

And she was *gorgeous*.

"Where are we?" Phoenix asked.

Imra was fiddling with a little card in her hand.

"Tanomar," she announced. "Arra gave me this guidecard when we arrived—I'd almost forgotten I had it. This island is called Tanomar, and it's bigger than it looks. A long time ago, the elves found natural sugarcane here. It started a culinary revolution."

"And now?" Elanil asked.

Imra surveyed their surroundings. "Now we'll have to explore. Nobody visits here anymore."

"It looks hospitable enough," Elanil said. "And if not, we do have two Prime Mages on staff."

"Three," Phoenix said. "Wait. Actually, we have *hundreds* of them."

They watched the approaching mages for another minute. None of them had said anything, yet. They were marching solemnly, almost religiously, as if they knew their lives had been meant for a great purpose.

"That's a *lot* of mages," Elanil said. "But without prime-wood, they're useless."

"Wait a minute," Rylan said. "The fires stopped."

Imra frowned. "Those Prime Palms…they're still here."

"I wonder…" Elanil said.

"Primewood," Rylan said. "It must be. Those Palm Trees must be a new source of power for us."

"Well let's get to it, then," Imra said. "Come on."

They trekked off the beach, hundreds of silent Prime Mages following them deeper into the island.

"WHY DID YOU DO IT?" Rylan asked. "Why did you die?"

They had found a tree that wasn't a palm, and wasn't a Prime Tree. It was just normal, with normal branches. Rylan wasn't sure what kind of tree it was. He and Phoenix were sitting on one of branches, feet swinging off the edge. Prime Mages milled about below, looking for food or materials or fresh water sources. Imra had taken charge of them, breaking them into groups and speaking to them quietly. She had taken to it quite naturally.

"I did what had to be done," Phoenix said. "I had to save the world."

Rylan moved closer to her, wanting her touch. It was still strange having her here, after all this time. A small part of him was angry at her for dying, but a larger part was just so happy she was back. She was real! He had a mother again! It felt as good as that Coke she'd given him on their last day together in the Under. Better.

He wiped a tear from his eye and snuggled against her on the branch.

"Would that volcano really have destroyed the world?" Rylan asked.

"Orym said it would have," Phoenix said. "Where is he, anyway?"

"No idea," Rylan said. "I haven't seen him since we left Earth."

"Did he at least end up being helpful?"

"Very. He's the one who made us fall out of the city. It's why we met the elves."

"Wait—you *fell* out of the city?"

"Blew up an entire room. Fell right off the bottom of the Edge."

Phoenix shivered at that. "I was under the Edge, once. It's not something I particularly recommend."

Rylan had never heard that story before. "The Remnant attacked us after that. Elanil and I almost burned down a building trying to get a few of them."

"Again? I thought we'd taken care of the People." She shivered again. "I know I killed enough of them."

"Some of them were nice, though. Jalnab was one. He took the elves somewhere else, to something called the Splinter."

"Jalnab always was different," Phoenix said. "Which reminds me. Whatever happened to—" She choked, as if she couldn't get the words out.

But Rylan had an idea what she was about to say.

"Beam." He let the word drop from his tongue. It tasted bitter.

"I miss her," Phoenix said.

"She left."

"What?"

"She left me, after you died. She ran away. She stayed on the surface, disappeared. I had to go back with Dill, and *he* kicked me out of the Crew. I almost starved to death, Mom, many times. If it weren't for a girl I met, I would have. Con. Now she's dead." Tears were threatening to come again, but he willed them away. "I hate Beam," he whispered.

Phoenix put her arm around him. "I had no idea she would do something like that. Beam was always hard— harder than me, anyway. I think she had trouble opening up to people, to her own feelings. She didn't go through the journey I did." Rylan felt her shiver. "But to just abandon her son..."

"I'm *not* her son," Rylan said, feeling anger driving through him.

"No," Phoenix said softly. "No, I suppose not. Well, I'm here now. And if I ever see Beam again, she might not survive the encounter." There was an edge to her tone that frightened Rylan.

"Please don't leave me again," Rylan said. "Don't die."

"I promise," Phoenix said. "I'll do my best to avoid using magic, or at least keep it to a minimum. Though I think it will take much more to soulburn me a second time—I feel my power reserves have grown considerably."

"You're a Prime Mage now. And so am I."

"Wait," Phoenix said. "*You're* a Prime Mage?"

Rylan nodded. "So is Elanil. And Arra, and Trey—or at least half of one. And Lorelei."

"I only recognize Arra from that list," Phoenix said. "When I last knew her, she was not a mage at all."

"She awakened," Rylan said. "Some kind of block lifted inside her. And it turns out she's actually twenty thousand years old."

"Wow," Phoenix said. "How is that possible?"

"I haven't even told you about the Under," Rylan said. "It's all connected now—all seven cities. All the underkids have banded together, living and working together."

"Wait—did you just say *seven* cities?"

Rylan laughed. "We have so much to catch up on."

Phoenix squeezed him. "And all the time in the world."

The darkness in her eyes was gone.

"Well," Rylan said, "we may not actually have that much time."

"Why?"

"Remember the Twins?"

"The...elven religion?"

"Yes. Well, they're real. And I'm pretty sure they're about to destroy the entire planet."

FORTY-NINE

RYLAN SPOKE with Phoenix for some time, doing his best to fill her in on everything that had happened. Her expression grew more sour by the minute, but she didn't interrupt. She didn't question him. It almost seemed as if she had expected something like this.

She'd fought a god and a volcano. She'd been connected to the source of magic itself.

It took a lot to surprise her.

When they were done, Elanil approached from down below. "They found fresh water!" she called. "There's a spring inland, feeding a little river. Also they saw some wild boar, or whatever they call it here."

"That's great!" Phoenix said. "Hey, do you want to come up here? I'd love to get to know you a little bit."

Elanil's face reddened slightly, but she nodded. Then she rose straight up into the air, turned, and sat next to Rylan on the branch. It all happened in just a moment.

"You're getting really good at that," Rylan said, reaching for her hand. One day back with her, and already he was as touchy as a girl. He'd never last a minute in the Under now.

He wasn't sure he wanted to.

"How'd you meet?" Phoenix asked.

"It was a bit over a month ago, I think," Rylan said. "When we fell out of New San Francisco. Elanil was there, with her sister."

"Arra," Elanil said. "Although she's not really my sister."

"Got it," Phoenix said. "Rylan did fill me in on some of this, though it sounds like I missed a lot. I take it you two have been on some adventures together?"

"That's putting it mildly," Elanil said. "I'm pretty sure we helped save the world. Or at least Rylan did. He lifted an entire Prime Forest by himself!"

Phoenix gave him a critical stare. "Really? I'm sure Beam couldn't have done that."

"I had a Book of Amplification," Rylan said. "And a hell of a lot of primewood."

"Still, it's impressive," Phoenix said. "What else?"

"She's a dancer," Rylan said. "Before she became a Prime Mage, she was a leafrunner."

"That's great," Phoenix said. "Do you enjoy dancing?"

"It's one of my favorite things," Elanil said.

"Do you dance, Rylan?"

He blushed. "Not really."

"I taught him a few steps," Elanil said. "He's really good."

"You're just being nice."

"I'm serious!" Elanil poked him in the side.

"You two are cute," Phoenix said. She put a hand to her head, then, as if in pain.

"You okay?" Rylan asked.

"I think I'm fine. Everything was hazy at first, when I left Ambarhal. But the longer I'm here, the clearer things are getting. I learned a lot while I was there. For example, I learned how to make Prime Mages."

"Ah," Rylan said.

"So. If you're both Prime Mages, that means at some point, both of you died."

They were silent for a moment.

"Shot in the chest by Lorelei," Elanil said. "Who is my fake sister's...aunt. It's hard to keep straight."

"I had my neck cut," Rylan said. "By Arra's real mother, Lorelei's sister."

Phoenix gave a low whistle. "Two sisters killed you. That's interesting. Dare I ask how old *they* are?"

"One hundred thousand years," Rylan said.

"Right." Phoenix looked around the island as if trying to decide where she fit in. "Maybe coming back wasn't the best idea, after all. Everything is different now. The numbers are larger. The evil is stronger. The stakes are higher. This isn't just a volcano, or an undercar race. This isn't one simple mindmaster. This is *alien gods*, ancient mages, three planets, magic I can't even comprehend. What am I supposed to do?"

Whatever had been affecting her when he'd first looked into her eyes seemed to have faded. She seemed normal now, like the Phoenix he had known. Maybe the effects of Ambarhal were wearing off.

Still, he knew the power was still lurking inside her, waiting to come out.

He wondered if any of that power had somehow been passed down to him.

"We'll help you," Rylan said. "I can't believe I'm saying this—*you're* the mage who stopped a supervolcano. But we'll help you if we can."

"We will," Elanil said.

"Thank you," Phoenix said. "I wanted to just sit here and talk. To learn about Elanil, to learn about your life, Rylan. But it seems you may be right—time is of the essence. If we want the time to do these things, we'll have to fight for it."

"You always were so smart," Rylan said. "What else did you learn while you were dead?"

A smile grew on Phoenix's face. "Many things," she said. "For instance, I now know that I'm the only mage to ever have discovered how to interlace emotions with forcefinder magic."

"I think Trey did it once," Rylan said. "Just a few days ago, when Arra was making a sandstorm in the desert, Trey made a firebubble."

"I'll have to speak with him about that," Phoenix said. "It takes a certain genetic makeup to do it. But that's not all—I'm also one of the only mages to have accessed the underlying particles of forcefinder magic. And that, my dear son, is a very important trick."

"Guruthos told you this?"

"The Twins did, actually," Phoenix said. "They were very impressed with me. They told me it normally takes about six thousand years for a person to train to the level I achieved in just ten. They said I had a remarkable sensitivity to soul-magic, that I almost didn't need to use the wood at all."

"Wow," Rylan said. "And you can teach me this?"

"I can try," Phoenix said. "I can try with you, too, Elanil. But the Twins told me that only certain mages have the strength and aptitude for this kind of thing. Since you're my son, Rylan, you stand the highest chance of being able to do it."

"Let's get started," Rylan said.

"Soon," Phoenix said. "I think Imra is trying to get our attention."

Elanil jumped off the branch first, sailing easily down to the ground below.

"She's cute," Phoenix said, nudging him.

Rylan felt his face heat. "Stop, Mom. You're embarrassing me!"

He leapt off the branch, Phoenix's laughter trailing behind him.

ELANIL TOUCHED down next to Imra, releasing the dark maple she'd been holding. All of this was so weird—they were on a beautiful island, but people were coming back from the dead. They were alive and well and by all accounts quite safe, but a great evil was bearing down on them. There were hundreds of all-powerful mages on Tanomar, but Elanil had never been more afraid in all her life.

Magic was the source of all of this.

"Come on," Imra said. "We need help hunting some boar."

"I'm not a hunter," Elanil said. Imra looked meaningfully at the pouch of primewood around her waist. "Oh. Okay, sure, I guess. Rylan?"

She turned to find Rylan standing right beside her, eyes shining. "I'm ready," he said. "I've never killed a boar, before. Or seen one."

"Me neither," Elanil said.

"This'll be fun," Imra said. "Coming, Phoenix?"

"You look like you have it handled," Phoenix said.

"Suit yourself. Let's go."

Imra motioned to a small group of Prime Mages and they headed out, traipsing deeper into the jungle. Imra had her customary bow and arrows strapped to her back, and no one else had any weapons of any kind. Elanil wasn't exactly sure what they were supposed to do, but she figured she could improvise. She *was* a Prime Mage now, after all.

The jungle was surprisingly easy to traverse. The vegetation wasn't as thick as she'd thought it would be. The big Prime Palm Trees took up the majority of the visible skyline, but the rest of the island was filled with trees of other varieties. Vines hung down everywhere, snaking over every surface they could find. The ground was covered in undergrowth: shrubs, smaller trees, ferns and mushrooms. Flowers poked their heads out here and there, but Elanil didn't have names for them. This was an alien planet, after all. While she was technically descended from the elves here, she couldn't call it home.

Still, it was beautiful.

They entered a thicker part of the jungle next, and everyone had to work to push through the plants that surrounded them. Then they broke through, and Elanil beheld the most beautiful sight she'd ever seen.

The jungle opened up into a clearing. They were standing on a bluff overlooking a sparkling, turquoise lake, its still waters leading up to a series of rocky cliffs at the far end. There was a waterfall pouring from an unseen source on high, glittering water cascading down to join the lake far below. The shore was made up of tiny rocks of all different colors: gray and brown and orange and even blue. Elanil bent to pick one up, holding it up to the sun to inspect it. It was clear, the sun shining through it as if it were glass.

"Wow," Rylan said, placing his hand on the small of her back. He'd certainly been touching her more, recently. Maybe it was because she'd come back from the dead.

Something else caught her eye, just then. "What is *that*?" she asked, pointing.

A shimmering circle of orange-white light was up on one of the cliffs. A gate, if she wasn't mistaken. She hadn't noticed it before because the sky was so bright, but it was definitely a gate.

"I don't know," Rylan said. "There aren't any mages up there."

"Why would there be a gate here, in the middle of nowhere?"

"It's beautiful," one of the Prime Mages said from behind her. It wasn't until then that Elanil realized what she'd been missing.

"Hi," she said, turning to one who had spoken. Three mages from Ambarhal were accompanying them, and as of yet she had not learned any of their names. "I'm Elanil."

"Alinar," the man said. "Imra tried to explain what was going on, but I admit I am confused. Now I find myself here."

"I am also confused," a woman said. "All I remember are purple skies, wavy Trees, and the Twins." She shuddered. "I'm Hycis."

"Vestele," the other woman said. "When did you all die? I can only assume we died to get where we were."

"Yes," Alinar said. "I died shortly after the Awakening, around 5 A.A. Killed unexpectedly by a thief who was after my silver."

"So you were a darkprime Tree," Elanil said.

"They said I had given my allegiance to Nelenor," Alinar. "That's all I know."

"Definitely dark," Rylan said. "What about you?" He was looking at Hycis.

"I died on Earth," Hycis said. "About 3,000 B.C., I think. I only know *that* from talking to other mages who arrived in Ambarhal, piecing it together. They didn't call the years that when I was alive."

"Wow," Rylan said. "That was a *long* time ago. Both of you."

"It was 20,000 A.A. for me," Vestele said. "I got into a fight with my husband in our apartment in Ilyrion. He said he wanted to kill me, and I said I would rather die than be with him a moment longer. Not the most willing of sacrifices, I guess, but it sufficed."

"You were one of the Prime Trees in Ilyrion," Rylan said.

"Oak, if I'm not mistaken," Vestele said. "Had a sapling in our house. I bled out over it, as it so happens. I remember that much."

"Wow," Rylan said. "I saw that Tree when I first arrived on Valaralda. It was really incredible—all the buildings were built around it, as if they were trees themselves!"

"How does it look now?" Vestele asked.

"Dead," Rylan said. "The Twins killed it."

"Twins," Vestele cursed. "Damn. I guess that curse doesn't work anymore."

"In my day we said 'moons,'" Alinar said. "It seems as good a curse as any."

"Some thought the Twins *were* the moons," Vestele said.

"It was as good a theory as any. Though I suppose now we know better. Did you all talk to the Twins while you were there?"

Everyone nodded, even Elanil and Rylan.

"Guys," Imra said, "we really need to be moving. And can we cut the chatter? Sorry, but everyone's hungry, including me. There's an animal trail over there, and I'm pretty sure it's boar. I can probably kill it, unless it's much larger than I'm expecting. Can you guys...help?"

"Of course," Elanil said. "For starters, I think I can make you invisible."

"That'll certainly do it," Imra said.

FIFTY

THE BOAR HUNT went a lot more easily than Elanil had expected. She used mistweaving magic to render everyone invisible—which was easy—and Rylan trapped the boar in place with leafrunning magic. The other Prime Mages branched out from there, levitating through the forest to find any boar nearby, using bladedancing magic to shoot branches through them.

They'd even found primewood to use. The Palm Trees, as it turned out, were indeed Prime Trees. Although they didn't visually match up to any of the Fourteen Trees Elanil was used to from Earth, they did impart the same differing powers. Nobody had any saws handy, but a little leafrunning magic did the trick for extracting chips of wood. And as with the Prime Trees on Earth, these Trees regenerated their wood almost immediately.

"We'll tell the others about the Trees when we get back to camp," Imra said as they were returning. They were carrying five boars between them, hovering them with magic. Everything was startlingly easy when you had this much power. Elanil couldn't help but wonder what the downside was.

There had to be one.

"Good," Alinar said. "There are at least two hundred Prime Mages here, by my count. We'll need a lot of prime-wood if we're expecting to do any magic."

"We'll need to," Rylan said. "The Twins are not something to be trifled with."

"I didn't know you even *knew* the word 'trifle,'" Elanil said. "So impressive."

"I'm not an idiot just because I was raised underneath the streets," Rylan said.

"That's not what I meant! Sorry."

"Maybe if my mother had been around, things would have been different."

"What do you mean?"

"She could have taught me things. Taken me places. Maybe we would have lived topside. Maybe then you wouldn't think so little of me."

Elanil stopped him, taking his face in her hands. The others continued trudging through the jungle, unaware that they had stopped. "I don't think little of you," she said. "I've seen where you lived. You're *strong*, Rylan. To have been through what you've been through? To have your mother die in front of you? To have Dill beat you up and leave you for dead? How many times did that happen? How many jobs did you do for him? And did you give up? No. You kept going. You kept surviving. That's what I love about you, Rylan. Because despite all of that, despite all you've been through, you *never* gave up."

Rylan was frozen, staring into her eyes. "You love me," he said.

Elanil felt herself blush. "I—well. Yes. I've barely known you, but I feel a—a connection, I guess. There's something that we share."

"What?"

"The way we look at life, I think. You've seen it at it's darkest, and you're still able to see the good in things."

"And you," Rylan said. "You're amazing."

"You're really going to have to be more specific," Elanil said. But she stepped toward him, conscious of how close their faces were.

"I've always liked dancers."

Elanil poked him in the stomach. "You'd never *met* a dancer before me."

"True. But I like you, so I—"

"You've always liked them. Very clever, you."

Rylan put his hands around her waist, drawing her in. It felt unusual, coming from him—he had almost refused to hold her hand the first time she'd tried. He felt different, somehow, as if this island had awakened him. It seemed like he was growing up before her eyes.

"The world got a lot bigger when I fell from the city," he said. "New places, new people. I was afraid." She saw a haunted look in his eyes. "But you said it. I always try. I never give up, no matter what happens. I learned that from my mother, you see. She never gave up for *anything*. Even when it killed her." His eyes were sad. "So when it came to doing the right thing, to helping you elves in your quest to save the world, I had to do it. I had no choice, right? Phocnix had shown me how. But I'll always remember *why*. The reason I didn't hesitate. I'll always remember the moment I first met you. You were *perfect*."

She felt her face heat, and it wasn't from embarrassment. Rylan pulled her closer. She could feel his body, feel his warmth. She stared into his eyes.

"That night when you were falling into the pit, when I

pulled you up but then you were trapped on that platform—I've never been so scared before in all my life."

"You saved me."

He smiled, the skin around his nose crinkling as he did. "What I'm trying to say, Elanil, is that I think I love you, too."

He kissed her, then, and it was like nothing she'd ever felt before. Not with Martan, not even with Rylan in the past. This kiss was different. More meaningful. She could feel the love in the pull of his arms, in the way his hand went up to touch her chin. And when he pulled back, she could see that he was crying.

When had Rylan become so sensitive? Maybe he always had been, but it had been lying beneath the surface. Killed by the Under. Sacrificed to survive.

Maybe Rylan was finally becoming who he really was.

"You are both too cute," Imra said from right behind her suddenly, and Elanil jumped, yelping. Rylan didn't let her go.

She took pleasure in that.

"We should get back, though," Imra said. "You guys good?"

"We're coming," Rylan said. "Just give us one more minute."

And he kissed her again, good and strong.

FIFTY-ONE

DINNER WAS ROASTED BOAR.

This was not something Elanil knew how to do, but Imra apparently knew all about it. She was really in her element, here, acting as the surrogate Hunter Mom for hundreds of people. She seemed a little frustrated, but she kept at it with a strong determination. Elanil thought she might know what was wrong.

Imra was missing Arra.

Elanil missed her, too. Her not-sister was gone, somewhere back on the mainland, probably traipsing around with Trey. Arra would have instantly taken charge, running everything on the island with perfect precision.

Maybe it was good she wasn't there.

"Can I help?" she asked Imra, coming up to where the woman was tending one of the boar roasting over a fire. The mages had rigged up a rotisserie of sorts, stripping branches and building a pair of tripods and a bar to rotate the animal on.

"You can help tend this pig," Imra said. "We just need to rotate it every few minutes."

"What do you think of all these mages?" Elanil asked.

Imra's brow furrowed. "I think there's a lot of power here waiting to be tapped."

"You never were the jealous type."

Imra looked at her, then, and Elanil could see anger written on her face. "I'm not jealous of her magic," she said. Elanil knew she was talking about Arra.

"I'm sorry," Elanil said. "You do know that Arra was always jealous of *you*."

Imra turned the boar. "It was mutual," she said. "Arra wanted my magic, and I wanted her beauty. Her strength. Her Twins-damned skill at every fucking thing she ever attempted."

It was unlike Imra to swear so strongly. "You loved her. Am I wrong?"

Imra gave a great sigh. "No. You're not wrong. I even told her, a few days ago."

"And?"

"She didn't exactly rebuff me. She just—"

"She's in love with Trey."

"I don't know. But I *do* know that she's not in love with me. Not in that way, at least."

Phoenix came up to them just then. "I'll never get used to real animals being killed," she said. "Need help?"

Imra surveyed her. "Turn this boar," she said, and she left.

Elanil couldn't help but wonder what had just happened.

"Prickly woman, isn't she?" Phoenix asked.

"Not usually," Elanil said. "She's maybe the nicest girl I know."

"This whole thing has all of us under strain, I guess."

"Yeah. Phoenix?"

"Yes?"

"Is it okay with you? If I'm with—I mean—"

"If you date my son?" Phoenix put a hand on Elanil's shoulder. "Of course it is! You are definitely the best thing that has ever happened to him. Under knows it's not me."

Elanil tried to smile, but it didn't quite work. "His friend," she said. "Con. Did he tell you about her?"

"A little."

"She's not here."

"No," Phoenix said. "From the sound of it, Con was not Talented. Only Talented people end up in Ambarhal. The others just...die."

"Oh." Elanil looked at the ground for a moment. "Does he know?"

Phoenix squeezed her shoulder. "He hasn't stopped looking for her since we arrived."

Elanil felt a sinking feeling in her stomach, but she tried to push it aside. Rylan loved *her*. He had just told her that! But a part of him had loved Con, too. He hadn't admitted as much, but Elanil knew. A woman always knew.

Maybe Elanil was a woman now.

RYLAN WAS JUST FINISHING his helping of roasted boar when his mother arrived.

"Like it?" she asked, settling on the ground next to him.

"I think I still prefer stew," Rylan said.

"Me too," Phoenix said. "Queen always served the *best* stew."

"Queen." Rylan felt his mouth twisting. "She was the beginning of everything."

"Of what?"

"This. You. What you became."

"What do you mean?"

Rylan was really wishing he hadn't started this line of conversation, but the boar was gone and he had no choice now but to continue. "I never knew Queen," he said, "but I know she made you into what you are now. Who you were when you—"

"When I saved the *world*?"

Rylan kept staring at the ground. "If you hadn't been there, what would have happened?"

"We'd all be dead," Phoenix said. "It's literally that simple."

"You believe everything Orym told you?"

"Don't you?"

"I don't know," Rylan said. "Dill beat me up, *hard*, the day before he let me into the Crew. When I asked him why, he said he had too much of his father in him."

Phoenix was silent. He dared a glance at her, but he couldn't read her face.

"I think Orym might be more dangerous than we know," Rylan said. "And I don't think that volcano would have destroyed the world."

"Magona," Phoenix said, drawing in a breath. "You think she would have stopped it."

Rylan nodded, feeling weariness setting in. He hadn't slept in a very long time. "She was in my mind, Mom," he said. "I feel as if I *know* her now. Magona would have seen the threat, and she would have neutralized it. She was at least as powerful as you are. And now we know that she *wanted* Earth to survive, to move here, in order to unlock the Twins. If that volcano had been allowed to erupt, none of this would have happened."

Phoenix was silent for a moment. "You think I should have let the volcano run its course."

"No. I'm just thinking about the past, is all. I'm not trying to change it. Sorry, Mom. I guess I'm in a morose mood, is all."

"What's wrong?"

"I'm not sure. The Twins, they…"

"What?"

"I feel like we're missing something."

"I might know what would cheer you up," Phoenix said. "Remember what I was saying about force magic?"

That did perk him up a bit. "Yes. Are you ready to teach me?"

"Are you ready to learn? Bring your girlfriend."

FIFTY-TWO

"LET'S BEGIN WITH REGULAR BUBBLES," Phoenix said.

She'd brought Rylan deeper into the jungle, finding a clearing they could work in. Rylan had asked Elanil to come as well, and she had obliged. The sun was still a few hours from setting, but the jungle animals were already out in force, screeching and jeering and chittering just out of sight. It was a far cry from the Under.

He liked it.

"You've done those before, right?" Phoenix asked.

Regular forcefinder bubbles. *Had* he done them before? He didn't think so. He might have used forcefinding magic when Cariel was in control, but he just couldn't remember. He pulled a piece of dark ash from his pocket, fingering it.

A forcefield popped into existence ahead of him.

"Good," Phoenix said. "That's the easy part. Now, you can make the forcefield either two-way—where nothing can go in or out—or one-way. Can you feel the particles of energy?"

Rylan looked at the forcefield he had made, wondering how he was supposed to do that. It was shimmery and silver, and it did look like there were little particles crawling around the surface of it. He peered at them, trying to imagine what they were like.

And suddenly he could *feel* them.

They were there, spinning just out of reach. Millions of them made up the bubble of light, and if he reached his mind in further, he could even feel *why*.

They were all connected. To each other, to him, to the wood in his hand. But the connection went further: into the air, into the world, shooting through space until it met some kind of big machine.

Subject 69327A49Z7 registered, a voice inside his head said. *Welcome to Xyclami. Operating system version 9.35375, last updated 100,000 years, two months, sixteen days, four hours and thirty-seven minutes ago, local system time. Last check-in with parent system was four million years, approximated. Significant time dilation detected. Please acknowledge your presence with the current system operators.*

Rylan dropped the wood he was holding, staggering back. The forcefield disappeared. "What—" he started.

A SUPERUSER, a new voice said in his mind. He knew this one—it was Nelenor. **WE HAVE NOT SEEN SUCH EXTRAORDINARY SENSITIVITY SINCE PHOENIX, AND CARIEL BEFORE THAT. HOW DO YOU WISH TO PROCEED?**

"I—"

"What's happening, Rylan?" Phoenix asked, concerned.

"I think I'm talking to the Twins," Rylan said. "Can you hear me?"

Yes, Velion said in his head. *You have been granted advanced functionality. Where is the Imprisoner?*

WHERE IS THE IMPRISONER?

"I don't—I don't know," Rylan said. "Can you tell me who it is?"

TAKE US TO THE IMPRISONER.

"I don't know."

"Stop talking to them," Phoenix said, an alarmed look on her face. "They're very dangerous."

Subject identified, Velion said. *Location: Tanomar, 104 miles due south-southeast of Ilyrion.*

FIND HIM.

I will go.

"Shit," Rylan said. "They're coming. They're coming here. We have to go."

"I need to teach you more," Phoenix said. "You need to know what I know."

"Emotion magic, right?" Rylan said, fishing out another piece of ash. "Wait—I don't need this." He put it back in his bag.

A forcefield popped into existence.

Phoenix's mouth dropped open in surprise. "How are you—"

"Quiet, Mom. Watch."

Fire erupted around the bubble, shimmering redly in the night. Then ice took over, freezing its way across the surface. Then the bubble turned green, little plants and flowers growing all over it. Then he flashed it gold, then violet, then blue in quick succession.

Then he flicked it out.

"What is—"

"You use emotion to activate it, right, Mom?" Phoenix nodded. "Neat trick. But you can shortcut it by directly accessing your Aspects. Actually—hang on."

Do you need to be a Prime Mage to do what I just did? he asked the machine.

Full Aspect unlock is required, Xyclami responded.

"You hacked it," Rylan said.

"What?"

"You got access to Prime Mage powers without *being* one. Incredible."

"How do you know all of this?"

"I...actually, I don't know how. There's a machine that's doing everything. Magic, everything. All I did was gain access to it. I think it's feeding me information now, subconsciously."

"You bypassed the Twins, like I did."

"I think so, yes."

"But you didn't die! You aren't soulburned."

"Mom," Rylan said, "who was my father?"

"Oh," Phoenix said. "Oh, *no*."

"What?"

"Your father was a very powerful mindmaster named Quynn. He's dead."

Rylan couldn't help it—he started laughing. Elanil had been watching everything silently, but now she looked really worried. "Are you okay?" she asked.

Rylan was really laughing now. "I'm perfectly fine," he said. "And Mom, Quynn is definitely *not* dead."

"What?"

"I'll tell you on the way. You're a Prime Mage now, so you can directly access the Aspects. I'll show you how. I'll show you both. Force particles are the underlying energy, the way the system works. They work similarly to regular prime magic, although it's more raw this way. Come on—we have to go."

"Go where?" Phoenix asked.

"Guys," Imra said, appearing from somewhere, "what's going on? I heard raised voices."

"The Twins are coming," Rylan said. "Why won't anyone listen to me?"

Imra stared at him for a moment.

"I believe you," Elanil said, coming up and slipping her hand in his. "But I'm a little scared of you now."

He looked down at her—she was only an inch shorter than he was, but it was still down—and saw that there was indeed fear in her face. And he knew instinctively that he could throw up red force—Destroyer magic—and alter her brain chemistry. He could modify her very thoughts. He could make her stop fearing him, stop fearing *anything*. He could control her just as surely as Quynn had controlled Beam.

Elanil must have seen it in his eyes. "Don't," she whispered.

Rylan shuddered, pulling away. "The power," he said. "Whoever this Imprisoner was, this must have been what he was after. It's...Elanil, it's *dangerous*."

"You're scaring me."

"I'm scaring myself. But we really do have to go."

"Where?"

"Back to Ilyrion."

"Wait—*back*?"

"Yes," Rylan said. "We need to defeat the Twins."

Elanil took a step back. "But *how*? And if you really think you can, shouldn't we let them come here?"

"Only one of them is coming to Tanomar. And I think that for this to work, we need both of them in one place."

"When are you going to tell me what is going on?" Phoenix asked.

"On the boat," he said. "Imra, can we get everyone on board?"

"It will take some time," Imra said, "but yes."

"Do it," Rylan said. "We need to pack it with anything we have. There's room for all the mages, but we need to bring any food we have left, and as much water as we can. I think I saw containers on the ship, belowdeck. Can you do that?"

Imra cocked her head at him as if wanting to ask a question. But then she nodded, a thin smile on her face. "Yes, sir." She spun and left.

"I feel as if you just grew up in front of me," Phoenix said.

"I think I did," Rylan said. "I think I just did."

Don't come to us, he thought at Velion. *We're coming to you.*

We look forward to meeting you, Velion said, and Rylan could feel the smile on the Twin's Anubis face.

PART
FIVE

FIFTY-THREE

ELANIL FELT like she was in a whirlwind. Mages were everywhere, hastily moving food and water onto the beached leafboat, looking bedraggled and tired. Rylan had completely changed before her eyes: now he was confident, seemingly older, with new powers beyond her ability to comprehend. Even now, Elanil and Phoenix were just standing there, unable to process what they were witnessing.

Was Guruthos really *that* powerful?

Rylan appeared suddenly, touching her elbow. "Hey," he said. "Sorry if I scared you, there. Before we leave, can I show you something?"

"Sure," Elanil said. His touch seemed genuine, but there was a new darkness in his eyes. She followed him out of the clearing and in amongst the huge Palm Trees. The sun was getting low, the shadows long.

"The machine speaks to me," Rylan said. "Literally speaks to me. It knows everything about what it can do, and I can query it with my mind."

"Okay," Elanil said.

"The only problem is, the Twins can hear everything we say."

"So they're spying on you."

"I guess. Anyway, I wanted to try something. Can you make a forcefield?"

"Sure." She pulled out a piece of dark ash, Willing a force-field to life. It shimmered around her in the night, shielding her. She felt suddenly safer, even though she wasn't sure why.

"Now, I want you to look at the little particles that make up the forcefield," Rylan said. "Look closely. Try to *feel* them."

"Okay. But, um, Rylan?"

"Yes?"

"What particles?"

"Oh," Rylan breathed. "Shit." His shoulders slumped. "You can't see them."

"I guess not."

"Okay, then, I guess your soul can't be directly attuned. Let's try the next best thing: put your hand on this Tree."

They were standing next to one of the massive Palms. She knew it was one of the Fourteen, but she couldn't recognize it.

She reached out to touch the wood.

She almost yelped when she felt it. The wood was warm beneath her fingers, as if the life inside it were responding to her. "It's a Prime Tree," she said.

"We knew that," Rylan said.

"Yes, but I hadn't touched one before. It's different."

Rylan smiled at her patiently.

"Here's the trick," he said. "This is something Cariel was doing, I have now learned. If you soulbind this Tree, you can access its power from anywhere in the world—without having any of its wood."

"Wow," Elanil said. "How?"

"Not everyone can do it, I don't think," Rylan said. "But you're strong. So let's try. I did almost this exact thing when I got us out of Ambarhal yesterday. All you do is reach into the Tree with your mind's eye, find its soul, and *take* it. Violently. Don't ask permission, don't be nice about it. It goes against your nature, Elanil. I know. But this is the only way."

"I'm not sure I want to do this," Elanil said.

"This fight we're about to enter will be tough," Rylan said. "We'll need every advantage we can get just to survive. Please try. For me."

She studied his face, so young and yet somehow now so old. Was it the same Rylan standing there, staring at her with his beautiful brown eyes? Was he the same boy who had cried for Con, who had cuddled with his mother, who had danced with Elanil at gunpoint? Was he the same boy who had saved her from certain death?

"Dance," he said, "please."

She smiled. "Okay, Wind. I'll try."

PHOENIX HAD NEVER SAILED BEFORE. Sometimes she had seen sailboats, hanging off the Edge of the city as she'd liked to do. They'd been visible in the distance, tiny triangles of white against the sea. She'd always figured they were ancient machines, something the nanovirus hadn't been able to destroy. It wasn't until much later that she realized the sailboats had been crewed by elves.

Now she was here on another planet entirely, surrounded by elves and her son—her son, who had somehow just become the most powerful forcefinder she'd ever seen.

Everyone was bustling about the decks, trying to find a place to sit or something to eat. Imra had caught her eye—

JEREMY THOMAS FULLER

she was pretty, less skinny than Beam, clearly skilled with her body. She wore a bow and quiver across her back, and she carried herself with a confidence that Phoenix found striking.

Imra caught her staring. "Want to help?" she said. "I'm trying to find places for people to get some rest."

"Sure," Phoenix said. "Just have them sit anywhere."

Imra gave her a look. "This isn't the Under."

"I'll get them settled," Phoenix said, smiling.

She went from group to group, assigning regions of the upper and lower decks for people to sit and sleep on if they wanted. The sun was just beginning to set, and many of the mages were tired. Phoenix was, too—nobody slept in Ambarhal, after all. She wanted nothing more than to sleep for days. But she couldn't. Not now.

There were no pillows or blankets on board, so they had to make do on the hard, silvery surface of the leafboat itself. Clearly the vessel had not been intended for overnight boarding, but it was at least large enough for the group they had.

They'd managed to store a lot of leftover boar and several barrels of freshwater from the lake belowdecks, just in case something happened to them during the passage. By all accounts it shouldn't take them more than a few hours to return to Ilyrion, but none of them had wanted to chance it. If they ended up stranded at sea for some reason, they would at least have supplies for a little while.

The Prime Mages—including Phoenix—were all stocked up with primewood from the Palms on Tanomar. It had taken some doing to extract it from the smooth-trunked Trees, but there was nothing like two hundred determined mages to get a task done.

And so they sailed, almost everyone sleeping fitfully as the sun set. The air was calm, but that didn't matter: leafrunning

328

ran this vessel. They were headed into sure disaster, but for a few quiet hours the world was hers.

Phoenix settled down against the gunwale, watching the setting sun.

Imra sat down next to her. Her face was flushed, her curly hair awry. She almost looked like an underkid, in that moment. Phoenix found it endearing.

They sat together in silence, watching the sky.

"That was quite the feat you pulled with that volcano five years ago," Imra said after a while.

"Thanks," Phoenix said. "I'd forgotten you were there." She kicked herself the moment the words came out.

"Happens a lot," Imra said. "I'm not the hero in this story."

Phoenix turned to her. "You really think that?"

Imra's green eyes were clear. "I'm never the one doing the big stuff, you know? The volcanos. The Forests. Three arrows at once. Prime Mage stuff. Most times I think I'm just along for the ride."

"That's how I always felt with Beam."

Imra regarded her with a careful expression, almost guarded. "When I met you two, you seemed like the strong one."

"I guess I became the strong one, over time. I don't think Beam liked me as much for it. She wanted the spotlight for herself." Phoenix sighed. "No, that's not fair. Beam was strong, and I loved her for it, but I think she wanted someone weaker to be with her. I'm just not that person anymore."

"You don't love her anymore?"

Phoenix felt storm clouds on her brow. "She left my son to the fucking wolves. He could have *died*. I didn't want him in Shock Crew, but I said nothing about Beam abandoning him. So no. We had grown apart in the years leading up to that volcano. We were hanging on for him, I think. For Rylan. And when I died, I guess it didn't make sense anymore."

"I want what you two had," Imra said. "At least at first. Not the growing apart. I could see it, sometimes. There was a glimmer in your eye when you looked at her. I want that for myself."

Strong *and* insightful—a trait Beam had lacked. And that explained Imra's reticence—perhaps she'd been rebuffed all her life.

"You're Arra's best friend," Phoenix said. "I could tell that the moment I met you two."

Imra's jaw was set firmly, as if she were trying not to cry. "She is still my friend."

Things were starting to make more sense. "You wanted her to be more."

Imra looked at her then, green eyes finally swimming. "I don't want to talk about her. We're going to die today, aren't we?"

Phoenix reached out impulsively, taking Imra's hand. "Not if I can help it," she said. "And I think my son really does have a plan."

They were still skimming over the waves, the leafboat gliding easily through the water. Rylan hadn't wanted to make the boat actually fly—it took too much energy, he had said. Even though he now had access to more power than he'd had before, he'd said that the old limitation was still in place: his physical fortitude.

And Rylan hadn't had a lot of sleep recently.

"I should help them sail," Phoenix said. "I keep forgetting I can do more than just forcefinding now."

"Stay for a minute," Imra said, squeezing her hand.

"Guys," Elanil said, appearing suddenly from overhead, "I think we've got a problem."

FIFTY-FOUR

"I'VE GOT one more thing to show you," Cresius said, ushering them into the elevator. This time it went backwards, but nobody seemed surprised.

"Do you really think the mages are being released from Ambarhal?" Arra asked. She was trying to puzzle it all out in her head. She felt like she didn't yet have all the pieces.

"We learned from you fine folks on Mar how Prime Trees are made," Cresius said as the elevator rumbled quietly beneath them. "Both dark and lightprime Trees require death. And from your friends Rylan and Elanil now we know how Prime Mages are made: by escaping Ambarhal. We know that Ambarhal is a world created by Guruthos."

"How do we know that?"

"It was in my translations," Trey said. "Although I got them wrong."

"Don't be too hard on yourself," Lashel said. "Anyone could have made that mistake."

"And let the Twins out from their Prison? I'm a fool, Lashel."

Lashel put a hand on Trey's shoulder, but they said no more.

"So you have all these people milling about Ambarhal," Cresius said, "and we know that *if* they manage to escape back into reality, like Rylan and Elanil did, they emerge as fully-formed Prime Mages. We know that just such a thing happened—repeatedly—to you three." He looked at Trey, Arra, and Quynn in turn. "The only question left is what will happen when the Twins leave the realm."

"I suppose we'll find out soon," Arra said.

The elevator door opened.

They stepped through into a room filled with desks, computers, electronics, and people. Screens lined the walls and the desks, and everywhere black-clothed men and women were sitting at their stations, speaking quietly into thin air.

"This," Cresius said, "is Army Operations. Come on in."

"What is this place for?" Trey asked.

"Our three thousand mages are very good at what they do," Cresius said, "but we aren't so backwards that we only use magic. All mages are equipped with ocular implants, giving them full virtual displays and wireless communications. The mages are also broken up into squads, and then into cells. Squad leaders are here, in Operations. Cell leaders are out in the field. With that and our proprietary software, we can very quickly deploy complex formations and battle tactics."

"Wow," Trey said. "Orym would love to see this."

"I'd love to show it to him," Cresius said. "Does anyone know where he is?"

Everyone shook their head.

"We coordinate using live satellite footage, as well as aerial drones," Cresius continued. "Each mage's ocular implant also transmits a constant stereoscopic video feed to us back here. It's a lot to take in, but our Operations Leads are *very* good at what they do."

"Question," Quynn said.

Arra was surprised to hear him speak up.

"Yes?" Cresius said. The sound of quietly murmuring voices continued to pervade the room.

"You've got mages training with formations that don't even work unless they're Prime Mages. You have thousands of soldiers in this army. You have this Operations room, full of very sophisticated tech and what looks to be a lot of highly trained operatives."

"Correct."

"Has there been a war recently? Or at all?"

"No."

"Has there been any fighting of any kind?"

"Not in the last thirty thousand years at least. We elves are generally a very peaceful lot."

"So...what is all this *for*? What have you been training for, all this time?"

Cresius ushered them back into the elevator. He pressed a button, and it began to rise.

"Our founder insisted on it," he said after a moment. "Aten wanted the very best for us in terms of facilities and funding. And he drove us *hard*, especially in the early days. He wanted us to locate cutting edge magical techniques, to learn how to combine magic in new and interesting ways. To leverage technology wherever we could, if it would help."

"But *why*?"

"I think," Cresius said, "it must have been because he knew that this day was coming, that one day the Twins would be released."

"You do realize what that probably means," Quynn said.

"I'm not sure."

"It means Aten was probably the Imprisoner."

"Aten is long dead."

"What if he isn't?"

ORYM ARRIVED IN NEKHRUMET, stepping through the whirling light of his double gate. He let the smaller gate dissipate first—he had been holding it to nowhere, which is something not many gatesenders knew they could do. Then he allowed the outer gate—the gate from Ilyrion—to disappear. It was a neat trick, one that allowed him to gate as much as he wanted without any of the nasty side effects.

If only he'd figured it out sooner.

His memories were back now. He knew who he was. He could feel the power crackling at the edges of the world, itching to be freed. He could once more feel the call of Guruthos—of Xyclami—of the magic that it held. He knew that, as before, just one thing stood between him and what he wanted.

The Twins.

Two things, then. But they were joined at the hip, or at least joined to Xyclami itself. And if he killed them, they had said, the device would be rendered inoperable. It was a failsafe against misuse. Probably against the exact scenario Orym was considering.

But he knew that even great, mysterious devices must have weaknesses. And so it was that he had labored long, constructing a device of his own making. A device that would rip the Twins from Xyclami without killing them, giving Orym the chance to step in and take the power he so craved.

He had called it the Pyramid Offensive System.

He chuckled wryly to himself. He hadn't known English when he'd named it, so long ago. So of course he hadn't realized what *else* that acronym could spell.

And it was true: the System really was a piece of shit.

It didn't work.

It never had, truth be told, or he wouldn't be standing here on top of his old palace in Nekhrumet, looking down at the world he'd created so long ago. It had changed, since then, but not too much. It was still his old city at heart: still rough around the edges, and pretty rough around the middle, too. It was still full of color and culture and chaos and sin.

Orym had forgotten how much he loved it here.

He slipped down to his old rooms, fallfoiling and leafrunning magic coming to him easily. He was a Prime Mage, after all. He'd simply had a block in place—a block that had lifted during his adventure in Atlantis.

He chuckled as he entered the room. Atlantis now descended into myth. Yes, he'd gone a little overboard with the decorations, the tests. Yes, that first room had been a little bloody. And yes, his stasis Artifacts really were impressive— though truth be told, he'd gotten the original idea from Cara. She'd always been better at manipulating the raw power than him.

But he was getting distracted. He was here to find the Entrance, which should be just over...there. He walked over to the northwest wall, pulling aside a tapestry to reveal a small grid of hieroglyphics. These he tapped in quick succession, his memory supplying the necessary code.

The whole wall slid away, revealing a dark room with a whirling gate inside.

He stepped into the room, eyeing the gate. Machinery lined the walls, electronics that seemed far too advanced for the surrounding area. But Nekhrumet was not as low-tech as it seemed, and it hadn't been for a very long time.

He'd created this room 99,300 years ago, after all.

The gate flicked as he watched, its destination changing. All he saw was swirling green inside. *Click*. The gate changed to swirling yellow. *Click*. Swirling white. *Click*. Back to green.

It went like that for some time, looping through three distinct possibilities. Orym wracked his brain, trying to remember what in the hell the gate was for.

"Oh," he said to himself when he finally had it, a smile spreading across his face. "I'll need help with this."

But first, he needed to figure out what was wrong with the System itself.

FIFTY-FIVE

RYLAN BOUNDED ACROSS THE DECK, responding to Elanil's call. The leafboat's momentum faltered as he ran, his concentration slipping. He was getting tired; he didn't know how much longer he could keep this up. And why was he the only one moving the boat, anyway? There were over two hundred other mages on board. He'd make them take over, just as soon as he'd found out what was wrong.

"There's a storm coming," Elanil said when he finally got to her. Phoenix and Imra were there as well, looking at her with alarm on their faces.

"You saw that in the air?" Rylan asked.

Elanil nodded. "The cloud system is obvious, even at this distance. Rylan, the storm is *huge*."

"Everyone on board is a stormwarden," Rylan said. "We can counteract it."

"You can do that?" Imra asked.

"I saw Trey do it back at Mirra's house. He used magic to create *good* weather, counteracting Arra's sandstorm."

"Worth a try," Phoenix said.

"I don't think this storm is natural," Elanil said. "I think the Twins sent it."

Lightning flashed in the far distance.

"Why would they make a storm?" Imra asked.

"Why would they destroy Ilyrion?" Rylan said. "Because they're insane."

A drop of rain hit him in the face.

"I'll get them organized," Imra said.

"I'll help," Phoenix said.

"Let's hope we can keep sailing in this," Rylan said. "Oh, and I need some mages to take over leafrunning for me."

"No problem," Imra said, looking at the sky.

BANZAB HAD BEEN in the desert for far too long. An entire day had gone by, and still there had been no hint of help, no water, no food or shelter. Magona had gated the People there and then abandoned them, without purpose.

They would die here, she knew.

The People were weak, sun-scorched, dehydrated and starving. She felt weak as their leader, helpless. There was nothing she could do.

They had not stayed still. They had marched south, near as she could tell, hoping to find an edge to this horrible place. They'd trudged through endless sand for hour after hour, growing weaker by the minute. But nothing was there— nothing but endless dunes.

Banzab had almost given up all hope.

It wasn't until night began to fall that they finally found it. The desert terminated at the sea, spreading out to the south all the way to the horizon. Salt water, Banzab was sure. Water they could not drink. They couldn't sail away, and they couldn't stay in the desert. The sea was a welcome sight, but it was not any help at all.

And there was one other problem. They couldn't actually reach the sea, because the desert ended in a sheer, rocky cliff.

Two hundred feet high.

Keleb was standing next to her. Her second-in-command was a huge man, towering over everyone else in Lusvunub. He was the *true* reason for Banzab's ascent—what she lacked in muscles and raw brutality, Keleb made up for.

And she didn't even have to fuck him to make him do it.

"Storm rolling in," Keleb said, looking to the east. "Looks big."

Banzab followed his gaze. Towering clouds thousands of feet high were gathering in the distance, roiling visibly in shades of white and gray. She saw lightning flash between the clouds as they approached. The last light of the sun faded beneath the horizon as the storm continued to grow.

THE SEA WAS GROWING INCREASINGLY rocky. Rylan was leaning against the bulwark amidships, trying to stay awake. He had overexerted himself running this leafboat, and now he was paying the price. Other mages were propelling the boat, mages who he did not know. He didn't think he'd ever be able to learn all their names.

But they had bigger problems now. The storm was about to reach them, the sky growing black before the sun had even completely disappeared. The wind was picking up, blowing furiously in almost every direction. It was like the gods themselves had created a vortex of air and water and lightning, intending to blast them out of the sea.

Elanil must have been right. It was the Twins.

Lightning crashed next to them in the sea. Rylan flinched as the boat began rolling up a huge wave, sea spray misting him as water came up over the edges of the boat. He turned, catching Imra's eye. She was the leader of this expedition, apparently, even though she was the only one of them who was not a Prime Mage.

"Get some mages to lift us," he said. "I have a little dark ash left. We should be close to Ilyrion, and I don't want to get smashed on all these waves."

"I'll tell them," Imra said, taking the double handful of dark ash from him. "This won't last long."

"I know. I'm hoping we're almost there. I can't see anything in this damn storm."

"We may not even be pointing in the right direction," Imra said.

"We'll just do the best we can."

She was right, Rylan knew. They'd tried to maintain course as best they could, but the sun was gone now. The storm had overtaken the sky, and there were no visible land-marks anywhere. They could be sailing *away* from Ilyrion instead of toward it.

They could be trapped out here forever.

The rain finally hit, soaking him instantly and chilling him to the bone. The wind whipped up even harder, but at least the rocking motion of the boat began to lessen. He peered over the bulwark and saw them rising out of the ocean, sailing on the wings of magic. He couldn't help but chuckle at the sight—Prime Mages really were so powerful.

But only if they got sleep. He slumped against the bulwark, closing his eyes for just a moment. He heard Imra nearby, shouting at a group of mages to begin stormwarding magic. They would counteract the storm if they could. Then they'd regain their bearings, sail to Ilyrion, and face the Twins. Everything would turn out okay.

Rylan just needed to sleep.

"WHERE DID THIS STORM COME FROM?" Trey asked. They were in a new conference room, and this one had windows. The sun had set, but the sky was roiling with a dense layer of clouds. Lightning flashed several times as he watched, the accompanying thunder only moments behind.

"Ops," Cresius said into thin air, "any information on this weather system? Respond at my location so the others can hear."

A screen on the wall flicked on, revealing the harried-looking face of a male elf. "We were just about to call you, sir," the man said. "*Caladmain* readings are off the chart all over the planet right now. This storm sprang up out of nowhere."

"Prime magic," Cresius said.

"Undoubtedly. This is an artificial storm. And sir, it's going to be huge. Valaralda hasn't seen a storm this large in— well, we've never seen one this large. Not in recorded history."

"Valaralda?" Cresius asked. "You mean Ilyrion?"

"I mean Valaralda," the man said. "Showing you satellite now."

The screen changed to an overhead view, far above the continent of Esara. At least Trey assumed that's what it was showing—all he could see were clouds.

"Give me a sense of scale," Cresius said. "What are we looking at here?"

"There is no scale to this," the operator said. "This is a planet-wide storm."

"Twins," Trey cursed.

"That's exactly what I was afraid of," Cresius said.

FIFTY-SIX

THE STORM WAS GROWING WORSE by the second. It was all Rylan could do to hang on to the bulwark—every gust of wind threatened to send him and everyone else flying into the ocean. The leafboat wasn't in the water anymore, but it didn't matter. The wind was out of control, buffeting everything.

"It's not working!" Imra shouted at him. "The stormwardens can't do anything against it!"

"It must be the Twins!" Rylan shouted. A huge wave crested below them, and the boat wasn't high enough. Water crashed over the sides of the boat, soaking everyone and flooding the deck. Two Prime Mages were swept off the boat in the chaos, but he glimpsed them using their magic to get back on.

This storm was powerful, but it was *very* difficult to kill a Prime Mage.

"Phoenix said you can talk to the Twins," Imra shouted at him. Rain was pelting them both, moving sideways in swirls as the wind direction changed.

"I can!" he shouted back.

"Then tell them to stop!"

"Don't do it," Phoenix said, suddenly standing beside him. "It will just tell them where we are. They're doing this for their own amusement—I know them. They won't stop, no matter what you say."

"There must be a way to get through to them," Rylan said. "But you're right—they won't listen to me. I can't!" he shouted at Imra. The woman gritted her teeth and clung to the side of the ship.

Rylan hoped they reached land soon.

"We need light," Phoenix said. "We can't see anything, and anything out there can't see us."

"Good idea," Rylan said. "But how?"

"Forcefields," Phoenix said. "Leave it to me."

BANZAB WATCHED HELPLESSLY as two more People flew off the cliff, propelled by wind. She had instructed them to stay low, to get ahold of a rock if they could, but not everyone had listened. The storm was hitting them with all its fury, and Banzab wasn't sure how much longer they would last. The driving rain and frigid wind made a strange counterpoint to the scorching heat of the desert.

Both were deadly.

This was water they could drink, at least, if they could capture it. Most of the People had their mouths open, trying to catch whatever they could directly. It worked, after a fashion. One problem solved, so many more to go.

A ball of red light suddenly appeared below them, somewhere out in the ocean. It hurt her eyes, at first, but she squinted at it anyway. Lightning slashed at the light repeatedly, but it had no effect. There was something *in* the light, Banzab saw.

It was a ship.

It was only then that Banzab finally recognized the red bubble sailing toward them.

She felt her blood run cold, and it wasn't from the storm.

FIRE SURROUNDED THE LEAFBOAT. Rylan squinted in the brightness of it, struggling to stay awake. "Can you move the forcefield?" he shouted at his mother. "It's too close! We can't see anything!"

"Sure," Phoenix said, and the forcefield blinked away. When it reappeared, it was a few hundred feet ahead of them in the air.

Illuminating the cliffs they were headed right towards at breakneck speed.

"Stop the leafrunners!" Rylan shouted, but Imra couldn't hear him. "We have to stop!"

But nothing happened. No one else had seen the cliffs, yet. They were shooting toward the vertical rock face at a hundred miles an hour, and they would be dashed to pieces.

Rylan had to do something.

He accessed Xyclami.

Forcefinder magic poured through him instantly. He accessed green first, suffusing himself with enough energy to make it through another few minutes. Then he pulled out violet—the Builder Aspect—sending particles into the ship. They induced weightlessness, a trick he hadn't known about until just now. Builder was the fallfoiler Aspect, so it made sense.

But the Mages were still propelling the ship. So he sent out red magic—Destroyer Aspect—not to hurt anyone, but to give them a light mindmaster nudge.

All the Mages stopped what they were doing.

The boat kept moving, momentum carrying it forward. The cliffs were close now, achingly close. Rylan could see everyone onboard reacting, finally seeing the danger right ahead of them, but there was nothing they could do. There wasn't enough time.

So Rylan flexed his mind, Willing white force—mergemelding magic—into the ship. If his next move didn't work, at least they wouldn't actually hit the cliffs. Phoenix had called this type of power an icebubble, and she hadn't known what it could do. But Rylan knew. He knew it all now.

He was all powerful, assuming he could stay awake.

The final magic needed to be movement. But all six Aspects of forcefinding magic provided movement for objects within them. The bigger the object, the harder it was to move. And with a ship this large, with so many people on it, and with Rylan's flagging energy, he knew it would be nearly impossible. He almost didn't even try.

"Let me help," Phoenix said, placing her hand in his.

He felt their souls connect, her energy intertwining with his. There was more power there now, but it still was not enough.

"And me," Elanil said, taking his other hand.

The cliffs were too close. It couldn't be done. The rocks sailed closer in his vision, growing brighter, distinct. Even in the midst of the storm he could see them looming, a craggy wall of death. He had about one second left to alter their course before they'd be plunging through it.

He made his move.

He directed the magic, pulling it out of Phoenix and Elanil, using their strength to augment his. He accessed all their Aspects—all six—pulling power from Xyclami and manifesting it there, in the boat. Particles of every color erupted all around them, cascading in glittering designs, filling every piece of the flying sailing vessel. Every kind of magic was with them, commanded by Prime Mages, fulfilled by the great power of Xyclami. And Rylan twisted with his mind, instructing all those millions of tiny balls of light and energy to rise.

They did.

The boat wrenched upward *hard*, sending everyone falling painfully to the deck. It sailed upward at a steep angle, trailing glittering pieces of magic like effervescent dust, scraping the top edge of the cliff as it crested onto land.

Rylan caught a glimpse of faces below him, of dirty humans with bedraggled hair clinging to the rocks. He faltered, then, his weariness finally winning out. He lost his grip on the magic, and the boat fell. He tried to stop it, but he had no more energy at all.

The world went black as Rylan finally went to sleep.

PHOENIX GRITTED her teeth as Rylan slumped over between them, eyes closed. The reins of magic passed over to her in that moment, and it was all she could do to ride them out. The sheer power Rylan had controlled—it was mind blowing, incredible.

Sure, this wasn't a volcano. It was a boat.

Still, he was probably the strongest mage she'd ever seen.

The leafboat had gotten up on top of the cliff, at least. Now it was just a few feet above the ground, listing sideways a bit as the magic streamed out of it. Phoenix did what she could to hold it in the air, but she was not strong enough. The boat was far too big.

So it fell, crashing into the ground, scattering people that she had not known were there from underneath it as it went. People that looked like...the People? But how in the hell would the *People* be here?

The boat slammed into the ground, careening forward a hundred feet, two hundred, three hundred before it finally ground to a stop on the cold, rain-lashed rocks. The storm was still raging all around them, but Phoenix was focused on the humans she had seen clinging to the rocks. She had recognized one of them, she thought. But it couldn't be. Not here.

She released Rylan's hand, and Elanil took the boy in her arms. Then Phoenix picked her way to the edge of the boat, pausing to help elves up as she did. Nobody seemed particularly hurt, at least. Things could have been a lot worse.

When she reached the edge of the deck, she peered down at the humans that were there. And sure enough, looking up at her with shock and maybe fear, she saw the person she had not thought to see. The person who would not survive their next encounter, should they have one.

Beam was looking up at her.

FIFTY-SEVEN

PHOENIX FLOATED out of the leafboat, putting up a forcefield around her in order to block the wind. The storm was still raging strongly, rain and lightning lashing against everything. But though the storm was strong, it paled in comparison to the rage Phoenix was feeling inside.

Her bubble turned to fire.

She released it when she got to Beam, then put a new one up to encompass the two of them. Silver, this time—she was doing her best to quiet her emotions. She didn't want to burn anyone to death.

Not on accident, anyway.

Beam looked different. Worse. She was haggard, dirty and sunburnt, with long jata hair that hung down nearly to her waist. There were new lines on her face since Phoenix had seen her last. There was a darkness in her eyes.

"Beam," Phoenix said. She didn't know where to begin.

"It's Banzab now," Beam said.

"Do you lead the People?"

Beam nodded brusquely. "I am Warlord of Lusvunub."

"That happened fast."

Beam nodded.

Phoenix gritted her teeth, not wanting to come out with it just yet. "Why are you here on Valaralda?"

"Magona brought us here," Beam said. "She needed us to fight."

"After everything we went through—after I *died* stopping the volcano Magona set off, how could you fight for her?"

How could you leave our son?

She couldn't say the words.

Beam bowed her head slightly. "I recognize it now as mindmaster magic," she said. "I was ever the weak one."

"Yes," Phoenix said, conscious of how cold her voice had become. "You were."

Beam looked at her then, and Phoenix saw that there was no love in her eyes. Whatever had been between the two of them was gone now, lost to death and the vagaries of time.

Beam was a different person now.

"Why the People?" Phoenix asked.

Beam barked a laugh. "Why anything? It seemed better than the Under. You know me, Megan, or you used to. You know I'm not one for nice things, for topside pleasantries. I could never have lived with elves."

"You could have stayed with our *son*," Phoenix hissed, feeling anger surging through her.

There. It was out.

She clenched her fists and watched Beam's face.

Rylan plopped down beside her then, flying right through her forcefield.

"Rylan," Beam said, a bit breathlessly.

"Ho," Rylan said, and Phoenix could hear the anger in his tone. Bits of shimmering light surrounded him, formless and floating in the air. He had woken up for this. He had wanted to face *her*.

Phoenix wasn't sure what was going to happen next.

"I see you have survived," Beam said.

"No thanks to you," Phoenix said.

"What is that light surrounding him?"

"Magic," Phoenix said. "My son has surpassed us all."

"Your son," Beam said. "*Your* son. You slept with a man to make him. An evil man. You fucked a mindmaster and had his kid."

Phoenix took a step forward, the forcefield strengthening around them. It was still silver. For now. "You were fucking Queen."

"I never slept with Queen."

"Bullshit. You were always the weak one, Beam. Always the slave."

"I don't have to listen to this." Beam turned, but the sparkling forcefield wall was blocking her in.

"Rylan almost died because of you," Phoenix said quietly.

Beam turned, and this time there was real anger in her eyes. "No," she said. "Rylan almost died because of *you*. *You* were the one who was always overextending yourself. *You* were the one who had to bring *emotion* into magic. *You* were the one who made Dill promise to kick him out of Shock Crew. What kind of parent does that? Why would you strip Rylan of the one thing keeping him safe?"

"I wanted to—"

"I don't care what *you* wanted," Beam said, biting off the words. "Rylan is *your* son. He was *your* responsibility. And *you* left him to die."

"No," Phoenix said, "that was you."

The bubble around them turned to ice.

"Moms," Rylan said.

"I am not your mother," Beam said. "Now if you'll excuse

me, my People are dying out there. We need to move on, find some kind of shelter from this unnatural storm."

"I'm not done with you yet," Phoenix said.

Beam flicked a finger in the air. "But I am done with *you*."

She took a step away, and Phoenix turned the bubble to fire.

"Stop this," Rylan said to her.

But Phoenix was too angry to listen.

She stepped forward, blue lightning between her fingertips, dark elm in her hand. She readied the magic, intending to strike Beam down. This woman, this *bitch*, had proven just how loyal she was.

She should have stayed with Queen.

Beam turned, readying magic of her own. Phoenix saw maple in her fingers, the metalwood shining in the firelight. Her lips were twisted, her body poised. Beam was ready to fight to the death.

So be it.

Phoenix hit her with everything she had.

"**MOTHERS!**" Rylan shouted, the sound booming, reverberating around them. Phoenix's forcefield splintered into chunks of energy, flying away into the wind. And particles of every color appeared around Phoenix and Beam, wrapping them tightly, jerking them apart. The light went out of Phoenix's hand. Beam looked very frightened.

And Rylan was glowing, his body lit a brilliant green. He was larger now, his body towering above them by at least a foot. His eyes were flashing, his mouth stern.

Shards of shimmering light were streaming from his hands.

"There will be no violence here today," he said, his voice still unnaturally loud. "Either talk this out as mature adults, or leave. I will not have you killing each other. Not now."

There was no wind whistling around them, Phoenix realized then. She looked at her son and felt something she had never expected to feel for him. He was so *powerful*, so commanding.

When she looked at him, she felt fear.

She caught Elanil's glance. The girl was standing behind them, staring at Rylan with a stricken look on her face.

Elanil was also afraid.

FIFTY-EIGHT

THEY SLEPT AFTER THAT, fitfully underneath forcefields erected by a rotating group of Prime Mages. The shields provided shelter for everyone, even the People. Even Beam. They were all worn out. Rylan was on his last legs. Now was not the time to be having emotional conversations.

And so they slept, while the storm raged on.

When Phoenix woke next, Imra was passing out the remains of the cold boar and fresh water. The People were grateful for their assistance—it had been over a day since any of them had eaten. The storm was still blowing and blustering unabated, so everything had to be done under the cover of forcefields.

They didn't have much darkprime wood left.

It was impossible to tell if it was day or night. Clouds covered everything, obscuring the sky. Lightning flared at random intervals; it was the only light they had.

"Are you ready to treat Beam civilly?" Rylan asked her as she stood, back aching from her time spent lying on the metallic leafboat deck.

"I won't kill her," Phoenix said. "If you forgive her, so do I."

"I forgive her," Rylan said. "She is not you. She is not self-less. She did the only thing she knew to do."

Phoenix put a hand on his shoulder, shivering as she remembered how he had looked the night before, glowing and magnified and strange. "Thank you for stopping me," she said. "I don't know what I was thinking."

"Let's go see her again," he said. "Maybe we can figure some way out of here."

"Okay."

They left the boat, using leafrunning this time. They had to conserve their darkprime wood, since there had only been lightprime available on Tanomar. The wind continued to gust dark circles around them as they alighted on the ground, still shielded by glimmering forcefields.

Beam was waiting for them, her face turned down.

"Ho," Phoenix said. "Can we start again?"

Beam looked up at her, then, and Phoenix could see that she'd been crying. "It hurt *so much* when you died," she said, taking a lurching step forward. "I couldn't think straight. I couldn't *do* anything. Every time I looked at Rylan, all I saw was you. I had to...I had to run away."

She stepped forward and collapsed, and it was all Phoenix could do to catch her in her arms.

They stayed like that for a moment, Phoenix stroking her dirty hair.

"The past is useless to us now," she said after a minute. "It seems that once again, we must save the world."

Beam sniffled. "I'm so lost," she said. "Magona just *left* us here, and I don't even know where *here* is!"

Imra strolled up to them, carrying her little white card. "The

Thesserin Cliffs," she said, "at the southernmost edge of the Thesserin Desert. The Airon Sea is to the south, and Ilyrion is to the east. If we were to walk—or fly—east-northeast, we would arrive in Ilyrion. It's only about two days on foot. Maybe three."

"Thank you," Phoenix said. Imra was watching the two of them, she noticed. Phoenix found herself pulling back from Beam, letting the woman stand on her own two feet. Beam wiped tears from her eyes.

Did she still have feelings for her old partner? Phoenix didn't know. She'd wandered Ambarhal for what had felt like decades, always alone. She had yearned for Beam's arms, then, wishing she could see her face. But now that she was back in the real world, she wasn't sure if the spark was still there.

Perhaps it had never been.

"I still love you," Beam whispered to her, and Phoenix finally broke down in tears.

"I HAVE SOMETHING FOR YOU," Beam said, reaching behind her. They were sitting on the rocky ground, watching the storm blow by as they talked. They did not touch each other. There were few smiles. Something unspoken had fallen between them, and Phoenix knew that despite her profession of love earlier, Beam would never be for her again.

She wondered if Beam had realized it, too.

"Here," Beam said, pulling out a pinblade and handing it to her.

Phoenix took it, marveling at its lightness. Pinblades were always the lightest of swords, but this one was even lighter still. The handle was made of something that looked like metalwood, she saw. Dark ash. "Is this—"

"I call it a fireblade," Beam said, "because of your fire-bubble magic. Try it."

Phoenix stood, wielding the blade in one hand. It was well-balanced and extremely sharp, and the wooden handle felt warm in her hand. She Willed magic through the wood.

It erupted into flames, fire shooting up and down the length of it, flaring brightly in the dark. "Wow," Phoenix gasped, almost dropping the blade in her surprise. It was forcefinding magic—she could feel it there, suffusing the metal with energy. But it was Aspected forcefinding—Destroyer magic.

She could do a lot of damage with this blade.

"That's really cool," Rylan said. He was approaching them, hand-in-hand with Elanil. The girl seemed recovered from her fear of him. "Is that forcefinding?"

"Yes," Phoenix said. "It's doing this without any anger or fear."

"I can feel it," Rylan said. "Does it have access to the other Aspects?"

"I don't know," Phoenix said. "Let me try."

She Willed the blade to change to white—Governor Aspect, Rylan had told her, used for strengthshaping and mergemelding. And the blade obeyed, ice scintillating across it like a breath of frozen air.

"I had no idea it could do that," Beam said. "How does Rylan know these things?"

"It's a long story," Phoenix said.

"I'm a superuser now," Rylan said.

"A super...user?"

"Beam, thank you," Phoenix said, reaching out and giving Beam a one-armed hug. "This blade is amazing—I don't know how you did it!"

Beam blushed. "You're welcome. I'd thought to carry this

blade with me always as a remembrance of you, but now I think perhaps a part of me knew you would return."

"You can access all fourteen powers with that," Rylan said. "You just need to learn how to utilize the Aspects."

"Can you teach me?"

Rylan nodded. "I think so. And if that blade is anything like Trey's Tree Ring Staff, you have an inexhaustible supply of primewood."

"Damn," Phoenix said. "What should we do with it?"

"Well," Rylan said, "we really ought to get out of this storm."

"I'm not sure that's possible," Elanil said. "I think the Twins are doing this on purpose."

"You're probably right," Rylan said. "But we can't keep forcefields up all the time. Hell, we can't even *locate* the Twins in this. What are we going to do?"

"Let's go back to Ilyrion," Phoenix said. "Imra, can you use that card of yours to orient us?"

"I think so," Imra said. "Twins—why didn't I think of that while we were sailing?"

"Not everyone thinks of everything," Phoenix said. "What's important now is that we use whatever we have."

"We can find supplies in Ilyrion, at least," Elanil said. "But how will we get there?"

Phoenix was staring down at her fireblade. "I think I have an idea."

FIFTY-NINE

ELANIL STOOD on the upper deck with Rylan as the leafboat sped through the air, red dust glittering behind it like millions of tiny fireflies. He had his arm around her, his breathing slow. But she could feel the immense power welling up within him, danger crackling every time he moved.

She wanted to love him, but she wasn't sure she knew him anymore.

The leafboat was packed to the brim with people—all 237 Prime Mages, plus another two hundred-odd Remnant from Lusvunub. It was nose to nose and elbow to elbow on board, and that was only because they'd stashed a lot of people belowdecks.

A glimmering violet forcefield surrounded the boat, giving it buoyancy and rendering it weightless. The shield also protected everyone within from the horrible storm that continued on incessantly.

Phoenix was doing all of this with her fireblade.

She held it out in front of her, flames rippling across its surface and dancing in her eyes. She Willed her force magic into being all around them, drawing the elements themselves into array. Elanil had never seen anything like it before. Not until Rylan had transformed.

He was a superuser now.

She feared what that might mean.

"Ilyrion is destroyed, you know," she said.

Rylan squeezed her waist. "I know. I'm just hoping we can find some supplies, maybe some food or darkprime wood. We can transmute food if we have to, but I'd really rather not." He looked at her, then, eyes shining in the violet light that surrounded them. "Are you okay?"

"Just tired, I guess," she said, shrinking away from his gaze. His arm around her felt too tight.

"I'm sorry if I scared you, back there. This power…it's too raw. I feel as if it might come out of me at any point."

"You don't even sound the same," Elanil said. "You never used to talk like that."

A moment of anger flashed across his face, but she could see him tamping it down. "It's Xyclami," he said. "It speaks to me, tells me things. I can't control it. It's giving me knowledge, Elanil. Things I shouldn't know. It has *deep* knowledge inside it, the ancestral learnings of its people. Of the Twins." His voice got quiet. "I think that's what its true power is."

"Please be careful," Elanil said. "I'm worried about you."

He squeezed her again. "I'll be fine. I'm the first human to have been granted superuser access—I know that much. Wait —" He cocked his head to the side as if listening.

"What's wrong?"

"Of course. How could I have been so stupid?"

"What?"

"Xyclami just reminded me of my heritage. My genetics. My father is Quynn, Elanil. That makes me half-elf."

"Oh." Elanil wasn't sure what to feel about that. Relieved? Concerned? She'd liked Martan before, and he was definitely human. Was that what had drawn her to Rylan in the first place? Was she looking for something other than her? Or had it been something else? "Are you okay?" she asked him.

He looked at her again, eyes bright, and this time she didn't shrink away. "I *love* the elves," he said, his arm still wrapped around her waist. "Finding out I'm one of you—or part of one, at least—it makes me very happy."

He kissed her, then, and she let him.

She could taste the power on his tongue.

THEY TOUCHED down on the Space Agency landing platforms that overlooked the city. Phoenix had eliminated all her colorful force magic before they got too near, switching instead to standard dark maple for lift and light elm for propulsion. They crept forward silently in the air, the wind and rain buffeting them relentlessly.

In the dark distance, Ilyrion was destroyed.

Elanil was clutching Rylan, shivering. She and everyone else was soaked through and freezing, and hungry and tired and just plain miserable. This was the new world the Twins had made.

"There's nothing left," Rylan said. All around them, mages and Remnant were disembarking the vessel, quickly filling up all the space on the platform.

"We need to figure out what to do with all these people," Elanil said.

"We shouldn't have flown here," Rylan said.

Phoenix came up to them. "Imra says they're just stretching their legs. We'll get them back onboard whenever we figure out where we're going next—obviously we can't stay here."

"We should take more leafboats," Elanil said. "If there are any left."

"Good idea," Rylan said. "Mom, see where I'm pointing?" He pointed to the east, in the direction of the ocean.

"Yes."

"Can you send a few mages over there, see if any leafboats are still intact? We can split up our forces that way, so we're not so crowded."

"Sure," Phoenix said. "Do you know those people?"

Elanil followed her gaze. Down below them on the deck was a group of familiar faces.

"Dill!" Rylan said. "What are you guys doing here?"

Dill, Small, Allain and Erodar were standing there, looking like bedraggled rats.

"Sleeping," Dill said. "That is, until you guys showed up. What the hell *is* this thing? And who are all those people?"

"Come up here," Rylan said, and force particles surrounded them.

Five seconds later, they were standing on the deck.

"Uh," Dill said.

"What the *hell* was that?" Small asked.

"Magic," Rylan said, beaming at them.

"My father would really like to see that," Dill said.

"Where *is* your father, anyway?" Elanil asked.

"No idea. We could try calling for him, though. I still have this radio." He pulled a black device from his pocket, heedless of the rain. "Oh."

Rylan popped a forcefield up around them, and instantly the rain stopped.

"Where are the Twins?" Elanil asked.

"They went north," Allain said. "Into the forest. I think they felt something in that direction—I don't know. We were trying to lie low, get our energy back, maybe scavenge around for things."

"Did you find anything?"

"Not really. I'm beginning to think there's nothing left."

"My home is gone," Erodar said. He had a haunted look on his face.

Elanil reached out a hand to touch his arm. "I'm so sorry."

"Let me see if this thing works," Dill said, fiddling with the dials on his radio.

"Let me," Small said, snatching it from him. "You never were very good with technology."

"Fine."

Small messed with the radio some more, and soon they heard a fuzzing sound coming out of it. He turned a dial, listening for anything else. "Nothing," he said. "Everyone in Ilyrion is dead or gone."

"Can we transmit to Dad?" Dill asked.

"Sure," Small said. He went to move the dial again, but a voice suddenly sounded.

"Again, if you're just tuning in, this is code-name Lightning. I've taken over the wideband transmitter at Piedmont Point, and I'm using the old-fashioned RF spectrum to send this signal. If you're within range of me, keep your head down. The Twins are here."

"What the hell is that?" Allain asked.

"Must be some kind of pirate radio," Dill said. "They used to have those, back on Earth. Before the—never mind. Let's listen—maybe this guy knows something."

"If anyone is out there," the radio continued, "the Twins left Ilyrion about three hours ago. They destroyed most of it, but they didn't go underground. There are still plenty of places to hide, and plenty of people here to take you in if you need help."

"Maybe the mages can—" Elanil said.

"Shh," Small said. She glared at him.

"The Department of Magical Research announced martial law yesterday, as you probably all know. What you might *not* know, because the broadcasts are all dead, is that they also fully deregulated magic. That's right, folks, feel free to do all the darkprime magic you want. Including gatesending. I guess the Believers finally got what they wanted. Now we'll see how long they stay alive."

The radio was silent for a moment. Elanil was about to say something else when it clicked back on.

"Citizens of Ilyrion," Lightning said, and this time his voice was quieter than before. "I fear we brought this on ourselves. We were too arrogant, too free with our use of magic. Whatever happened during the Great Awakening, it really pissed off the Twins. So I urge you, fellow citizens—if you know who this Imprisoner is, or *where* he is, do us all a favor. Turn him in." There was a crackling sound. "I'm not sure how much longer this planet will survive."

SIXTY

A FEW HOURS LATER, the storm was still raging. Rylan paced the decks of the leafboat, listening beneath a shield as others made their plans.

"The mages are safe in the underbelly of Old Town," Allain was saying. "Jassin, that bartender I met, was very helpful."

"He's a good man," Erodar said. "They'll be safe there, for a time. Is there any way we can radio the DMR, tell them where they are? I have a feeling they'll be able to put the mages to good use."

"I sent someone," Imra said. "He knew where DMR head-quarters was."

"Good," Dill said. "Now what?"

The group was silent for a moment.

"Now we leave," Rylan said.

Everyone looked at him.

"What?" Elanil asked.

He stared at her, trying not to let the particles show on his skin. It was getting increasingly difficult to hold the power at bay. Xyclami was still speaking to him.

"This planet has nothing for us now," he said. "With this storm, there's nothing we can do."

70.3% probability of failure to exit the atmosphere, Xyclami said.

"Shut up," Rylan muttered.

"What?" Elanil said again.

"Nothing. I just think we need to regroup. We need to get out of this infernal storm. We can't fight the Twins."

"I thought you said we *could*," Elanil said. "You're the one who made us leave Tanomar. You're the one who said that we could fight."

Rylan had to force his hand to stop shaking. "I'm scared," he said. "I don't know what this power is doing to me. I don't think I can control it."

Elanil took a step toward him, concern growing on her face. "Maybe we should go to the DMR."

"No," Rylan said. "I want to go home. I want to go back to the Under. I can't do this anymore."

202,469 souls currently in residence in the United Sky Cities Under. 42,112 of them are capable of connecting to me.

"Wow," Rylan said.

"We can't just leave," Elanil said. "We have to solve this! We have to stay and fight!"

"Maybe he's right," Dill said. "There's nothing for us here, after all. On Earth, we have the entire Under. All the elves. Even the topsiders—President Greyson will help. We could leverage an army, not to mention thousands and thousands of mages."

"It might be our only chance," Rylan said. "I can't do this on my own."

Elanil was glaring at him. "I thought you *wanted* to do this on your own."

He held out his hands toward her in entreaty. "Please."

She sighed, but he saw the love return to her eyes. She came the rest of the way forward, wrapping her arms around him. "You just need to talk to me," she said, nuzzling her head against his chest. The wind howled outside their shield. "Tell me what you're feeling."

"I'm afraid."

"You'll always have me," she said. "Do you know that? I'll always take care of you."

Visions of Phoenix flashed into his head.

"That's what I'm afraid of."

THEY FOUND a man by the name of Stilmyst hiding in an abandoned spaceport building. Captain Stilmyst, he told them, and that's what he was: a spaceship captain.

With him, they could get off the planet.

But he wouldn't fly. "This storm is too bad," he said. The man was sitting on a piece of luggage, dark hair slicked back and soaked. His face looked gaunt, as if he'd just been through hell.

"Have you seen our forcefields?" Rylan asked. "We can protect the ship."

"Why do you want to go to Mar, anyway?"

Rylan sighed. He didn't want to have to convince this man. He could just mindmaster the guy, make him do what he wanted him to do, and all of this would be over.

But he glanced at Elanil, and found the idea repulsive. He couldn't betray another person like that. Not even if his life depended on it.

"For starters," Rylan said, "it gets us out of this storm. And we know a lot of people on Mar—we can get reinforcements."

"What if the Twins follow you there?"

"Can they *do* that?" Elanil asked.

Rylan nodded. "If we can get to Earth, you can sure as hell believe the Twins can. They can just gate anywhere they want."

"Why don't we do that?"

"Too dangerous. Don't want to lose our memories."

"Oh. Too bad there's no way around that limitation."

"Will you do it?" Rylan asked the captain. "I give you my word: we will get out of here safely. I'll protect the ship myself. This might be your only chance to escape the Twins."

84.9% chance of failure, Xyclami said.

"Include a forcefield in your calculation," Rylan said.

"What?" Stilmyst said. "I'm not calculating anything."

42.1% chance of failure.

"Okay, include *two* forcefields—one outside the other. One from me, a superuser, and one from Phoenix. She has that fireblade."

"Rylan," Elanil said, "are you talking to the machine?"

He nodded.

9.5% chance of failure with amended variables, Xyclami said.

"Good. Let's do it. Captain, are you in?"

"I—" Captain Stilmyst looked at all of them as if they were insane. But then his face fell and he stood, tugging at his luggage. "Let's go. Maybe we really can outrun the Twins."

IN THE END, it took *three* forcefields to get them safely off Valaralda. The wind was incredibly strong in the upper atmosphere, strong enough that Rylan and Phoenix weren't able to maintain their shields' position in the sky. Luckily, Elanil stepped in to help.

Then they were free, transitioning into zero gravity without any more hitches. They were on their way to Earth, settling in for the long flight. Rylan hoped they had made the right decision. He wondered where his father was.

He hoped the Twins would leave them alone.

Enjoy your flight, Xyclami said, and Rylan couldn't suppress the shiver that rippled through him.

SIXTY-ONE

ELANIL WATCHED with some trepidation as the spaceship landed in New San Francisco, settling down in a huge open area just west of Old Fisherman's Wharf. Rylan was feeding her information as they landed, telling her about this area of the city. Apparently its analogue in Old San Francisco had been the city's biggest tourist destination. Now it was mostly just a storage place for heavy vehicles.

There had been no peep from the Twins since they'd left Valaralda—or Rylan hadn't mentioned anything, at least. He was still getting information from Xyclami constantly, and she could tell that it was wearing him down. She wished there was something she could do.

The trip to the Under was uneventful, even downright boring. With the city no longer under Cothellon control, all the Monitors and Civil Service agents were gone. The Under was a bustling place now, and all its entrances were wide open.

A lot had changed since Elanil had first visited here.

"Wow," Phoenix said as they entered Shock Crew headquarters. "This is...not what I expected."

The room had been expanded since Elanil had seen it last. Had it only been a month? Apparently there was no end to what tens of thousands of determined kids could do.

Shock Crew headquarters was now hundreds of feet high and thousands of feet in every other dimension. The rope rigging had been enlarged to match, strings of nets and rope houses and ladders and things filling the airspace above the ground. Colorful lights hung everywhere, banners and ribbons adding decorative touches throughout. Underkids scrambled all over the rigging, shouting to each other, tossing balls around, hooking up new lanterns, and just generally creating chaos. A few of them saw the new group entering the room and set out hollering at them.

Dill let out a whistle. "Reminds me of Trash City," he said. "Never thought I'd see anything like it again."

"Shot did all this?" Small asked.

"How many underkids live here now?" Phoenix asked.

"I have no idea," Dill said. "It must be *thousands*."

"Ho!" a voice said, and Shot himself swung down from the rigging. He was followed by two others: a tall, spindly teenager and a spiky-haired girl. "Friends, meet Stick and Spike, my seconds-in-command. Whatcha guys doing here?"

"Ho," Dill said, reaching out and clasping Shot's hand. "Quite the place you've got here."

"Thanks, Captain," Shot said.

"You're the boss now."

"And you'll always be the Captain. So what's the deal? This looks serious. Wait a minute." He was staring at Elanil, looking as if he'd seen a ghost. "Weren't you *dead*?"

"Long story," Rylan said. "We've just arrived from Valaralda, and we need your help. Let's do some introductions, first. You know Dill and Small and me and Elanil. You know Allain, right?"

Shot nodded. "Ho, Allain. Where's your twin?"

"I ate him," Allain said.

"Uh."

"This is Erodar," Rylan said. "Another mistweaver. Imra, from Sylrantheas."

"Pano Sylrantheas," Imra said. "Nice to meet you."

"Ho," Shot said.

"Imra is a bladedancer," Rylan continued. "And that brings us to the last few members of our group." Elanil could see that Shot was already staring at them with intense interest, but he didn't know who they were.

"I'm Beam," Beam said, stepping forward. "This is my second, Keleb."

"And I'm Phoenix."

Shot's mouth dropped open. "The forcefinder, right?" Phoenix nodded. "I've heard of you. We *all* have. You were around during the age of Queen."

Phoenix didn't seem happy to be recognized. "That was a long time ago."

"But you—you're *alive*!"

"And so is Elanil," Rylan said. "You might want to get used to it—a lot of people are coming back from the dead."

"Not my mother," Elanil said softly.

Rylan didn't hear her. "Is there a place we can talk?" he asked.

"Sure," Shot said. "Follow me."

THE GROUP WAS TOO big for Shot's tent, even though it, too, had been enlarged. So they took the meeting topside—*way* topside.

Into the Upper Apartments.

Professor Greyson's chambers were huge, taking up half of the eighty-fifth floor of the Park Building, so named because it existed where Golden Gate Park had been in the ancient version of the city. The apartment was opulent, with ornately-carved wood paneling reaching to the ceiling, depicting stags and archers, strong men and naked woman, vicious beasts and demons and angels.

Elanil had never seen anything like it before.

President Greyson wasn't there, but Shot had the key and knew where everything was. It was strange that the President's son was the one in charge of the United Under, but Elanil figured stranger things had happened.

She looked askance at Rylan.

He was staring out the huge floor-to-ceiling windows in the next room. Elanil went up to join him, taking his hand when she arrived.

The view from way up there was *incredible*. Buildings and bridges stretched all the way to the horizon, jutting spires floating in the sky. There were seven cities now, interconnected like a massive spiderweb of metal and glass. They could see the New Golden Gate Bridge beginning to take shape to the northwest, bridging the gap between New San Francisco and New Paris. The New Eiffel Tower was visible beyond that, obscured slightly by clouds. What other wonders were up here, just waiting to be found? Elanil wished they had more time.

She wished there were fewer gods trying to kill them.

"Got a treat for us today," Shot said, raising his voice so he could be heard. "Come on into the dining room."

The dining room was equally massive, lined with wall-to-wall windows and covered in beautiful marble floors. A long, oak table took up most of the room, its edges carved in curves and curls, its surface varnished to a brilliant gleam. Everyone filed in, making their way to the table, unsure what was about to happen.

"No," Rylan said. "It *can't* be."

"My god," Phoenix said. "How?"

Elanil looked at the table again. In front of every seat was a red can with the word "Coke" emblazoned on it.

She had no idea what that was.

"Found a new stash on the ground," Shot said. "Come on, take a seat. You're gonna *love* this—it's even refrigerated!"

"This shit is three hundred years old," Spike said. "It'll probably kill us all."

"It'll be fine," Shot said.

"We should have come back to Earth a lot sooner," Rylan said.

Shot clapped him on the back as he sat down. "Anything for my old friend."

Elanil caught a grimace on Rylan's face, but the look disappeared as quickly as it had come. She knew the history, though. She knew that Rylan had not been welcome in Shock Crew for quite some time before recent events. The pain still lingered, she knew. He would always have that with him.

"I've got food coming," Shot said. "In the meantime, fill me in."

Everyone from Valaralda exchanged a look, as if weighing who should speak. Dill glanced at Rylan. "May I?"

Rylan nodded. "Sure."

"The Twins are real," Dill said. "It wasn't just an elven religion. We don't know anything about them yet, but we do know that they're immensely powerful. They completely destroyed Ilyrion."

"Damn," Shot said.

"They're searching for someone they call the Imprisoner. We assume this is the person who locked them away to begin with, but we don't know who it is or even if that person is still alive. We don't know what they'll do once they find this Imprisoner. All we do know is they keep destroying everything around them. It's only a matter of time before everything is gone."

"So we have to fight them," Shot said.

"Just so," Dill said. "Damn. My father always says that—I guess it rubbed off. Anyway, yes. We came here for two reasons: because we know a lot more people on Earth, and also because the Twins created a planet-wide storm."

"That sounds fun."

"Not really. Makes it impossible to get anything done."

"So what's the play?"

"The play is—well. I'm not sure. Rylan? This was your idea."

Rylan sat up straighter in his seat. "I'm a superuser now," he said, lifting his hand over the table. Multicolored particles drifted above it, sparkling.

"I don't think I want to know what that means," Shot said.

"It means I'm very powerful. But I'm not sure I can defeat the Twins alone—they *control* the device that gives me this power. Maybe nobody is powerful enough, but we have to try. So the plan is to get as many mages as possible together, and beat the shit out of the the Twins."

Spike smiled at that. "Just my kind of plan."

"There are a lot of mages in the United Under," Shot said. "We haven't run a full census yet, but—"

"There are 42,112 mages in the Under," Rylan said.

"I—but how did you—"

"Correction," Rylan said. "42,113. One was just born."

"What in the fucking—"

"Rylan is a superuser," Elanil said. "He speaks directly with Xyclami."

375

"You guys really got into some weird shit on that other planet."

"Xyclami is the device that powers all magic," Rylan said. "The elves call it Guruthos, but that's not its real name. It leverages soulmagic to connect with its users, and it's highly sensitive. That's how it can count the mages, even from such a long distance away."

"Okay. Well, that's definitely a lot of mages. So what do you propose?"

"We get them," Rylan said, "and everyone we can from Pano Sylrantheas. Neighboring elven villages, too. And we figure out a way to ship all those people over to Valaralda—probably via gates."

"What about the memory loss?" Elanil asked.

"Nothing we can do about that," Rylan said. "We only have one spaceship."

Dill's radio suddenly emitted a harsh buzzing sound.

"What the..." he started, fiddling with the knobs. The buzzing sound grew louder, then it abruptly changed to words.

"If anyone can hear me on this primitive device," a male voice said, "know this: we *will* have the Imprisoner."

"How did they—" Dill started.

"That's Nelenor," Rylan said. "I'd recognize his voice anywhere."

"The Twins have a *radio* now?"

"If the Imprisoner does not show himself," the voice continued, "we will be forced to continue destroying everything around us, including but not limited to the Seed Planet Valaralda."

"What does he mean by 'Seed Planet?'" Shot asked.

"No idea," Rylan said.

"How are they even on the radio at all?"

"They're gods," Rylan said. "They're not stupid. Xyclami is a *machine*, remember?"

"Oh."

"Wait a minute," Nelenor said, his voice crackling over the radio. "Is this true?" There was a shuffling sound, and muted talking could be heard. A moment later, Nelenor came back on. "Velion is sifting the sparkthreads. We have found a descendant of the Imprisoner. We will find him and make him tell us where the Imprisoner is."

"That doesn't sound good," Dill said.

"It's not me," Rylan said. "Quynn isn't the Imprisoner, is he?"

"He could be," Phoenix said. "We don't know anything about him."

"I doubt it," Dill said. "Quynn and my father go way back. It's probably not—"

He stopped.

"What?" Rylan asked.

"Just a theory. Dammit, that's something else Orym always says. But it is—I mean—Orym might be the Imprisoner."

"That's ludicrous," Phoenix said.

"I never trusted him," Imra said. Everyone looked at her. "He discovered darkprime magic here, remember? He lied to Trey when he first met him. He sanctioned it when Dill kicked Rylan out of the Crew. And let's not forget that Orym was the Scientist General for the Cothellon—by all accounts, he is a bad man."

"He's my father," Dill said, "but you're not wrong. There have always been mysteries lurking in his past. He never speaks of it. I'm not sure he even *knows* his past."

"We don't have enough information," Phoenix said. "If the Imprisoner really *is* Orym, what does that mean?"

"It means *I'm* the descendent," Dill said. "It means they're coming for me."

The radio crackled again. "The descendant is on Mar," Nelenor said. "I will travel there. Be ready to divulge the whereabouts of the Imprisoner, whoever you are. I will be there soon."

Everyone began to panic, and Elanil realized she still hadn't tried a sip of Coke.

SIXTY-TWO

"I HAVE AN IDEA," Rylan said. They were still seated at the big dining table, trying to figure out what to do.

A Twin was coming to Earth. Just one of them, from the sounds of it, but one would be enough.

One Twin could do a *lot* of damage.

"Spit it out," Dill said.

"Right. Hang on." He took a long drink of his Coke, spluttering a bit when he put it down. "Holy hell, that is even better than I remember it."

"Easy," Dill said, laughing. "You look like you've just—never mind, you're too young."

Shot and Small erupted into laughter. Phoenix glared at them.

Elanil had no idea what they were talking about.

"My idea," Rylan said, looking at her and blushing, "is this: we use the United Sky Cities as a weapon."

Everyone was silent for a moment, digesting that.

"Think about it. We know the cities were designed to channel energy from the planet's core in order to create a gate. I was there when it happened. It was really powerful."

"We all were there," Shot said.

"Not me," Phoenix said.

"But that was taking energy *from* the planet," Small said. "Are you suggesting the opposite?"

"Yes. Remember all those Power Storage chambers? You had me and Small get some power for you, Dill. We only took the tiniest fraction of one of those batteries."

"Oh," Small said. "*Oh.*"

"You want to reverse the device," Dill said. "Turn the city's power against the ground."

"If it can be done. And not just this city—*all* of them."

Small was rubbing his hands together enthusiastically. "I love this plan."

"You would," Dill said.

"It may not kill Nelenor," Rylan said, "but it could stun him, buy us some time to do something else."

"What else?"

"Magic," Rylan said, and particles of light began rising from his hand.

"Are you as powerful as the Twins?" Dill asked.

Rylan cocked his head as if listening to something. It was Xyclami again, Elanil knew. "No," he said. "I am a superuser, one step below the actual owners of the system. They can stop me if they want. Shit—they can turn magic *off* if they want."

"What?" Dill asked. "That's insane!"

"They control the device. And yes, it has an off button."

"How do you know all this?" Shot asked.

"I told you: it talks to me."

"I always thought you were a little crazy."

"Hey," Phoenix said.

"None taken."

"Guys," Small said, "I think it will work. But I'll need

access to all the Power Storage chambers, plus access to whatever central power plant they have in each city—there must be one. Permission to make changes, and a whole bunch of underkids to help."

"Done," Shot said. Everyone looked at him. "What? My dad *is* in charge."

"I wonder if there are more batteries in the mystery rooms," Small said.

"We gave up on that," Shot said. "Nobody knows what the rooms are for. We tried to get inside for a *month* with no luck at all."

"But it's a *third* of the Under!" Small said. "There has to be a reason for them."

"Closer to a half," Shot said. "We mapped out the perimeters when we were trying to fit all those underkids in."

"*Half* the Under isn't used?" Rylan asked.

Shot nodded. "Total mystery, and it's like that with all seven cities. Back when we were barely surviving down there, nobody cared. But now, everyone's curious what it's all for."

"We'll probably never know," Dill said. "But let's make this plan happen. Shot and I will work on getting the underkids here organized, especially the mages. We'll have a fighting force in no time. It'll be like the old days—from like a month ago."

"The Prime Forest," Rylan said.

"Just so. Shit—I have to stop saying that."

"What will we do?" Phoenix asked.

"I want to visit Sylrantheas," Elanil said. "I haven't been back since I...died."

"Pano Sylrantheas," Imra corrected. "And I want to go there, too. We will be the emissaries to the elves, getting them ready to fight."

"Good," Dill said.

"There are warriors left in Lusvunub," Beam said. "Magona only took half of them. Also, we have war machines."

"Destroyers," Phoenix breathed.

Beam winced. "Yes. Only these are bigger now. We have had time to make improvements."

Elanil could see Phoenix suppressing a shudder.

"I'll stay up here in the Under," Allain said. "Pano Sylrantheas has no place for me, anymore."

"I'll stick with Allain, I guess," Erodar said. He didn't look too happy to be here on a planet he didn't know.

"Alright," Dill said. "That leaves Rylan and Phoenix. Where will you go?"

"You do realize Nelenor might be after *you*," Rylan said.

"We don't know that for sure," Dill said. "But I'll tell you what: I'll get out of the city as soon as I can. That way, if I *am* the target, I can lure him to a safer location. Okay?"

"Okay," Rylan said. "I want to stay up here."

Elanil looked at him. "I'd like you to come with me."

He stared at her, and for a moment she thought he would refuse. "I want to be with you," he said, "but I'm afraid."

"You won't hurt me," Elanil said. "You would never hurt me."

Rylan flexed his fingers, watching purple particles explode around him in the air. "I'm not so sure."

"Phoenix?" Dill said.

"I'll go with Beam. I've always wanted to see Lusvunub."

Imra was staring at her. "On second thought," she said, "I think I'd like to see Lusvunub, too."

Elanil recognized the look Imra was giving Phoenix. It was so soon! They'd only just met. But Imra was *definitely* jealous of Beam.

"Then it's settled," Dill said. "Shot and his Crew, Small,

Allain, Erodar and I will stay up here. Rylan and Elanil will visit Pano Sylrantheas. Imra, Phoenix, and Beam will head to Lusvunub. Here"—he rummaged about in the bag he was carrying—"I've got radios for some of you, that way we can keep in contact. Our goal, ladies and gentlemen, is to whip up some serious armies. We'll get the Fennas Elenathon device reversed up here if we can, and then we'll be ready."

He gave one radio to Rylan and one to Phoenix.

"Let's hope we have enough time," Rylan said. "Nelenor might have just gated over."

"I suspect we'd know if he had," Dill said. "Maybe he's taking the scenic route."

"I hope so," Rylan said.

"Good luck, everyone," Dill said.

"Question," Phoenix said. "Just how exactly are we getting down to the ground?"

SIXTY-THREE

IN THE END, they used magic to get down. Not gatesending—
it was still too dangerous. Apparently they'd discovered some
severe memory side effects after Phoenix had died. She shivered, thinking of the gates she'd been through. She wondered
what memories she might have lost.

She'd said a teary goodbye to Rylan before she'd left. She'd
only just come back, only just saw him again, and already
they were parting ways. Part of her wanted to go with him, to
visit the elves, to see where they lived. But another part
wanted to stay with Beam, to see what had driven her these
past five years.

She and Beam used leafrunning and fallfoiling magic to get
to Lusvunub. They used forcefields to protect their bodies from
the wind—they were moving *quickly*, after all. And Phoenix
had the added responsibility of Imra, who was not a Prime
Mage. She could tell the woman was annoyed at always being
inferior, but there was nothing Phoenix could do about it.

It only took them a few hours to get to Lusvunub,
touching down just shortly after noon. Beam had taken Keleb

with them, who was not a mage but was apparently her right-hand man. Phoenix knew she wasn't sleeping with him—Beam *never* liked men—but there was still some kind of connection between them. She wasn't jealous, though.

Apparently she was over Beam.

Lusvunub looked a lot like Gulthurub did, except bigger. It had the same barbed wire walls with the turrets and the Gatling guns, the same ramshackle buildings that didn't quite look like they fit together. But there were other buildings, too —wooden buildings in a perfect state of repair. And from the air, Phoenix could see the outer regions of the city.

They were filled with Destroyers.

After they had landed, Beam took them directly to her command quarters.

"Keleb," she said, "round up whoever we have left. And see if Weaponmaster Galab is around. Bring him here if he is."

"Of course," Keleb said.

In English.

"What..." Phoenix began.

"Let me show you around," Beam said. "Imra, you coming?"

"I wouldn't miss this for the world," Imra said, looking at Phoenix, curly hair bouncing as she turned.

Phoenix found herself blushing.

"THIS IS MARTIAL SQUARE," Beam said, leading them through an open area filled with gravel. A few tents dotted the ground, revealing desks and barrels and crates full of unknown things. "Not much here, right now. This is where we gathered the army before we...well, before we gated to Valaralda."

"Was Magona really here?" Phoenix asked.

Beam nodded. "I didn't even know she was mindmastering me. Not until she died."

"Magona is *dead*?"

"Didn't Rylan tell you?"

"Oh. Yes, he did. You're right. I got so confused—Magona had so many names."

Beam barked a chuckle. "She had at least three of them when we first met her five years ago. Apparently she never quite gave up that whole 'god' thing."

"She was a monster," Imra said.

"You fought her?" Phoenix asked.

"I helped *heal* her," Imra said. "I'm not sure how, but—we had a soulcircle, amplified by the Books. I felt power coming out of me, healing her eyes."

"You did it, too," Phoenix said. "You accessed Aspects you hadn't unlocked. Like a Prime Mage."

"I think we all did," Imra said. "Even Allain."

"If we'd known all this," Phoenix said, "if we'd known how the magic worked, who the players were, what they wanted—if we'd known what we know now, do you think things would have turned out differently?"

Imra's green eyes met hers. "We can't change the past."

"No," Phoenix said, "but I'm pretty sure the past can change *us*."

They walked on, following Beam.

"Second District is just through here," she said, leading the way out of the vast graveled square and through a small curtain of trees.

"You have trees here?" Phoenix asked. It seemed incongruous. She didn't remember seeing any trees in Gulthurub.

"Sure," Beam said. "We don't cut them down because we *hate* them. Only if they're in our way."

It was not quite the same approach the elves had, but Phoenix let it slide. Beam was clearly at home here amidst the humans and their wreckage. Humans. Phoenix was human, too, but once again she found herself siding with the elves.

Beam stopped just past the trees, looking upward and breathing heavily. "There's something here, I think," she said. "Almost like a spirit, or something. Sometimes I think I see a ghostly tree."

"What happened here?" Phoenix asked.

"My, uh." She looked at the ground, obviously embarrassed. "My...lover...killed herself." Phoenix saw her face contort, grief overtaking her.

She reached out, putting a hand on Beam's back. The gesture didn't feel genuine, but it was the best she had. "What happened?"

"Her name was Lalban. She was special." Beam looked up at her.

"What happened?"

"She wasn't satisfied down here. The People are...hard."

"I know."

"She didn't fit in. I guess maybe that's why I liked her. But it all got to be too much for her, one day. She hung herself right here."

Beam pointed above them. A beam of wood jutted outward from a nearby building, the perfect place to loop a rope over. Beam. Beam's name.

"What's your real name, Beam?" Phoenix asked. She couldn't believe she'd never asked it before.

"I found her here," Beam said. "Her body was still warm. It must have just happened. And through my tears and screams, I swear I saw a tree forming. Like it did when you died, Phoenix. I thought I was hallucinating."

"What happened when I died?"

"A tree appeared. Like a ghost tree. Huge, and growing larger and larger until it took up the entire island and just kept going. Then it...disappeared."

"I'm sorry," Phoenix said. "I'm sorry she died. She must have been special."

"I should have seen the signs," Beam said. "I've always been too self-absorbed. I was trying to lead the People, dammit! I didn't know. I didn't realize she was hurting."

Phoenix wanted to comfort her, but she didn't know how.

"I watched her hanging there," Beam said, "her soul ascending to the heavens. I saw her spirit in that tree, and then it disappeared."

Everyone was silent for a time.

"Angel," Beam said.

Phoenix cleared her throat. "What?"

"My real name is Angel. Come on, I'll show you where we make the bourbon."

Phoenix followed, trying to choke back tears.

SIXTY-FOUR

WHEN ELANIL ARRIVED in Pano Sylrantheas, she was shocked at how few trees there were. The whole village looked completely different: the streets were straighter, the buildings larger, the people more diverse. She saw Remnant humans mixed with elves everywhere she looked, putting houses together or sitting on the grass, chatting. It was beautiful, seeing the two races coexisting like that. But it was also terrible—so much had been lost.

"Come on," Elanil said as Rylan touched down beside her. "We need to summon a Council meeting."

"Can you do that?" Rylan asked.

"I think so. Father is dead, so..." She choked up suddenly, unable to continue the sentence.

"We'll find someone else," Rylan said, putting a hand on her shoulder.

They found Daylor in Meriel's, drinking a beer. The tavern had been rebuilt larger than before, and one wall was entirely made of glass. Elanil liked it—it let a lot more light into the space.

"*Elanil?*" Daylor said when he saw her.

She was going to have to get used to that reaction.

"Hi," Elanil said. The Regulation Mentor was looking her up and down as if doubting his eyes. "Yes, I'm really alive."

"But...how?"

"We need to speak with the Council. Can you get them together? It's an emergency."

"I—sure. Give me an hour. You know where the new Town Hall is?"

"I'll find it," Elanil said.

"Good. See you then. And Elanil—you look good."

"Thank you, Daylor."

"Twins guide you, daughter."

"No," Elanil said, and surprise registered on Daylor's face. "No, I do not think we do not want the Twins guiding us anywhere."

THE COUNCIL HAD CHANGED a lot since Elanil had died. Three of them had been killed: Silanar, Eloen, and Orist. Two had volunteered for the Prime Forest: Nuvian and Belstram. Those two might yet be alive, but they would be on Valaralda with the other Prime Mages if they were. Kharis had resigned from the Council, having fallen into a deep depression. So of the original eight, only two remained: Bellas, the Organization Mentor, and Daylor, the Regulation Mentor.

New elves had risen to take their place. New Mentors had been assigned. And in a shocking turn of events, one of the humans had ascended to the Council itself.

Jalnab.

He was the Instruction Mentor now. Despite his lack of English skills, it turned out he had a certain knack for it. Plus he was one of the quickest learners the elves had ever seen.

Nuala, Elanil's aunt and the Cultivation Mentor, had taken the Protector spot on the Council. Chasianna, the Architecture Mentor, had taken Orist's place as the Builder. Ellarian, the Musician Mentor, had taken Nuvian's spot as the Creator. Lorsan, the Penetration Mentor, had replaced Kharis as the Destroyer. And the new Council Leader, the one nominally in charge, was someone Elanil had not expected at all.

It was Meriel, the tavernkeeper.

She smiled as Elanil and Rylan entered the Town Hall. Meriel followed Conflagration—cooking and brewing—and she wasn't even a Mentor. Hadn't been, anyway, when Elanil had been there last. And Destroyer Mentors were never Council Leaders, in any case. But maybe desperate times called for desperate measures.

Or maybe Meriel was just the best woman for the job.

"Greetings," Meriel said. "It's good to see you safe and sound."

"The Council sure has changed," Elanil said. "It's good to see you, too."

Meriel gave her a smile. "I guess rounding up bar guests all day made me an ideal candidate for running the village. Anyway, Daylor says you have something important to tell us. An emergency."

"Yes," Elanil said. "It's the Twins."

She explained the situation as best she could, Rylan interjecting when needed. When she was done, the Council was staring at her in disbelief.

"Twins," Nuala said. "That was quite the story."

"Be careful the curses you use," Elanil said.

"Is it true?" Bellas asked. "Are the Twins really back?"

"Aren't I here? Alive? There's a lot we didn't know."

"We don't have time for this," Rylan said. "Nelenor is coming—may already *be* here, in fact. The Twins destroyed all of Ilyrion—a *huge*, high-tech city—in less than a day. What do you think they'll do to Pano Sylrantheas?"

"I don't like this," Meriel said. "There's too much we still don't know. Who is this Imprisoner? Why do the Twins want him or her so badly? What will they do when they locate him? I find it hard to believe they'll just go away."

"That's why we have to fight them," Rylan said.

"And just how do you propose to do that?"

In response, Rylan began floating in the air. He drifted upward slowly, multicolored lights glittering around him. He raised one hand and the particles formed a gentle curve, arcing toward the Council where they sat at the front of the room.

And the Council started floating, too.

"Put us down," Daylor said.

"Where is your wood?" Lhoris asked.

"Where in the Twins' name are all those bits of light coming from?" Meriel said.

"He's a superuser," Elanil said.

"A what?" Daylor asked.

"A superuser," Rylan said. His voice was loud and rich, echoing throughout the chamber. His body was glowing now, standing larger than before. "I'm connected directly to the device. I no longer have need for conduits such as wood."

"He's a Twin himself," Bellas said, still floating in the air.

"I am not a Twin," Rylan said. "Nor am I a god. But I *am* just underneath them—the first and only person on either planet to attain this status."

"He's the Prime Mage," Daylor said. "The one Quynn was trying to breed."

"I am a Prime Mage, yes," Rylan said. His fingers were still twisting, making little curls of light in the air.

"No," Daylor said. "*The* Prime Mage. Before we threw

Quynn in jail, we questioned him. He told us he'd been trying to create a Prime Mage for centuries, breeding people like dogs. He told us of his conquests: with Lorelei, with Phoenix, with many others. He had intended to breed Trey, get him to have kids. But you—you're Quynn's son, aren't you?"

"Yes," Rylan said. "I'm surprised you knew." He twisted his hand again, and the Council settled back to the floor, the particles of light fading. Rylan himself grew smaller again, darker. Elanil found herself swallowing nervously. How often was he going to do that?

"It was you," Daylor said. "Quynn's big project resulted in you."

"I'm not strong enough to defeat the Twins on my own," Rylan said. "I need your help. Will the elves and humans here agree to act for this great cause?"

"Let us put it to a vote," Meriel said.

SIXTY-FIVE

AS ELANIL HAD EXPECTED, the Council vote did not go their way. The elves were ever reticent to act without provocation —their first foray against Gulthurub five years ago had taught them that lesson. And so Elanil and Rylan had had no choice but to leave the Town Hall and regroup.

"There must be something we can do to convince them," Rylan was saying. They were walking through the newly-straight streets of Pano Sylrantheas, hand in hand.

"I can't think of what," Elanil said. "We told them every-thing we know. Short of somehow *proving* that the Twins exist, maybe showing them the ruins of Ilyrion, I'm not sure what else would work."

"When Nelenor arrives," Rylan said, "then they'll believe."

He took her into a sudden dance position, bringing her a few steps closer to him. Her hand naturally went up to his shoulder, her other hand to his. His dance frame was actually pretty good.

"What's gotten into you?" she asked.

"If the world's about to end," Rylan said, giving her an awkward twirl, "I wanted to have one last dance."

For an underkid who'd never danced before, he was doing remarkably well. She strengthened her grip, taking the lead, helping him through a few steps. They were dancing in the middle of the village, right there on the street, but nobody was around to see.

"Rylan," Elanil said, "have you ever wondered what your life would have been like if you'd had this magic sooner?"

Wisps of gold traced beside them in the air as he took her into a turn, her head ducking under his arm. He was a natural.

"I hadn't thought of it in all the chaos," Rylan said. "I sure as hell wouldn't have been beat up so often."

"You would have been a force to be reckoned with."

"What am I now?"

"Surprisingly good at dancing," Elanil said. "Did you take lessons while I was in Ambarhal?"

"Nope," Rylan said. "But ever since I became a Prime Mage, I feel...awakened. As if the other parts of my soul are stronger now."

"Interesting," Elanil said. Did she feel that way, too? She hadn't thought about it. She hadn't really tried doing anything uncharacteristic recently. Maybe she should. Maybe she could finally be an archer, like Arra. "Do you think we'll really defeat the Twins?"

Rylan's step faltered for a moment, running into her. Elanil strengthened her grip, leading him back into place. "Honestly?" he said. "No. I don't think they can be killed. They control all the power—how could we possibly go up against that?"

Elanil frowned. "But you're willing to get all these armies, bring all these people? For what, some kind of false hope?"

"We have to at least *try*."

"I know. I just can't help but think there's something

we're missing. We missed so much for so long—do we really know everything now?"

"Maybe we'll never know. That doesn't mean we should give up."

"I know. I'm just scared, Rylan."

"Me too." He pulled her closer, their bodies moving perfectly together. The dance had turned into just a sway, Elanil staring deeply into his eyes.

"Whatever happens," she said, "promise me we'll stay together. I want to go through this with you."

She caught a hint of fear in his eyes for just a second, but then he leaned in and kissed her, softly. "I promise."

They stayed like that for several minutes, just swaying on the street as the sun began to set.

Then the magic began to take hold of them again.

Violet sparks of light filled the space around their legs, and Elanil felt herself becoming nearly weightless. She spun with Rylan in the air, feet tracing patterns in the sky. He held her tightly as they rose, their chests together, breathing in tandem. She looked into his eyes as Pano Sylrantheas fell below them, wreathed in purple sparkles.

And they danced. Gold came out to join the violet, shards of energy effervescing in the air around them. She felt a sense of beauty welling up within her, the forest in the distance becoming greener, brighter. Rylan himself grew stronger, more handsome. Her legs and their arms and the feeling of the sun transformed into an exquisite heaven, a paradise made just for them.

Then green entered in.

Flowers erupted around them as they twirled in the air. Lustrous vines and a carpet of grass appeared, dewdrops glinting in the sun. Birds and butterflies flew around them, twittering, wings flashing. And still they danced, their patch of sky filled with rainbows and waterfalls.

He kissed her again, and she felt her heart leap inside her chest. She was breathless when he broke away. She wanted to chase the fire in his eyes. She wanted him to clutch her, to move her, to take her where she'd never been. Their flight continued to ascend as stars appeared around them, brilliant bursts of color popping in the night sky that was suddenly there, and a sliver of the moon reflected on a glassy lake, and Rylan's hands were on her back, and his head was close, his breath hot in her ear, and he was whispering things to her and she felt herself stirring and a buzzing sound roared up in her ears and

he was *inside* her—his thoughts inside her mind! She could feel him there, love and lust burgeoning, and the power —*oh, the power*—filled his very soul and hers up to the brim

and the sun and moon shone down together, and the world was hot as hell

and the rainbows broke,

and the stars bloomed,

and he was trying to kiss her again, but something was wrong. Her head was wrong. The sparks had gotten inside it, and she could feel her mind *twisting*, her will no longer her own.

She saw flashing light inside her eyes, and she knew it for what it was.

Red.

"No," she tried to say, but a darkness clamped down on her thoughts, and the illusions that surrounded them whirled into chaos, into nothingness, into magma and sound and bright pinpricks of pain,

and Rylan's hands gripped her arms tightly, too tightly, and she tried to scream, was screaming,

and light and sound crashed down upon them but—

"Lani?" a voice cried out from down below. "Lani, is that...you?"

Instantly the magic shattered, fragments of light raining out of the sky. And Elanil fell, still held by Rylan, and they were falling hundreds of feet to the ground, and she saw Martan standing below them, a look of shock on his face. The Remnant boy had come to find her, and now she was falling, and there was no more time, and—

She found a piece of dark maple in her pocket and Willed it to life. She and Rylan crashed into the ground, just hard enough to send shooting sparks of pain through her feet and legs.

Rylan backed away from her immediately, a look of terror in her eyes.

"Are you...okay?" Martan asked.

Elanil stared at Rylan, realization dawning. He had controlled her, up there. He had mindmastered her. His magic had gone horribly awry, and Rylan hadn't even seemed aware it had been happening.

He had almost taken away her entire *being*.

She shuddered with revulsion, and Rylan saw the look on her face.

He fled.

SIXTY-SIX

ALLAIN STEPPED INTO MISSION CONTROL, voices and electronic sounds washing over him. The wall at the far end of the room was one gigantic screen, split into segments showing various video feeds, charts, and indicators. Wide rows of desks lined the room, filled with thin computer monitors and keyboards and equipment he didn't recognize. Operators were in every seat, dressed in white and wearing small, black headsets. There had to be at least thirty people in the room, all elves.

Most of them were Cothellon.

But they worked for President Greyson now. Shot's father. They were the good guys now. Or so Allain hoped.

There were some Valaraldans here, as well. They operated new stations that controlled the gravitonic engines that held the city up, and the massive electric jet engines that oriented and positioned the cities in the sky. The elves had in a short time eliminated as much magic from the city operations as possible.

Lives were too valuable to waste.

Shot was standing at a desk, speaking to a computer screen that showed a pixellated version of Small's face. Shot beckoned Allain over when he saw him enter, then returned to the screen.

"Sorry," he said. "Continue."

"Power Station 17 is online," Small said, his voice tinny over the connection. The video was jiggling as he talked, as if he were using some kind of handheld device to transmit it. "The conversion is pretty easy. We should have the rest of them up and running across all seven cities within a couple hours."

"Nice," Shot said. "That sure as hell was easy."

"Been studying these systems for a long time," Small said. "They're not that complicated."

"Keep up the good work."

"You got it, boss. Small out. Or...something." The screen went dark.

Shot straightened, looking over at one of the other stations. "How's the reversal looking?" he asked an elven woman.

"Feasible," the woman said. "The gate collector should work just fine as the entry point for all the Power Storage systems. From there, it's just a matter of forming a coherent beam of energy. That's the part we're not sure about—we have most of the hardware already in place, but the real beamforming was accomplished on the receiver site on Earth."

"Can it be done?"

"Probably. The device on this end was designed to capture and focus a tremendous amount of power. We've got every engineer we have working on it."

"Good. Keep at it. We may need it soon."

"Yes, sir."

Allain had missed the part where Shot had somehow been put in charge of Mission Control. It seemed strange to see him ordering around all these scientists. Allain couldn't help but wonder where Orym was, and why he wasn't here.

"Sylvis," Shot said, and another female elf perked up from two rows away. "Can we move the cities if we need to?"

Sylvis frowned. "All the cities were designed to move," she said, "but now that they're all connected, I'm not sure how safe it would be."

"We don't know where this Twin is going to land," Shot said.

"We should conduct a test, then. Move a few miles off from where we are, see how things hold up. If that works, we should be able to get ourselves anywhere we need to be."

"Do it."

Sylvis nodded and returned to her screen.

Shot hit a button on his desk, and Spike's head came into view. "Ho, boss," she said. She was carrying another handheld camera, and she was looking offscreen. Allain could hear the sound of what must be thousands of people talking in the background.

"Ho, Spike," Shot said. "How's it going?"

"The underkids are itching for a fight," she said. "Got twenty thousand of them, at last count. About half are mages. More are coming in every minute. We're about to move topside so we can get them all in one place."

Shot pursed his lips. "Let me get Dad on the line first, make sure the topsiders are warned. Where are you putting them?"

"Old Fisherman's Wharf," Spike said. "That's where all the remaining fallcars are, anyway. Figure we'll need them to get down."

"True," Shot said. "Good thinking. Thanks."

"Boss? You know when all this is going to happen?"

"Not yet. Just be ready."

"Got it."

He clicked off, just in time for his radio to buzz. "Shot here," he said, hitting the transmit button.

"Shot?" a voice said. "It's Rylan." The boy sounded shaken, as if something had just gone terribly wrong.

"Ho, Rylan," Shot said. "How are things on the surface?"

"Not good," Rylan said. "The elves don't believe me about the Twins. They won't fight."

"Damn," Shot said. He was silent for a moment, thinking. Allain had no ideas of his own. The elves could be stubborn—of that, he had no doubt. "Let me get Dill on the line, see if there's anything we can do."

"Okay," Rylan said. "I take it Nelenor hasn't arrived, yet?"

"Not that we know of," Shot said.

"Thanks." The radio went silent.

Shot hit transmit again. "Did you hear that, Dill?"

There was no response for a moment, then the radio clicked on. "Sure did," Dill's voice said. "I think I know what might convince the elves. Can you get me transportation to the surface?"

"Sure can," Shot said. "How many do you want to bring?"

"Let's start shipping these Crews down now," Dill said. "Get me some of the big droplifts, if you can. We'll keep them down here with us in case we need to move quickly. As to the rest of the Under Army, we may need to resort to gates. There are just too many of them."

"We'll do what we can," Shot said. "I'll get a pair of droplifts to you now. You at headquarters?"

"Just so."

"I'll have them there in ten minutes. Any idea why Rylan sounded so scared?"

"None," Dill said. "He seems...different now. I hope every-thing's okay."

"I hope so, too. Shot out."

SIXTY-SEVEN

ELANIL SAT ON THE GROUND, feeling suddenly cold. What Rylan had almost done to her—what he *had* done—was unthinkable. She had heard of this mindmaster power, but she had never felt it. She felt dirty. Used. She didn't know what rape felt like, but she imagined it must be something like this.

She didn't know if she'd ever be able to forgive him.

"Are you...okay?" Martan asked, sitting cross-legged on the dirt road next to her.

She peered at him, unsure exactly what to say. Martan seemed different, and it wasn't just the short hair and the clean, fitting clothes. No: he had an air of intelligence about him, as if the month since she'd died had somehow been long enough for him to learn wisdom, truth, and a lot more of the English language.

Jalnab, his father, was the Instruction Mentor now. She wondered if the two things were related.

She gathered in a deep, shuddering breath and let it out slowly. "I think I'm fine."

"What...happened?"

"Rylan used magic on me. Mindmaster magic."

"Oh." He didn't ask what it was. Could it be that he already knew?

"I don't think he did it on purpose." But could she be sure? Rylan's new powers seemed to be taking over everything. Xyclami was worming its way into his mind.

"I think..." Martan said. "I think he loves you."

Elanil stared at him, not quite blushing. "I thought I did, too."

It wasn't until she saw the crestfallen look on his face that she realized her mistake.

Martan had liked her. *Really* liked her. And she'd liked him, for the brief few months they'd kissed and danced in the forest, unknown to the Remnant so nearby. Until that night when Jalnab had found them, and everything had changed. Then her world had turned to machines and magic and guns and death. But then she'd met Rylan, and thoughts of Martan had simply fled.

She didn't feel that way about him. Maybe she never had.

"I'm sorry," she whispered, knowing it was not enough.

But Martan had recovered. He gave her a kind look, even half a smile. "You two are...cute...together."

"Thank you." This time she blushed. "Your English is so good!"

"I study hard. Father...good teacher. Lani, will you ever... dance...with me again?"

She almost reached out for him, but she knew the gesture would be too far. "Once this is over," she said, "I promise we'll dance again." She looked around at the village being reassembled. "Maybe I'll even be a Mentor, someday."

"I would...like that."

They stared at each other wordlessly as the sun dipped lower in the sky. She wondered what life would have been like if Martan had been all she'd had. If fate hadn't come to take her away. If magic and flying cities and a dirty boy hadn't separated them forever.

Maybe they would have been happy.

There was a whirring sound behind her, and Elanil turned to see what it was.

Huge flying vehicles were descending from the sky.

"Ho!" Dill shouted, waving from his position at the back of one. "We're here to see the Council!"

Elanil got to her feet, reaching out a hand to help Martan up. He didn't seem frightened, to his credit. They were both strong now.

"Ho," Elanil called back. "I'm glad you're here."

"NELENOR IS COMING," Dill said, standing at the front of Town Hall, addressing the Council. Elanil was with him.

"We've been through this before," Meriel said. "The Council voted against any intervention."

"It's not that we doubt your story," Nuala said. "It's just…"

"I have proof," Dill said, holding up his radio. As if on cue, it began blaring.

"We are still sifting the sparkthreads," Nelenor's voice said. "We know the Imprisoner is somewhere in this system, but we cannot seem to locate his thread. Again, I ask anyone who is listening to surrender him to us. We must have him."

"Is that—" Meriel began.

"Nelenor," Dill said.

The radio continued. "Since we cannot find him, we will proceed with his closest kin. Whoever you are: we demand the same from you. Give us the Imprisoner. I will give you six more hours to deliver him, and then I shall travel to Mar to find him."

"Shit," Dill said. "Six hours is not very long."

"What should we do?" Nuala asked.

"We have no choice," Dill said. "We must get ready to fight."

ORYM SHIVERED, suddenly feeling cold. Something had touched him for a moment. He could have sworn something had been inside him, touching his soul. It felt like a brush with death, as if a great power had almost found him.

He'd reacted instinctively, putting up a gate to nowhere around his body. He could feel it working, isolating his soul-strand from the outside world. Now nobody could find him. Now he would be safe.

Now he could finally finish his plan.

But first, he wanted to see if any of his bourbon was left.

SIXTY-EIGHT

ELANIL LEFT TOWN HALL, not wanting to be there while the Council made their plans. She didn't have anything to offer, anyway. All she had was magic and dancing. She wasn't any good at strategy, or at war. Twins, she was only fifteen.

She needed to find Rylan.

The sun was setting when she finally found him, sitting under the oak tree Arra had always loved. How had he known to come out here? How had he even found the way? She surveyed him from the edge of the forest, seeing the forlorn slump of his back, the way he was staring at the ground. His magic had clearly hurt him as well as her. Xyclami was taking over. Could he be blamed for the things he'd done?

She stepped into the clearing, making her way toward the tree.

He didn't lift his head as she approached, but she saw him move his hand, setting it in the grass next to him. A few green sparkles erupted from his fingers and he jerked, anger clouding his face.

Magic was getting the better of him.

"Ho," Elanil said, sitting next to him underneath the tree. She didn't touch him. She was scared to even be this close.

"Ho," he whispered, and she could tell that he'd been crying.

She didn't know where to start. "It was a good dance."

"I'm sorry," he whispered.

She turned to him, and for an instant she could see the motors working behind his eyes. His brain was struggling to keep up with Xyclami and the world outside. "I can't—" she started. "I don't—" She couldn't get the words out.

"I didn't mean to get inside your head," Rylan said. "Without the wood to filter it, the magic is just so *raw*. One power blends into the next, and I almost have no concept of which is which. If I want something to happen, it just *does*. Sometimes that means red."

"Red?"

"Destroyer Aspect." He sighed. "It burns people. Hell, I've seen my own mother do it. But what she didn't know is that it's also mindmaster magic."

"Oh."

"The Aspects, the Ways, they're all the same thing. I can access all of it, flitting from thing to thing. Flitting. What the hell? I'd never even *heard* that word before. Fuck. What's happening to me?"

He turned to her, eyes brimming.

She reached out to him.

She couldn't help it. She couldn't bear to see him like this, so alone and afraid. Mysterious powers were taking hold of him, and all because Phoenix had asked one simple question. All because Rylan was somehow *special*.

Now magic was ruining his life.

She took him in her arms, letting him cry on her shoulder. It was a gentle, quiet moment. A moment without pretense, without expectation. No dancing. No magic. Just him and her and the night and his tears.

The sun dipped below the horizon.

"Six hours," he whispered after a while.

"You heard?"

"I heard. Must be more like four hours now. Why such an arbitrary time?"

His vocabulary really was getting better. How was a machine on another *planet* capable of granting him so much knowledge so quickly? Elanil shuddered, and he felt it, and pulled away.

She reached out to him again.

And he kissed her, right there underneath the tree. Just a small, chaste kiss. Their lips connected for but a moment, and she could taste his tears. One spark flew between them. One gold spark in the growing gloom.

"What does gold do?" she asked.

He paused for a moment, as if distracted. When he returned his gaze to her, she thought she saw gold dancing in his eyes. "Beauty," he said. "Creator Aspect imparts raw energy and beauty. You can shoot people with it, like with shockstriking. Or you can make things appear more beautiful. I guess leafrunning isn't needed, since all the Aspects grant movement."

Creator Aspect was hers. "Did Phoenix ever make a gold bubble?"

"Not that I know of. She could have, if she'd used creativity. That's the emotion that would trigger it."

"Creativity is an emotion?"

"More like a state of mind. Every Aspect has one."

"Have you ever used gold on me?" She thought he had, while they were dancing in the air. She remembered golden light sparkling around them as they flew.

"Yes." He hung his head.

She lifted his chin up with a single finger. "And what did you see?"

"I saw you."

She frowned. "Then why the ashamed look on your face? Am I ugly now? You can say it."

"No," he said, laying a hand on her knee where she sat cross-legged next to him. "Do you really want to know what I saw?"

She nodded, suddenly scared.

"I saw you five hundred years from now."

"What? But I must have been—"

"You were *beautiful*. You were a Mentor—more than a Mentor, actually. You were...I don't know the word for it. Mature, I guess you'd say. You were so full of knowledge, of grace, of poise. Everyone looked up to you. Everyone wanted to hear what you had to say. You were just so full of *life*. Like you are now, but just...different. Better. As if you were a fine wine, getting better with age. I just wish I could be there to see it for real."

"Have you ever even tasted wine?"

He blushed. "I didn't even know what it was until about five seconds ago."

How could he do this? How could he speak so eloquently to her while the machine was speaking in his head?

"What do you mean?" she asked. "You wish you could be there to see it for real?"

"I'll be dead in five hundred years."

"But you're Quynn's son. Remember? You're half an elf."

"So you think..."

"You could have an elven lifespan. You might live to see me that old." She looked at the ground. "If you stay with me that long."

His touch on her knee grew firmer. "If we survive the Twins."

"A lot of ifs."

"Elanil, I want you to know how sorry I am. Truly. I didn't mean to hurt you back there. I didn't mean to mindmaster you. Hell, I *never* want to hurt you like that. I was just so happy, you know? There was some kind of...energy, I guess."

He was cute when he got like this, when his words failed him. Those moments were becoming rarer. "I forgive you," she said. "Do you think it's possible to control?"

"I hope so," he said, his eyes faraway. "I hope so."

"Come back to me."

She touched his cheek, drawing a line with her finger down to his neck. When he looked at her again, the golden sparks were gone.

"You should leave," he said. "I'm dangerous. You should be far away from me."

"I don't want to leave," she said, shifting closer on the ground. "I want you to kiss me again."

He swallowed. "I don't think that's such a good idea."

"Please. I know you can control it if you want to. Can you try? For me?"

He nodded, his face moving closer to her own. She was conscious of his lips, of her own chest rising and falling, of his hair, perfectly awry. The sun was gone, its light fading upwards from the forest, reflecting in his eyes. The moment grew, their lives pausing in the glow. Their lips were there, hovering in the sky, connected by a thought.

They moved together as one.

Then his hands were in her hair, his lips pressed fiercely to hers. She felt heat rising to her face and she opened her mouth, tongue questing for his. She didn't know how she knew to do that—she just did. The passion of the moment overtook her and she surrendered herself to it, her body no longer her own.

She was Rylan's, through and through.

Her hands went to his face, around his neck, her head changing angles as she tried to drink him in. His mouth was motion, his touch fire. She was dancing with him, choreographing their connection beneath the tree. Her heart beat the steps as her hands found his.

Then he was pulling her toward him, and she was lying on top of him on the ground. His hands were low on her back and his lips broke away, kissing her cheek, her neck. She felt sparks of energy leap inside her as he kissed her there, as a breath of wind blew over the wetness on her skin.

His hands went lower, and she let them. She was touching his chest, feeling the developing muscles on his small frame. He was strong—stronger than he looked. And his mouth was just so sweet, his hunger for her more powerful than any magic could be.

She pulled back an inch, breaking his kisses, looking at him in the night. She saw love there in his eyes, and lust, and a spark of red.

Mindmaster magic.

But it hadn't erupted from him, yet. "Stop the magic," she said. "Focus on me."

And she sat up on his chest, peeling off her shirt.

She had no idea what had come over her. Now she was topless, bare breasts exposed to him and the wind. She hadn't thought this through. She didn't even *like* her breasts. She'd never shown them before to *anyone*, and she'd barely known Rylan any time! Mother would *kill* her if she knew what she was doing.

Mother was dead.

And Rylan was looking at her as if she were the most beautiful thing he'd ever seen.

She fought against the urge to cover herself. She sat there, back erect, lips parted, willing herself to let him see. She *wanted* this. She wanted his eyes on her.

She wanted more than that.

"You're...*incredible*," he whispered. "Can I—"

She nodded.

Then he was touching her, the contact sending sparks through her spine, between her legs. She felt giddy, as if the moments were clustered all together, the rush of feeling almost overwhelming. Then she was leaning down toward him, his hands still on her breasts, and their lips connected again.

It was the most beautiful thing she'd ever done.

She was here, in this moment, with this boy she loved, sharing with him the tenderness and connection that only they could share. The night wind caressed her bare back as she pressed her chest into him, as she rubbed herself against him on the ground. She felt a bulging in his pants, a hardness where there hadn't been before.

It heated her face even further.

That was when sparks erupted in the night, spinning outward from them and exploding. Gold and red and purple and blue, white and green and silver. Bits of light shimmered in the air, surrounding them, embracing them. She felt her emotions and her skin expand, his touch and his lips and the warmth between her legs growing warmer, stronger, her need for him all-encompassing. She reached a hand down to his pants, feeling his need for her. She wanted him—she wanted him *so badly*. She wanted him to live inside her forever.

She saw red dancing in his eyes.

"No," she said, trying to push away but failing. Her breath

was coming shorter now, heat suffusing her lungs. His grip on her breasts was stronger, too strong, painful. "Stop," she said, but he didn't stop. He sat up, pushing her back, grasping hungrily for her, lips fighting for her own.

Magic filled the night.

"This isn't you," she said. "Please stop."

But he was too far gone to stop. Red and golden sparks cascaded over them. She saw his beauty amplify, his face becoming impossibly pretty. She looked down and saw her own breasts protruding larger from her chest, her nipples taut, inviting. She felt the sudden urge to strip completely, to let him take what was his, to give herself fully to this boy. This man. This powerful demigod lying there beneath the tree.

Mindmaster magic was inside her brain.

She yelped, struggling against it, pushing against him, hitting his chest. But it did no good—he was far too strong. He wanted her, and he would have her, no matter what she did.

He was going to take her against her will.

So she slapped him, as hard as she could.

And he sent everything he had at her, particles of every color slamming into her body. They launched her back, flying *quickly* through the air, the world sliding away from her in harsh rewind. She hit a tree, then another one, her left arm snapping like a twig. Pain shot through her and her head hit another tree, then she slammed *hard* into a big, unyielding piece of wood.

A branch pierced through her stomach.

She gasped, unable to make a sound, pain filling her entire mind. Her bare breasts heaved as she tried to breathe, as she tried to do *something* to save herself. Blood fell hotly from her stomach where the branch protruded. Her arm hung uselessly at her side. Her head felt like it had been squeezed by a thousand vices. Her skin was ripped and torn.

But the worst pain was inside her mind.

Rylan had almost taken her. He'd almost *raped* her, mentally and physically. He'd almost done to her the most unforgivable thing a man could do.

The magic had taken control.

"Elanil!" she heard him call, and the particles were gone. "What have I done?" She heard the plaintive tone, the horror in his voice. She knew he hadn't meant to do the things he'd done.

But he couldn't change what had happened.

Now she was there, half naked on a branch, dying on a tree where he had put her. She would die there, having tasted passion and its bitter end.

But something called to her.

A strand of light, invisible except in her mind. A strand of energy. A soulstrand, connecting her to a Tree.

A Prime Palm, on another planet. It was calling to her now. It was the one she had bound to her.

She could take power from it, if she wished. Though the distance was great, she knew that she had not yet exceeded its bounds. She could Will it to life, imparting magic in this world. And now, finally, she knew which type of power that Tree held.

Soulsoothing magic.

She sighed, and shed a tear, and Willed the magic to appear.

As she slipped off the branch, her wounds repairing, her skin rebuilding, she reflected on the person Rylan had become.

She would never be able to be with him again.

SIXTY-NINE

"I *KNOW* our best warriors are gone," Beam was saying to Keleb. "That's why the women and children must be ready."

"Have you actually *seen* these Twins?" Keleb asked.

"Phoenix has," Beam said, motioning to the woman. Phoenix just looked at them with a blank expression. She didn't speak their language. "Listen—I trust her, okay?"

Keleb gave a great, heaving sigh. "Everyone is already ready," he said. "They're at Feed."

"Then why all the arguing? It's not like you."

Keleb kicked a piece of gravel. "Magona already tricked us once."

"You think *I'm* Magona?"

He glanced at Phoenix.

Beam gave an abrupt laugh. "If *she* were Magona, we'd all be in a hell of a lot of trouble." She stepped forward, gripping Keleb's shoulder tightly. "I appreciate your candor, and your carefulness. But Phoenix is on our side, and the sooner you realize that, the sooner we can fight as one."

"Yes, Warlord."

"Thank you. Now tell me of the bourbon."

"The...bourbon? But surely *trade* is the least of our concerns, what with the—"

Shouting erupted in the distance. Beam turned her head toward Martial Square, where the sounds were coming from. Harsh, white floodlights illuminated the area, revealing the towering form of a man with a fox for a head.

Nelenor had finally arrived.

Phoenix was grasping at her radio. "He's here," she said into it in English. "Nelenor is here, in Lusvunub."

The radio crackled, but nobody replied.

"Greetings," Nelenor said, his voice easily carrying across Lusvunub. "Where is the Imprisoner's kin?"

She could hear more shouts, but nobody fired any weapons. Yet.

"Dragons," Nelenor said, making the word sound like a curse. "This is the wrong place. The energy here..." He looked down at the ground, as if there were something underneath it. "I must investigate this."

"Quick," Beam hissed to Keleb, "go talk to that Twin."

"What?" Keleb said. "What do you want me to say?"

"Anything," Beam said. "Just distract it. Him. We need help. We need reinforcements."

"Phoenix?" a voice said over the radio. "This is Dill. We read you. Can you keep him occupied? We'll be there as quickly as we can."

Phoenix looked worriedly at Beam.

"Just try," Beam said to Keleb. "Maybe be nice to it. Maybe you can sweet talk it."

Keleb snorted. "You think I know how to *sweet talk*?"

"I'll get as many troops as I can find," Beam said. "Go."

"Yes, Warlord. The troops are at Feed."

"Thank you."

Keleb left.

And Beam ran toward Feed, where they held communal meals, Phoenix trailing behind her.

Ilyrion had been reduced to rubble—she'd never seen the city in its prime, but she recognized ruins when she saw them. She hoped they could muster some resistance before Nelenor did the same on Earth.

ELANIL STUMBLED into Town Hall just as things were getting crazy. Council members were jumping and gesticulating, arguing over things she didn't care about or know. Battle plans, it sounded like. They sounded like a bunch of humans.

She'd put a new shirt on. She could still feel the branch where it had pierced her body, the blood where it had crept down her cold skin.

She could still feel Rylan inside her mind.

But she brushed it away, intent on moving forward. She couldn't deal with what had happened. She couldn't face what it had meant. All she had now were the others: the Council, and Dill, and that was really it. She had no family, anymore. Arra was not here. And Rylan was gone.

Rylan could be with her no more.

She swept back tears, rushing to the front of the room, just trying to stay ahead of her emotions.

"Nelenor is here, in Lusvunub," a voice said over Dill's radio. He fumbled with it, doing something with the controls.

"Lusvunub?" Bellas asked. "What in the Twins' name is he doing way out there?"

"You do realize you just invoked the Twins' name about a Twin," Meriel said, her tone dry.

"Old habits are hard to break," Bellas said. "Can we get there in time?"

"Goddammit," Dill said. "I can't get this stupid thing to work. Bellas, the droplifts we have can go maybe five hundred miles an hour at the most."

"That's around...five hours," Daylor said. "Too slow."

"All we can do is try," Dill said.

"Or we can use a gate."

"No gates," Dill said. "Oh, for fuck's sake." He rotated a dial on the radio. "Wrong transmission channel. Phoenix? This is Dill. We read you. Can you keep him occupied? We'll be there as quickly as we can."

The doors burst open suddenly, and Rylan appeared. He looked more disheveled than usual—twigs and leaves were in his hair, and his clothes were rumpled.

"I can help," he said, studiously avoiding looking at Elanil. "I can make the droplifts go *much* faster than that."

"Well, folks," Dill said, "it looks like we have our plan. Get everyone together. Now." He changed the dial on his radio. "Shot? Nelenor is in Lusvunub. Can you get the United Sky Cities over there?"

The radio fuzzed for a second. "Yes, Captain," Shot said. "We'll move as quickly as we can."

"Send the underkids down when you get there," Dill said. "And, uh...godspeed."

"Which god?" Shot asked over the radio.

"I have no idea," Dill said. He lowered the radio, looking around the room. "Well, folks, it seems as if we have a Twin to kill."

"Or try," Meriel said.

"Or die trying," Bellas said.

Elanil and Rylan finally exchanged a look from across the room, and she felt fear shivering across her soul.

PART
SIX

"If you prick us, do we not bleed? If you tickle us, do we not laugh? If you poison us, do we not die? And if you wrong us, shall we not revenge?"

— *William Shakespeare*
  1596 A.D.
  420 years before the Sundering

SEVENTY

LORELEI WAS STUCK USING her feet. She couldn't gate, for obvious reasons—it would fuck with her mind. And she didn't have a car or a spaceship or a train or anything, not that any of those things were still running. Everyone had fled Ilyrion, and now nothing was left.

Lorelei had fled, too. She and Elasha had managed to find a place to sleep, huddled in a ruined building in Old Town with several newly homeless elves and a few who were not newly homeless at all. Everyone smelled like shit, but that didn't matter.

Ilyrion was destroyed.

She should have left the city, following the line of refugees north into the Faedori Forest. The Twins hadn't gone there yet, but Lorelei was under no illusions that the forest would be safe. Still, she should be running away.

Instead, she was heading *toward* the Twins.

"This is a terrible idea," Elasha said. "You're going to get us both killed."

The storm was blowing over and around them, making it hard to hear or speak or walk or breathe.

"You're welcome to leave," Lorelei said. "Nobody is making you come with me."

"And go where?"

"I don't know. But if you're not leaving, stop complaining."

"I see why you have so many friends."

Lorelei stopped walking abruptly, turning to face Elasha. "This is a matter of life or death."

"I know, I know. I'm sorry. Let's go."

They resumed walking.

When they finally arrived, only one of the Twins was there: Velion. Lorelei recognized him, though she didn't know how. Perhaps it was because she'd been there when the Twins had first arrived. Though they hadn't, in fact, been in this Anubis form back then. What had happened? Why did they look like this now?

She shook her head, steeled herself, and stepped forward, trying to ignore the wind whipping through her hair.

"A little one approaches," Velion said, his voice loud. "Have you brought me the Imprisoner?"

"Almost," Lorelei said, doing her best to keep her tone even. "I know who he is."

"Good," Velion said. "And who is he?"

"Where is your brother?"

"Ah, a quid pro quo. Very well. Nelenor has traveled to Earth. The Imprisoner's kin is there."

That would be Dillon. She felt her heart sink as she realized Earth might be facing the same destruction the Twins had just rendered here. She didn't want to have fought so hard to save that world only to lose it in the end.

She had to bring this saga to a close.

"Your turn," Velion said.

"Orym," Lorelei said. "You knew him as Aten. Later he was known as Akhenaten, the king in the desert."

"And where is this Akhenaten now?"

"I don't know."

Velion roared, raising his arms over his head.

"I can help you find him!" Lorelei shouted.

Velion lowered his arms. "I am sifting the threads. Now that I know his names, it will be easier. I will find him, little girl. It is only a matter of time now."

"What happened to you?" Lorelei asked. "When I first met you, you were a pair of scientists. You were calm. Reasonable. And I could have sworn you were a girl. Or was it your twin?"

Velion laughed, the sound uproarious. "Have you ever been Imprisoned?" he asked. "Have you ever been lost for a hundred thousand years?"

"Worse," Lorelei said. "I lived a hundred thousand years *and then forgot it all.*"

They were silent for a moment.

"Then it would stand to reason," Velion said, "that you would understand our position. Akhenaten stole pieces of our *souls.* He shouldn't have known how to do that—*couldn't* have. He is power-hungry, greedy, dangerous. If he somehow attains Xyclami, there will be no end to the destruction he can wreak."

"I agree," Lorelei said. "Orym must be stopped, and I'll help you do it. But do you really think destroying our cities— our *civilization*—is the way to go about it? When you first arrived on this planet, you told a story of your own home. How it was destroyed by outsiders. How you barely escaped. Is that what you want for us? Have you become that which nearly ruined your existence?"

Velion peered down at her, Anubis face expressionless. "We will find the Imprisoner, and we will kill him," he said. "Then and only then will we stop this destruction. Your kind has been nothing but horror for us. We should never have come."

"But Velion," Lorelei said, "we are *you*."

Velion stomped, the ground shaking as he did. "Silence." Then he cocked his head, looking to the north. "Ah. A new thread has appeared. The one who freed us is still alive. That is well—perhaps he can help us find Akhenaten."

"Trey," Lorelei whispered.

"Trey," Velion echoed. "Thank you for the information."

"Please don't kill him."

"I will make no guarantees."

And Velion left, taking great strides to the north. He didn't give Lorelei another look as he receded in the distance.

"You've really got some balls on you," Elasha said. "Weren't you scared?"

"Terrified," Lorelei said. "And it didn't do us any good. Velion came out ahead in that exchange."

"Should we warn Trey?"

"We don't know where he is. The only thing north is... Errenmel, but I doubt he's there. The Department of Magical Research is that way, too. And he *was* with Cresius. That's probably where they went.

"I hate the DMR," Elasha said, shuddering. Clearly there was some kind of history there.

"He'll be safer there than anywhere else on the planet," Lorelei said. "Come on—maybe we should go to Earth."

"Why?"

"Nelenor is there. Maybe we'll have better luck with him —or maybe we can at least help fight. I don't want to see my beautiful cities destroyed."

"Fine," Elasha said. "But how?"

"Let's hope there's a spaceship left, and a pilot willing to fly."

MISSION CONTROL WAS IN CHAOS. Allain stood next to Shot's desk, hoping nobody would run him over. Nelenor had finally arrived, but he was apparently in the wrong place. They'd expected him to follow Dill, or at least show up where the most people were. They hadn't expected him to arrive in Louisberg.

"We need to move, Sylvis," Shot was saying. "Now."

"Our test was successful," Sylvis said, "but you're talking about jetting at full speed. I must strongly recommend against this."

"Not full speed," Shot said. "We need to go *faster*."

"The cities could rip apart."

"That's a risk we'll have to take."

"Sylvis," an elf named Grathgor said, "you don't have to take orders from him."

Grathgor was a Cothellon, formerly on Lorelei's Small Council. Allain had learned that just a minute ago. Now he was wary.

Sylvis sighed. "Actually, Grathgor, I do. President Grayson himself gave the order. We are to do everything in our power to meet this threat from the Twins, and Shot here is in charge."

Grathgor ground his teeth. "Then get it done," he said. "If we're to die, let us die quickly."

"We won't die," Sylvis said. "At the worst, it will simply require years of extensive repairs." She gave a curt nod to Shot, then turned in her chair. "Helm, give us a bearing on

Louisberg, in the former state of Kentucky. All ahead full—to start."

"Aye," the helmsman said.

Allain took a seat as the floor lurched underneath him, the city moving ponderously in the sky.

He hoped they would reach Nelenor in time.

SEVENTY-ONE

THE STORM WAS STILL BLOWING as Trey twiddled his thumbs at the conference room table. The Twins were no doubt still rampaging about Valaralda, causing who knew how much desolation, and all they could do was sit there and *talk*.

They were getting nothing done.

"Here's the plan as best I see it," Cresius was saying.

"*Finally* he gets to the plan," Arra muttered from her seat next to him. Quynn had a dark glare on his face, and Lashel looked supremely bored.

"As I said earlier, we actually have somewhat prepared for this sort of situation," Cresius continued. "In fact, we've been preparing for millennia."

"You thought the Twins would come back to life?" Trey asked.

"Not exactly. We reasoned that with enough magicians, eventually someone would grow more powerful than the rest. We've witnessed great power variances across our history, and we at the Department figured we hadn't seen it all. Someone would come along, eventually—someone that was too powerful for us to fight."

"But you have an Army of Mages."

"Indeed we do, though none of them are Prime. But we were worried that even our Army might not prove to be enough. So we spent a long time preparing something... special."

"Go on," Arra said. "Don't make us beg for it." Her tone was uncharacteristically snide.

"I suppose we're all short on temper," Cresius said. "This infernal storm isn't doing much to help matters." He spread his hands on the table. "There is a place to the north of the Thesserin Desert, where the sands bleach white. Where endless spires appear, hundreds of feet high, leading down to brutally sharp rocks below. Pillars made of pure salt. We call this place *Singwa Lingwe*: the Salt Spires."

"Sounds hospitable," Arra said.

"The very opposite. Nothing grows there. Nothing can. There is no water, no way up if you fall. The sun beats down on *Singwa Lingwe* incessantly, so hot it's almost impossible to breathe. But that's not all."

"There's *more* to this?"

Cresius nodded. "We've spent thousands of years laying devastating magical traps throughout *Singwa Lingwe*. We used every artifact we could find, every bit of power we knew to use. There are traps there that could kill men by the thousands—by the millions, even. There is power there that could render even a god powerless."

"Great," Trey said, "but there's just one problem. You just described what is probably the worst place on the planet. Nobody will ever go there."

"That's where you're wrong," Cresius said. "The plan is to

find the Imprisoner, bring him to *Singwa Lingwe*, and lure the Twins there."

"You want us to *lure* the Twins?"

"Yes."

"You're insane."

Quynn barked a sudden laugh. "You've got more guts than I took you for."

"Thanks, I think," Cresius said. "Listen. We have technology that lets us easily survive out there on the Spires. And with magic to protect us, we'll be fine—providing we avoid the traps."

Rain beat against the windows, an incessant rapping sound that was driving Trey crazy. "Something is bothering me," he said. "And it's not just this storm. I feel like we don't have the full story, yet. Who are the Twins? Where did they come from? Why are they so mad?"

"The Imprisoner," Cresius said. "We know this."

"Yes, but what about the Believers? How do they factor into this? You said yourself, they were right to predict the Twins' second coming. If they were right about that, what else might they know?"

"There's something else," Arra said. "Something I saw in the forest, when I tried to save Lorelei." She shivered. "Gray mages, performing some ritual. They brought a person back from the dead."

Cresius pursed his lips. "The Eglaria," he said, sounding the word out like a curse.

"Aren't they the ones we met in Nekhrumet?" Trey asked.

Arra nodded. "They saved your life, as I recall."

"They taught me that anti-storm trick. I wonder what else they know?"

"Perhaps it would behoove us to consult them," Arra said.

"I agree," Cresius said. "Let's go."

"Just like that?" Trey asked.

"Just like that. I've long meant to pay our brothers in the west a visit. Now seems like the perfect time."

THE STORM BUFFETED them as they touched down in Nekhrumet. The ship managed to navigate without crashing, at least. Quynn winced as his butt bounced in his chair. They could have sprung for better padding.

Soon the ship's doors opened, disgorging everyone into the raging storm. Quynn couldn't even really see Nekhrumet through the wild rain. He couldn't see damn near *anything*. He was instantly soaked through.

"This way!" Cresius shouted, pointing to the left. There was a shadow of a building of some kind in that direction, with a sign made out of stone. Quynn could barely make out a circular symbol on it. The Eglaria.

But Quynn didn't want to go to the Eglaria. He didn't want any part of this insane plan. He wanted to leave, to escape before anyone got any bright ideas about merging Trey and him. He wanted to get his own life back, and now seemed as good a chance as any. If the world was about to end, he wanted at least a few last moments for himself.

He took off running to the right.

"Quynn!" Aira shouted from behind him.

"Let him go!" Cresius shouted, barely audible over the rain. "We have bigger problems!"

A smile grew on Quynn's face as he ran, leaving the motley crew behind. Maybe he could find a horse, a camel, whatever kind of animals they had in this place. Maybe there would even be a car. He would find what he could, steal it if he had to, and get the hell away from these mages and their stupid plans.

SEVENTY-TWO

ORYM STROLLED along the barren upper deck at Turovoite, reveling in the storm. The restaurant was the only building left standing in Ilyrion, ironically. Perhaps the Twins had heard of the bourbon he'd sold them. Orym gave a wry laugh, the sound lost to the fury of the storm.

The woman he hadn't married would have liked this storm. Tiala had always loved the rain.

He stood there for a long minute, lost to the dust of memories. It made sense now, why Tiala had left. She must have felt the Akhenaten that was buried within him.

If only he'd felt it himself.

He held the nowhere gate around him still, feeling the slow burn of dark willow as he did. He had plenty of the wood, at least—he'd stocked up heavily from the supplies under the city. The Department of Magical Research hadn't regulated magic nearly as well as it thought it had; the only effect of all their rules was to drive darkprime magic underground, where thieves and criminals could fetch higher prices. He had seen the same thing time and time again on

Earth. It was pitiful, really. Even here, in the *enlightened* city of Ilyrion, even here they made the same mistakes.

The nowhere gate had another side effect: it prevented him from getting wet or blown around. It disconnected him from reality, as if he no longer existed. It made it so the Twins couldn't find him. It prevented him from losing or gaining memories when he traveled through another gate.

And it acted as the world's most effective umbrella.

He paced the deck, picking his way through toppled tables and unused silverware, wondering if there were side effects to not being real. If he held this gate around himself too long, what would happen? Would he cease to exist in truth, lost to the ethers of time? Or would he grow more powerful, becoming like the Twins themselves? He laughed, the sound going nowhere in his gate. No, he would never be as powerful as the Twins. Not unless he stole their power.

Which was exactly what he planned to do.

"The Pyramids of Souls," he said to himself. Sometimes it was easier to think when he spoke out loud. "I know the capture side works, at least."

It did work. The pyramids on all three planets acted as a sort of sponge, an attractor for the etherial energy that made up souls. Orym had never *quite* been able to define what that energy was, or how it worked. It was physical, and yet not. He was sure there was some kind of physics to be described, but the concepts were far beyond him. Soul energy was at the core of all magic—he knew that much. It was what powered Guruthos, connected people to it. It was how you told it what to do.

And with enough of it gathered in one place, Orym had reasoned that he might be able to break some rules.

Like the one preventing the Twins from relinquishing

their device willingly. It was just a theory, of course, but he was confident in it. His theories had a history of success.

"But it doesn't work. Why?" He continued pacing, peering out at the ruins of Ilyrion whenever the rain parted for an instant. "I know soul entrapment works. I know the pyramids work on an individual level, transmitting that energy back out. I tested each of them after they were built. It's only when they *connect* that there's a problem."

He was missing something. He must be. There was some mechanic here, physical or magical, that was stopping his network of pyramids from working together, from shooting out their soul energy as they had been intended to do.

He just needed to figure out *what*.

Maybe he shouldn't have killed himself, eons ago. He had needed to be free of Edrafen, of the constant presence of the Twins in his mind. And it had worked, but had he lost something else in the transition? Had his suicide somehow fomented the problems he now faced?

He growled to himself, frustrated. He was getting nowhere. He needed more data. Perhaps he should visit the others, reintegrate into their group. As long as Lorelei hadn't found them yet, no one would know what his plan truly was. No one would know the role he'd played in the Twins' demise.

No one would know that he was the Imprisoner.

He allowed himself a minute to fantasize about what would be. To picture the future, if his plan were to succeed.

He closed his eyes, and envisioned what his life would be like.

Respect. That was first. He had respect now, though it had taken him so many millennia to attain—but it wasn't enough. He needed more. He'd always needed more, back when he was a Junior Professor trying to get his idiot students interested in astronomy. He'd been smarter than them then, and he was smarter now. But the world insisted on never giving him his due.

Well, he would show them what a smart person could do.

Power. Power was next. Power was how he'd gain his respect, how he'd show the world what he was capable of. But that wasn't the *real* reason he wanted the power.

He wanted it for the *possibilities.*

What could he do with the raw power Guruthos held? He knew the Twins shaped it, made it into the Fourteen Powers that everyone knew today. He knew that the machine actually wrought something more primal, more indistinct. That once he held the device in his grasp, he could do with it whatever he wished.

He could create worlds in his image.

He would be a god, though gods were overrated. He didn't want to be a *god*, exactly. Yes, he wanted respect. He wanted people to respect him, even to love him. He wanted the Selenias and the Loreleis and even the Arras and the Treys of the world to look up to *him*, to know that he was their better.

Okay, maybe he did want to be a god.

But oh, the things he would create! Cities the likes of which none had ever seen. Places that defied all natural laws. Transportation, commerce, science—everyone's way of life would be completely changed. The Fourteen Powers were far too limiting. Without them standing in the way, there was no bound to what he could do.

That was his plan.

He just had to get the Pyramids to work.

QUYNN HAD MANAGED to find a camel in Nekhrumet. It hadn't been hard to steal it, what with the storm pervading everything. He'd taken the camel west—it was impossible to tell without any points of reference, but the natives in Nekhrumet had been able to help. So he'd gone west, heading toward what he hoped were the ruins of civilization. Maybe from there he could finally get off this planet.

Sometime after that, he'd found a caravan in the whirling rain. A dozen wagons laden with food and gear, driven by camels, looking sodden and forlorn as they trudged through the wet sand. He was surprised they could move at all, what with the wind and everything. He was frozen to the bone.

The caravan was easy to mindmaster. He'd palmed some darkprime wood from Trey when he wasn't looking. The man was always the stupid one, ever unaware. At least Quynn finally had some inkling as to why.

And so it was that Quynn was sitting inside one of the wagons, enjoying the relative shelter from the storm, trying not to wince every time his body jolted on the hard wood as the wagon bounced and moved. They'd been heading to Ilyrion, the caravan leader had said. Evidently they hadn't heard about the Twins.

The wagon stopped suddenly, and Quynn could hear shouting in the strange Nekhrumetian language. He didn't understand a word of it, of course, but he could tell panic when he heard it. He grumbled, rolled over, and got out of the wagon.

The Nekhrumetians were all off their camels, standing in a group and pointing in a single direction, shouting at each other. Quynn squinted, trying to make out what they were looking at, but all he saw were murky shapes in the wind and rain.

Shapes that looked like monsters.

He didn't cringe. This was Valaralda, after all—who knew what wonders it held? He should know—he'd lived here, after all. But many of those memories were gone now, and besides: he was always up for an adventure. If these monster things proved dangerous, he always had magic to defend himself with.

So he stepped forward in the sand, leaning into the wind, passing the Nekhrumetians and their gesticulation. He wanted to make out the shapes better, to see what they could possibly be.

For a moment, he thought he saw claws.

SEVENTY-THREE

NELENOR WAS GROWING INCREASINGLY AGITATED. Phoenix watched as Keleb and some others tried to reason with him, speaking in halting English. The Twin seemed to understand the language, which was interesting. Probably from a hundred thousand years in Ambarhal.

"This isn't going to last," she said to Beam. "He's on the edge."

"I know," Beam said. "And once he starts attacking, we're dead."

"Should we run? Maybe we can quietly evacuate people."

"That'd probably just piss him off."

"Well, we can't *fight*."

"We can try."

"We'll die, Beam."

"Aren't you the one who always said to never back down from a fight?"

Phoenix was beginning to regret saying that.

"Anyway," Beam said, "it's too late to run now. Look."

Phoenix looked where she was pointing, her mouth falling open in surprise.

Two massive vehicles were flying through the air, huge bursts of rainbow particles streaming out around and behind them. They were distant, but they were moving *fast*, and as they approached Phoenix could see people on them.

Hundreds of people.

Phoenix's radio blared. "Phoenix?" It was Dill. "The elves from Pano Sylrantheas are arriving. You should be able to see us now. I'm with them."

"Rylan must be, too," Phoenix said. Then she clicked the radio on. "You're just in time," she said. "Nelenor looks about ready to attack."

"We may not be able to hold him off for long," Dill said. "The United Sky Cities are coming, but they're slower than we are. We have an idea that might work to defeat Nelenor, but we need to stall for time."

"Okay," Phoenix said. "Everyone has enough primewood?"

"Just so," Dill said. "Do you?"

Phoenix nodded, then realized he couldn't see her. "Yes."

"And Phoenix, I know you were reticent to use magic when we last fought together. We'll need you now."

"I won't hesitate," Phoenix said. "I'm not afraid of dying any longer."

THE DROPLIFT LANDED in a cloud of colorful light. Elanil fought to keep her feet as everyone streamed from the vessel, running off the flat platform in the back and down a ramp that had appeared. Rylan was in the other droplift. She was careful not to look his way.

Lusvunub looked a lot like Gulthurub, only bigger. And this time she was *inside* it, well inside where she would normally have been killed. The Remnant didn't take kindly to unexpected visitors, after all. At least not before.

Times had really changed.

She saw Gatling guns on towers around the outer wall, itself made up primarily of barbed wire and steel. Harsh, white floodlights illuminated most of the city, and the place felt empty, as if everyone had fled. One part of the city in particular stood out more than anything else.

Nelenor was standing there.

He towered over everything, vulpine face somehow angry in the floodlights shining up at him. He was tall and well-muscled, his humanoid body at least thirty feet high. Hadn't he been bigger before, in Ilyrion? She could have sworn she'd seen the Twins towering over the other buildings. Maybe he could change his size at will. He *was* a god, after all.

She shuddered and followed the group of elves.

Phoenix, Beam and Imra arrived suddenly, finding Dill and beckoning to her. Elanil ran up to them.

"What's the plan?" she asked.

"The People here are mostly women and children," Beam said. "But they're good fighters all the same. They're hiding out in Feed right now, armed to the teeth."

"Feed?" Dill asked.

"Where we have our meals. All we need is the signal, and we'll attack."

"What about the Gatling guns?" Dill asked.

"Unmanned," Beam said. "That's our first priority. I've already assigned People to those positions. Let's hope they get there before Nelenor strikes them down."

"Once we start this, it will move quickly," Dill said. "Our mages will throw everything they have at Nelenor simultaneously, but it's not likely to do much good."

"There's got to be something else we can do," Phoenix said.

"There is, once the United Sky Cities arrive. They're almost here—we just have to hold him off."

In the distance, Nelenor was looking at them. "More children?" he rumbled. "Ah, I see the Imprisoner's kin has arrived."

He was staring right at Dill.

"Shit," Dill said. "So I was right. But…"

"It doesn't make sense," Phoenix said. "Orym hasn't even been alive that long!"

"Maybe Orym is related to the Imprisoner," Dill said. "Maybe I'm more distant kin."

"That makes sense."

Nelenor was taking a slow step toward them, a smile growing on his face.

"Guys," Beam said, "I think it's time."

"Just so," Dill said. "Consider this your signal. Go!"

Elanil ran to the south as quickly as she could, her hand inside her primewood pouch. Everyone else scattered immediately, running in opposite directions. Beam was speaking in a radio she had, and Elanil heard the shouts and screams of Remnant as they flooded out from somewhere to the north.

The fight had finally begun.

"DON'T TELL me you're going to fight," Nelenor boomed. "That would be…foolhardy."

Phoenix had ducked inside a building, the walls made of corrugated metal haphazardly connected together. The People who remained were streaming out from Feed, yelling and screaming at the top of their lungs. But they were just a distraction: the *real* fighters, and especially the Gatling operators, were converging silently on their intended positions. In just a moment the true fight would begin.

Phoenix fingered the dark ash in her hand. It was warm, as all ash was. As all wood was to her now. But ash was all she needed: with it, she could access every Aspect. With it she could destroy bridges and heal volcanoes.

She didn't know if she could stop a god.

Gunfire erupted, finally. The huge Gatling guns mounted around the edge of Lusvunub had been turned on their mounts, facing inward. Now they were firing, each of them pummeling Nelenor with huge slags of metal.

And Nelenor, in all his glory, laughed.

Bullets from handguns and Gatling guns alike bounced right off of him, the air shimmering as bits of forcefield connected. The shield itself was invisible, somehow, but she could see it fuzzing whenever an object hit it.

The mages struck next. Lightning flashed, striking Nelenor's invisible shield. Arrows and blasts of shockstriking magic flew through the air, but they, too, were deflected. A wind sprang up, but it didn't even ruffle Nelenor's clothes. Phoenix could imagine other powers at work, fallfoiling and leafrunning and strengthshaping and more, but nothing touched the Twin. Nothing affected him at all.

He was impervious to their puny magic.

"Give me the Imprisoner," Nelenor said, "and I won't destroy each and every one of you."

"We don't *have* him," Phoenix muttered, anxiety beginning to rise. The situation was simmering on the edge of total chaos—all Nelenor had to do was raise his hand.

He raised his hand.

Everything blasted away.

The buildings, the people, the Gatling guns and their towers. The fences. The gravel. The ground.

Everything flew outward, a circle of total devastation rippling from the center of Lusvunub.

Phoenix had a forcefield up, but even that was not enough to hold her. She was ripped backwards, forcefield and all, the building shattering around her as she flew wildly through the air.

She landed in a heap, flicking the forcefield to green as she did. Healing magic raced through her, soothing bones that may or may not have been broken in the fall. She picked herself up from the wreckage, doing her best to avoid the sharp pieces of metal all around her. She hoped some people had managed to survive.

It was clear that they could not fight this Twin.

"Phoenix, Rylan," her radio blared. "This is Dill. Do you read?"

Phoenix fumbled with the radio, clicking it on. "Phoenix here. Where's Rylan?"

"I'm here, Mom. I'm okay."

"Oh, thank the Under."

Phoenix looked around. Beam and Imra were picking themselves off the ground about two hundred feet away. Beam was bleeding from her arm, but the wound didn't look too serious. They'd been lucky. *Very* lucky.

She didn't think they'd survive a second attack.

"Do not shoot at me again," Nelenor said. She could see him there, towering over the flattened ruins of Martial Square. It and the outlying areas had been destroyed, but the rest of Lusvunub was still intact. Perhaps it would stay that way, as long as they didn't provoke him any further.

"What's the plan?" she asked into the radio.

"It's here," Dill said. "They made better time than I expected."

"What's here?"

"The United Sky Cities."

SEVENTY-FOUR

ELANIL WATCHED with gaping mouth as the glittering spires of the United Sky Cities arrived over Lusvunub. Seven cities sprawled across the sky, larger than she could possibly imagine. All she could see were the undersides of the cities from where she was, thrusting downward like skyscrapers of their own. It was difficult to contextualize just how *big* the assembly of buildings was above her. How many people lived up there, unaware of why they had just moved thousands of miles through the sky?

How many of them knew that death was now upon them?

"Impressive," Nelenor said, looking up at the cities. "I had not thought to see such feats on this planet. But why have you brought this here? You know you cannot stop me."

"Shot," Dill was saying over the radio, "Get everyone down here now!"

"Already in progress, Captain," Shot's voice said, and Elanil saw gates flashing into existence on the ground.

Hundreds of them.

"YOU TWO NEED TO get down there," Shot was saying.

Allain was still in Mission Control. He and Erodar had stayed there while the cities moved, glued to their chairs.

The cities almost hadn't survived the trip.

"What are we supposed to do?" Allain asked.

"Fight," Shot said. "Use that magic you were telling me about. Splinter-something."

"What will you be doing?"

"I need to stay up here, make sure everything keeps running."

"We're almost ready," Sylvis said, interrupting. "Gate Control reports that they were able to reverse the beam. They haven't tested it at scale yet, obviously, but I gather we don't have time for that."

"We don't have the power for testing, either," Shot said. "When we use this weapon, it'll drain all our power supplies. Small?"

"Yes, boss?" Small's head said, bobbing about on one of the screens on Shot's desk.

"Is everything ready on your end?"

"Sure is, boss. I saved one Power Storage chamber in each city for emergency power, but we'll need to recharge the vast majority of them before the cities can resume normal operations."

"Works for me," Shot said. "Grathgor, have we made our announcement to the public, yet?"

"It just went out," Grathgor said. "No rioting—yet."

"Wait until emergency power goes into effect," Shot said. "Then we'll see the riots."

"We could lose the cities," Sylvis said.

"We *will* lose them if we don't do this."

"Let's hope it works."

"Let's hope. Allain? Erodar? You guys ready?"

"If we have to," Allain said.

"Nothing better to do," Erodar said.

"That's the spirit, bros," Shot said. "Now get to work."

ORYM'S outer gate dissipated as he stepped through into the forest surrounding Lusvunub. Nelenor was there for a reason, after all—Orym figured it had to be something important. For a moment he was confused by what he was seeing: were those *gates* sparkling all over the night? There must be *hundreds* of them, with people streaming out of them by the thousands.

He moved closer to one, careful to keep his nowhere gate active. He didn't need Nelenor finding him, especially now that he was so close. People continued running through the gates, brandishing makeshift weapons and screaming as they went.

That was when he finally realized they were underkids.

Every Under in every city must be arriving on the ground, kids from all over joining in this fight. Orym tried to suppress a laugh as he stepped through the forest. Did these *kids* really think they stood a chance against the Twins?

PHOENIX WAS with Beam and Imra, and Elanil had arrived shortly after. The four of them were standing together, breathing heavily, hoping Nelenor wasn't about to destroy everything around him. There were no more gunshots, at least.

Gates had appeared everywhere, underkids piling out of them by the thousands. Phoenix wanted to stop them, wanted to warn them that they were marching to their deaths.

But there was nothing she could do.

"Shit," Elanil cursed, the word sounding strange coming from her. "I just realized something. The Books of Amplification! With them, we might have a shot. Where are they?"

Phoenix thought about that for a moment. "I think we left them back on Valaralda," she said. "We stowed them belowdecks."

"That was stupid," Elanil said.

"We were all very tired."

"Let's hope they're not lost forever."

The radio blared suddenly, Dill's voice coming over the speaker. "Everyone!" he shouted. "Get out of there! Get the underkids away!"

"We're getting ready to hit the button," Shot's voice said. "All personnel should clear the area immediately."

"Spike here," a new voice said on the radio. "I've directed the kids to the forest outside the city. Will that be far enough?"

"Should be," Shot said. "We've got eyes on Nelenor from up here. Why is he just standing there?"

"No idea," Dill said. "He nearly wiped us all out with one flick of his hand, but he seems to need provocation now."

"I sense you!" Nelenor shouted, as if on cue. "The Imprisoner is here!"

He stomped his foot, and the earth quaked.

"We have to go now," Dill said. "Shot, give us thirty seconds. Anyone else listening to this, get the hell out of Lusvunub!"

Phoenix and Elanil exchanged a look.

Everyone ran.

RUNNING WASN'T FAST ENOUGH. So Elanil added magic to the mix, carrying herself and Phoenix and Beam and Imra up and out of Lusvunub. She saw underkids streaming out of the city, heading for the forests. More of them were still arriving from gates placed further out, and she caught sight of the Pano Sylrantheas mages to the south. They looked no worse for the wear, thankfully. All was not yet lost.

"I'm going to set us down in trees," she said, and Phoenix nodded. "That way we can get a better vantage point of this."

They landed in two trees, neatly spread out across several branches. Elanil was proud at how easily she'd managed it—this Prime Mage thing was starting to come more naturally for her.

Too bad it wouldn't do any good against the Twins.

"T-minus ten seconds!" Shot said over Phoenix's radio.

A hole opened up above them in the middle of New San Francisco. That city was at the center of the United Sky Cities, positioned directly on top of Nelenor. As she watched, the hole began to glow bright blue.

"9!" Shot said.

"I do not recommend this course of action," Nelenor said.

"8!"

Elanil huddled against Phoenix on the tree, fear growing in her mind.

"7!"

The underkids finished scuttling away into the forest, leaving the area clear.

"6!"

"Stop this," Nelenor said.

"5!"

The light in the city grew brighter and brighter until Elanil couldn't look at it anymore. She shielded her eyes from the glare.

"4!"

"Power Stations active," Small's voice said over the radio.

"3!"

"Gate Control ready to fire," Sylvis said.

"2!"

"You have been warned," Nelenor said.

"1!"

A brilliant light pierced the darkness, slamming down directly onto Nelenor. Energy coursed through him, rippling visibly through his body. Elanil could see his frame distort, light piercing him with devastating brightness.

For a moment, she thought he paused. His image flexed, moving in the air as if it were about to explode. For an instant, she thought the plan might just succeed.

Then Nelenor started laughing.

The sound of it was rich, rolling out of him in waves. "Electricity," he said, his voice easily audible from so far away. "I might have known you'd try that." He gave a great, heaving sigh. "Well, you've left me no choice."

He raised his hand, and the energy beam turned red.

It shot upward, and Elanil could see the city glowing red in return.

She put out a hand as if willing him to stop, but it was far too late.

There was nothing she could do.

Gate Control exploded, great billows of orange light and debris shooting outward from it. Then the areas around it exploded too, fire and hot gas spreading faster than she could track.

"We have a problem..." Shot said over the radio, but it was overtaken by static.

The explosions continued, rippling outward from the center of the city. The Under was ripped apart as she watched, massive pieces of metal and cement flying off and falling to the world below.

"No," Elanil whispered. "Quickly!"

She captured the women near her with her magic, wrenching them off the trees and flying them eastward. Explosions continued to rock the city up above as they flew. Great holes appeared in the Under, revealing streets and cars, pedestrians and subway trains. Everything was falling through the holes, and still the explosions continued on. Skyscrapers were next, ripped apart by the devastating energy Nelenor had unleashed. Hot wind whipped through her hair, burning embers singing her body as she flew away, fleeing the destruction.

Great creaking and groaning sounded up above as skyscrapers tilted, their foundations destroyed. Energy rippled through the city, red light flashing along metal surfaces, around cars, even along the very streets. Fires broke out everywhere, smoke streaming into the air.

Elanil kept flying, doing her best to dodge falling debris. An entire building sailed through the air in front of her, dozens of stories of flaming metal and broken glass shooting downward like a falling star. She flexed her magic, willing them sideways, just barely avoiding the building as it fell. It hit the ground as they passed, dust and broken trees and shards of metal ripping outward from the impact, a cloud of horrible destruction.

And still the city was being destroyed. It was falling apart, chunks of it breaking away and streaming to the ground. She saw burning people, flaming cars, pipes and infrastructure, more explosions. The screams were everywhere now, all around her, above her in the air. Tears streamed down her face as she flew, as the hot wind blew, as the sound of all that destruction assaulted her.

Smoke filled the air.

Then the largest explosion of all rocked the sky, the sound deafening. Elanil winced, looking up, and saw the biggest fireball she'd ever seen engulfing the entire city, spreading outward. She increased her speed, frantically pushing through the air, adding soulsoothing magic for herself and Phoenix, who she was still touching.

Then the air cooled. They had escaped the blast radius. Elanil paused, rotating everyone in the air, floating as she looked at the destruction behind them.

Seven great cities had been up there, united together in the sky. Now there was nothing in the middle but twisted, smoking metal, flames, and smoke.

Six cities remained.

New San Francisco had been utterly destroyed.

SEVENTY-FIVE

"SHOT?" Dill was calling over the radio. "Shot? Are you there? President Grayson? Sylvis? Anyone?"

The radio was silent.

Elanil fought back tears. Phoenix was gripping her arm tightly, her face white. They and Imra and Beam were still floating in the air, watching burning embers falling down to Lusvunub below.

"This is Hammond," a male voice said on the radio, "City Director for New Manhattan. I'm sorry to report the complete destruction of New San Francisco. All hands lost."

"No," Phoenix breathed.

"You were warned," Nelenor said. "Do not dare attack me again. Give me the Imprisoner, and all of this will be over."

"Commencing detachment protocol now," Hammond said. "Good luck down there."

One by one, the six remaining cities began disconnecting from each other in the sky.

"All these kids," Phoenix said. "Now they have nowhere to go."

"The other cities will take them up," Beam said. "If they survive this."

"If *we* survive this. You know we can't attack him now. That weapon was our one, best shot. What are a bunch of kids going to do?"

Evidently Dill had the same thought, wherever he was. "Spike," he said over the radio, "stand down. I repeat, stand down."

"Fuck this guy," Spike said.

And the underkids attacked.

ALLAIN FLITTED THROUGH THE AIR, flicking his carving knife. He'd started a new piece just now, something he'd never thought he'd carve.

It was a city.

New San Francisco was destroyed. Just gone, leaving nothing but a huge tangle of blackened metal. New Paris and New Manhattan were still connected to it, dragging it away in the sky. He assumed they'd drop it in a safe place when they could. Then that would be it: the beauty and majesty of San Francisco would be no more.

It hadn't deserved to meet its end like that.

Now the underkids were streaming inward from the forest, screaming and gesticulating at Nelenor. And the Twin himself just stood there, staring out at them. All this time, all this destruction, and Nelenor had not even moved.

He'd only lifted his hands.

"They can't win," Allain said, splinters leaping around him in the night.

"No," Erodar said. He was splinterleaping as well, only he

didn't need to carve anything to do it. "You heard Spike. She's insane."

"I would be too, if my city had just been destroyed."

"They're going to die, you know."

"Maybe we should try to help."

"Then we'll die, too. Wait a minute. What in the name of the moons are they *doing*?"

Allain peered downward, trying to make sense of it through his flickering vision. "They're mages," he said. "They're all *mages*."

Underkids were flying through the air by the thousands, popping upward from the forest with reckless abandon. They were all fallfoilers, or at least thousands of them were. And they were all carrying ropes with them as they flew.

The ropes interconnected in the air, wrapping around each other, wrenching them to the side. Allain had never seen anything like it before. And there were just so *many* of them! They quickly formed a sort of net, a tapestry of rope in the sky. Everything was in constant motion, ropes rising and falling, looping and curving in the air. He saw little hooks placed here and there, floating with fallfoiler magic. The hooks helped station the ropes in places throughout the sky, giving the whole thing shape.

"Where in the *hell* did you learn to do that, Spike?" Dill said over the radio.

"It's rigging," Spike said. "Like we have in Shock Crew."

"Incredible. What's the plan?"

"Watch," Spike said.

The ropes kept coming, spiraling out and over and around, filling the air above Nelenor. And as Allain watched, the complex constellation of rope began to drift lower.

Nelenor was looking upwards, his vulpine face looking

faintly amused. "You have very strange habits on this world," he said. "Is this supposed to stop me?"

"Now!" Spike said over the radio, and all the ropes began pulling taut. New mages vaulted up out of the forest, shock-striking magic glimmering on their fingertips. They released their bolts of blue toward the ropes, and Allain saw force-fields shimmer into existence, capturing the energy as it hit the ropes. The whole skein continued growing tighter, pulling inward toward Nelenor. Curves of glowing blue filled the air, surrounding the Twin.

It was a hell of a display.

"Creativity!" Nelenor boomed. "This is very well done."

"Nice to get a compliment, at least," Erodar muttered from his position next to Allain in the air.

"Odds of success?" Allain asked.

"Zero."

The energetic rigging continued collapsing, underkid mages popping up and down in the air as they drew it in, feeding it more energy. It was an incredible, choreographed display. Allain wondered how the hell they had practiced it in the Under—or who had even had the idea to begin with.

"Now!" Spike said again over the radio.

The ropes released their energy. Magic cascaded inward, inundating Nelenor with blue and white. Force-fields collapsed, unleashing shockstriking magic. The fields themselves remained active as they broke apart, shimmering light falling onto Nelenor from above. The ropes were tight now, almost touching the Twin. Then they were burning, suffused with shockstriker magic, the blue glow impossibly bright. Allain had to shield his eyes.

For a moment, Allain thought the underkids' plan had actually worked.

PHOENIX WATCHED the glowing ball of magic surrounding Nelenor. It was bright, impossibly bright. She'd never seen so much magical energy in one place before.

Actually, wait. She *had* seen something like this before. She herself had been the one to do it, at the Golden Gate Bridge. And again on Stromboli.

Maybe it would work.

But Nelenor finally laughed, as she knew he would. He seemed to almost be enjoying the attempts on his life, as if curious to see what the denizens of Earth could accomplish without his aid. But now he was laughing, and Phoenix knew that even though she couldn't see him, he was probably raising his hand.

The magical ball of light and energy burst apart, fragments of it flying everywhere, dissipating into the night. Then Nelenor was visible again, face gleeful, towering at least a hundred feet above the ground.

He had grown.

And he still did not seem angry.

"You would have loved it on Starmist Prime," he said. "Your creativity is almost a match for them."

"Is everyone okay?" Dill asked over the radio.

"Seriously," Spike said, "fuck this guy."

"Don't do it," Dill warned.

"Too late."

Underkids appeared again, this time launching themselves directly at Nelenor. Phoenix saw knives and machetes in their hands, brass knuckles and even a few pinblades. They flew toward the Twin, screaming, and Phoenix found herself flying forward as well. She needed to get closer.

Imra, Elanil and Beam followed behind her in the sky.

Elanil was carrying the three of them, a worried expression on her face.

"They're going to die," she said.

"I know," Phoenix said. "I want to get closer in case I can help."

"The volcano," Beam said. "You want to try that again."

"It might work."

"It's too dangerous."

"All we can do is try."

They approached the center of Lusvunub, flying close to the ground. The first underkids finally reached Nelenor as Phoenix watched, their faces twisted with anger.

And Nelenor just swatted them away.

By the hundreds.

Phoenix could hear them scream. She could see their broken bodies, blood streaming away in the air. Limbs were torn from limbs, bones cracking audibly. She watched as hundreds, then thousands of underkids flew at Nelenor, only to instantly meet their doom.

They were all dying. It wasn't even a fight.

"Pull them back!" Dill was shouting over the radio. "What are you *doing*?"

"It's too late," Spike said, her voice sad. "They wanted this fight."

"It's useless," Dill said.

"It is," Phoenix echoed in the night. But inside, she felt a kind of calm. A sort of peace descended on her as she realized what she must do.

She alighted on the ground in front of Nelenor, underkids streaming through the air above her, and the Twin looked down to meet her gaze.

"The superuser's mother," he said, his voice quieter than before. "This should prove interesting."

SEVENTY-SIX

PHOENIX HELD up hands filled with dark ash. She was conscious of the other women arrayed out next to her: Beam was to her right, legs slightly spread, a drawn sword in her hand. It was Beam the way she'd always known her: resolute, firm, a little angry. Imra was standing to Phoenix's left, a fierce expression on her face, bow drawn and arrow nocked. She was gorgeous as she stared upward at the Twin, but Phoenix could tell that she was just as strong as Beam.

And Elanil, the girl Rylan loved, was standing next to Imra. She, too, was beautiful, her young face stern as she held primewood in her fists. She was good for him, Phoenix knew in that instant. She was at least his equal, if not more.

Now if only they could all survive.

She turned back to Nelenor, preparing to unleash her magic, but then she remembered something. Something that was still attached to her waist, swinging.

The fireblade that Beam had given her.

She put her wood chips back inside her pouch, pulling the fireblade out instead. It instantly flared to life, flames rippling across the surface of the metal.

"Very pretty," Nelenor said. "Do you wish to stick me with that sword?"

"No," Phoenix said. "I wish you to stop this madness. There is no *need* for all this destruction. Do you know how many people you have killed?"

"Blame the Imprisoner," Nelenor said.

"No," Phoenix said. "I blame you."

She had less need of emotion now. The trick Rylan had taught her, to access the Aspects directly, made sense to her now. Perhaps it was because her soul had fully Awakened while she was in Ambarhal. Perhaps being a Prime Mage was all it took. Now she could access all the colors.

Now she could feel the world without *feeling*. It was a welcome modicum of control.

She unleashed the magic all at once, channeling it out from the Artifact in her hand. Unshaped particles of light filled the air, forming glowing rainbows in the night. The magic surrounded Nelenor and the space beyond, and Phoenix Willed them to be *stronger*, to be *more*, to strike out against Nelenor. To kill him, if possible. Or to heal him, like she'd done with the volcano. She needed him to stop. She needed him to *change*.

She needed this power within her to somehow win.

BEAM WATCHED Phoenix's magic swirling in the air. It wasn't doing anything to Nelenor, not that she could tell. And Nelenor himself wasn't reacting to it yet. Instead he just stood there, Anubis face looking mildly amused. Perhaps he was curious to see if Phoenix could actually hurt him. Or maybe he was just waiting for the right time to kill her.

She wondered if there were anything she could do.

But then something strange happened. New light shimmered into being in the air—light that wasn't driven by Phoenix's magic. It was silver, this light. It covered a space thousands of feet in every dimension, strange ghostly lines and textures taking shape in the middle of the square. It grew and grew, the figure revealing itself as Phoenix's magic interacted with it. She saw colored particles of magic merging with the silver light, and she looked up to try to take it all in.

When she realized what she was seeing, she took a sudden, sharp breath.

It was a Tree. A ghostly Tree, shining above them, larger than any Prime Tree, larger than Lusvunub itself. The shimmering image towered over them, looking somehow sinister in the night.

She had seen all this before. Her mind flashed back to the memory.

BEAM STUMBLED, the fog of mindmaster magic fading. Around her she saw the other mages shaking their heads, confused as to what was going on. Magona had fallen to the ground, watching the volcano ahead of them in awe.

Beam looked for Phoenix.

She saw her there, facing the volcano, eyes fiercely concentrating. What was she—oh, no. Beam scrambled to her feet, but she was rocked by another earthquake. She fell, cursing as her hands were caught by stones. She had to get to Phoenix.

She tried to get up, to run, but the world was moving too slowly. She wanted to stop her, but she was far too late.

Phoenix had a beatific expression on her face.

And the volcano *reversed*.

The smoke and detritus melded back together, a great wide plume of gray and black sucking into the volcano from whence it came. The mountain took it all back in—then it, too, was repaired.

Then there was a sudden flash of brilliant light, and a spear of white energy shot out from Phoenix's chest, blinding as it raced away into the heavens.

And Phoenix pitched forward, a great, gaping, smoking hole in her body.

She was dead.

"No!" Beam screamed, and she saw Rylan falling to his knees.

But then another strange thing happened.

A Tree appeared.

She knew she should capitalize it, that this Tree represented great power, great magic. It was white and strangely ghostly, appearing on the island right where Phoenix's dead body lay.

She was laying *inside* the Tree.

"Ash," Orym breathed. "It's *beautiful*."

The Tree grew as Beam watched. It grew and grew, ghostly silver branches getting larger and higher, waving in a wind she couldn't feel. It grew until it was a hundred feet high, two hundred, and it just kept growing. Orym and Rylan and Dill stumbled away from it, shading their eyes to watch as it towered over them.

And the Tree continued to grow.

Rays of light began playing on Phoenix's skin. White bursts shot out from her body, shimmering as they interacted with the ghostly Tree. And as Beam watched, Phoenix's body began shimmering, too.

The light played along her form, growing so bright that Beam couldn't see. She squinted, trying to discern anything inside the light. She thought she saw Phoenix's form change, crumbling into brilliant dust, like ash, blowing up and melding with the Tree.

Then the light was gone. The Tree was gone.

Phoenix had disappeared.

She was gone, like a phoenix to the ashes of the world she'd saved.

Beam burst into tears.

ORYM BLINKED. The huge Tree towered over them, bigger by far than the entirety of Lusvunub, reaching all the way up to the sky cities that remained overhead. It moved faintly in an unseen wind, particles of light shimmering across its surface. Phoenix had unleashed it somehow. Her unshaped magic, her force magic, had unlocked its existence.

But what *was* this Tree? How had it come to be?

He weaved an illusion of invisibility over himself, creeping closer to the four women standing in front of Nelenor. Beam was speaking, and he had to know what she was saying.

"I REMEMBER," Beam said. Particles of light were still floating in the air, interacting with the ghostly Tree. "When you died, Phoenix, a Tree like this appeared in your place."

"I died because of...magic," Phoenix said.

"But that wasn't the only time I've seen a Tree like this."

"Ah," Nelenor said from up above. "Another who has taken the path of self."

More memories surfaced in Beam's mind.

"WHERE IS LALBAN?" Banzab asked.

Keleb shrugged. "Haven't seen her in a few hours. She seemed upset, earlier. You should go talk to her."

"That's what I'm *trying* to do," Banzab said, "but I don't know where she is."

"Maybe she went to the rickhouses? You know she likes it there."

"Maybe. Do you know what's wrong with her, Keleb? She hasn't been herself, lately."

"Life here has been wearing on her," Keleb said. "Think nothing of it. She will get over it soon."

Banzab wasn't sure if that was true.

She went to the rickhouses, and that was where she found her.

Hanging from a beam of wood.

"No!" Banzab shrieked. Lalban's body was swinging slightly, her face white. Her neck looked broken. She must have climbed onto the beam and jumped, with the rope around her neck.

Banzab couldn't understand.

Lalban, her lover and her friend. Lalban was gone. And worse, it was by her own hand. What had come over her? Had life really been that hard?

Had Banzab not been enough for her?

But then something strange happened. A Tree appeared in the air, ghostly and strange, shimmering as if it wasn't quite real.

As Banzab watched, the Tree began to grow.

ORYM LISTENED to Beam's tale, still hidden by mistweaving magic. He was nervous being this close to Nelenor, but so far the Twin hadn't seemed to notice him. His nowhere gate was still working, even though it was shrouded in mist.

Beam's story had been interesting. Lalban had committed suicide, and a ghostly Tree had formed. The same had happened with Phoenix, when she had died. By her own hand, Orym realized. Magic had killed her, but Phoenix had done it to herself.

In a way, Phoenix had also committed suicide.

"It is a Soul Tree, young ones," Nelenor said. "An artifact of life on your worlds. Trees have great significance for you. They are your only conduit to magic. And so it seems that when one of you takes the path of self, a Soul Tree forms in your place."

Orym felt like he was missing something. If a Soul Tree was anything like a Prime Tree, it would be a great source of power. But it was ghostly, different, apparently invisible until activated by unstructured force magic. And if force magic activated it, then...

A theory began to form.

That was when Orym finally realized what he'd been missing all this time. His mind cast back, dim memories forming from just before his own death.

SELENIA SMOOTHED OUT HER DRESS, the transparent fabric leaving nothing to the imagination. Her cheetah padded around her, watching her from all angles and purring with approval. She looked good. It was time.

She stepped into Aten's room, freshly lacquered finger-nails holding the object she had brought to commemorate the occasion: a golden ring. She opened her mouth, ready to utter the words she had prepared. Her cactus wren flew in from a side window, adding its eyes. All was ready. All was about to fall into place.

Selenia let out a horrible scream.

Aten. He was in his room, where she had expected him to be. But he was not in his bed.

He was hanging from the ceiling.

His eyes were bulging, his face white, distended. A thick rope was wrapped about his neck, choking the life out of him. His legs were kicking as she watched, his mouth wide and struggling to breathe.

It was in that moment that Selenia realized she actually had *feelings* for Aten.

"No!" she screamed, wishing tears could fall from her destroyed eyes. She reached for him, trying to lift him up, to hold his weight.

But it was too late. It was not enough.

Aten gave one last, final kick before he died.

Then something strange happened.

A tree appeared on the floor underneath Aten's body. It was small, glowing a brilliant, shimmering white, the outlines of it brighter than anything she had ever seen. She / the cheetah shrank from it instinctively, afraid of this new source of light. She / the bird shrieked, flying out of the room, disobeying the bond.

And she / Cariel shielded her eyes, as if the glow of this tree could pierce into her very soul.

Then it grew. The brilliant glowing outline of it became larger, more mature, filling all available space, cutting through the room. Its scintillating image flew right through her body, filling the air, growing and growing. Soon it was so large that she imagined it towering over the palace, over

Nekhrumet, over everything. Her cactus wren was still outside—it confirmed what she suspected.

This was the largest tree she had ever seen. It was as big as the entire city, and still growing.

But it wasn't real. It was a ghost. The image faded into nothingness as she watched through the wren's eyes, leaving her alone with the corpse of the man she'd loved.

THERE WAS a Soul Tree in Nekhrumet, Orym realized. He had been the one to put it there, when he'd committed suicide all those millennia ago. And if that Tree was as big as this one, it might even touch some of his pyramids.

"Just as Prime Trees grant you access to magic," Nelenor was saying, "Soul Trees cancel that magic out. Soul energy has no effect, here. You can use magic, yes. But if you try to access the higher-order functions—soulbinding, soulspecting and the others—you will fail. It is a very interesting phenomena, I must admit. Velion would like to study it, I suspect."

Nelenor's scientist side was finally beginning to come out. Would it ever take over from this murderous personality they all now faced?

Perhaps murder and science were not so different from each other, in the wrong hands.

Orym smiled. He had his answer now. The Soul Tree in Nekhrumet was preventing the Pyramid Offensive System from working.

He just needed a way to eliminate the Tree.

SEVENTY-SEVEN

WAS IT ELANIL'S IMAGINATION, or was Nelenor finally softening? He was giving them information—information that she didn't understand, but it was still information. Maybe they wouldn't have to fight much longer.

To her right, Phoenix was still wielding her fireblade. Particles of force magic continued emanating from it, colliding with the massive Soul Tree that had unexpectedly appeared. Maybe it should be called a Suicide Tree—for that was what it was.

Elanil shivered.

The particles of magic continued interacting with the Tree. And as she watched, parts of it began to fade.

Interesting.

But something else was happening. There was motion in the sky, things flying in from the sides.

"He's distracted," Phoenix's radio blared.

"I am never distracted," Nelenor said, but it was too late.

The remaining underkids were attacking. Again.

Elanil watched them come, flying in from every angle. It

was suicide, she knew. Perhaps thousands of new Soul Trees would form after Nelenor had had his way. But no—this wasn't suicide. It was murder, and Nelenor didn't seem to care.

Well, Elanil cared. She didn't want all these poor kids to die. They should be free to live their life, not destroyed by some vengeful god. Their Under had already been taken away. Must they also pay with their lives?

No. It wasn't right. She had to try to stop him.

Wood was in her hand in an instant. She lashed out with it, not entirely sure what she intended.

Leafrunning was the first thing she tried.

It was her strongest Aspect, the one she'd naturally Aligned with. It had been her first love, flitting from tree to tree. And now, when her final moment came, it was the magic she chose to meet her doom.

She sent leafrunning magic against Nelenor with all her might.

But Nelenor just laughed, and pointed his finger at her, and she knew that it was finally her turn to join the corpses on the ground.

"Stop," a voice said, and suddenly Rylan was standing in front of her. He glanced at her, his expression pained, then returned his face to the Twin.

"Ah," Nelenor said, lowering his hand. "The superuser. I trust you have not come to fight me."

"You can't kill my friend," Rylan said. "Stop killing *everyone*. You don't have to do this."

"Oh, but I do," Nelenor said, and he pointed his finger at Rylan.

Elanil screamed.

But magic burst into being around Rylan, shooting outward with impossible speed. Particles of light shot into

Nelenor with reckless abandon, and the Twin actually stumbled back.

Rylan took a step, back hunched forward, hands splayed out ahead. Magic flooded from him, pummeling Nelenor, an endless stream of wild energy. It was strong, *so strong*, stronger than anything Phoenix had been doing. And it was bright, and uncontrolled, and Nelenor took another step back.

For a moment, it looked as if Rylan were actually *winning*.

"You...must...end...this!" he shouted, stepping forward toward the Twin. Magic lit his face, erupting from his fingers in a torrent of particles. His expression was stern, his body taut. Wild energy was everywhere, flitting across the Twin and out into the night. Elanil felt the heat of it singe her skin, and she unconsciously pulled on her Prime Palm to give her healing.

The night had gone insane.

But Nelenor was angry now. He took another step back, bringing his hands up to bear. "You...dare...not...attack... me!" he said, his voice roaring. Raw magic continued flooding into him, and Elanil thought she smelled burning hair. "Xyclami made you," Nelenor said, "and Xyclami can *unmake* you!"

"No," Rylan said, and Elanil could hear the fear in his voice.

"Xyclami," Nelenor said, "please unregister subject 69327A49Z7."

"Oh, no," Elanil said, and suddenly all the magic disappeared.

"I—but—" Rylan said. "It's gone!"

Just like that, Rylan was no longer a mage.

"You shouldn't have done that," Nelenor said, and he struck against Rylan with a hand made of light.

SEVENTY-EIGHT

"NO!" Phoenix screamed, and she threw a forcefield up around Nelenor.

It worked.

The shield stopped the Twin's strike, the magic splattering harmlessly against the edge. Phoenix could feel the strength of it hit her shield and she winced, gritting her teeth and strengthening the magic. Nelenor fought back, piercing through her shield with magic of his own.

He was just so *strong*.

So she added a second forcefield, and a third. She stepped forward, sending magic from her fireblade, Willing energy into the shields surrounding Nelenor. He was trapped, for now. Her shields were actually working.

"Xyclami," Nelenor began.

"Oh, no you don't," Phoenix said, sending a dart of targeted energy right at Nelenor's face. Red energy: Destroyer Aspect.

It actually hit him in the face.

He flinched, spluttering, his command to Xyclami momentarily forgotten. He had the ability to delete all her magic, Phoenix knew. He could turn her off like a switch. But in order to do that, it seemed he needed to issue a command.

Phoenix wasn't going to let him do that.

She exercised her magic in the blade, putting a shield around herself. She flipped it to green—Protector Aspect—and added buoyancy. Then she was floating, propelled by a circle of living things, and Nelenor was glaring at her from inside her shields.

So she turned the shields to red.

Fire burned inward toward Nelenor as Phoenix sailed over him. She added gold to the mix: Creator Aspect. Something Nelenor had said earlier had inspired her. He'd mentioned creativity, that they'd be at home on Starmist Prime. She doubted that was true, but he had been right about one thing.

She *was* creative.

A spear of sparkling gold sliced down inside her layered shields, striking Nelenor across his body. The Twin winced, slashing out against her. Raw power swept past her, ripping her own shield apart and scintillating across her skin. She felt it burning, but she already had a green shield up again, healing power filling her. It wasn't going to be that easy to kill her.

She floated further to the north, sending a rain of blue energy at Nelenor, unformed. They took the shape of lightning strikes, thick bolts of electricity discharging in the air. It was storm magic, she instinctively knew. Scholar Aspect. She added to it and a wind sprang up, cold and harsh and *incredibly* strong. The wind blew only inside the shields she had placed around him, and she could see him stumble as it hit.

"You are...strong," Nelenor said, making a slicing motion with his hand.

Brilliant light seared her vision, but her green shield corrected it almost instantly. Then a thousand sparks of red flew at her out of thin air, ripping through her body. She healed through the first of them, putting up five shields in quick succession, surrounding herself in a cocoon made of light.

"You are almost a superuser yourself," Nelenor said.

"I don't *want* to be a superuser," Phoenix said, fireblade still held brightly in her hand. "I want you to go away."

She dropped all her shields except for one beneath her, pointing her blade directly at Nelenor.

Fire streamed out of it, raw Destroyer energy blasting Nelenor with everything she had. She pushed it *hard*, putting every bit of herself into the magic. Nelenor seemed surprised —he stumbled backward, raising his arms as if in fear.

And Phoenix just pressed on.

She hadn't wielded this much magic in quite some time. Not since the volcano had she sent out so much energy, given so much of herself. She'd been trying to save the world then, and she was trying to do it now. It seemed her life was destined to be forever dying so that others might live.

So be it.

She increased the flow, a piercing sound rising in her ears as the beam of energy grew stronger, brighter, taking over the entire night. Nelenor was leaning away from her in fear, pure magic pushing him back. She could do this. She could actually win.

All she had to do was push harder.

The sweetness of it finally arrived. The dangerous edge of sugar, the feeling that always precipitated death. She'd been soulburned before—she knew what it felt like. She was close to it now.

But she had to kill Nelenor. She had to get this done. So she ratcheted her magic up to a new level, pouring every ounce of fury and passion and hate and need into the magic.

She felt her heart swell, her emotions growing out of all control. She would end this, finally end what had been started so very long ago.

"Ambarhal is no refuge for you," Nelenor said, wincing as the energy continued striking him. "If you die here, your soul cannot return."

"It doesn't matter," Phoenix said. "If you won't give this up willingly, I'll force you."

"You won't win," Nelenor said.

"Yes," Phoenix said, "I will."

And she sent every ounce of her remaining Will, flooding the sky with light.

Rylan was suddenly next to her in the air. "Mom," he said. "You can't do this." Tears were in his eyes. "I can't lose you again."

"I have him," she said, gritting her teeth against the flow of magic, against the unbearable sweetness that was encroaching on her mind. "I can do this."

Beam appeared, fallfoiling allowing her to float. "This isn't a fight you can win," she said. "You have to back down."

Nelenor was still unmoving. He just stood there, one arm raised, watching as Destroyer Aspect flooded his being. Could it kill him? Phoenix wasn't sure. But she knew she had to try.

She had to be stronger. She had to take this all the way.

"I can't," she said to Beam. "I can't back down."

"No," Beam said, "and neither can I."

She pushed Phoenix, *hard*, and kicked her in the hand.

The fireblade fell to the ground, and all of Phoenix's magic went wild.

Particles of red sprayed everywhere, flooding the sky. With nothing to hold her up, Phoenix began to fall. She looked upward as her body slipped away, and beheld the strangest thing she'd ever seen.

Destroyer particles were spreading out, creating the distinct outline of a Tree. The Soul Tree reappeared, fading into being, glowing silver light filling the entire area. And her Destroyer energy—her wild, unfocused magic—joined the Tree, scintillating across its surface. In moments, the Tree turned red.

And then it exploded.

She was dimly aware of Elanil grabbing her with fall-foiling magic, arresting her fall. Shards of strange magic were suddenly everywhere, tearing off the Soul Tree and flooding the night. A piece of it hit her, sending searing pain across her mind. No—it was her *soul*. The magic was hurting her soul.

"Shields!" she shouted, but nobody around her was quick enough with forcefinding. She saw a chunk of strange red magic slam into Beam, sending her careening backwards in the air, the light instantly leaving her eyes. She saw one glance by Elanil, but the girl had finally gotten a forcefield up around herself.

The bulk of the energy was flying into Nelenor.

"What *is* this?" he shouted, but already he was on his knees.

Shards of the Soul Tree pummeled into him, blobs of viscous, wispy red slicing and curling through his body. Then Phoenix thought she was seeing *people*, souls flying through the air. Hundreds of them flitted from place to place, their cries piercing into her heart.

"Stop this!" Nelenor shouted, stumbling, hands around his head. "The soul magic...I cannot contain it!"

Then Nelenor was screaming, and the souls were screaming, and the Soul Tree's shards were exploding everywhere, discharging their awful presence into the sky. Souls were wheeling around and around in the air, crying out in remembered agony, ghostly apparitions sailing on the wind. They struck at Nelenor, wailing at him as they sliced his skin. Nelenor could do nothing against their strange, unearthly power.

He fell, fists beating against the ground. And still the souls hit him, hurting him again and again, their shrieking energy the only thing Phoenix could see or hear. Nelenor's face was a grimace, his Anubis skin glowing with ethereal energy. He tried to get up but failed, the soul magic pummeling him over and over. The Tree was still disgorging bits of itself, an infernal rain of horrible, powerful magic.

It looked like Nelenor was dying.

"This is not...over!" he gasped, struggling to lift his hand. His fox-like teeth were bared, his eyes filled with pain. He gave one glance at Phoenix before a gate overtook him and he disappeared.

Nelenor was gone.

And the remains of the Soul Tree fell out of the sky, cascading to the ground. The souls flew away, their unearthly shrieks fading as they left.

Phoenix finally reached the ground, Elanil beside her.

Beam was there, too.

Her body was lying on the earth. She wasn't breathing. Phoenix knelt beside her frantically, using the last remains of her energy to Will soulsoothing magic into her from the pouch at her belt.

But it was no good. The magic had no effect.

Beam was dead.

SEVENTY-NINE

ELANIL COULDN'T SLEEP. It was the early morning hours now, and she was tossing and turning in a tiny tent the elves had brought with them to Lusvunub. They had set up camp in the forests just outside of town, and the Remnant had let them be.

They were allies now. Even with Beam gone.

But she couldn't sleep. Too many things were bothering her. New San Francisco, so cruelly destroyed. Nelenor, who had retreated through a gate and not come back. Beam, who had died from the strange soul magic that had come out of the Soul Tree. Many others had died, too—elves and under-kids and Remnant alike. Whatever that magic was, it had been *strong*. Nelenor almost hadn't survived.

Suicide, it seemed, carried with it a great deal of power.

She was also worried about herself—she had tried to fight Nelenor, but her performance had been pathetic, weak. She was nothing compared to powerful super-mages like Phoenix and Rylan.

Rylan.

That was what was truly bothering her.

She missed him. She missed his eyes. She wanted to hold his hand again, to hear his voice. She wanted to dance with him onboard a ship, to hear him call her Dance.

She wanted him to be okay.

Their last few encounters together had not been good. He was scary. Dangerous. His magic had been out of control. He had almost taken her against her will.

His magic was gone now.

What did it mean? What did it mean for her? She still loved him, of that she was sure. She missed him so much, even now. He was sleeping in his tent at the far side of camp, probably dreaming. Was he dreaming of her? Did he miss her as much as she missed him?

She'd seen his face, back there when she was fighting Nelenor. She'd seen the love on it, and the worry, the fear of rejection, the guilt of his betrayal. Even through all that, even though she'd run away, he'd still defended her. He would have died for her—she knew that. And she would do the same for him.

He could learn. They could both learn. He could control his power, given time and practice. If the Twins could control it, so could he. He was young, hormonal, attracted to her. Giving a boy that age such immense power was an incredible mistake, but she had faith that he could learn to master it. She would help him, if she could. She would guard herself, but she would be there every step of the way.

If he ever got his magic back.

Yes. That was how she felt. That was what she wanted. She had made her decision: she would go to Rylan, she would talk with him, she would ask him to try again. Slowly. Carefully. They would be together, and together they would learn control.

She crept out of her tent, bare feet padding on the forest

floor, heading for where she knew Rylan was. She'd kept track while they were building camp. Even then, she'd already known what her decision would be. Her face flushed as she imagined what it would be like, what he would say. He would take her in her arms, speaking to her lovingly. He would kiss her, but not too strongly. She longed to feel his lips.

But when she got to his tent, Rylan wasn't there.

A piece of paper was on his blanket, scrawled with handwriting that was barely readable.

She hadn't realized Rylan knew how to write.

DANCE,

I'm so sorry I hurt you. I didn't mean to. It was the last thing I wanted. Ever since you left, I've been hurting inside. It kills me to think of what happened between us. I don't know how to go on.

I'm too dangerous to be around. Even with the power gone, I can still feel it inside of me. If it comes back, Lani, I don't know what will happen. I don't know if I can control it.

When I was fighting Nelenor, something happened. A part of me latched onto him, connecting us. I know where he is now. He is close. He is brooding. Recovering. But it is only a matter of time before he returns and this destruction continues. I can't let that happen.

I'm going to him tonight. I'm going to try to talk him out of this vengeance. If that fails, I'll try to get my magic back and fight him on my own.

I do this for you. For everyone who fought for me. For New San Francisco. For me. I hope I am successful,

but I am not disillusioned. I will likely die, but at least I will have tried.

I will have tried for you.

I love you.

—Wind

A TEAR FELL from Elanil's eye, landing on the paper as she finished reading it. The message was so eloquent, so heartfelt. Xyclami truly had worked wonders on his mind.

If only it hadn't irrevocably damaged their relationship in the process.

Now Rylan was gone. She might never see him again. He was gone on a noble quest, and she was sure he would never return.

The floodgates finally opened, great sobs wracking her body. She cried for what had come before, for what was yet to come. For lives lost, for cities destroyed. For the love of her life, so briefly found now extinguished in the night.

She wept that she would never see her Wind again.

EIGHTY

ORYM STROLLED through the woods outside Lusvunub as the sun began to rise. He was still cloaked in double invisibility: once with his nowhere gate, to sever his soulstrand from existence, and once with mistweaving magic, to make him visually hidden. With those two things he could travel anywhere, go anywhere, and no one would ever know the difference.

He knew the secret now.

He knew how to get the System to work. All he had to do was access raw Destroyer magic in the vicinity of his own Soul Tree, letting the power go wild. And it would destroy the Tree—and thousands of people, most likely. But the block would be removed. The Tree was preventing the System from working, of that he was sure. Removing the Tree was his primary imperative.

Accessing raw Destroyer magic would be tricky for him. He was a Prime Mage, but he was not a superuser like Rylan. He had never expected the boy to have such power—witnessing it had been incredible. But his mother had been something else entirely. She was the one who had discovered the ultimate secret, the way Orym could finally obtain every-thing he'd ever wanted.

He would use forcefinding magic to destroy his Tree.

He grinned, thinking of how it would be. Of the glory. The power. How it would feel to finally wield Guruthos himself.

It was interesting how Soul Trees worked. They were invisible, even to elves, until raw force magic interacted with them. But he supposed it made a kind of sense: Prime Trees themselves were invisible to humans, after all. You could even walk right through them. Wouldn't there also be a kind of Tree that worked the same way for elves? If only he had realized that long ago, perhaps things would have been different.

But no matter. He knew what he had to do now.

Fixing the System was only the first step, though. There was also the matter of *activating* it. He hadn't wanted Selenia—or anyone else—to use it, after all. And so he had hidden the Control Center somewhere that was very diffi-cult to find. He had known the secret to it, once. But the memory was now lost to time. Cariel's magic had not returned it.

And so he needed help. He needed guinea pigs. People who would attempt the Control Center gates, triggering the traps he'd laid. People who would die for the things he'd made.

The elven camp began to stir awake, and Orym smiled.

He lifted his illusion, allowing himself to be seen.

QUYNN BLINKED, rubbing his eyes as the storm finally cleared. Had something happened? Why had the storm gone on for that long, only to mysteriously vanish? Maybe someone had finally been successful at attacking the Twins.

He looked ahead of him, paying no attention to the Nekhrumetians who were standing in the sand, gesticulating.

There were monsters in the desert.

They looked like upright wolves, like werewolves, completely covered in hair. They had broad chests and snouts and dark eyes, and they stood on two feet like men. Their arms were well-muscled and equally hairy, with long, sharp claws at the end of every finger. He could hear them growling to each other, but it sounded like there was structure to it. They were speaking a language, he realized. They were intelligent.

And they looked *very* dangerous.

But then something else captured his attention. Something in the distance, far away across the desert. A line of Trees had appeared near the horizon, Trees of every shape showing up where none had been before.

They were on fire.

And people were streaming out of them. Not people, exactly—they looked more like ghosts. Like souls, newly released from their otherworldly prison.

Millions of them streamed out across the sand.

JALNAB SAT in his little office at the edge of Lusvunub, looking out the one-way window at the destruction Nelenor had caused. It could have been worse. It could have been so much worse.

"He found us," he said into thin air.

"He doesn't know what he found," a voice responded. "The others drove him away."

"Still, it was a near thing," Jalnab said. "This threat could be the end of us."

"You and I both know there's nothing we can do. If we could have fought against magic, we already would have done so."

"I know. Still, the elves are in over their heads. They need our help."

"We can't help, Jalnab."

"You may be right. Still, I think it's time."

"Time for what, old friend?"

"Time to tell them who we really are."

RYLAN STEPPED QUIETLY OUT of the forest into a clearing, heart beating wildly in his chest. Nelenor was asleep, huge Anubis body laid out on the ground. He was maybe fifty feet tall now. His height kept changing to suit his mood.

Rylan wasn't sure what he should do. He took another step with trepidation, wondering if he would know the right things to say. He had no magic now. All he had were words.

He had never been very good with words.

Not until recently.

He missed his mother. He missed Elanil. He wished it hadn't come to this, that he had had to run from the damage he had caused. Now he only wanted to make amends. Now he wanted to do what was right.

He would convince Nelenor to stop, or he would die trying.

He would probably die.

He took another step, and Nelenor opened his eyes.

The Twin smiled.

THE

END

TO BE CONTINUED...

THE STORY CONTINUES

Excerpt from THE SPLINTER SOUL, book ten of The Metalwood Saga:

There was an army of souls in the desert.

Quynn stood, not quite slack-jawed, and watched them come. Millions of ghostly people were streaming out from burning Trees which had appeared out of nowhere in the sand. They milled about almost randomly, with no particular purpose or intent. But despite their ghostly appearance, they seemed real enough—he could see them kicking up sand, sliding down the dunes, even fighting with each other.

They were real and yet not real, as if the dead were coming back to life.

What could they be? What source of magic was this? Quynn didn't know—and unless these strange souls decided to attack him, he realized he didn't care.

He was far more interested in the monsters standing right in front of him.

"Greetings," one of the wolf-man things said. The voice sounded like a cross between a growl and a cough, but the Eldrim language was surprisingly recognizable, nonetheless. "My name is Falgr."

He held out his hand, claws and all.

Something about the creature seemed familiar to Quynn. Not that he'd seen anything like it before, just that he'd *heard* of it. He pictured jungles, a walking stick. Magona, her blind eyes everywhere.

Oh. Of course. Saul had described the very figure standing before him. It was called a rylak, and it had been the intelligent life on Eryn, before the Sundering there.

Not an *it*, then. More like a *he*.

"Greetings," Quynn said. Evidently this Falgr wanted to shake his hand, but the razor sharp claws would prove quite dangerous. Surely these creatures didn't shake each other's hands in the human tradition? They must have picked the habit up somewhere. He thought it through, the gesture hanging in the air.

Then he reached for the rylak's hand.

Falgr withdrew his claws just as Quynn's hand met his own. Quynn thought he caught an expression of some kind flicker across the wolf-man's face—respect? He didn't exactly know how to read the man.

The handshake was firm and brief, then Quynn stepped back. "How are you here?"

"Cariel," Falgr said. "She took us from Ambarhal and led us here. She kept us on Tanomar for millennia, breeding us like rats. None of us remember our home, but we have kept the stories alive."

"Damn," Quynn said. "I've been to your home world. Eryn is beautiful, if you like jungles."

"Cariel kept us training, kept us sharp. She wanted us in fighting shape for when her...war...started."

"Is that why you're here in the desert?"

"Yes, though the war never actually happened. All we had was a short fight against a few small elves. Then they defeated Cariel, and her control of us ended."

"You're not interested in killing elves?"

"All we want," Falgr said, "is to go home."

"That's all I want," Quynn said. "Perhaps we can be of

some use to each other."

"I managed to send a message before her soulbind made me come here," Falgr said. "It was a word of warning. I believe I sent it to you. Are you Tarathiel?"

Quynn almost said no, but then he realized that the answer would be wrong. Quynn *was* Tarathiel—albeit half of him. Perhaps there would be something to gain for owning up to his original self. He didn't want to reintegrate with Trey— he would *never* do that—but it couldn't hurt to be honest, here.

"I am Tarathiel," he said. "Thank you for the message." He hadn't read the message, of course, but he might as well play the part.

"We have heard that Tarathiel knows great magic," Falgr said. "We had hoped you might be able to grant us our return."

"Great magic," Quynn said. "Yes. Yes, I believe I can help."

Magic was what had brought everyone here. Magic was what had created all this conflict. It was why Quynn was half a person—the better half, but still not whole. Magic and splinters were dangerous toys, perhaps not best played with.

A new rylak appeared suddenly, stepping in from somewhere to Quynn's right. He looked bedraggled, possibly injured, and he hadn't been standing with the others. The figure towered over him, teeth bared, claws extended.

"Ah," the new rylak said, "I see you have finally come to pay us a visit. My name is Talon."

Quynn narrowed his eyes. Something about Talon didn't seem right.

Elanil hadn't slept. How could she? So much was wrong with the world. New San Francisco had been destroyed. The Twins were still on the loose, and no one was any closer to locating this Imprisoner they were so keen on finding. Worse, the Twins couldn't be defeated. Not with ordinary magic, anyway, or any technology they had. Only a mysterious power that no one understood had affected Nelenor, and that same power had killed Beam.

Rylan was gone.

He had hurt her, and he had left her. He was too dangerous to contain.

But all his magic was gone now.

So much was wrong with the world.

So she sat, huddled beneath a tree, shivering. It had rained, but she had let it fall, soaking her to the bone. She couldn't bring herself to do anything more.

Rylan was gone.

"Elanil?" a voice said, and she looked up to see Phoenix approaching. The woman's eyes were red, her hair wet and bedraggled. She looked like she hadn't slept, either.

"Ho," Elanil said, weakly.

Phoenix sat beside her. "I can't believe he left."

Elanil was silent, trying not to cry.

"What did he mean in his note?" Phoenix asked. "What was he apologizing for?"

"He..." Elanil wasn't sure what to say. Could she really tell his mother what had happened between them? What had *almost* happened? "His magic is—was out of control. He mindmastered me. He started to make me do things I...did not want to do."

"Oh, no," Phoenix said, her voice filled with dread. "No, no, no."

"He didn't mean it," Elanil said. "The magic was just too much for him. He said the Aspects all bleed together."

"It sounds like emotion got the better of him," Phoenix

said. "Perhaps there are still things left that I can teach him."

"I would like that," Elanil said, laying her head on Phoenix's arm. "I wonder if Nelenor has killed him yet."

"Shush," Phoenix said. "We have to stay positive. There's a reason he went to Nelenor, and it wasn't just to get away from you."

"It may have been."

Phoenix put her arm around Elanil. "He loves you," she said. "I've seen it on his face. He left so he could protect you."

"I don't *want* him to protect me."

"I know. But I think he has another plan. He might actually have a way to stop this Twin from hurting us."

"Do you really think so?"

"I hope so," Phoenix said, squeezing her. "I hope so for all our sakes."

Another face materialized in the gloom, stepping out of the trees. Imra.

"Couldn't sleep either?" she asked, coming over to sit beside Phoenix.

"I can't believe the city is just *gone*," Phoenix said. "What else could these Twins do, if they had a mind? Are entire planets within their reach?"

"Their machine created magic," Imra said. "There's no end to what they can do."

"All those framekids," Elanil said. "Who will answer for their deaths?"

"We will," Imra said. "We who couldn't stop what was coming."

"I hate magic," Elanil said.

"I started hating magic a long time ago," Phoenix said.

They were silent for a time. Birds began to wake up around them in the forest, sparrows and starlings twittering. A pair of squirrels moved about overhead, scolding each other. The sun was beginning to rise, the camp stirring. There was still life down here, Elanil knew. The world had not yet ended. Why, then, could she only think of death?

"I miss him," she said.

"I miss him, too," Phoenix said.

"I don't understand what that red magic was," Imra said. "How could the Soul Tree just kill Beam like that?"

"It hit me, too," Phoenix said. "I could feel it inside me, as if it were tearing at my soul."

"What even *is* a soul?"

Phoenix shrugged. "I don't know, but apparently it powers all this magic."

"There were souls in that Tree," Elanil said. She shivered —both from the cold and from the memory.

"Poor Beam," Phoenix said. "To lose two people she loved in so short a time. I can't imagine what that must have been like. I hope she's happy, wherever she is now."

"Do you think there is a beyond?" Imra asked.

"There was, before the Twins were released. But now? Now I don't know."

"I guess we'll all find out, sooner or later."

"Maybe sooner," Elanil said. "If Rylan isn't successful."

"Elanil," Phoenix said, "are you okay? Did my son hurt you?"

"He almost killed me," Elanil said, remembering how the branch had felt piercing through her body. "But I'm stronger than I appear. I can heal myself without any primewood now."

"You soulbound a Tree."

Elanil nodded. "Rylan made me do it, before we left. I guess he's the reason I'm okay now."

"Emotions run strong in our family," Phoenix said.

"How well did you know his father?"

"Not well. And anyway, the person I knew wasn't Quynn —it was an illusion. He was putting on an act."

"I knew him," Imra said. "A little, at least. I watched him fight. He was vicious. Evil. Selfish."

"Wasn't he working for Lorelei?" Elanil asked.

Imra nodded. "And Lorelei was working for Tarathiel, in the end—even if she didn't remember it."

"Weird," Elanil said. "Strange how it comes full-circle. But how do the Twins factor in?"

"What do you mean?" Imra asked.

"I mean, why are they here? What do they want, besides the Imprisoner? They must have arrived here for a reason, back when they were imprisoned."

"I don't think anybody knows," Imra said. "If they did, it's been lost to memory."

"Maybe that's Rylan's plan," Elanil said.

"What is?"

"Maybe he's going to ask them what they want."

"What should *we* do?" Phoenix asked.

"You should come with me," a man's voice said, and Orym stepped out of the shadows.

To be continued in THE SPLINTER SOUL…

To purchase, head to **jtf.link/metal10** or scan the QR code below.

ENJOY THE BOOK? HELP SPREAD THE WORD

Reviews are the most powerful tools in my arsenal when it comes to getting attention for my books. Much as I'd like to, I don't have the financial muscle of a New York publisher. I can't take out full page ads in the newspaper or put posters on the subway.

But I do have something much more powerful and effective than that, and it's something that those publishers would kill to get their hands on.

A committed and loyal bunch of readers.

Honest reviews of my books help bring them to the attention of other readers. If you've enjoyed this book, **I'd love it if you could leave a quick review.**

Head to **jtf.link/metalreview9** or scan the QR code.

ABOUT THE AUTHOR

Jeremy is a fantasy and science fiction author, living and writing in the San Francisco Bay Area. Fantasy is his first love —there's something about magic and mayhem that has interested him since he first cracked opened Lord Foul's Bane in the seventh grade. Also archery.

There always seems to be a lot of archery involved.

When not writing, Jeremy is a graphic designer, software developer, game designer, and music composer. He makes a really great Old Fashioned.

Check out his other work and sign up for his newsletter at **www.jeremythomasfuller.com**.

facebook.com/JeremyThomasFuller
instagram.com/jeremythomasfuller
amazon.com/author/jeremythomasfuller
bsky.app/profile/jeremythomasfuller.com

www.ingramcontent.com/pod-product-compliance
Lightning Source LLC
Chambersburg PA
CBHW021837010726
47493CB00005B/1431